Diary of an Ageing Sexual Adolescent

The Harsh and Brutal Truth of Firsts, Volume 1

Angelina Kennedy

Published by Angelina Kennedy, 2018.

Dedications

To the people whose
memories are still with me.
Even though you are no longer
walking next to me, you share my story.
Until we meet again.

A x

Prologue

My parents always told me that there were lessons to be learnt in life, but surely this is taking the piss! I suppose I should just be grateful that I've had such an eventful life. Full of house moves, different boyfriends, not to mention fiancées, wedding arrangements, falling in and out of love, making and breaking friendships, various employee positions and occasionally, sex! Put it this way, if I lived on Albert Square, Coronation Street or on the Chatsworth Estate, I'd be the one with all the heart-wrenching storylines.

Perhaps I am just finding it hard to differentiate between real life, or should I say, 'my life' and the soaps. This could be due to my abnormal obsession with said 'soaps' or more likely down to the fact that my life is so dramatic that at times I swear it's set up. I'm thinking *Jeremy Beadle* or *The Truman Show,* or for you, young peeps, a more recent example may be *Ashton Kutcher's Punk'd*. I can relate to those people in the soaps, you see I feel like them, a life full of torment and hurt. What sets me apart from them is, I occasionally visit the toilet and always brush my teeth. I suppose you may already be thinking, well doesn't she feel sorry for herself? Let me tell you, feeling sorry for myself is one of my specialties and if you do not mind my saying so, I am very good at it!

Yesterday, I was browsing through one of my many packed boxes and came across some of my old diaries. Adorned across the front of a black leather book were the words 'Shannon Black's Memoirs'. Holy fuck! This was going to be funny shit! Filled with reminiscent excitement, I eagerly peeled open the heavily graffitied cover and delved straight into my immature scribblings of adolescent life. It quickly became apparent that said 'diaries' actually resembled suicide notes rather than day to day events and feelings. Maybe my destiny was affected, when at 10-years-old I wrote that I 'held a special light' for the guy that has now turned out to be the local drug rat? Similarly, I must question why at primary school we all acted like Mormons and happily shared boyfriends?

After my initial fits of hysterical laughter, over how pathetic myself and my counterparts were, I began to enter deep thought regarding my later experiences in my adolescence. Had everybody been as unfortunate in love as I? Does anybody have that magical first kiss? Do people actually enjoy losing their virginity? And I am pretty sure no adolescent girl thinks that a penis is an attractive body part!

I laid awake that night thinking of all the mistakes that I had made, or for want of a better word let's just say 'Past Events'! Was my past really a normal experience of adolescence?

Hence, I have decided (drum roll please) that it's time to take my life experiences, significant and insignificant, and to share them with the world. Maybe then I would know! Brave step, I hear you cry! Well let's face it, we have all been there; I'm just brave enough to admit it. So, my most sincere apologies go out to anyone, and everyone, that I have to take down with me, in sharing this with the world.

Welcome to my Adolescence!!!!

Introduction to Adolescence

I was one of those class jokers at school. You know, one of those kids who are always frantically searching their heads for something funny to say or a good way to embarrass the science teacher. Yes, those students who were hilarious to their peers, fucking annoying to the teacher types, that was me! It was my way of feeling popular I suppose. I would have much rather have had attention for my stunning figure and to die for looks but unfortunately, that didn't ever happen back then.

Without heading down the 'placing oneself in a tightly labeled box', I can imagine my sexuality might well have been questioned by many. I was a tomboy; you know with the short locks and baggy clothes. Maybe that was just my way of drawing myself away from the average girls in the school, my way of being different. Yes, that is right, my way of being different was being a heterosexual girl who actively dressed like a lesbian! Adolescence is indeed a confusing time.

Ok, I will help with the imagery here, as if the stereotype above isn't enough, as I don't feel that you could realistically understand my trials and tribulations of adolescence if you are not clear of the hurdles I faced. From my Northern upbringing, my dowdy appearance, my second-hand clothes and my obsession with boys, I will quickly fill you in on it all.

Whilst, in contemporary society, girls face a backlash if their photos aren't 'on fleek' on Insta, I need to transport you back to a time where eyebrows were there to keep the dirt out of your eyes, it was not possible to photoshop your fat rolls away and before dating was carried out through inboxes and the exchange of nudes and dick pics.

Now if you are super eager to get to the sex bits (although if you remember the beginning of your adolescence the way I remember mine, there may be no hurry to revisit it) then you need to skip to the middle of the book. I mean, I didn't start my life out as a confident nymphomaniac handling the phallic tools with ease, you know. No, this is no 50 Shades of Grey, a more apt title for this book may be '50 Shades of Fuck Ups and another 50 Shades of Disappointments'.

Clearly, the most obvious thing that I need to point out to you is my name is Shannon Black and I'm now withering in my agedness. Whilst I could spend a chapter or ten mooning on this, I will attempt to carve sufficient imagery of my much younger and slightly more stupid 14-year-old self.

I lived with my mam and step dad slap bang in the middle of the ghetto. We moved around from council house, to council house dependent on my mam's ability to pay the rent that month. I was lucky enough to have a brother and a sister. I say lucky because if it wasn't for their hand me downs, I am guessing I would have had to endure life naked. Truth be known, we all argued like cat and dog, and there may need to be a prequel one day if I am to spill the details of our upbringing outside of my sexual adolescence, but even so, I loved the bones off them both and my childhood would have been all the poorer had they not been a part of it. Although, admittedly there would have been more money to go around, so maybe the sacrifice would have been worth considering at least?

Whilst my dad stayed in my life, when he left to move to London in a very rash attempt to avoid laying his eyes on my mother ever again, he wasn't around that much and aside of the odd letter that dropped on the mat, I was doing this growing up lark without him.

What did I look like? It pains me to be this honest, but I wasn't even remotely pretty. Yeah, I know everybody says that about themselves, but this was fact, not opinion. So, let me give you the facts.

Well, to start, I was whiter than white, and this is no reference to my clean-cut personality, oh no, I mean my skin. It was the bane of my life. I know it doesn't sound like a major image issue but believe me, it was. I was so pale that you could see the veins on the side of my head, which made me look like some urchin that had rarely seen the light of day after being raised in a box and therefore was suffering from a condition worsened by a lack of sunlight. Back in the Victorian Era, I would have been considered as beautiful (and rich actually) with that kind of rare paleness.

It didn't help that in my wisdom I decided to be a peroxide blonde. After all, blondes do have more fun, right? Wrong! Not sure what possessed me to take style tips from Eminem, but I thought it turned me into a fox at the time. In all fairness to myself, my adolescence took place in the nineties; makeup availability and services were somewhat limited (as was money) compared to what is available today. I mean there were no tutorials for smoky eyes back then, nope! We relied on copying Auntie Edna's sparkly blue eye attire when dressing up for a night at 'The Club'.

Oh, and did I mention my height? How could I forget? Put it this way, I would like to thank my mother for her twenty a day habit since it rendered me five foot nothing as a fully-grown woman. Hence, at the tender age of 14, you can just imagine what a little stunner I was. Being the size of an 8-year-old girl is, in my opinion, one of the most un-sexiest features of a growing girl, surely? Although, to be fair, it never did Kylie Minogue any harm. Especially when my breast size matched the age group. Unless you were Nudge the Nonce from the local park, then I just wasn't girlfriend material. When you are small you just don't get noticed and when boys did notice you, it was a case of "Oh, how cute are you."

CUTE? I wanted to be 'damn fine' or 'some hot shit', not fucking 'cute'!

Maybe the bigger issue was my own self-confidence. To be frank, I did have an aversion to small men and therefore the irony that I myself was small, was just a problem to me.

On top of the serious issues of skin tone and breast size, there was my body shape. Did my body shape make up for the height of which I lacked? Of course, bloody not: I was so thin that my brothers and sisters called me 'lucky legs'! Yes, that's right, lucky they don't snap! I still find it ridiculously hilarious after all these years – not! My body shape was, well I suppose it was non-existent.

I resembled a young prepubescent boy, which did me absolutely no favours when it came to styling myself. Remarkably, this is how I came to the dumbfounded conclusion that since I looked like a frigging boy that I might as well god damn dress like one. Yeah, I know, not exactly the best idea I ever had. I had the strange tendency to think that if I wore my clothes baggy enough nobody would notice that I had string legs or that my breasts were so non-existent that they may have been inverted. And ladies isn't it always the case that if you are lumbered with the smallest mountains ever to be, all your friends have massive baps. Yes, and my friends were no exception to this rule. The cruelness of this rule means that even more attention is drawn to the fact that you have yet to sprout. The jibes about my tiny boobies are still with me to this day! You can be as cool as a cucumber, but when a young man used your breasts as the joke of the day, it is very disheartening, not to mention cruelly embarrassing.

So, taking the above physical description into account, I will now provide you with a summary. I resembled a lanky streak of piss, who was as big as Tyrion Lannister (Game of Thrones), who dressed like a wannabe gangster, was deathly pale (think Lord Voldemort), with bulging veins out of the side of my head, owner to two tiny lumps of which God intended to be my breasts and this was all nicely topped off by my Eminem style peroxide hairdo complete with the 'Golden M' (McDonald's) trademark quiffs set in with days' worth of 'Insette' hairspray. This was a typical nineties hairdo, not just my weird style sense. As you can tell, I was the centre of attention for all the right reasons!

What was my life like? Hopefully much like yours, or I really did not have a normal adolescence and I may recall this book. I grew up on a typical English council estate in the village of Detton and I attended the local comprehensive, just outside Sunderland, England. Sounds quaint, doesn't it? It wasn't. It was a fucking shit hole! Employment was at an all-time low and people were still busy blaming Maggie Thatcher for their refusal to find employment. Having said that, it was my home and I loved it. Although I have to say that, so no one puts my windows through.

It was the early Nineties. The nineties were just that era that consisted of the worst fashion mistakes ever. For anybody lucky enough to have been a teenager in this era, it will no doubt conjure up memories of The Sweater Shop, Eclipse Jeans, Fat Willies Surf Shack Merchandise, shell suits, Fruit of the Loom and, who could forget, Global Hyper Colour T-Shirts. What was the big deal about being able to touch a T-shirt and it change colour? I will never understand. I didn't worry about that trend, as my family were too poor for me to ever lay my hands on one of them anyway. I mean if they didn't do it at the YPO, then I wasn't having it: end of! No big loss there is my reckoning.

For those not familiar with the term YPO, it stands for 'Yorkshire Purchasing Organisation'. Sounds posh? A bit like Detton Hill sounding 'quaint', it wasn't. It was basically a shop where the poor families went to collect their school clothing so that they wouldn't have to go to school naked! It was all free, you just had to go and pick your delights! Unfortunately, since half of your school went, it was like we had a uniform for the poor: easily identifiable by a pair of shoes and a coat. It was rather Hitleresque. As if queueing in a separate line to get your free dinner wasn't embarrassing enough, we all had to wear the same 'your mam and dad are losers' clothes too!

Anyway, out of school, whilst I didn't have wardrobes bursting at the seams with clothes, my friends and I did have a style of our own. Okay, so most of my attire was hand me downs (not good when you have brothers) but it was better than hanging out in your free clothing, believe me. Our wardrobes consisted of: baggy jeans, tucked into our socks; Air Max, with socks pushed under the tongue to puff them out plus untied shoe laces; Nike hoodies and Sweater Shop jumpers; Caterpillar boots (yes not all my friends were as poor as me) and the trademark crop top, teamed thoughtfully with the checked shirt left open to catch sight of our pubescent tummies – pure class!

Some of my individual style statements consisted of my 'BITCH' necklace (oh I was hardcore alright) and my bandana which I used for various purposes, be it a headband or just hanging off my jeans. I had to have it dangling somewhere, it defined my dedicated hip hop status. You will be shocked to know that I switched the colour of my bandana often, therefore making a mockery of the gang colours the bandanas represented. I was just that kind of rebel.

All this, coupled with my bright green Reebok puffa jacket (of which I had spent months working at a cruddy discount supermarket for), finished off with my chunky gold chain complete with The Lord's Cross 'delicately' hanging from it, I was ready to roll! I probably can't skip by this without clearing up the 'Lord's Cross' reference. No, I hate to disappoint you, I was not religious. Why did I choose it then? Because I was a fucking idiot, if truth be known. I do have to snigger at the irony of expensive gold jewellery for people like me that grew up in the ghetto. The irony that we didn't have a pot to piss in yet wore hordes of gold jewellery to prove our wealth, that we didn't have. I suppose nobody needed to know that I had starved myself for weeks living on bread and butter to be able to finance it under layaway at the local pawn shop.

As mentioned previously, my mam rarely purchased any new clothes for me (remember we had the YPO), but one rare day she lovingly purchased me the 'must <u>not</u> have' of the nineties, a fake NAFF NAFF coat! Oh yes! We were that poor, that I had no option of telling my mam that I just could not wear it for fear of being ridiculed (not fear actually, fact), it was the coat or the cold, I obviously opted for the cold. How the bloody hell was I supposed to pull in that frigging thing? Was she so unaware of an adolescent's quest?

I suppose looking on the bright side I should have been grateful since last year it was my older brother's coat that I was lumbered with. Not good when he was in the year above me at school, which ultimately meant that people didn't even have the time to be able to forget that he had worn it the year before. I still shudder at the thought of walking into our social block at school, with the 'Naff Naff' coat on whilst trying to block out the laughter that the coat had drawn. And here I am trying to work out why it took me so long to find somebody to hook up with?

Oh, there were so many more fashion mishaps, but I will have to be careful not to stray from the topic here. Although perhaps our sexual adolescence is shaped by the way we dress, I'm sure Susan Boyle wouldn't deny that, after her dramatic X Factor transformation. If only the girls with the slug eyebrows would realise this.

Last but not least in these memoirs, we need to discuss friends. Whilst this book is specifically focusing on sexual adolescence, one of the most important aspects of a young adolescent's life is their best friend, so it is something that we have to explore.

My best friend was a girl that I had known all my life: Anna. We were both so similar and yet so different, all at the same time. We liked the same clothes (not the YPO ones) and the same music: old school American hip hop, a sprinkling of R n B and occasionally a bit of Reggae and Hardcore Jungle. But our taste in men couldn't have been more different. For this reason, our friendship was a flawless recipe, we never fancied the same boy: perfect. There is one thing I can say, I wouldn't have made it through my adolescence without her. Let's not forget that this was long before the days where you could wack a self-pitying status on Facebook and tons of randomers would comment 'I'm here for you hun', 'Inbox me bae', 'UR my world' – you know the drill, right? Yes, in those days, a girl without a Bezzie was, well, she was lonely, that is what she was.

I had other friends, I'll introduce some of them as we go along. However, girls and friendships just may be a whole other book and it would take me far too long to detail them all. It might sound strange, but it was mostly boys that we befriended. Really, it wasn't strange though, the reasons were pretty simple. 1) we preferred to hang out with boys (red blooded females), 2) men are easier to please than women (we wanted an easy life), 3) the boys were 'less' likely to sleep with our boyfriends. There you have it! Those were the main reasons anyway, there were countless motives but that would take me all day and I would offend too many people. I mean it is only chapter 1!

Adolescent Hunting

Locally, my friends and I were known as the 'Hill' crew. Okay, okay! I know it sounds sad but don't be mistaken, it wasn't some lame gang name, it was more of a piss-take of a label that had been forcibly applied to us by others, in essence, it reflected that Detton Hill was our stomping ground. Okay, so maybe we did unwittingly adopt gangland mentality at times, but it was minus the extreme aggression and violent weapons, except when it came to our boys. I suppose a better comparison than *Ross Kemp on Gangs* would be the T. Birds and the Pink Ladies. Let me try to explain this notion a little better to avoid looking like a total prick.

Basically, the boys who we hung around with 'belonged' to us and we 'belonged' to them. Yes, you read that right. We were effectively each other's property and woe betide anyone that crossed that line. You may scoff my loyal reader, but we both know you did the same thing. The problem with me was, I was a major flirt, or a desperado, depends on which way you look at it I suppose. Hence, one set of special friends was never enough, and I was never massively into flirting with the girls. I liked to think of myself as a social butterfly but I'm not sure that my old entourage would agree. Although without my social butterfly persona, I wouldn't have been able to write this book and more to the point, my friends and I might just still be virgins!

At this point in my adolescence, I had next to zero experience with boys. I had never willingly kissed anybody, and I was now an ageing 14-year-old. I'm telling you the truth! Strangely enough, the folk of Detton never believed that about me, not even my mam who constantly lectured me about getting AIDS. Maybe she would have been better off giving me the birds and the bees lecture, or even better, advice on how to pull in the fucking first place so that at least I had a chance at catching some kind of venereal disease.

My only experience was that I had a rather pitiful kiss forced upon me previous to this point, whilst I was a mere 12 years of age. A particularly naive 12-year-old at that. I still liked to manhandle Barbie and Ken and sing into the mirror using my hairbrush as a microphone. I had known the 'kiss stealer' all my life really, he was my brother's best friend, Joel.

Joel was a regular fixture at our house throughout my childhood and my mates and I adored eavesdropping on him and my brother through the walls whilst romanticising over being his girlfriend, how sickeningly sad. I hate to admit this, especially so early in the book, but I think I cringingly remember writing him love letters and shoving them through his letterbox before hop footing it around the wall.

I love you, why don't you love me back?
We could run away together if you like?
Tick box yes or no if you will go out with me.
Yes/No/Maybe
S.W.A.L.K (sealed with a loving kiss) xxx

HOW TOTALLY EMBARRASSING! Especially when I think back to the fact that he looked like Pookie from *New Jack City*. For those of you too young to remember, I am referring to a very sick (poorly if you're of northern origin) Chris Rock in an early nineties gangster film. I suppose I should take solace in the fact that it is nowhere near as embarrassing as how young people trade dating notes these days. I mean how offensive can a 'tick box love note' be, compared to a pubescent dick pic?

One particular day, I was innocently singing into my hairbrush and admiring myself in the mirror when he abruptly appeared in my bedroom, interrupting my visions of entertaining the masses on MTV. Although I had hoped and prayed for (and no doubt had even acted it out at some point: you know, role play, *Barbie*s?) this moment since like forever, I obviously didn't really want it to happen. I wanted Wesley Snipes to molest me too but had he appeared at my door, wanting to stick his hands down my pants, I would have called 999!

So, I quickly sat down on my bed and did the only thing nervous girls know how to do, that's right, I giggled. As he seated himself next to me, my very angry big brother walked in and demanded to know why his friend would prefer to be in my room than his. Don't misread this situation, whilst I am sure he loved me dearly (as did I him), he had no concern about my safety, it was just an episode of enraged jealousy over his friend. Unable to answer him, my brother responded by furiously slamming off my light switch and dramatically stormed out. I know, switching off the light, what a rebel. Joel took this darkened room opportunity to dive on top of me on the bed and force a very inexperienced heavy kiss upon my lips. And we all know that heavy kissing can only bring on one thing, yep that's right, teeth smashing – nice!

I pushed him off instinctively and hysterically ran downstairs to my Mam who was tediously washing the dishes. Why did I flee? Don't ask me to rationalise this, I just panicked. Maybe I just needed to share the burden with somebody?

I casually raised the subject of the teeth smashing incident.

"Mam, Joel has just come into my room and tried to kiss me," I blurted out.

"Ooooh that's lovely love, you've always fancied him, haven't you?" she responded nonchalantly.

Yeah, that wasn't exactly the kind of response I was looking for. Think 'The Gallaghers' of *Shameless* and you won't be far wrong. And so, the journey into adolescence began.

MILESTONE = BOY'S INTEREST GAINED

Although Joel had scared the shit out of me, he hadn't put me off boys. Oh no, just him! I know what you are thinking, how could you stop liking somebody that you so ardently desired? Seriously? Didn't you think that the teeth smashing incident was enough? Joel had given me more confidence to properly embark upon my path of sexual adolescence, ok maybe not sexual yet, but I did fancy a snog with a guy who wasn't going to remove my front chompers. I was so done with snogging my own hand. I knew the secret to handling this species was simply experience and that I had no choice but to get myself some of that, if I wasn't to end up some old spinster. I mean I was 14 already!

If you thought this next paragraph would detail my successes in nailing the opposite gender, then you obviously had a much better time during your teenage years than I did and perhaps you should be the one writing the book. Nope, in reality, Anna and I spent the 'Year of 14' trawling our village looking for suitable snogging partners.

Heartbreakingly so, there was a close call with a mid-batter (a mid-batter being somebody semi-worthy) during that time. He just happened to drop by where I was babysitting one day. Now whilst I was ready to find my match, I needed time to prepare, both physically and mentally, and perhaps what was required was the physical presence of my friends for moral support (not as a perverse dogging session). This was, however, totally out of the blue and I was alone! Alone was dangerous, as anything could happen, and I clearly would absolutely shit my pants should he expect 'anything' to happen.

As he began to cosy up on the sofa behind me, perspiration took over my entire body. My throat was closing and believe me so were my thighs. He began to gently kiss the back of my neck and whilst I understand from the porn my friends and I had managed to oogle whilst babysitting, this should have been an enjoyable experience, it didn't feel enjoyable to me as the fear had begun to set in. I stiffened more with every kiss and instead of focusing on pure ecstasy, my mind was racing to find a plan to get this guy off of me and out of the door. His hand began to move around my body as he spun me around so that we were face to face. Never mind face to face – lip to god damn lip!

"Oh god, is that the time?" I blurted out whilst jumping up off the sofa, "they will be back any minute."

He shifted himself rather sharpish, planting a 'peck' on my cheek as he left. Damn, I really liked him too. Confused? The complexity of a woman I am afraid. Sorry, you are all still pondering on the porn? If you didn't do this, I doubt you grew up pre-noughties. It was a complex activity watching somebody else's porn, especially in the days of VHS Tapes. First of all, it was imperative to take note of the counter on the tape to avoid being caught. Then when finished, it was quite a task to rewind back to exactly where it was before you laid your hands on it.

Anyway, back to the wasted year, it seemed the problem we had was, that I couldn't really find anybody in Detton that I wasn't scared of but that I liked enough, nobody that was in my low league anyway. Think back to my physical description of myself, I wasn't exactly 'catch of the century', I had to be realistic about this mission. Unfortunately, the crusade was much harder than I had ever envisaged. It was a fine balance between so 'hot' that they brought with them an air of fear and 'not hot enough' for me to desire them. My friends and I had slowly exhausted all the various groups of boys in our colony looking for suitable prey. I contemplated kissing lots of frogs to meet my prince, but it is hard to kiss a toad when the yearnings were missing.

Before I knew it, I had reached the end of my first 14 years on earth and the situation was getting more desperate by the day. I was now 15 and still had zilch experience with boys! I knew we had to move onto new hunting ground if we were ever to find suitable boyfriends, or even a simple kissing partner would do. What better place could we choose than the adjoining village of Combe?

Travelling to Combe, or Comby as we called it meant we were treading on dangerous ground. We were adolescents, so it is the law to shorten all names, whether it be a person or a place and stick a 'Y' or an 'O' on the end. Again, I make reference to the gangland mentality we were unwittingly exposed to. It wasn't 'our' village and so in an unwritten law, we were forbidden to step foot on their land. To create adequate imagery here, you could visualise the treatment of immigrants entering the channel tunnel. The hostility and desperation to prevent refugees from entering, should create a sufficient enough representation. Consequently, it was imperative to our safety that we had allies amongst the female population in order to save ourselves from a brutal kick in. Some people would have called us traitors for passing to the other side, but in fact, we were cool and calculated and we were merely following our master plan. This involved the art of manipulation upon the rival gang's bitches into sharing their men with us, and, I'm happy to report, yes, it worked!

Philosophy – Female Friendships
Forgive me if, throughout these ramblings of mine, that I share with you some deep thinking on adolescence and life, won't you? Let's start with making

'new' female friends. I believe this concept is unusual for young ladies within the adolescent period (especially in opposing villages), but making male friends is a breeze for any confident girl. A bat of the eyelashes and a few swigs of cider and the conversation easily flows. But girl friends: that is totally different! Not only are they harder to speak to but they are a total threat when it comes to luring the opposite sex. Pubescent girls, no matter how pretty, are never satisfied with their appearance and, as a result, will always feel threatened by other girls. The competition was not what I needed so early on in my adolescence. The NAFF NAFF coat was enough of a hindrance, I really didn't need competition added on top. To cut a long thread short, I too, usually, tried to keep the girl friendships to a minimum, purely for selfish purposes.

Consequently, I'll explain from the beginning how we managed to infiltrate Comby as easily as we did. It can all be attributed to our first ally, Susan. I was already acquainted with Susan as she had previously dated my cousin, so when she suggested that we join her on her home turf of Combe, we jumped at the chance. Her flaming red hair may have made her appear fiery but in reality, she was a cool chick and couldn't have done more to make us feel welcome. As soon as she passed us 'her' cider bottle, I knew we were safe. It's not only the lure of money and diamonds (of which neither of those were an option during our childhood) that makes women's eyes sparkle, the lure of new totty can do just the same. Especially when you were a teenager in the nineties, your mam and dad weren't exactly rolling in it and you grew up on the shittiest of council estates. Notably, there was never a question of having any money, you just knew that you had none and you accepted it. But with boys, that was an entirely different story. You want – You seek – You find!

The crossover to Comby went quite well considering the danger of the situation but hey, who cared? All I knew was there were new boys to be had and I was blinkered to anything else. What was a bit of a beating from a couple of girls if it meant that I 'got' a boyfriend? I was willing to take it. Brave? Nah, just desperate!

Covering New Ground

Despite my reservations about girls, I actually did have girlfriends, carefully picked though. We had tended to keep most girls at least a fist length away as a rule, however, the girls of Comby were just as cool as Susan, and we quickly became great friends. There, we hung around with a combination of boys and girls and they weren't even jealous of us hunting their herd on their own territory. In fact, they gave us free rein upon their land and allowed us to hunt whatever, wherever, whenever (if the *Shakira* song entered your head there, you are perfectly normal). You would think this was good enough for us, but being a typical young female adolescent, I eventually bit the hand that fed me. It seems I was a little insatiable.

There were around ten of us girls altogether, and we got on (shock, horror). Somehow, we had managed to make more female friends in this village than we ever had in Detton during the course of our whole life. Maybe I had the wrong impression of this particular gender altogether. In all honesty, these girls were fun, unlike many of the girls we had the displeasure of growing up with. By fun, I am referring to the fact that they too had no other aim in life than to get smashed and bag a boy. Whereas the girls in Detton, although they may have liked getting smashed, also held a great fear of any other female who may have been more attractive or even dared to be better at anything than them. If I am honest, I too suffered from this ailment. I was perhaps then, a product of my environment too. This sickness (named jealousy) made them nothing more than a bore and were simply unable to enjoy themselves. Instead of being able to throw themselves around a dance floor, or, maybe at this age, a field, they were too busy scowling at you in a corner. A bit like one of those birds that sticks out of all its feathers and puffs out its chest before it starts running at you and spitting to ward you away from its mate or babies. But Comby girls were nothing like that and the antics we got up to more than proved it.

Where do I start? Maybe I could introduce you to a couple of the relevant boys. Firstly, there was Josh. Josh was your typical teenager: tall/gangly; wore tracksuit bottoms, the shiny ones (this was the nineties don't forget); trackie top to match, or not in some cases (I'm not sure what was worse); baseball cap..... oh, and lots of spots! But then again, it was rarely the physical appearance that appealed to me, I more relied on personality which was an equal phenomenon. This was probably because I was hardly surrounded by Brad Pitt and 2pac doppelgangers (a bit of a juxtaposition there I realise) or could have been due to the fact that I myself was hardly Angelina Jolie.

Philosophy – Hot Boys
This piece of philosophy doesn't just stem from my adolescent experiences but my experiences as a woman full stop. Whilst hot boys are simply delicious to the eye, they are nearly always fatally flawed in other ways. Mostly with a huge ego and love for their cock. You must decide which you value more, a beautiful bit of aesthetically pleasing fluff on your arm or a personality: it is very rare find to find a man/boy that possesses both attributes. The other issue with hot boys is that they are not usually boyfriend material. Mostly because they don't ordinarily have an issue finding a partner, in fact several partners, usually at once! I mean surely it is selfish of a woman to expect to keep such a jewel in a jewellery box.

On that very note, there was Shane. And boy was Shane in a league of his own. He was your typical adolescent variety of 'hunk'. He was dark, handsome ... okay, he wasn't particularly tall, but since I was a midget, he could just about get away with it. I even put aside my aversion to small men for him. I'm sure you won't need me to describe his persona to you, as the description 'hunk' sums up much more than his visual appearance. He was just too good looking to be a nice person. I suppose having an abundance of women (or girls realistically) throwing themselves at you on a daily basis could make it a trifle difficult to stay in a relationship. He wasn't just your run of the mill slag though, oh no he was a 'smooth' slag. He could have talked Margaret Thatcher into bed, I'm sure of it. Put it this way, he had me at 'Hello' and nobody stole my cool the way he did!

I'm sure you can gather from my account of this boy, that I wanted him, which was a tad of an understatement. Yearned, sobbed, pleaded, and begged to a higher being even, are all better adjectives that would much better fit the circumstances (refer back to above philosophy on 'hot boys'). Yes, in a typical teenage way, I would bang on the love songs and sing into my hairbrush whilst day-dreaming about him. Which is rather sad since other than a peck on the lips, of which we all shared at the end of the night, he had given me nothing to day-dream over.

The variance between the two aforementioned boys is evident. Be that as it may, Josh was always there (unfortunately), whereas Shane would appear and disappear like Houdini, leaving me constantly on edge, heart racing, and waiting for his short visits so that I could stare at him, chin on the floor, tongue out!

But when he was there, oh was he there. He barely spared me a second, but what his presence did to my body was a lust that I had never experienced. Whilst my mam had taught me about the unrealistic views of love that poured out of the movie world in the nineties and prior, she had evidently never experienced this. When this guy plonked himself next to me on the soggy grass of the school field, asphyxiation quickly kicked in. His face could have easily adorned the front of a magazine and his smile made me turn away with timidity. Eye contact with him was best to be avoided: think Kaa in Jungle Book.

My heart paused in time and my hormones raged as I began to imagine a future of waking up to that every day ....

Philosophy – Want What You Can't Have

Everybody knows exactly how this feels. It could be that you don't even like somebody that much, but the minute they don't want you, they suddenly become the only thing in the world that you need. You can literally be ready to leave somebody but if they suggest it first, you are very likely to break down into floods of tears and beg them to stay, only to realise in the morning that you fucking hated them yesterday. Similarly, you can be in a room full of people that want you, but some of us are just destined to want the only person that doesn't hanker after us. Why? I said this is philosophy – deep thinking – it doesn't mean I have all the bloody answers. Who knows why? Because we are insatiable tossers probably.

Think toddlers. They can have the toy they have been desperately crawling to, but if somebody else takes a toy they have just put down … then shit is going down!

It would take me too long to introduce you to the rest of the boys in our little gang, especially if I keep lapsing into philosophical mode, but to sum them up, just like the girls, they were nice lads (yes, those types do exist). The boys of Detton were nothing more than players really. When they were bored of 'playing' or realised they weren't going to be 'playing' at all, they would move on: a complete lack of understanding of the concept of a relationship. In contrast, Comby boys were nothing like that. Hold your breath, I think these boys saw us as friends. Yes, get that, teenage boys and girls all being friends together. I know, this was a new concept to us too and we loved it. It was all quite *Secret Sevenesque*.

We were all quite innocent then I suppose, as we should have been at 15 really. Our days consisted of anything from camping out in the dead of winter, without a tent may I add, to good old-fashioned spin the bottle. I say innocent, I did end up sharing a sleeping bag with one of the lads on one of the camping trips once, but it was purely about comfort rather than sexual chemistry or a desire for a fumble. It all happened on one of our many 'camp in the woods without a tent' trips. When the thunder and lightning hit, we quickly realised that our quilts would get wet with our lack of tentage therefore we headed off to find to find some shelter. After hours of trekking through the midnight winter rain and slipping down huge mountainous mud ramps, we found ourselves on the local nature reserve and cosied ourselves down in the shelter of one of the bird huts. See bird huts do have a use after all, shielding the youth of today from the rain. One of the lads, Alan, had no covers and I agreed to share mine. Alan was a lovely guy, but by no means was he a fanciable type. He was skinny, small and …. nice!

"I can't get it up," Alan blurted out.

"Pull it harder then, for fuck's sake," I began to give up.

"You fucking pull it, you lazy bitch," he snarled, "why is it me that has to pull it?"

"Because you can reach it," I told him "in fact, I can't even find it, it's not exactly massive is it?"

"Why don't you get on top, we might be able to get it up that way?" he suggested.

As we shuffled about in the sleeping bag and I attempted to climb on top of him, Anna interrupted us.

"Shannon?"

"What?" I snapped in a flustered state.

"What the sodding hell are you two doing?" she sniggered, as the whole bird hut erupted with immature giggling.

As we wriggled to try and pull the zip up on the single sleeping bag, the rest of the darkened hut thought we were being anything but innocent. At that point it was the closest that I had been to a boy's body. Whilst we were fully clothed (a bonus), we were still writhing around on top of each other, which I am not going to pretend wasn't horrendously awkward. Luckily there were no protruding nether regions, so I guess it could have been worse. And I didn't mind that our friends thought I was getting some action. Maybe if they thought I was 'getting' some action, we could stop being obsessed with 'finding' some action.

Not sure that particular embarrassing memory would outlive my friend's experience of spin the bottle though. Whilst the boys were partaking in a bit of bonding time blowing up condoms on their head, we decided to entice them into a game of 'Spin the Bottle'. They were up for it, especially because it wasn't exactly a thrilling experience in the first place to blow a condom up on your head. I mean come on, blowing a condom up on your head may be funny the first time, but why do boys insist on doing something repeatedly, if they managed to raise a few laughs the first time. Because we were inventive, we decided to use our recently emptied cider bottle as a prop for the game. I'm sure you are all familiar with this game, but just in case my target audience for this book has managed to stretch to any old age pensioners, maybe I should explain. You simply sit in a circle and spin the bottle, twice. The two people it lands on then must kiss each other. Simple.

The game began. Unfortunately, one of the boys decided he had become quite comfortable with the condom on his head and thought he would leave it there, simply leaving his mouth uncovered. The bottle then just happened to land on him and my friend. Asserting her authority, she demanded he took the condom off his head if he was to kiss her. I'm thinking she wished she hadn't bothered!

They must have only been stood a couple of inches apart from each other when he pinged it off his head. Unfortunately, as he did this (probably due to the over excited nose blowing required to blow the condom up) the longest ever snot line flew off the protective device and landed straight across her face. Eeeewwwwwwwwwwwwwww! Oh yes, it really was that disgusting, and funnily enough, we never played that game again.

This may have been immature fun, granted, but it was innocent. But just exactly how long can innocence last in adolescence? Let's find out!

Edging on Coupledom: The first boyfriend

I ronically enough, although we were very fond of our new stomping ground and the boys that stomped on it, it was at school that I had my first taste of that wrenching sensation called 'Love'. Whilst I adored the boys we hung around with, it was all very platonic, except Shane of course. I mean how sexually attractive can you find someone who plays games with jonnies (of which are condoms, for you young folk)? I had all the trademark symptoms that would indicate that I was in love. Butterflies – check, feelings of insecurity – check, extreme clumsiness around said victim – check, inability to focus on anything except <u>that</u> boy – check, ability to make any love song fit my circumstances – check. Yep, it would well and truly seem that I was head over heels in teenage adoration. I spent my school days checking the clock, anxiously waiting for the end of the lesson so that I could grasp a quick glance of my desired one in the corridor. This encounter would give us something new to talk about for the next week.

"Oh my god, did you see how he looked at you?" my friends would say. "You could tell he was dying to ask you out."

When in fact the reality probably was that, he happened to glance past me in a crowd of fifty people. The sad truth is that most young girls (adults too) will make any situation fit into the box they want it to, aided by their well-meaning friends.

Looking back now, I hardly remember his name (okay, maybe I do), but I certainly do still remember that first electrifying kiss, especially that feeling that you might not do it right. Unbelievably, I still hadn't managed to bag myself a first kiss at 15! How had it taken me that long? Shane used to plant a peck on my lips occasionally but he did that to most of the girls as he was leaving. So, I am not talking about those 'pecks', I am talking about full on 'French Kissing'.

Considering the amount of 'kissing the hand' practise that I had experienced, it should never have been an issue. Come on, we have all practised on our hands at one time, right? I have lost count of the times that I stood in front of my mirror, peeping through one eye as I tried to give my most seductive kiss to my very available left hand. I would ensure that I had the correct music on to get me, myself & I in the mood and I might even try to chat myself up in the mirror. Okay, maybe I'm going a bit too far there, cringe! I did keep my foot up against my bedroom door, just in case, I should be caught out by 'the parents'. I never fancied explaining that one.

I look at practising on your hand as one of those things that you just needed to do through puberty. Just like lying about not being a virgin to your highly sexually active, attractive fifteen-year-old female (and sometimes male) friends. Come on, I'm sure 50% of you did it too. Is it such a crime? I just simply didn't want to be known as the frigid one. After all that just wasn't the case, I wasn't frigid! I just didn't have much luck in finding myself a man and I decided since that wasn't either my fault or my choice then I would lie about it. It saves all the awkward questioning and obviously humiliation. Until you grow up and then you realise that losing your virginity at fifteen was not such a cool thing after all! However, hindsight or the reassurance of Google not being an available option at that time, I felt that I only had one option: lose it and lose it fast! I suppose the longer I held onto my first kiss, the harder it was to let it go. Aaarggghhh, how complicated is having your first kiss?

The problem was, I really didn't want my first attempt at kissing to be on the boy I was, at that time, hoping to spend the rest of my life with. More realistically perhaps, maybe the rest of that week if I was lucky. Let me explain myself. Obviously, boys talk, and there was no way that I was going to be the gossip of the boys changing rooms during double P.E. No way. That was just the worst. Just let me remind you that I grew up in a mining village in the North. That means that gossip, especially bad news which is principally totally inaccurate or completely made up shit travelled at the speed of light, whether it be true or not.

Philosophy - Gossip

Don't be mistaken in thinking that gossip news arrives in the original state, as it makes it way from one gossip spreader to the next. No such luck. Each Chinese whisperer adds in their own bit of sugar, meaning that the truth will be so sugar coated at the end of it that the bad truth will be even 'badder' than you ever imagined it could be and to the receiver, the sourer the better.

It is easy to see then, why I, at least, wanted a quick trial run. The irony of my virginal status is that I was constantly referred to as a slag by the highly educated in Detton. For those not familiar with this term, I think the dictionary definition goes somewhere along the lines of:

An individual who cares not for relationships beyond the realm of the sexual, these people sleep with many partners not caring about anything, save for the moment of climax.

This derogatory term (for a female anyway, it was cool for boys to be slags – obviously) was tossed in my direction, particularly by the girls of Detton. We have discussed the lack of girlie solidarity before, haven't we? They certainly did claim to know me, when in truth they knew absolutely nothing about me. Sadly, at the time, I felt like their hatred came from something that I had done wrong. It clearly wasn't sex, since getting laid was somewhat of a hurdle to little old me. However, being a naive young girl, I wasn't offended anyway. I kind of thought being called a slag was a badge of honour. I thought it was an indication of my dedication to gaining skills in the bedroom department and I was most definitely up for that. If only I could find somebody that I wanted to be the other inductee!

Although, I must admit, it did totally freak me out, and fuck me off greatly, the number of individuals who told tales that they had slept with me, amongst other claims. Understandably (although it wasn't true), I was more than willing to lay claim to the good-looking ones, but there were some goons who I would not have touched with a barge pole and I was in awe of why they would totally fabricate a story of such content. But, this is something that I became entirely used to as the years went by, especially as I began to slightly improve aesthetically. I was like a good wine, slowly improving with age I suppose. Not in a beautiful swan way, just slightly more alluring than before (which wasn't hard).

Philosophy – Boys Who Brag

So why do boys brag? Is it some caveman remnants that makes them think that they will become more popular to the opposite sex? Like a blow fish puffing out its chest they spit their conquests hoping the rumours will make them sound more appealing to their next victim. Or a peacock lining up its notches rather than its feathers. I mean what do boys really think happens? A female overhears a rumour that said boy has slept with a good-looking girl and therefore their cock now sounds more attractive?

"Oooohhh Stacey, did you hear Jason has just slid his cock in Sabrina, I just have to get my jaws around that now." Yep boys, that is exactly what fucking happens!

And this is without considering the fact that they lie about who they have laid their serpent to. I mean isn't that slightly embarrassing? Surely phantom shagging is in fact a mental illness? Admittedly, we all lie in adolescence, myself included, many times, but I never dragged anybody else into it.

Back to the story of my first victim then. We went to the same school together. The one hitch being he was in the year below me, which landed me with the undeserving title of cradle-snatcher.

Philosophy – Age Gap

Ah, age gaps. They seem to have little importance in the grown-up world. That is unless 90-year-old Derek ties the knot with 16-year-old Destiny. But in the uncertain world of adolescence, age gaps are reputation destroyers. And I am not talking about the filthy goings on between Dirty Derek and Super money hungry Destiny. Even I am intrigued of how things work between their sheets, I am talking about a mere 'year gap'. Yes if you dream to date a boy in the 'year below' then you are a laughing stock. In reality, a boy in the year below could be only a few weeks younger, but that didn't matter, the fact remained that he was in Year 10 and you were in Year 11, and that definition made the matter of a relationship – disgusting!

I remember vividly, walking into my friend's maths class. I was in the 'duggie' group and was sent by my teacher to their class for some equipment. As if coming from the bottom set group sent to the higher group wasn't enough, being greeted by jeers of 'Cradle Snatcher' from my so-called friends convened at the back of the class was the worst.

I felt like screaming, *"Listen, I would get off with a 13-year-old if it helped rid myself of this curse"* but I kept it to myself. Instead, I made some clever, yet cruel, comment to the maths teacher to take the heat from myself.

"Miss, why have you styled your hair in the shape of vaginal lips? Have you been to a sex convention this weekend or does your husband just want to have sex with something else?"

Obviously, after this comment, the class had turned their attentions away from my love life and onto the watery-eyed teacher instead, which obviously was the plan. I won't go into the trouble this landed me in at school.

I had observed Kayden (yes, my victim had a name) from afar for a couple of weeks by this time. Ok, I was stalking him, but I will have you know that it is perfectly normal and acceptable in adolescent relationships. Admittedly, we weren't in a relationship but there is no need to be pedantic. Obsession is healthy when you are under 18, I have it on good authority. Besides being only 15, I only stalked him at school, in the corridors. I might have stretched to stalking him at home if he had lived in Detton, but he lived in one of the surrounding villages that could only be reached by bus, and that was just too much effort. Catching a bus also meant money and let's face it, that was something I just didn't have. Even if I had, it wasn't going to be wasted on buses, I had cider to buy. I do feel a little jealous of the younger generation these days when it comes to stalking, it is so easy, safe and productive. Cracking open a can of Coke whilst browsing social networks diligently gathering information is bloody easy. Back in my day, the art of stalking meant hard bloody graft with often little or no gain.

Mine and Kayden's romance started like most juvenile relationships do, my mate fancied him, and I thought I would dive in there first! Oh, come on, can you really tell me you have never done the same thing? It is yet another part of adolescence that just must be passed through, let's call it a milestone? As most of the girls reading this will agree, growing up as a girl, you tend to trade your female friends in every so often. There can be numerous explanations for this (briefly discussed before), such as, lack of compliance when you want them to do something, inability to get on with your boyfriend's friends, or the most palpable reason being far too pretty, hence gets much more attention than you! Readers, it is a dog eat dog world out there and adolescence is hard enough without constantly being sidelined for one of your friends.

MILESTONE = STOLE MY FRIEND'S CRUSH

My friend had been writing *'Katy 4 Kayden'* on her maths books for quite a while, even ending it with I.D.S.T (if destroyed still true) which made it 10 times more serious. And during her 'stalking of him' stage, I noted that he was actually not that bad. Decision made. I needed to ditch her. Although I was aware that under our teenage unspoken laws, I shouldn't have had yearnings for him, but I did. It was simple, she had to go.

I don't know if I fell in love with him or just in love with the idea of being in a relationship. The fact that I can hardly remember what he looks like suggests the latter. I do however remember the desperation of needing to find someone to rid myself of my extreme pureness. I mean not only was I a bloody virgin, I still had unkissed lips, never mind had the pleasure of any other kind of sodding foreplay. I remember each and every little step of the relationship though, specifically the moment that he first acknowledged me … properly.

It was after my Monday Maths lesson: he had Science. The maths classes were on the floor above the science rooms, at the top of a five-floor high block. After our lessons, my friends and I would take our time coming out of class, to allow Kayden, the time to get on the stairs that we all needed to use to get down to the ground floor. Surprisingly, I would appear behind him on the extremely steep stairs that just happened to be lined with full-length glass windows. To create the opportunity to flirt, we would push each other on the stairs, in a playful loving kind of way. You know that old crack where you attempt to beat each other to death in a vain attempt to flirt with each other? The fact that the potential of pushing each other down the stairs could lead to one of us falling through the glass windows never crossed our minds. Why would it? The most important thing to teenage girls is boys and vice versa, so obviously some risks had to be taken and if that meant the risk of us falling out of windows, hey ho. It was all in the name of love and that was all that counted.

Thank god we grow out of that, it could become quite a problem, don't you think? I mean picture it. You are in a wine bar primly sipping champagne out of a crystal flute with a Donna Karan white number draped around your perfectly tanned body when the gorgeous brown Adonis to your right pushes you off your bar stool, you proceed to fly halfway down the bar, after which you gleefully pick yourself up off the floor knowing that you are about to get laid! See it just wouldn't work, would it? The bouncers on the bar doors would get confused between brawling and flirting. It would be a catastrophe but fun, I guess.

Anyway, after lots of playground tapping between Kayden and I, we got together in the most common way 15-year-olds do. My mate asked him out for me and he agreed! I had been boasting to my friends that he would be my next victim, but I obviously had no intention of doing anything about it (those who talk about it….), since I was a petrified, perfectly preserved Veronica Virgin. However, Anna had ideas of her own. Hence, at the end of the school day whilst strolling down the corridor, she announced to me that she had asked him out for me and he had said yes! Could this be real? Could I really have a boyfriend? Oh, this shit was big!

MILESTONE = GIRLFRIEND STATUS ACHIEVED

Once the excited butterflies fluttering in my belly (from being able to say I had a boyfriend without needing to lie) began to simmer, the fear began to set in. This meant that I would have to do 'the kiss' for real. No starting again when I had made a false start, no peeping in the mirror to check I wasn't eating my fist (I mean his face). The perk of myself being the only judge had gone. I knew in my heart it was going to be a disaster. But I had to do it sooner or later, so total humiliation or not, I just had to go for it!

As I'm sure you imagined, our first meeting was an awkward one, to say the least. I couldn't stop panicking that I would kiss him wrong, he would then proceed to inform the whole school of my inability to entertain or at least satisfy at this early stage, the opposite sex. I would be destroyed. Obviously, with my reputation in tatters, my life wouldn't be worth living and I would just have to kill myself: there would be absolutely no choice! This was it, my whole life was hanging in the balance.

He was walking down the hall in front of me. Fuck, Fuck, Fuck!!!! The last five years of stress, worry and practise climaxed at this point. I would liken this situation to something like waiting for my driving test or maybe even giving birth (although my situation was obviously much more stressful). As I was too slow off the mark to incite communication between us, my 'beloved' friends decided to fucking interfere. I knew they weren't doing this to aid my love life and to help me find lifelong happiness, but they just loved to see me squirm. Bastards! Unfortunately, I am pleased to say, they didn't get their circus show after all, but in contrast, I did get my wonderful moment.

My friends shouted down to Kayden and he turned around in haste. That was it, I was trapped, I had no choice but to enter *his space*. Remembering that I was supposed to be this experienced girl with a tirade of followers thanks to my elaborate lies, I was sure they expected a spectacle of fireworks and a tango routine. I was, therefore, bloody petrified! With great hesitation, but armed with my blasé attitude and shaking legs, I strolled straight up to him and blatantly asked, "So we together or what?" whilst seriously avoiding eye contact and kicking the ground where I stood.

"Suppose so," he batted back at me, enthusiastically.

I looked up from the ground and we locked eyes for the first time. I had never really noticed just how gorgeous his eyes were, brown and bashful just as I liked them. His eyes met mine and the moment seemed to last an eternity. Right there and then, in that moment, I didn't feel inexperienced or unworthy, I just felt like a girl who had finally found the treasure. As my stomach was doing flips, I couldn't take my eyes off him. I even forgot about my bloodthirsty friends watching. The crowd who had gathered to watch were no doubt waiting to give us marks out of ten. I didn't want to let myself down, so I had to stage this well.

You may have cringed at the fact people had gathered to watch. I suppose it does sound strange in the context of 2017. But with a lack of YouTube for guidance on such important matters like snogging it was maybe the way to learn the art. I am not suggesting however people gathered around to watch a full on sexual session, although when you consider the activity of 'dogging' exists, maybe there is little difference. Albeit, I am aware that to some it may not have been a lesson, but more to simply get their own rocks off.

My body began to enter meltdown, I couldn't decide whether I liked this feeling or not. Tingly electrodes shot through my body and I didn't quite know what to do next and seemed to have simply frozen. He stepped towards me and pulled me closer by placing his arms so gently around my waist. He looked down at me (as everybody had to since I was about the size of one of Norton's *Borrowers*) and began to slowly pull me closer. I couldn't quite catch my breath! There was a very short awkward moment, which you expect with your first kiss. It was all down to technical stuff, you know like head positioning, noses, tongue action and stuff.

Any other thought that may have been occupying my headspace at that moment disappeared, as I was completely lost in the moment. We could have been Kim Kardashian and Kanye West on a Caribbean beach for the way I felt at that second. My want for him was indescribable and he made me feel desired for the first time in my life. The kiss was electric, I never knew you could derive that kind of pleasure from a measly kiss! My legs shook uncontrollably but my heart told a very different story. I felt like part of him and could never imagine that anything would ever be as important to me in my life as the person whose arms I found myself in that second. All this from a kiss you ask? No, not 'a kiss' – 'The First Kiss'.

The reality was that this guy was a stranger, but in that moment, I felt like we knew each other better than anybody else on this planet. My hands and lips turned pro and you would have never have known this was my first time (okay, I had practised enough on my hand but that's between me and you). I molested him to the point of no return as my friends began to urgently drag me away from him. Maybe I thought it was just quicker and easier to lose my virginity right there in that corridor, right then. My eyes were closed, and I could never imagine a need to open them again but inevitably I did, as my friend eagerly tugged at my arm and assertively pulled me away down the hall.

"See you later," I managed to call out, whilst being dragged away from the serenity that I had just found. Wow!!! I wondered if he realised that he had just given me my first kiss. He had earnt a place in my adolescent history. It was over, I had done it. Victory!

MILESTONE = THE FIRST KISS

I suppose Kayden was never what you call a looker to most. I mean he had a mop of greasy curtains for hair and to be totally frank, his face was nothing to be admired either. Firstly, there was the big nose, not to mention he was covered in teenage acne. Strangely enough, though, I didn't ever stare at the yellow swellings on the top of the red mountains adorning his face with repulsion. In fact, I barely noticed them. He wore scruffy, old trackie bottoms and the same Adidas jumper day in and day out, but none of this mattered because I was infatuated with him. I wasn't exactly that fit myself and besides, it wasn't particularly his looks that I was smitten with.

He had just the sort of persona that I am still attracted to now, minus the puss laden physical aspects. He was so shy and for some strange reason, that just turned me on muchly. Maybe there was something sadistic about it, like I could be the one with the power. Maybe, just maybe, it signalled an opportunity for me (yes, I know me, the virgin queen) to bring him out of his shell, mmmm, power! Ironic isn't it, I had only just had my first kiss and already I was a demon possessed with lust.

His cheeks would blush when anybody spoke to him causing him to look so cautious and vulnerable. The irony was, I knew him well and boy could he lose it should he want to. He had been excluded from school for fighting, numerous times, and as immature as it might sound now that I am old as shit, I bloody loved this. Think Tom Hardy in Lawless. The juxtaposition of his shy persona versus his Mr Hyde psychotic side did it for me. That to me was some horny shit and I loved it. Who gave a toss that he was no Brad Pitt? His personality would be around long after his looks had faded and even at a naive age of 15, that was what I was clinging to. It seemed I now had a type. Adolescence was clearly evolving me.

Kayden seemed to idolise me from the word go. Yes, not only had I finally bagged myself a boyfriend, he was nice to me too – hurrah! He would ride his bike forty-five minutes from his house to mine to spend twenty minutes with me, come rain, hail or shine. You may not be impressed but I'm hailing this guy as a hero. He called me every night, they were the longest calls I have ever had in my life. I have no idea what we spoke about for hours upon end, but we managed to run up epic bills, so it must have been enthralling. And let's not forget, we are talking about pre-mobile days. Hence, there was no privacy. Oh no, I had to seat myself on the cold hard floor in the passage (or hallway if you are posh), where one would find a wall mounted mahogany telephone table adorned with a green phone. Underneath lay shelves laden with telephone directories and a plastic book that you have to spin the dial on the front to open, not to mention the device was firmly attached to the wall, no wandering around with this baby. Every man and his dog would trundle through the passage as you were pouring your heart's content out to your loved one, but we cared not!

From here the relationship went from strength to strength, for a short time anyway. We had embarked upon adolescent milestone heaven. He was the first boy I French kissed, the first boy I held hands with. Although there was David and Carlton when I was 8, my friend and I alternated them as our boyfriends on a weekly basis. It was an early, more innocent version of wife swapping. His was the first penis I saw, except my dad's (explanation to follow) and ultimately, he was my first sexual experience. Oh, hold on .... you want to know about the penis touching. Oh, you do, do you, you filthy fuckers. Stay patient, we didn't rush into it, you know. I may have now turned 15 but it didn't add to my confidence, that I can tell you.

At first, we seemed madly in love, meeting each other at every available opportunity for a quick snog and fumble. Between Technology and French lessons, at the bottom of the Design block, behind the bike sheds, only joking, we didn't have bike sheds. I didn't have a bike! We hadn't long been out of the mining strike, for god's sake. Anyway, I think you get the picture, we were fast becoming inseparable and although I was undeniably perfectly happy, I still wanted more. The males reading this are now thinking, *"And you want us to be shocked?"*

Do you recall me telling you about our crossover to Comby in search of new totty? Anna and I were still visiting the forbidden land, even though I had seemingly found love on home turf. Nasty me? Maybe. I was young and insatiable for attention. It wasn't that I was a 'slag' How could I be? I was a bloody virgin in every sense of the word, my sexual experiences were limited to a snog with hands on hips really. I just loved the attention. It was my addiction and I suppose my downfall!

Boys + Cider + Attention = Naughty Behaviour.

It was the aforementioned formula that landed me in it really. I suppose if I could have laid off the booze I wouldn't have made the mistakes that I did. Bloody hell, lightbulb moment. Why am I still suffering from this flaw? I'm clearly not a very fast learner. Anyway, back then we were 15, we were inflicted with a serious lack of funds coupled with a lack of parental guidance. Therefore, we couldn't busy ourselves with horse riding or snowboarding lessons. We could barely afford bus rides never mind anything else. So, we were limited to getting smashed out of our minds on a nightly basis on a £1.99 bottle of cider and making memories that we would never have made sober, in order to be able to reminisce when we were sober. Yep, that was it, our social activities consisted of getting smashed and when we weren't smashed, reminiscing about being smashed. I often wonder where the social misconception surrounding us council estate folk starts. Who says we aren't cultured?

However, now that I belonged to one who belonged to my homeland, it was obviously not the done thing to trot/sneak (depends which way you look at it), to the neighbouring village. Even back then, as an inexperienced woman, there was no way a mere boy was going to tell me what I was going to do. Yes, it seems now I had a boyfriend, my claims to be the perfect girlfriend were waning a little. Besides, as young adolescents generally are, I was constantly torn between the needs of my faithful friends and my desires to spend every waking moment of my life either thinking about boys, being with boys, dreaming about being with boys etc. All this kept my social life extremely busy and as a result, I often found the stress a bit hard to cope with. For this reason, and this reason only, I kept my friends, and, ok, myself, happy by cross communicating with the aborigines of the next village. I suppose we better call it sneaking. Maybe it would be the correct definition to use? The fact that we had to lay down on the back seats on the bus whilst passing my lovely boyf and his friends, who were hanging out on their regular corner, indicates that it may have been quite a sneaky move to make.

Maybe you are giving me the benefit of the doubt and are questioning whether this was indeed a sneaky move or whether it was just my inexperienced way of trying to keep everybody happy and not hurt other people. I sure would like you to think that; nobody likes to be thought bad about. However, when I began to jot these memoirs for you, I swore to stick to the whole truth and nothing but the truth or as close to the truth as I could get. Firstly, because this is all obviously only from my own perspective, which is clearly very biased, and secondly, I don't want to land myself with a libel lawsuit. So ultimately, yes, there was always something in it for me. I was/am quite selfish like that, and in this case, it was (taking a wild stab in the dark) probably boys.

Do you recall the 'crossover'? And Susan? It was Susan that was to bring the downfall of our ideal status of grazing on both grasslands. I know, I had been so fond of her too. Although I am not sure that I can lay the blame entirely at her feet.

She was dating one of the boys that I detailed to you earlier; Josh. Ahh, Josh. Maybe we could, in fact, blame Josh and leave both Susan and I free of any wrong doing at all? Yes, Josh was confident, a trait that can easily manipulate a young woman's mind, and confidence was something that I liked. Don't get me wrong, I didn't like cocky confidence, eeewwwwwwwww, no! That was more of a turn off than picking fleas off a dog's belly, but I did like the shy type of confidence. The 'I have confidence when it matters' type of mantra. The 'when it matters' would be when it came to handling me. I liked a man that could talk the talk, he had to be able to walk the walk too. I liked someone that would tell me the things I wanted to hear, even now I still don't like a man that keeps the important things to himself. For god's sake, what is the point in that? What is the point of having thoughts if you are not going to share them?

Susan and Josh were a great match, to be fair, though Susan was more interested in her cider than she was in keeping an eye on Josh, so surely, she was to blame for his unavoidable roaming. May I make it clear here that I never chased him. That just wasn't my style. Even in my desperate 'I need a boyfriend' days, I would never have humiliated myself in such a fashion. I played the cool and calm role with my exterior blase attitude. That may have been my persona, but it definitely wasn't a true reflection of the emotions I went through inside. They were for me, and only me, to know.

The problem was Josh never left me alone, he made his intentions very clear. He would lure me into the closest and darkest corners and declare his undying love (albeit it was obviously lust). So, I'll admit it, I loved the attention, who wouldn't have? I was young! And now you are questioning my loyalty to my friends and my boyfriend? Loyalty between 15-year-old girls is generally very thin on the ground and being the selfish beings us young girls are, loyalty was only an issue when the loyalty was towards me.

Reluctantly, I gave in. Look it really wasn't my fault, his advances were so forceful that I was given no choice. I saw it as a 'get it over and done with thing'. That and the fact that I was so plastered on cheap cider that even hijacking a bus would have seemed like a good idea. Hence, we snogged! To be totally honest, it was not a nice experience. I didn't find him particularly attractive and the fact that he had chased me to the death just really put me off him.

The other issue was, I liked my boys to be physically fit, of which he was not, and the stench of cigarettes on his breath was a major, major turn-off. At that age, the chase was definitely more exciting than the actual deed. In the end, he felt like a booby prize as I began to embark on a whole new experience. I was beginning to have feelings! I sobered up quickly and started to think about the friend who I had let down and my lovely boyfriend who I had ultimately cheated on. Maybe it was time that I accepted that we were no longer in junior school, openly sharing boyfriends, quite acceptedly. I had waited so long to enter coupledom and then I had gone and defiled it. Jesus Christ, what was wrong with me?

MILESTONE = CHEATED ON A FRIEND

I knew even that night that this one could never stay a secret. We were out in a group of about thirty people and we were not exactly hidden in the bloody Amazon. We had positioned ourselves around the corner of a brightly light school and since we were extremely pissed, I doubt very much that we were even remotely careful or for that matter the slightest bit quiet. For this reason, I was not surprised in the least when I received a call from Susan the very next day. To say I was nervous would be a major understatement. It wasn't that I feared her, no, instead it was this new feeling of guilt that I was experiencing. Okay, so she wasn't my best friend by a long shot but she was a friend and one that I liked a lot and I had betrayed her. Yes, with a spotty, scruffy tracksuit wearing loser, but it was still betrayal in all its glory.

She asked me what had happened, and I told her the straight truth: no John Bull.

"I did nothing, it was all him," I blurted out.

Surprisingly enough, she was quite okay with it, to a certain degree. Maybe she was grateful that I helped her see him in his full loser status, maybe she saw me as a bit of a hero? Obviously though, she proceeded to tell me what a total fucking slag, bitch, whore, crap friend (etc) I was. Then she gave me THE ultimatum.

"You tell him, or I will," she stated firmly, and she bloody meant it.

She was referring to my lovely Kayden. The mother fucking bitch was going to make me destroy myself. Did she think that we are the movie set of fucking *Saw*? Well, she can tootle off on her tricycle because that shit was not going to happen. Did she bloody realise how long I had waited to get to this point in my youth? Did she seriously want me to take ten steps back at such a crucial stage of my adolescence, all because her boyfriend forced his spotty faced, fag breath upon me? It wasn't my bloody fault, I was pissed, and he took advantage. I was the mother fucking 'victim'. My plea fell on deaf ears.

"I have given you the ultimatum and the choice is yours," she said smugly.

What the fuck was she talking about? How the fucking hell was it a choice? Either way, he found out, so really there was no sodding choice! It was a bit hard to decide which option to take. I mean if she told him, at least I wouldn't have to stand there and witness the look on his face when he found out what I had done. Neither would I be the first person in the firing line should he decide to kick the total shit out of someone. I also wouldn't have to be the one who uttered the words to him that in reality labelled me with a title that I felt I just totally didn't deserve. For all you doubters reading this, you must realise that I was so young that I was inevitably going to make mistakes, otherwise how would I ever learn? Mistakes are inescapable in the growing up process and therefore fate states that they must be made. Taking this important information into account, did I truly deserve to lose my Kayden? Did the punishment actually fit the crime?

On the other hand, if I did pluck up the courage to tell him myself, then I would be able to lay on the floor hold on to his legs whilst sobbing and begging forgiveness and refuse to let him go until he had pledged his total undying love for me regardless of any behaviour I may have displayed. I could possibly even bend the truth in my favour a little. All for love and saving his feelings, obviously.

To that end, I decided to bite the bullet and do it myself. Since I was only 15, this obviously wasn't going to be done over a romantic meal with some fancy gesture to make him forget. Similarly, since I was still a Virgo Virgin, neither was I going to offer him a blowjob or parade in stockings and suspenders whilst seductively sucking my fingers. No, this time my only weapons were my wit coupled with a whole barrage of begging and pleading words.

Clearly, it would seem I had more control over the situation if I opted for the latter. So, whilst sat on our hill, huddled together with his arms wrapped lovingly around my shoulders and mine desperately, tightly clasped around his waist, I began to prepare to tell him my sordid secret. The truth was I loved every second of being with him. I had the trademark butterflies and I wanted to rip his clothes off so there was no doubt that he was the one for me. Could I be about to lose him?

As I looked into his eyes and confessed, I did not enjoy seeing the look of anguish on his face. He looked puzzled like he couldn't believe or didn't want to believe that I would do that to him. He didn't even remotely release his grip from around my shoulders, he didn't even loosen it. He didn't even move his gaze from me, he just continued to look straight into my eyes. It seemed like an age before he spoke, and I had never been more nervous. I waited with bated breath for his reaction, with everything including my toes crossed.

"So, was it a one off?" he finally probed as he stared way past my eyes and deep into my soul.

"It wasn't even a one-off," I fired back, "I can barely even remember it and I feel sick with guilt."

My heart began to race in anticipation. Could he be about to forgive me?

"And you won't ever go down there again?" he asked calmly.

"No fucking way," I answered back quickly, scared that he may change his mind before I had a chance to finish my sentence.

He casually waited a few minutes as if he was pondering over which CD to put on. Slowly, he shut his eyes, leaned towards me and kissed me more passionately than he ever had before. It wasn't just a kiss. It was a symbol, the symbol of the sealing of a deal. One of the first signs of real love that I had ever felt.

Tensely, this seemed to be moving from lust to love. Fucking hell, I didn't think for one minute I could ever feel more for him, or anybody, than I already did; this was a whole other level. I could barely feel my legs, they were like jelly bags. He was so calm. It was just the biggest turn on ever. Readers don't mistake this for lack of feelings, for I could tell by his eyes that I had cut him deeply. I could also tell from his kiss that I meant more to him than some stupid pissed up 'kiss'. We were clearly falling in love!

Luckily for me, I never saw Josh again. I say luckily because of the misery I caused myself because of him. As for Susan and I, we fell right back into our friendship like nothing had ever happened. Teenagers seem to be able to do this much more easily. As I said earlier, I think anybody can fall victim into the cheat trap at that age. As an adult, no friendship would ever survive such turmoil and betrayal. When you are that young, I suppose, it must be easier to forgive? Either that or you base your friend's loyalty on how much cider they bring along to a damp cold winter night when huddled in a muddy field?

The First Sexual Experience

A lthough Kayden may have forgiven me, his friends were less convinced. He had two friends in particular, that he spent a lot of time with (therefore so did I): Micky and Mitchell. I had known Micky a long time, he used to live over the backs from me. He claimed to 'know' me, just like many of the other boys in our gossip ridden village. So, he felt himself to be well versed in filling Kayden in with the far from factual material that he felt that he had a right to dole out. You know snippets of information like, I was a dirty whore and that I had slept with most of the estate. Hence obviously, he found it very strange that I had not slept with Kayden. He also thought it his duty to convince Kayden that the fact that I had cheated with Josh meant that I was obviously going to do it again, and again, and again (you get the picture). The basics here, they weren't exactly top of my fan club list.

I suppose I deserved their interference following the sorry situation of my infidelity and couldn't help but think about the fact that neither of them had ever been in a boyfriend/girlfriend relationship clearly showed that they were just jealous and wanted to free their mate from my clutches just to get him back all to themselves.

All that aside, what was more than obvious was that I was in lust at the very least, with Kayden. As I had previously mentioned (yet another drum roll, please), it was with him that I had my very first sexual encounter. I must say, it didn't seem dirty or seedy with him, just like the teachers and your parents led you to believe it would be. Oh no, this was pure, good, clean loving!

As with most teenagers, our first experience was whilst my friend was babysitting. I sense the gasps from the readers who regularly employ such services. If, by any chance, you didn't experience the kind of adolescence that you are poring over within these pages, then I feel that I have a moral duty to awaken you to the 'babysitter movement'. To you – you are innocently employing the services of a young person to care for your children as a temporary replacement for a parent whilst you pour copious amounts of liquor down your throat in a drastic attempt to forget that you are overworked, underpaid and (let's be frank) to forget that you have children altogether. Whilst I am sure that you have made this very clear during the employment process of said 'babysitter', looking after your children is actually the last thing on their mind. In a bizarre kind of cross providing of services, your babysitter has not only hired your premises, but cleverly, they have even been paid for it, quite entrepreneurial really. They have one aim only - to get themselves some mother fucking ass, in privacy and total and utter comfort.

So once again, I was about to embark upon a total class experience. After getting completely wrecked on my usual medication of Special Red cider and a tipple of Red Thunderbird for good luck, I was ready to be welcomed into the broken woman crew. Eagerly, I invited him round whilst my friend was babysitting and I was ready for whatever should happen. Let's be totally honest, I was hoping to give away my cherry that night but knew in reality that I was so petrified that I might have to add half a bottle of vodka into the mixture before I gave that special fruit away. Besides, it was just a quiet gathering whilst I was babysitting, I was aware that the hustle and bustle of a party may have been needed to distract from the love making spells being cast from the bedrooms above (having my friends listening with the glass against the door just didn't do it for me). For now, I was more than happy to just go with the flow and see what did or didn't happen.

Waiting for him to arrive, me and my girls went through the saga of situations that may arise just to ensure that I was educated and prepared for all eventualities. Problem was, my friends really believed that I was much more experienced than I actually was. All right, I hold my hands up, maybe I may have led them to believe that I had already been deflowered. Therefore, as a result of my fable telling, real advice in this situation was in short supply. They wrongly assumed I was versed with the tales of the serpent, so gave me general Kayden advice and not the much-needed penis tackling advice. Arrrggghhhh. I had hoped that all would be remedied after that night, with any luck.

My Kayden arrived (god, I loved saying that), and with my legs eagerly shaking and my heart in my mouth, I led him straight upstairs. What was the point in wasting time? I might sober up after all and fail to go through with the process. This could only lead to disaster, in the form of me retaining my virginal status. So, I decided to get onto it whilst I was at my most drunkenness and my courage was at its top. Looking back on it now, he probably felt like he was about to be raped or 'used' at the very least, which I'm sure (being of the male variety) he did not mind one little bit.

Philosophy – The Process of Sex

Yes, I did use that word 'process'. Ok, admittedly I agree that there is a middle ground. However, embarking upon the beginning of the journey of sexual adolescence, the act is definitely a 'process', and equivalently, so is the end: there is no denying we get to the point in relationships where sex once again becomes 'a process'. I am desperately trying to think of a more positive lexis, 'procedure' is about as good as I can get, and I think that it is worse. Thank the fucking lord for that period in between, where terms such as magnetism, lovemaking and shagging, fit much better. Even more abhorrently, the truth is that it is a frigging process that we have no idea about, there is no fucking manual (not for us internet less generations anyway). To put this into layman's terms, imagine trying to put up flatpack furniture ... actually hold on ... the other participant is actually the flat pack furniture, yeah, that's right, you are trying to put this human flat pack furniture together, as an adolescent (just about as inexperienced in life as one can be) .... naked.... without the bloody instructions. So yes, a process it is. Modus operandi at its best!

I opened the door to the master bedroom (somebody else's master obviously, but who cared about that for tonight) and laid him on the bed. God knows what I thought I was about to do with him but fuck it, I was pissed. Maybe I was using role reversal, or it was more likely that I was just too pissed to control myself. Luckily, he seemed much more experienced then me (praise the fucking Lord that I don't believe in), he confidently grabbed me and seductively spun me around, slamming me down onto the fluffy bed. Turned on was an understatement. So how was I feeling? I loved a boy who could take control, especially when I had no fucking idea what I was doing, it really helped. Praise the non-lord!

I lay there on my back as he slowly lowered himself on top of me (I know I'm making this sound very mechanical, aren't I?), looked into my eyes and whispered, "I can't believe I'm actually here with you."

That was it, that was enough for me to decide it was time to rip my knickers off, dive on top of him and get on with the deed. The thing was, I was no longer doing this because I wanted to lose my virginity, I was doing it because I felt I needed him, besides I wanted to be as close to him as physically possible. He just made me feel so special (no, not that kind of 'bus' special) and so important. Cliché? Agreed. And let's face it, he wanted to get laid.

In my naivety however, it was clear that I had never felt like this in my life and it just supplemented the intensity of the moment. I wanted him more than I had ever wanted anything in my entire life, which wasn't too hard since I could realistically only remember the last 5 years or so in detail. The pace and intensity increased as he totally took control and pushed me backwards onto the bed, my head narrowly missing the solid oak headboard (disaster averted) and began to slowly take my clothes off. His seemingly experienced fingers began to fumble slightly with the button on my jeans. I wasn't willing to wait, I pushed his hand out of the way and ripped the bleeders off myself.

We did the normal teenage thing, lots of snogging and rolling around the bed, whilst rubbing our bodies on each other. Come on what did I know? He suddenly stopped kissing my lips as he made his way around to my neck, then my ears, mmmmmm. I loved it. Why hadn't somebody told me about the existence of such pleasure before? I began to writhe about the bed in pleasure. Although regarding pleasure, I was about to be schooled!

He began to slowly work his way down my perfectly flat stomach (I had to get that in there, seriously it's true), towards my nether regions. Oh shit! I had been so pre-occupied (ok petrified), I had to take a moment to remember whether I had in fact shaved my legs this week or whether he was about to enter cactus zone? I didn't at this point have to worry about the spreading bush, being so young, I didn't yet have spider's legs spreading their way down my unwilling legs, just yet.

Those worries, and thoughts lasted all but a second. In fact, any thoughts and worries vanished as his wet tongue touched my vagina. The mere contact of his mouth onto my skin made it hard to breathe. Sweat began to appear in places it had never before. I had always thought that the moaning women made during sex scenes in films was fake and here I was, screaming, like an out of body experience, unable to stop myself, unable to rein this new me in. As if the mere contact was not enough, he began to move his tongue slowly (and expertly it seemed) up and down, I glanced down quickly to check what he was using, surely this feeling could not be created from his tongue? I looked away quickly, I was embarrassed to watch him do it, but not embarrassed enough to make him stop. The more I moaned, the more enthusiastic he got. Oh, so that was how it worked? A bit like a vocal remote. I suppose it is a bit like an 'Alexa' with a tongue.

Clearly, he wanted to show me what he could really do, so he grabbed hold of my behind firmly with his hands and pulled my groin even closer to his face, inserting his tongue as deep inside me as he could. I wailed with pleasure as he refused to ease off his tight hold, as if I would have wanted him to. My breathing deepened taking me far away from the reality of being laid on somebody else's bed and instead exploring caverns of pleasure I could never have imagined even existed. Oh, this is adulthood?

Imagine my frustration, and hopefully his, when he pulled himself away from me to check his watch. WTF?? Who gave a shit about the concept of time when we were circling in orbit out of this world. Surely a telling off from 'mammy' was worth it in order to extend this feeling for as long as humanly possible? It would seem not. I must admit, I didn't like this mammy boy side of him or the fact that he chose the mother over me. I suppose with years of hindsight, I can clearly see that had he have ignored his curfew, this would have meant that he was to be withheld from meeting me due to the literal enforcement of retaining adolescents within one space (usually the home) that is generally referred to as 'grounding' by us northerners.

"I'm so sorry babe," he said as he began scrambling for his clothes, "I've got to go."

"No fucking way," I announced as I attempted to drag him back onto the bed. Nobody was going to stop this. I was so close to ridding myself of the curse of virginity that I couldn't let a silly thing like a curfew get in between me and the target.

"This isn't the end, it's only the beginning," he said to me with that oh so cute blushing face and the sneaky smile.

I immediately let go as I melted back into the pillow floating on absolute lustful bliss. Who needed drugs, when this kind of high could be achieved through a few flicks of a tongue? I think I had just found my new favourite pastime and I knew just who I wanted to be my playing partner. Could this boy be any more perfect?

I have always said from that day forward that no person has ever known pleasure until they have experienced oral sex from a woman's point of view. I can honestly say from thence forth, I saw the whole world (yes, the whole world, it really is that dramatic) in a different light, I suppose I had my first taste of womandom, and I fucking loved it! The moment was so intense, and I finally understood the meaning of closeness from one human being to another. I had never been this close to anyone.

We never got as far as doing the actual do. Let's face it with the hormones pumping through a 15-year-old boy's body, my virgin routine was never going to tie him down was it? At least this meant it wasn't my fault that we didn't reach the point of penetration. It was Stagecoach's (bus company) error, with a sprinkle of his mam's rules. The last bus that ran in order to get him home for his curfew of 10 o'clock was 9.30p.m.

MILESTONE = SEXUAL CONTACT

Words wouldn't be able to bring to justice my feelings at that moment in time. I was riding the waves of sensual desire, and to be totally honest, have never felt a high like that since. At the time I contributed it to the fact that I had finally found my soul-mate, and this is what it felt like to be totally and truly madly in love. Now having had much more experience of life, I think it's obviously more to do with the intensity of experiencing those feelings for the very first time.

Unwillingly, I began to redress myself and my attire was completed with a cheesy smile plastered across my face. I couldn't stop staring at him, which was clearly embarrassing him as he was blushing like a bloody beacon. I was a smitten teenager and he was my victim. He grabbed my hand and slowly pulled me up from the bed close to his chest and then wrapped his arms, so tightly, around me. As we stared into each other's eyes for a moment, I had to catch my breath. I suddenly realised that those so called 'Silver Screen' moments were in fact real. For teenagers with no notion of the real world they were. And I was lucky enough to just be embarking upon that very journey and bloody hell, was it exciting.

Then he said it!

"I love you babe," he declared as he leant down and kissed me.

My chest ceased to move ... who even needed to breathe? He said what??? I would like to tell you what was going through my head in that moment, except I couldn't think, my body was concentrated on feeling. An overwhelming feeling of love that I never knew was possible.

MILESTONE = I AM LOVED

I wanted to tell him *'right back atcha'* but the not breathing thing kind of hindered me. That and the fact he was now snogging my face off, hence making it very hard for me to speak. Maybe that was his plan? He would declare his love for me and just in case it was not reciprocated, he would snog my face off so that there were no awkward silences. I may need to remember that trick for future use. He really need not have worried! He had me hook, line and sinker. I felt like a totally different person. Dare I say it without sounding like a complete clichéd drip? Oh, sod it, here goes: I just felt so complete!

Philosophy – Hearing 'I Love You'

I know that your parents may have been uttering those words to you all your life. That is not what we are talking about here. We are talking about those overwhelming words being proclaimed from a partner's mouth for the ... very .... first ...time! The collywobbles stem from one obvious reason. The fact that this person doesn't have to love you (unlike your parents), they choose to. Now that is one hell of an amazing thing. Basically, what they are saying is not just 'I love you' they are really saying 'you are just fucking awesome'. Now don't tell me that hearing that, doesn't make you feel like a rising god?

As we walked to the bus stop together we barely spoke. We didn't need to. I can only speak for myself, but I was so encompassed in this new world that I had discovered, that I needed to take it all in. He held my hand so tight and kept giving it a little squeeze every now and again. I supposed at the time he did that just to let me know he was still there even though he wasn't speaking. Now, I wonder if it was to check I was still alive. I was never quiet and most definitely never shy, he probably wondered what the hell had happened to me.

We stood in that bus shelter, totally oblivious to the smell of urine surrounding us. His bus came far too quick. I really couldn't bear to let him go. It was a real *Titanic* moment. Fair enough, I wasn't dropping him into the bottom of the ocean, but you know how dramatic teenagers are. It really felt that way, honest. I would have run away with him there and then, any sensible ideas I had ever had about my future went out of the window that night.

Philosophy – First Sexual Contact

I suppose Kayden could have been anyone, to an extent anyway, and I would have felt exactly the same. It is the first time you have felt those emotions and experienced that pleasure. Let's compare it to something else. The first time you have alcohol, it only takes a few mouthfuls before you are slaughtered. Why? Your body isn't used to it. The more used to it you get the harder it is to get pissed. Similar analogy? I think so. And so, I suppose we could say, the more tongue action we get, the harder it is to please us. I'm not sure it's that complex for men (if I am going to be totally honest). Maybe that's why even as an adult we allude back to these early relationships and wonder why we don't love with the intensity and sincerity that we did back then. It ultimately makes us question the relationships we enter as an adult, as we obviously compare them, stupidly! Take the 'perfection' of these relationships, chuck in a mortgage, screaming kids, lack of sex and they are all doomed to the same fate aren't they, irrelevant of how it felt back then?

I remember after the first time we got intimate with each other, I was convinced that people could tell. I presume that you are smiling here, as you thought the very same thing, didn't you? I just felt different. I suppose I felt grown up, like I too knew the secrets of the adult world like all the other women around me I know it's a strange thing to say, I felt so superior, like that one event had somehow matured me. Let's face it, all that had really happened was a quick fumble in the dark. Nonetheless I regarded that event as my transition of girl to woman.

Kayden was a golden find to me and the perfect match for me in terms of my ideal fella (only at 15 mind), but he was by no means a goody-goody. He got himself into so much trouble, but that only made him even more attractive in my eyes. The most attractive thing about him was that he wasn't a bragger or somebody that wanted everyone to think that he was the bee's knees. No, he was the total opposite. He liked to blend into the background and hated being the centre of attention. Although he was often up to no good, fortunately, he more than knew how to look after himself. This I found very attractive.

In contrast, I'm sure I would have been perceived as cocky, mouthy (foul mouthed at that – and nothing much has changed in that department), rude, arrogant and loved being the centre of attention. The sad thing about this is that none of the above was what I really was at all. Inside I was so unconfident about anything and everything and since I was always the centre of attention for the wrong reasons, I didn't enjoy it at all.

Following our successful night of passion, we were both desperate to pick up where we left off. This however, was easier said than done. We both still lived with our parents and since none of them had jobs, it was highly unlikely that we were ever to be able to grab the house to ourselves.

Ok so I catch your thought vibes and I know you are thinking, *'Come on you were a teenager, what was wrong with a field or even behind a bush?'* Let me stop you right there. This wasn't that kind of relationship, I'll have you know. We didn't want a quickie. We wanted time and space to explore each other. Ok, 'I' didn't want a quickie. I don't suppose he gave a toss as long as he got his fill. Personally, I just wanted it to be remarkably perfect, I wanted to remember every detail, I no longer wanted to be pissed and unable to re-count the event detail by detail, this was a memory I already knew I would want to savour.

Finally, bingo, the gods had shone upon us! My mam had asked me to baby-sit my siblings on one of her rare outings out of the house. The W.M.C was calling her with its alluringly smoky atmosphere. That was our chance, perfect! Eagerly, I made the arrangements. Nothing complex, just made the call to him and told him it was on.

I had been pacing all day, heart in my mouth. My mind had been racing. Was he going to turn up? Would it go ok? Would it be what I wanted? Would I still feel the same? More importantly to me, would he still feel the same? I couldn't bear the thought that I would never feel again what I felt that night. I set about the all-important losing of the virginity preparations: bathed the tush, defurred the legs, tamed the bush and lathered the Constant Caroll on my face. No, there was no revealing outfit: this was the nineties. As revealing as it got was that I unfastened the top few buttons on my checked shirt!

Startlingly, he did arrive and abruptly ended my misery. Oh yes! I still felt the same alright. I opened the door and he smiled cheekily at me. He was dressed just as I liked, trackie bottoms and the trademark baseball cap. He turned me into some shy schoolgirl that I had never been before. Ironically, I was more nervous than the first time. Why? Because, maybe (just maybe) I was beginning to fall for him. I felt so nervous around him, I was so desperate for everything to go perfect.

The first hour or so was torture, as I actually had to baby-sit and not focus my attentions on him. By the time I finally got the children to bed, the sexual tension had built between us so high that there was absolutely no time for niceties and definitely no time for polite kissing or foreplay. No way! I shut the stairs door and dived straight on him like a woman possessed. I'm sure we smashed teeth a few times in my desperation to just get as close to him as possible. If it was embarrassing, I don't remember because I was so turned on that I could barely stop myself from passing out.

All this aside, he was here, I had let him in and once again we were in our own little bubble, we were right back where I wanted to be and once again we were totally in tune with each other. Now this is no *50 shades of Grey* and neither was he *Christian*: we were far too inexperienced to start knocking shit out of each other during our nervous fumbling session. We could barely make eye contact, never mind start tying each other to the bed and inserting love beads! For his years and his inexperience, he sure seemed to know what he was doing!

We were quickly lost within the exploration of each other's gums and molars, his hand began to wander around to the front of my leggings. Looking back, I guess he was ecstatic at the easy access wear, I was totally oblivious in that moment. I was suddenly not lost, I was there ... there and very aware and very fucking petrified! Curious and excited, a whole myriad of emotions spilling from my pores. Frantic thoughts and questions were circling my head: do I need to move closer, higher, open my legs, will it hurt? My thoughts were broken as he wrapped his arm around my hips and hoisted me closer to him. As our bodies made contact, my eyes widened as I felt his fingers slide in between my legs. Ooosshhh! Without any warning the floodgates opened. WTF? It should go without saying that this had never happened to me before! Was this supposed to happen? Or had I just pissed on my boyfriend's hand? I figured it wasn't the latter since he continued to plunge his fingers towards my cervix.

I would love to divulge to you all here, about how I writhed about with excitement as his fingers eased in and out of my vagina bringing me subliminal joy beyond earthly comparison. I would be fucking lying. It was nothing he had done wrong but clearly my vagina was expecting a little more, considering her rendition to the fucking Bellagio Fountains upon finger entry. To be fair, my experience since has not fared me any better. It wasn't terrible, I am not saying it was painful either. I'm just saying it was a bit shit. Totally twatting pointless for the female. So, if I was to describe it to somebody who had not yet engaged in such an activity, I would explain it as somebody poking you in a playful way. It is neither irritating nor enjoyable, it just happens.

So, what is the official term for this sexual engagement? Fuck knows, but I do know that any term would be better than the street term, fingering?! I cringed when people said it then and I still cringe now. Why hasn't somebody come up with a fucking acceptable alternative? I completely understand how the term was attributed to it – it is pretty bloody self-explanatory (as is the term fisted –we are not going to venture there either) but come on. It is foul! This was one of many very literal terms that we used as youngsters. We were so classy. I do however know a girl who didn't understand that BJ wasn't a literal term but that's another story; along with my cousin getting confused when asked to bend over, it seemed the crab wasn't what he had in mind.

MILESTONE = REALISATION NOT ALL SEXUAL ENGAGEMENT IS GOOD

As before he took control and he picked me up and laid me gently on my living room floor. He wasn't even put off by the 1990's vomit style patterned carpet that he was about to lay me on and neither was I embarrassed about it for the first time ever. I hated taking people back to my house normally for a multitude of reasons. The flower-patterned wallpaper that revealed the large white cracks in between (detailing the unprofessional décor), coupled with the yellow ceilings and doors from an obsessive amount of nicotine released into such a small space, was just too much to bear. You may think that doesn't seem too bad, but I haven't mentioned the brick fireplace yet. You know, the ones that spanned from one side of the room to another encompassing not only the fire (of which surely was the only purpose of a fucking fireplace) but surrounding the T.V as well, leaving a space for the video. Wait, it didn't stop there, no this mammoth fireplace also housed a massive tropical fish tank. No, my parents didn't have a job and couldn't afford new clothes for us, but they could spend tenners galore on elephant fish. Bloody nineties!

He started kissing my neck as my toes curled and my legs seemed to automatically wrap themselves around of him. I recalled back to our first encounter and longed to skip the pre-foreplay and get down to the 'real foreplay'. As I locked myself around him with my ankles, I felt his erection push against me and my heart began to race. Scared as I may have been, I wanted it! My body was telling me that. My temperature rose and my core pulsated! I felt so hedonistic and was happy to lay there and let him do whatever it was he wanted to do to me. As he slowly moved his tight grip from the back of my neck and ran his hands slowly and professionally down my side, my whole body tingled with desire. I was beset with an eagerness to have him as close as possible to me, inside me even.

He began to follow his hand movements with small gentle kisses down my body that made me writhe on the floor with pleasure, probably coating myself in dog hair from our rarely brushed Alsatian that mostly lived under the worktop in the kitchen (sorry it was getting a little serious there and let's not pretend that it wasn't). Every time his lips touched my body, electrodes travelled down to ensure that I was more than ready. Nervous I may have been, willing I undoubtedly was. I didn't want this to end.

And then 'it' happened! He lowered the front of his bottoms to release his penis. My eyes largened as I took in this complete unnatural sight and I hoped that my face hadn't revealed my utter distaste of the view. As natural as this might sound whacked in the middle of a sex scene, I may have to confess that I had never actually seen a penis before, not really. Initially, I wondered if he had injured the end of it due to the large bulbous swelling (maybe he had been masturbating far too much) and I was absolutely certain that the veins should not be protruding it in the way they were! It looked unhealthy, but I am embarrassed to say, I was still happy to proceed.

I doubt that anybody ever forgets the first time that they lay eyes on their first donger! Admittedly the millennials of the world are far more prepared for their first penis viewing then we ever were. I am sure that we would be hard pushed to find a girl that hasn't laid her eyes on a picture of a cock after the age of 12, thanks to the media of the world, whether she was searching for it or not. If I am going to put over an honest portrayal of this experience, I would have to admit that my first time I saw a willy was not a sexual partner. Instead it was my dad! I hasten to add that I reckon most of us are in the same boat on this one. Maybe that should make the understanding of dicks more natural, I am afraid it really doesn't. I remember catching sight of my dad's parts as he ran into the bedroom to deal with my sister's projectile vomiting.

Here I was comforting Clair during her moment of need (which was imperative since we shared a double bed) and the next thing I knew, I was faced with a floppy, deep brown beak encompassed by a mass of shiny black locks. What was this curio? Whilst I was admittedly taken by surprise, this was purely down to the colour (I mean my dad was as Scottish and as Caucasian as they come, so why was his willy such a different colour?). Other than that, as a six-year-old, I just thought it looked a bit fucking stupid and if you want me to cut to the chase – I still do.

Now, I don't claim that vaginas are attractive at all, I would go as far to say that they are intriguing, although you may disagree. I think it terms of description you just couldn't claim the same for penises. They simply look hilarious at best and at worst, weak and feeble. Even when faced with a stern and erect penis, it doesn't look intimidating or even powerful, it just looks ridiculous. Now forgive me for being pedantic, the weapon that is seemingly responsible for the continuation of the entire species of humanity, maybe should just NOT look either feeble or ridiculous! And even if we look at it on a more personal level ... if they are designed to capture the affections of the female/male counterpart shouldn't they at least look good? I mean it's hardly comparable to the feathers of a majestic fucking peacock is it?

Anyway, lets uncomfortably move over from musing over my father's penis and its ageing colour and get back to me being laid on the floor (possibly covered in dog hair) with Kayden, knob in hand. He grinned as he let go of his asset and leaned down to reassure me with a kiss, when the unthinkable happened. No, not that (you dirty buggers), no, the door flung open.

Fuck! It was my older brother; his timing was impeccable. Kayden frantically jumped to his feet attempting to put his protruding weapon safely away into his tracksuit bottoms, which is easier said than done with blood being pumped wildly to its tip. Reminiscing about this does make me wonder how today's girlie boys would cope with such an experience. In effect, Kayden had it easy, he had expandable tracksuit bottoms on (shiny Kappa for the sake of imagery), so whilst his erection was noticeably obvious, my brother still didn't have the opportunity to lay his eyes on 'it' in its raw glory. With today's trend of skin eating trousers, trying to put away a stonking hard cock when they barely have enough room to tuck their bush away from the painful teeth of the metal zip, must be quite a challenge. Maybe they need to add that one to the challenges on *The Crystal Maze*!

As much as I loved my brother, I envisioned jumping up and bludgeoning him to death. How dare he ruin this, did he not know how desperate I was to have sex with this boy, it wasn't even a want anymore, it was a total need. As much as Harry Potter needed his wand, scarily so, I now completely needed cock! It took me a few minutes to rid myself of this mentality and realise that I should in fact be worried that my big brother had just caught me with my pants down, or at the very least I should be embarrassed. Luckily, it finally clicked, I pushed Kayden away from me and grabbed at my underwear to cover what was left of my modesty. His face was a picture though and since Kayden had burst out laughing, so did I. My brother didn't find it humorous, but neither was there much he could do. I knew more secrets about him then he would care for me to mention.

Although there wasn't much he could do physically, there was no way he was going to turn back around and leave us to it. So, after the half an hour lecture of which Kayden and I sat on the sofa and giggled through (typical teenager response), he decided that he would spend the rest of the night with us. He had to be joking, right? He made himself a hot drink, grabbed the remote control and settled down all snug in the armchair. Kayden wasn't laughing now, and neither was I. His face quickly changed. I hadn't quite seen him like that before. I mean I wasn't exactly impressed with the situation, but he seemed angry with me? He quickly found himself to his feet and began to make his excuses to leave as he awkwardly fiddled with the zip on his coat. He wouldn't even look at me. I could have punched my brother in the fucking face as I turned around and saw him smirk.

Sensing issues arising, I span back around to try to convince him not to let my brother win, but he had made his mind up and it wasn't in my favour that was for sure. He seemed so cold and this worried me. Normally, I would have followed him, so I could have enforced sexual advances upon him and I would have quickly changed my stance on not fumbling in bushes or fields. Sod it, I was willing to do it anywhere now. How could I chase him when I was babysitting? Something told me then and there that he was slipping through my fingers and if shagging in a field could save it then who was I to argue? I had already planned out the entirety of my life out with him, which was clearly going to happen, and I wasn't going to let a little issue like my virginity, stand in the way.

He didn't want to listen to me, he just wanted to leave. I tried to kiss him goodbye and he just gave me a married kiss. Surely you know what I mean? Where one of the parties tries desperately to kiss the other passionately and maybe slip the odd bit of tongue in here and there and the other just keeps refusing the tongue entry by placing a series of pecks upon the other party's lips it's a way of saying *please don't touch me, I can't bear to have sex with you tonight and therefore don't want to give you the wrong impression by passionately kissing you*. I told you you'd be familiar with this, didn't I?

Maybe you now understand where my concerns stemmed from. When I received one of these kisses from my boyfriend of only a few months, not forgetting that we hadn't even had the pleasure of consummating the union yet. I was bound to be a little more than worried. He casually walked away down my garden path without so much as a glance back. I was immediately heartbroken. I stormed back into the house, slammed the door behind me and could no longer contain the emotion within me.

"You mother fucking prick," I screamed at my grinning brother of whom our closeness was now being challenged by the vile passion that he had eagerly evoked in me, before stomping back up to my bedroom.

Maybe I wasn't ready for sex after all? I was still retreating to my room like a 13-year-old.

I laid on the bed sobbing for what seemed to be an eternity. I gave him enough time to get home and then I made the call. I punched the numbers into the corded phone as my heart sat cradled fragilely in my mouth. It was an elongated wait. Did he not want to take the call?

"Is everything ok?" I probed.

He assured me that it was, maybe it was just me after all, I'm sure he just felt embarrassed and perhaps he just thought that to save knocking my brother out, he would just go home. I was sure it was just that. It was conclusive – he still loved me!

As human beings, we have the ability to turn any situation to fit what you want it to fit (and any song while we are on the subject) and you tend to believe what you want to believe. That's definitely what I did that night when I chose to trust it was all going to be okay. Now, I can clearly see that this young boy was so sexually frustrated and totally pissed off that he had spent months trying to get this girl to sleep with him and when he finally had managed it, some dick head came along and fucked it all up. Now at my age, I totally get it! Back then, I didn't yet realise the female vs. male issues. I didn't then yet understand that men don't have the same feelings that women do. It was going to take me about 10 years to work that one out. I thought that he was devastated because he wanted to feel close to me, that he wanted to make love to me. How laughable.

Philosophy - Sex for Men vs Sex for Women

It would be ludicrous of us to pretend that sex means the same to all humans, ok forget humans – I am clearly talking about gender. Sex for a man is mostly a physical entity, whereas for a woman whilst it might still be a physical entity, it is more of a physical way to explore their emotions as a rule. It is that intangible realm that we just can't reach otherwise. That is not to imply that there is no physical pleasure, there is, but it is completely fired by their emotions in the first place and hence fuelled by them throughout the process. And unfortunately, after! Which is clearly a women's fatal flaw. Let's have some honesty then, sex (even for men who are madly in love) is not an expression of emotion of any sort – it is purely about them: a pure physical release. Now admittedly it can be confusing when they are so eager to please us, seemingly for no physical pleasure of their own. Don't be so naïve, you silly fuckers. It is all still linked back to their ego. They are physically aroused by seeing you writhing around the bed in pleasure. That and the fact they want you to be able to place them as number 1 in the skills department. Whichever way you look at it, there is nothing 'selfless' about sex for men!

The Green-Eyed Monster

Regrettably, we had partook in two failed attempts. Firstly, interrupted by a curfew, secondly by the big brother, what on earth could be next? Kayden decided we would try our luck on his home turf next. Who would have imagined that it would be this complicated? Esh! Where's the problem, you are thinking? He didn't exactly have the upbringing that I did. As you know I was raised in the ghetto and he came from the neighbouring posh village. Therefore, obviously in posh villages, you have posh people and posh I was not! Although my mother gleefully informed me that his mam was too also nothing but a hood rat but she was far more skilled in the leg opening department and had managed to bag herself a bit of social mobility (a common occurrence within the middle-class suburbs of England).

Apprehensively, my girls and I climbed aboard the bus and we just knew it would end in disaster even before those bi fold doors had screeched shut behind us. It didn't help that he still knocked about with his ex-girlfriend, who I was convinced would be a far cry from myself and I couldn't have been more right. She was the epitome of what a girl should look like I suppose. Tall, slim with curves, smartly dressed but above all, she was well spoken – and quiet, I noticed that more than anything else. It took all of 30 minutes of us stepping off that bus for us all to be reassured that this was not a good idea by anybody's standards.

Why? To be frank, a load of hood rats had just been dumped in an affluent village where they felt socially inferior and therefore went into defence mode. If you are struggling to understand this, it is no different to Big Brother. You watch the first people arrive, they feel suave as fuck, strolling around like they own that shit! But you watch those close-up camera shots as the bit of hot shit with the plastic tits/solid six pack walks in: they begin to shrink like the guy's head in 'Beetlejuice'. It is almost painful to watch, as you physically see them writhing in their uncomfortableness, all because somebody is hotter than them.

Unfortunately, we were no different. So, we dealt with it the only way we knew how. We insulted everybody by ridiculing their posh little village. We were clearly just embarrassed in terms of the way they lived to how we existed. I mean, I didn't once see a car on fire at the kerbside the whole time that we were there? There were no women in leggings and short tops with their muffins spilling over as they pulled hair and ragged each other around the street because their man had been sharing his serpent with the neighbours. Plus, they had all the trendy gear and hadn't even had to steal it. They just oozed confidence.

Kayden's ex-girlfriend (who just happened to be the hottest of the bunch – bitch) was obviously still too fond of him and was very touchy feely, and far too giggly. I couldn't just sit there and watch them flirt with each other, so I did what any committed girlfriend would do. I threatened to smash her fucking face in if she so much as looked his way again! That was obviously a step too far and without doubt not something that Kayden found attractive in his girlfriend. I was absolutely gutted when he seized me by the arm and hauled me around the corner. Ok I was gutted, but I was also very turned on, weird I know. I found it attractive when he was very angry. I couldn't help it, I just liked it. Remember, I did confess that to you in the beginning. Seriously, I had only been there literally five mins!

Philosophy - Jealousy

Growing up is hard. It is even harder when other people have something that you don't have. Now, this can encompass such a range of things from cash, clothes to high cheek bones and tits! Tits are the most enviable feature ever – right? When all is said and done, it is about insecurity isn't it? When somebody comes along with a better resume then you, it is daunting, and you don't have to pretend to me that you don't feel inferior -we all do. You can feel hot as fuck, despite your tiny titties, when you have finally purchased that must have dress. But if some bint, rocks up with a giant rack, you check your watch to see if it is time to go home. We all want the best resume we can get, and I think that is only natural. When somebody outshines us, all the memes and inspirational messages on Facebook don't really take away that feeling of failure.

Anyway, he told me that I was out of order and I was embarrassing him and humiliating myself! How dare he speak to me like that? I knew that he was right. Still, didn't he know how lucky he was to have me? It would seem that he didn't, he ordered me to go home. What the fuck? Ok, I was mortified and heartbroken, he didn't have to bloody tell me twice. I shouted my girls and told them we were leaving. Although they were clearly confused, they didn't question me, they just hurried along. I walked back over to him, and for the first time ever in our short relationship, I showed him exactly what he could expect from me. I went to kiss him goodbye and as he lent down to give me a peck on the lips (that's all I deserved after my behaviour he supposed), I pulled back.

"Fuck you, who the fuck do you think you are, you 'La di da' mother fucker?" I said angrily through gritted teeth. "You may think you are too good for me, but I'll tell you now you're not." I glanced over at his little female fan base who were looking very smug with their night's work.

"Girls, if I were you I would be very careful," I screamed over. My tone expressing the extreme violence I was promising to them. "you won't always have MY

boyfriend to barge in on his white BMX and save you and I promise to be there exactly when he is not."

Nobody said a word: not them, not Kayden, and not my friends. I took one last look at him and our eyes locked. His eyes bored deep into my soul. He glared past the hard exterior and right through to my insecurity.

I could tell by the look in his eyes that he knew just how hurt I was. As the tears began to prick my eyes, I knew it was time to leave. As I turned my back on him to walk away, he hesitated before he shouted my name. Even though I wanted to turn back and run into his arms, I just couldn't. The tears were flowing down my face and there was no way he or his snotty nosed friends were going to see that. Instead, I chose to make a mature move and raised my arm as I held my two fingers up to him. There that would show him, eat your heart out. This time it was my turn to fail to glance back.

As we sat awkwardly in defeat on the back of the number 56 bus, my friends tried to comfort me. I just wasn't one of those people. I didn't like the 'arm around you 'situation, or the pitying looks, it just made my cry more and I didn't like crying. I wasn't about to show any weakness, instead I began to prepare myself for the eventuality of the situation and ensure that I could come out of this with as much of my pride in tact as possible.

"You know what guys, I have totally gone off Kayden. I think it is time I finished with him," I blurted out.

He called me that night to tell me he loved me, but sadly, the cracks had appeared. I could tell by his voice that he was more apologising because he felt bad for seeing me upset. I didn't want him to feel like that. I wanted him to be sorry that he had taken their side over mine. I craved for him to understand that I had reacted in that way over him because I loved him so much and I was being protective. If the situation was reversed, I would have been in my bloody element. I loved it when a man was willing to prove just how much he loved me. As previously discussed, he didn't find the same aspects attractive as I evidently did.

That was it, just like the back of a taxi after a very good party our perfect, unblemished relationship had been stained. Ok, so maybe my snogging somebody else did that too. Regardless of the reasoning, whilst I was still majorly in lust with him, I just recognised that the feeling was no longer mutual. I began to protect myself. There was no way he was going to get the better of me. So, when my friends suggested that we go back to the village of Comby of which we had promised to never frequent again (due to my promiscuity) I jumped at the chance. Why? Because I fucking could!

I enjoyed defying him and lying to him too. I know how that makes me look. I was still so angry at him that I really hoped that it did hurt him. Surely then we would be equal. I know you are shouting at the book that this isn't a game. That is where you would be very wrong. Adolescence is most definitely a game and love is very, very much a game, therefore putting the two of them together is like opening a compendium of games and you are right in the bloody middle of it, you are officially a sodding pawn. Let's think about it as '*Jumanji*'.

I will even go as far as saying that I even thought it funny as we passed Kayden, Micky and Mitchell at the bus stop. They clearly saw us even though we all scrambled to lay down on the seats to avoid being spotted. I found it hilarious and I hoped in a way that he had seen us, so that he could lay awake that night worrying, the way I had done over him. This was the beginning of a change in me. I had begun to build the walls of protection around me –

something that would affect me for the rest of my life. We should never underestimate how these early experiences can shape your whole life.

This was the onslaught of a real battlefield drama for my entire adolescence with Micky and Mitchell. I had probably given them more than enough reason to hate me already but when Kayden did finally get around to demanding to know if it was me on that bus, I obviously blagged my way through with some fantasist story detailing how there was no way I could have been on that bus, because my brother's, dad's, grandma's, friend's dog had a seizure and my brother's, dad's, grandma's, friend had nobody else in the world but me to stay with it whilst the paramedics arrived to care for it as the vet couldn't make it on time. And if he didn't believe me, then he could just go and speak to my brother's dad's grandma's friend's dog and ask him to confirm my attendance at the dramatic event!

Despite my elaborate story telling (maybe I could grow up to be a writer, who knows?), something more important was happening. This time, I failed to feel the enveloping guilt that I had felt the first time that I had lied to him. Maybe this was evolution and I simply should embrace it? Maybe this was part of becoming a woman?

I don't really know if Kayden every really believed me over this one, he said he did, but I'm sure it tipped me onto the slow ramp to the end of the line. The sad thing is, I wasn't sure that I cared that much. His friends categorically did not believe me and made no bones about telling me this. Micky and Mitchell positively hated me and would encourage him to finish with me, even whilst I was sat there. I laughed it off and tried my best to convince him that they were just jealous. The fact that later in my adolescence, both tried it on, might have proved that I was right. Boys have even less loyalty to their mates than girls once the pleasuring of one's willy moves from the realm of the right hand. Ok so maybe that's a bit harsh. Perhaps it's just that they are less dramatic about it.

Philosophy - Bromances
You see if a girl dated one of her friend's ex-boyfriend, it would be friendship over but boys; they are a different kettle of fish. If their friends happen to 'fall' into an ex, they just get on with it and turn the other cheek, seemingly disaffected. Loyalty wains when their dick gets hard and it is therefore an acceptable part

of the male friendship. They have to accept it, right? I mean they are bound to want to do one of their mate's girlfriends at some point, so it is just like stashing the 'Top Trump' or trading 'Pokémon' cards.

I think the final nail in the coffin (or so I thought then) was the incident at the local youth club. The youth club wasn't somewhere that me and my friends frequented. We didn't see ourselves as youths (as you don't when you are in fact a youth) and didn't particularly enjoy hanging out with people who saw themselves as such.

This particular night, we were pretty bored. Please remember I was ridiculously poor, before you pass judgement. 20p to get into the youth club was about as far as my pennies would travel, although there would probably a bit of change for some wheat crunchies and a carton of pop. At least there were things to do here. We could slob out on the furniture that had been donated but would have been much better suited to a skip due to the abundance of foam that was on display. It was therapeutic to pick away at it, lobbing chunks at passers-by. If that didn't take our fancy, we could go into the disco room and sit awkwardly around the walls refusing to dance to Mc Hammer because nobody could dance as good as him. The black cloth nailed against the window attempting to block out the fact that it was still broad daylight outside was fantastic to hide behind if you just needed a little break from your pals. Or if you were really pushed there was the arts and crafts section, where us older kids would use the pipe cleaners to write profanities in pretty shapes on the card and sprinkle it with glitter just to finish it off *'Fuck off Bastard'.*

And finally, if you were having one of those days, there were always the slightly weird youth club workers who would try to entice information out of you as sensitively as possible about your lifestyle so that they could assign you to the appropriate services. More often than not they would deem that you were not being sexually abused, your drug use levels were acceptable for now and you weren't responsible for setting the school on fire this week and therefore would just encourage you to take a handful of the condoms out of the woven basket on your way out. I couldn't help but notice an excited glint in their eyes when there was a potential problem identified during one of their 'casual' chats. Something to take back to the meeting I suppose.

Anyway, this day, chilling on the foamless sofas was the choice for us. Although I can't say I wasn't a bit excited to drop in to the youth workers, that I was now 'sexually active' so would be needing those condoms after all. Soooo exciting. We hadn't even had chance to fill the room with foam chunks before things started to take a downward turn. Silliness prevailing, one of the group decided to challenge me to a dare. I leapt at any chance to be naughty and I loved a laugh as much as the next person, unless that next person was Kayden. Regrettably, my boyfriend didn't share the same idea of what was considered comedic material and what wasn't.

Philosophy - Laughter

Maybe this isn't philosophy at all and instead is just an expression of my favourite type of guy. I have had plenty of hot guys and clever guys too. And very, very rarely, you are rewarded with a guy who has both extremely favourable traits. I can promise you, this is nowhere near as comparable to the guy who makes you howl with laughter. Kevin Hart has proved this. Primarily, he wouldn't be my type because he is small. I like to be protected by my man, so being pocket sized just doesn't leave me with the feeling that this will happen. Yet I would look beyond his petite, dainty stance and would so still throw that midget about the room. Note this down, boys: humour is the fastest knicker ridder, fact!

The dare was given. I was to set off the fire extinguisher in the tiny room in the youth club. That to me seemed an easy dare and a not too damaging one. Without a second thought I grabbed the offending weapon and began to blast our friends. The room was dripping with foam but more importantly, so were the occupants. As people eagerly gathered up bits of foam to make beards and eyebrows on each other's faces and we rolled around with laughter, I caught sight of Kayden's disapproving glare.

Now whilst Kayden was certainly no angel, his unruly behaviour involved more formidable crimes and therefore this seemed far too immature for his liking. The volunteers at the youth club didn't find it very funny either, which is funny as they were always telling us that it was our space and to use our imagination. It was only about 3 minutes before we all got kicked to the kerb. What a waste of 20 fucking pence.

Whilst we could all barely stand for laughing, I glanced towards my boyfriend only to catch an utter look of disgust that he was aiming right in my direction. In all honesty this did put me off him a little. Actually, fuck it, it put me off a lot, the boring cock womble! I liked someone who knew how to have fun, someone that was daring and someone that did stupid shit for a laugh; a bit like myself. I approached him to talk, surely this was some misunderstanding and the narrowing of his eyes was due to a stomach ache or some other pain he must have been experiencing.

"What's wrong babe?" I asked unable to hide the fact that I was smirking. I know, I know, somebody who laughs at their own jokes is the worst kind of comic.

He didn't speak at first, he just looked me up and down like an over-reacting parent that had learned you had used profanities for the first time.

"I'm going home," he finally replied, applying a matching disappointed parent tone too.

As he turned and walked away, I just stood there confused and a little bemused. I let him go, I didn't want to go after him. I was past that point. I looked over to our crowd of friends who were still laughing and then looked at him sulking off for his 9 o'clock bus and decided where I was better off. It wasn't that I didn't like him anymore, far from it. I just knew, in my heart, that we were drawing to a close and I wasn't up for making a fool of myself in the process, not yet anyway, I would save that for later.

After that night we didn't see each other for nearly a week. During our infatuation stage we saw each other every day, so this temporary separation was a fucked-up thing. It seemed like forever. Remember when you are young, going out with someone for a week, it felt like it was nearly time to get married. Usually when Kayden was grounded (of which he often was), we overcame the obstacle of not being able to physically meet up, with the wonder of technology and phoned each other every night. Now admittedly we weren't lavished with the wonders of filters, streaks and Tinder but we still had the good old 'landline'.

He was always the one who called me first, which I found so sweet. I completely took it for granted. So, on the first night that he failed to call me, I was more than a tad stubborn and decided that neither would I call him. By the sixth night of no calls, I decided that I would make the effort to call him.

Ok, I need to stop sounding so blasé here. I had been itching to call him since day one of the absent calls, but I just knew I had to fight it. Nonetheless, it was this call that would shape the end of this chapter of my adolescence.

I'm sure you have guessed, he ended our relationship: following a short conversation that mostly consisted of awkward silences and myself desperately trying to get him to talk to me. He never explained to me why and I was simply left heartbroken, trying to work out the answers for myself.

What happened? You bloody tell me? It was all so perfect! As girls we spend our childhood waiting to be old enough to experience the feeling of falling in love. And here I was ... finally falling in love! It was everything I had ever wanted. I had my Patrick Swayze, my Danny Zuko, albeit in the guise of a 15-year-old boy. He introduced me into the world of womanhood and showed me that exploring each other was not seedy, dirty or something to be ashamed of. He paraded me through sexual adolescent milestone heaven and I so badly wanted him to help me through the third and final step: the one.

I was sure that he had been sent to me for this purpose by the universe. Why was fate trying to snatch him away so cruelly now? One moment in time, we were lovingly gazing into each other's eyes at the bus stop, floating on lustful bliss of our sexual engagement, a few months later and I was binned like Oscar the Grouch (*Sesame Street*), binned and green with love sick (not as furry though, not at that point anyway). All right, so we had a couple of bad days, but in the grand scheme of things though, we got on more than we didn't. And besides, the sexual tension was so intense that it was worth an argument or two, surely? We had even been together for a long three months before we had even crossed a bad word with each other; surely that was good going?

Philosophy - Gaslighting

Don't worry if you haven't heard this term before. All it actually means is, being a total and utter cunt. In society, we can't just tell the truth about people and their personalities, we have to dress it up in a nice fancy way to make it both acceptable to use the term in public and to peoples' faces and additionally, because, let's face it, everybody loves a good label, don't they? Anyway, gaslighting is a professional term used for people that purposefully use tactics to manipulate power over their victim. To be fair to Kayden, I don't think he was ever clever enough to 'gaslight', I think he just chose to withhold the information as to why he was leaving me because he couldn't be arsed to get into the conversation as it took too much energy. I can see to an outsider how his behaviour could be deemed as such. It was, after all, a ridiculous turnabout of emotions in such a short space of time and I am sure that it would have took minimal effort (yet maximum balls that he may not have had) just to tell me the truth. This purposeful withholding of information ensured that I stayed within his control just desperate for the answers to close the door.

Breaking up him was my first taste of heartbreak and oh my god did my heart break. I quickly decided that suicide was the only option. The only problem being I was far too scared to even venture down that route. So, since that option was out of play, I had no option but to choose the 'curl up in a ball on the floor between the wardrobe and the bed' option, naked (because shivering is even better), wailing in emotional agony of the torturous torment of what would never be.

I even tried the begging phone call approach. That didn't work. Ok, you are right – I even used to call just to hear his voice and put the phone down again. I was desperate guys, I loved him. Strangely enough the stalking approach didn't seem to work either. I would regularly make my friends walk past his house repeatedly, just in case he was hiding inside. I didn't even just stop at his house, we would also sit on the street and wait for his bus to pass by (as the major attraction of our night) and brazenly follow him around school despite him very obviously trying to get away from me. Oh yes, getting a glimpse of him on the back of the bus meant the world to me and I had long since stopped caring what he thought of me during the process. Why did my friends even agree to come and sit with me, why didn't they make me stop?

MILESTONE = CARRIED OUT SOME SERIOUS STALKING

It's strange that when you are young, you are convinced that if you can just get that certain person to lay their eyes on you that everything will be fine, and they will lay at your feet. There is little doubt in my mind that this is exactly why Zuckerberg invented Facebook. He can lay on this thick story about how he wanted to compare hotties to uglies, but really, he wanted to stalk people. That never mattered to me in regard to Kayden in the end. Because no matter how much I stalked past his house or lay in wait on Detton Hill like a hungry predator, I never ever saw him again.

It didn't take long for the rumours to spread at school of our now lack of togetherness. Do not underestimate the embarrassment of being dumped at school. Dumping someone is totally acceptable, in fact you obtain quite a cool status if you take this option. Being dumped, that is just total humiliation and not something that you can ever, ever, ever overcome. Stop right there if you are thinking that I am being a drama queen and am turning a total normal teenage experience into something more dramatic because I have not yet begun to disclose to you the rumours that began to circulate my school quicker than foot and mouth disease.

Just think of the most humiliating reason as to why a girl could be dumped. Okay not that, not yet anyway. Yes, he had allegedly left me for his mates 'MAM'. And no, that was not a typo! And note that I did not type MILF, this was no *Stifler's mom*. Not to mention the fact that this made her a bloody nonce!

Can you believe it? Some people might claim I had been a bit frigid and he was sick of playing the perfect gentleman, but his mate's mam?? I would have coped so much better had he dumped me for one of the annoyingly good-looking girls in his year, or even a college girl, but not this. I was totally and utterly ashamed to leave the bloody house. No wonder he had used his disappointed parent tone over the fire extinguisher incident. Should the only hose that I wanted to play with, have been his?

In all honesty, I knew it had to be about sex, why else would he be with this old woman? I still can't get my head around that. Why did he want to sleep with a woman who had experienced childbirth three times, over, well, somebody who hadn't? Now, I was taking a wild stab in the dark to be fair never having given birth before, but I could not imagine that it was a preferable sight in comparison to one such as me. Obviously, I was wrong, very wrong. Lesson noted! Please take note of this readers and spare yourselves the shock and embarrassment that was thrown upon me. Always, always expect the unexpected during the rocky road of adolescence.

Philosophy – Older Woman v's Older Man

Whilst my heart broke and no doubt you lot are pissing yourself laughing, surely there is a more serious tone to this. How could she get away with grooming a child in her own home whilst he was staying at her son's sleepover. Let's face it, if it was a dad doing it to a daughter's friend then his windows would be going through. Clearly none of the boys will be complaining in the slightest and neither would they appreciate me fighting their corner, why are the rules so different from female to male? To be honest, if any of my friend's dads looked like Channing Tatum, I would be straight in there myself and would most definitely not be crying paedo. But that aside, I am still trying to figure out how luring an underage boy from his sleeping bag after you have sent them to bed with hot chocolate can be justified, especially when said boy was my fucking boyfriend.

A Taste of the Older Man

Kayden may have managed to bag himself an 'older' partner first but he certainly wasn't going to be the last. That may have been the end of that chapter but as with anyone's adolescence (or life in general to be fair), the next chapter was already beginning. And this may have been the time for me to find a nonce all of my own (take that, Kayden). I found it to be so true through my younger days that as one door shut another door opened. What I was still yet to learn was, to be more careful that I actually let the door close before I walked through another. In fact, maybe I needed to learn to bolt and deadlock that fucker.

You will not be surprised to learn that I was to move on quickly to my next victim. He just happened to be one of the local undesirables. To parents and the police anyway. To the teenagers in our village, he was some hot stuff. He was much older than me, I was 15 and he was 23 (we probably had the same maturity levels though).

Philosophy – Going for a Younger Partner
I don't think that it is accidental that older men go for young girls or vice versa. Fuck knows what Kayden was thinking, because I am not sure it works the other way around, I just think that he got this concept confused. I'm sure the whole world understands the lure of a younger woman or man though. Younger partners are easier to control, more grateful, less likely to say no and putting the bitter stick away, let's just admit it, they are hotter too.

I am not proud to say that I spied this one on one of his many visits to the local drug dealer's abode, who unfortunately happened to be housed straight across the road from me. At the time I thought this one was quite good looking. Saying that, another teenage peculiarity, is that you tend to fancy whoever everyone else desires. It's true. You don't hear many people stating that Brad Pitt is ugly, yet surely, he can't be everyone's type? People just tend to agree on an archetypal sexy stereotype and for adolescents this couldn't be truer, especially as we rarely manage to find any Tom Hardy types sat at the back of our classrooms.

I remember stating that I fancied some of the ugliest boys in school, just because my friends said they did and I was convinced that I must have bad taste if everyone else thought that this boy was good-looking, and I didn't. Subserviently, I would agree just for the sake of it and if you are honest, you probably did the same.

My new guy was stocky (which I loved), short (which I didn't love), To swing the deal though, he was confident, very confident (which I most definitely did like). He just so happened to have a look of Brian from *E17*, which was ironic as Brian was his name. His style was similar too. You know, baseball caps that they couldn't quite fit on their heads, underwear that that they liked to show to all who passed, trousers that they forgot to pull up and dresses instead of t-shirts. Have you all turned to google to remember who Brian was? Clue: his girlfriend's nose collapsed once due to an over excitable powder habit. For all of those of you who are still very much largely unaware of who the hell I am talking about let me do a more recent comparison – 50 Cent – but a scruffy 50 cent without the style and definitely without the millions in the bank.

Although we had all fancied Brian from afar for such a long time, that was all it was ever meant to be, from afar. Girls tend to desire this physical idol that they can stalk, talk about incessantly and write their names on their school books, bus stops and market stalls etc. Professionals call them tags: I am not sure our immature scribblings could be counted as such. But we sat for hours designing our own, just part and parcel of life in the nineties.

Shannon 4 Brian FE (forever) I.D.S.T. (if destroyed still true)

To boot, since I couldn't afford to buy magazines, I wasn't really the kind of girl that adorned her room with posters of the latest hunk (not then anyway), so a village idol was the perfect focus for my hormonal longings. It didn't matter if you didn't fancy anyone, you just had to find somebody, or your mates would on your behalf. It was the law! Fail to heed to it and you would be left in solitary and isolated from all conversation. I mean what could you possibly contribute to a conversation if it wasn't about boys? Therefore, what happened next was just never in my plan.

My friends and I were laid out on Detton Hill, no doubt pissed, causing havoc and practising our tag on the benches, when Brian and his equally fanciable (admittedly this was questionable as per my previous confession) mates began to approach us. Now, please don't be imagining the cast of '*Twilight*' here, a more effective imagery might be the cast of '*Trainspotting*'. Although we had all dreamed about this moment a million times, it felt a lot scarier than any of us had ever imagined. I felt about 5 years old! My heart was in my mouth as Brian waltzed directly up to me and playfully asked after my wellbeing. What the Fuck? I searched my head for what to say. My options were, sweet young girl or laid back carefree bitch who just didn't give a fuck. I had to make a decision and I had to make it fast.

I wanted to choose the latter and that was my intention, but as he added, 'So, we are going for a little late-night stroll together babe."

I'm afraid I crumbled.

Come on readers, you know me by now, how could I resist such assertion and confidence? I tell you, I couldn't. My knees buckled, and I was totally and utterly at his command. As my friends' jaws dropped to the floor, he took my hand and led me off the market. To be fair, I think that it was more of a rhetorical question and I had little choice.

I guess the question is, why didn't my friends stop me from being whisked away from this potentially dangerous situation. I suppose we would like to think that the answer to this is quite a positive one. Maybe there is a choice:

a) It could be that they are completely over the moon for you and they are going to ensure that nothing will stand in the way of your happiness?

b) They think you are completely trustworthy and that instinctively, you will not only know that you are in danger but will handle it like the master that you are.

c) They think you are a complete bell end and whilst eaten up with their own jealousy, they think that if you are murdered then it will serve you fucking right!

I will not discuss these outcomes with you all – you must be strong enough to apply them to your own predicaments and accept the ugly truth. Yes, it may just be that Smiley Sharon is an absolute cunt and is to be fair, your worst enemy.

As we began walking my heart was beating so fast I was worried he would bloody hear it. I really felt small, immature and very young (maybe because I was). I was absolutely petrified that he was about to ask me to participate in some kind of sexual activity with him and this I can tell you I was not ready for, not with him anyway.

Whilst at times, I wanted to lose my virginity, it wasn't going to be like this, it had to be with someone I cared about and someone that cared about me. Either that or I had to be totally fucking plastered. This situation didn't fit into either of these categories, hence the heart about to burst out of my chest. I was so nervous and (unusual for me I know) couldn't think of anything to say to break the extremely awkward silence. It did cross my mind to pull my hand from his and leg it as fast as my trainers could carry me, but I was just too cool for that wasn't I. He was one of the most popular lads in our village, much older than me and I was, after all, surely honoured to be in his presence. So, I would go ahead with the walk and what would be, would be. I epitomised the pathetic glory of young girls.

Philosophy – Popular

What does that phrase even mean? The truth is, it means a variety of different things. It should in its most basic sense, mean that somebody is a pleasure to be around. It rarely means that because most popular people at school are twats. Nobody wants to be around them for who they are, it is usually because it's easier to be friends with them then not be friends with them. That and they throw the best parties and have money for the tuck shop. The other explanation is that everybody wants to sleep with them. Girls would also then want to befriend them in order to ensnare the boys who the popular female refused entry to her nest. Easy prey you see.

Anyway, to put all your minds at rest, I couldn't have been more wrong, Brian could not have been more of a gentleman. Yes, you read that right; 'Mr Wanna Be Drug Dealer', the gentleman. Either that or he was effectively grooming me. He was just nothing like I had imagined, albeit I am sure all groomers start out with this technique. It was like he was reading my mind and knew exactly how panicky I felt as he interrupted my thoughts with an affectionate squeeze of my hand. It instinctively made me look up and I was pleasantly surprised as I raised my head and our eyes met. He wasn't dishing me the usual psycho look that he gave out, instead as he smiled at me so did his eyes too. I couldn't help but grin back at him. This ignited the butterflies in my stomach as I gulped to catch my breath. Unexpected, to say the least.

Philosophy – Desiring the Undesirables

Ok so this philosophy could cover a whole tirade of issues, but I am focusing here on adolescent girls. Girls adore a bad boy. Bad boy being code for total fucking loser usually. If only we could infer that golden nugget of information sooner. Girls think that these kinds of men are the top of the pyramid yet can't seem to link the fact that they are the furthest away from potentially owning that Ferrari that she so masturbates over! I mean maybe there is something in it when we are talking about pure gangsters. I am referencing the likes of The Kray Twins (especially when played by Tom Hardy) or Al Capone. The power they held and the money they oozed was bound to have some lure on the ladies but these hood rat men dealing a bit of fluff from their trackie bottom pockets, bitch please!

We continued to walk in absolute silence, except for the sound of the gravel crunching beneath our feet. We made our way to the local 'beauty' spot which was an 'idyllic' pond teeming with wildlife. You had to be a fucking moron to go there at night. Tonight, I didn't have to worry about that. I was with one of the feared, the ironic thing is that I didn't fear a thing; in fact, I had never felt quite this safe.

"So, what you been up to tonight," he blurted out, interrupting both the silence and my trail of thought.

He took me by surprise as I had been focusing on the crunchy gravel and ok maybe some of the deliberations occupying my mind, were whether he was going to rape and murder me once we were at the pond, at worst, and at best, what the fuck did he want with me? However, once he had uttered a few ice breakers, my fear subsided. And as he fired question after question at me as if I was under interrogation, I answered, as honestly as I wanted to anyway.

As we reached the pond he pulled me down to sit upon a wall and as he wrapped his arms around me, I felt overwhelmed. I had felt totally consumed with lust and maybe even love with Kayden, but this was a whole different kettle of fish. Brian was the kind of boy/man we (not 'we' as in society, just me and my friends) all looked up to. He was a fantasy, like the posters on a teenager's wall. He was never supposed to come true, yet here we were, and I couldn't quite believe it.

Especially the part where he looked straight at me, placed his freezing cold hand on the side of my cheek and said to me, "Jesus, you are so beautiful."

He didn't give me time to answer, not that I would have known what to say, this was not a conversation I had prepared for and I did not have a clever arse reply for this one. He quickly leaned towards me and began to kiss me.

I can't express how glad I was that this was quickly. Had it been slowly I might have had time to absolutely shit myself and leg it. This would have been a disaster for two reasons, (1) I would have looked a total dick and would have never lived it down (2) I would have missed out on a wonderful experience with a guy who treated me like a complete princess.

When away from the pond and back in public he was a little different to how he had been when shaded by privacy, but he was still attentive. He didn't hold my hand, but he kept reassuring me with a quick gentle squeeze before he would let go again. Neither did he kiss me goodbye at my gate the way he had at the pond. Instead he placed the most perfectly passionate, non-tongue, kiss I have ever had. It sent tingles down my spine and when I caught the look of lust in his eyes, tingles through my loins. I couldn't wait to tell my friends about this one. Bragging rights or what?

Philosophy – Bragging Rights

This is one of those topics that is very different for us '80's babies. Bragging rights now is so easy to achieve. You simply type a few lines into a virtual system and the world knows what a god you are. Shit, it is even easier than that, a simple snap of idealised life shared with the masses and you have reached 'Zeus' status. Back in my day, you had to do the real leg work. If you were lucky, the village would do the leg work for you.

Our next meeting was, let's just say, less romantic. As me and my friends were sick of getting wet in the ever-pouring English rain (hence ruining the hours of work we had spent preparing our lovely locks), we decided to take drastic action. Tragically, we were strolling/manly aggressive swaddling down the street with plastic bags on our heads to shield ourselves from the rain. Considering the poverty trap that my family were engulfed in, my carrier bag adorned the 'oh so not cute' Westie dog with his black basket adorned on a bright yellow background (yep, *Netto*) and I had arranged it around my head like a turban. Attractive and mature as I'm sure you can imagine. So, when Brian and co. pulled up at the side of us in their sodding fiesta we nearly suffocated ourselves in the urgency of removing our mock turbans from our heads.

"You coming for a ride, babes?" he bellowed out of the car at me from the passenger seat.

I would have preferred for him to be the driver (*TLC No Scrubs*). There was something sexy about a driver when you were an adolescent. Maybe it is the fact that they can do something that you legally can't? I'm not sure it was as fickle as the fact that you would have an on-demand taxi service, more to do with the driver having the ability/brains to work two things at once; the peddles and the steering wheel. You may well scoff at this way of thinking guys, but I didn't grow up with a crowd of Harvard Graduates. Brains were important to me; I didn't love Eminem for his crooked nose, it was his word play. His innate ability to manipulate and control the people around him with words. He built an empire out of nothing and that level of intelligence and motivation just drives me bat shit crazy.

My answer to his proposition is obvious, I'm sure. Because, firstly, I absolutely wanted to, and my alternatives for entertainment for that day were non-existent. This was the nineties, entertainment was something you sought out for yourself. Usually it had to be free and you had to have one god damn funky imagination. Now, adolescents have 'hobbies'. Yes, that is right, structured entertainment sessions largely organised and paid for by a willing and enthusiastic parent. I didn't have either of those, so I eagerly climbed into the back of the car.

Our relationship started right then and then. It was the strangest relationship that I had and have even been in. We never discussed our status, or really even mildly spoke about it: it just was, and that was it. You might be asking yourself how I knew that this was a relationship? The fact that he picked me up from the school gates most nights, barely let me speak to anyone else and appeared up at every corner I turned around, kind of made me feel like I was in a relationship.

Over the coming weeks, I learnt all about the real Brian. He was not at all the gang member I had thought him to be whilst growing up. My impressions of him were not helped by the Christmas card I received from him stating 'From Brian B – One Time!!!' Classic! For those of you unfamiliar with this slang terminology, let me enlighten you. It is an old gangster term, fondly referring to the police. Mmmmmmm, it was easier to disregard his Christmas card in the bin and try to forget ever reading it. I liked him better without that memory. It was hard to imagine this seemingly tough guy who didn't give a shit about anybody and anything sat at his writing bureau, neatly filling out his Christmas cards with his fountain pen to help spread the joy of the season. The juxtaposition of this just amused me.

It was seriously big stuff to us in those days though. The millennials are used to seeing people's affections written down, how else can you communicate with somebody if not by text or a slutty message on Facebook? In the nineties, if you received a card/letter from somebody, you kept that shit! You could then pull it out to explore it over and over, tracing the letters with your fingertips because somebody wrote those words down, just for you. Now, there is nothing special about receiving a text, you can't even trace the fucking letters properly, and unless there is something special in there (and no I don't mean a dick pic), then it is hitting the recycle box.

Admittedly my rendezvous with Brian heightened my street cred, but it just made the girls hate me even more. That's normal isn't it? The more popular/attractive or clever you are, the more of a victim of hatred you become. I suppose that's how you could look at being despised as a positive, it clearly must mean people want to be you, or you have something that they too desire. But having somebody like Brian laying claim to you is not always a good thing.

My friends and I were reaching the stage in our life where we were ready to move beyond drinking in a darkened field. Hiding with hoodies up was all well and good to avoid the gaze of potential grassers, but now my parents had given up trying to parent me, I was so ready to take this to the next step and hit the town. Not that I enjoyed drinking per se. I enjoyed the effects of the drink but not the drink itself. This may have been due to my alcohol selection during those poverty-stricken days. Anna and I usually opted for the following: Special Red, White Lightening/Star or of course Frosty Jack's and of course Mad Dog 20/20. For those of you that haven't heard of these very unique drinks they aren't forms of exclusive Moet, so expensive that you have never heard of them. No, they are just rank plastic bottles of shitty cider (mostly produced for teenagers and alcoholics), yum, yum.

Pub drinking in the nineties was in some ways easier and some ways more difficult. To start off with there were only a handful of pubs and not all of them had bouncers. Towns must have been used for such things as shopping back then, who knows. But on the flip side, the pubs with bouncers were usually the ones you wanted to get into more than anything. Now for the young girls of contemporary society this is a breeze with the amount of fake additions one can easily add to your body and face. It is hard to refute that 15-year-old girls back then, do not look like 15-year-old girls now. With my baggy jeans and bandana as a headband, I would certainly not rival the highly tanned, contoured puffed lipped girls of today. It is a bit embarrassing really and I certainly wouldn't want to do a picture comparison. I am so thankful that this is not a picture book.

Despite these hurdles, we did our very best to look the part. Swapping my *Karl Karni* jeans for a satin slip skirt with huge buttons adorning the front and the only thing a pubescent girl can wear with a skirt – a short top! Not very stylish or imaginative, but Primark was not the beast that it is now, so choices were limited. I was inexperienced at applying make-up, but I did know the thicker the better. I was sure that nobody would notice the orange tide lines around my chin, it would be dark anyway. I brushed mounts of brown eyeshadow up the sides of my eyes/face (it was more dramatic that way) and used a white eyeshadow to brighten the outside rims. Sounds strange doesn't it but I suppose it is akin to the highlighters we use today, we were so inventive. And like a professional I flicked that eyeliner up the side of my face (movie star, eat your heart out). My lips just so happened to be my trade mark. I had seen the style on a poster in *Boots* once and I had prepared my own lips in the same way ever since: nude lipstick sealed with some white eyeshadow and outlined with a plum lip liner (probably stolen from the chemist). I banged on the wedges and I was so ready to attempt some grown up drinking, until my brother entered the room. It seemed he was eager to protect me, since I wasn't doing a great job of it myself.

"Where the fuck do you think you are going?" he demanded to know.

"Why the hell do you only turn up to destroy my life, why can't you offer something constructive to my adolescence other than being a pain in the bloody ass," I retorted.

"You look like a fucking slag," he yelled as I pushed past him. I needed to leave as quick as possible before he grassed to our mam.

"Good, since you totally bolloxed up the popping of my cherry, maybe this is my chance to finally get laid. Toodle pop," I snarled from the front door.

Mine and my friend's hysterical laughter at just how fucking funny I was, was abruptly brought to an end when Brian appeared in front of me, hands on hips (fucking diva).

"Was he talking to you?" he said through gritted teeth.

Now this was an opportunity to give my brother a bit of payback, so I can't say that I wasn't tempted to use my new-found power, but I loved him too much for that and knew he was just eager to keep me on the straight and narrow.

"No!" I assured him as I pecked him on the lips and began to walk quickly down the street, we had 5 mins until the bus. I hadn't even stepped another 10 steps before I heard the yells and turned around to watch my brother hit the deck as Brian shook his injured fist. What a complete cunt!

In regard to Brian, maybe this is also the time to mention one teeny weeny minor detail. So, erm, I was not actually his only current relationship, oh no he had many. Listen, it was something girls, like me, were just willing to except. I mean he was very popular and we average girls couldn't deny him filling his boots. That just wouldn't be fair on him, would it? I know, it's much more than cringe worthy isn't it? What was I thinking?

I do remember having this particular conversation one night with him though as he kept trying to smooch me in the street and I was petrified of one of his other 'girls' would spy us and kick my sodding head in. As I was trying to explain to him that I felt it best that our rendezvous was kept a bit more discreet, we were inconveniently walking past one of these said 'girl's' house, before I could finish getting the sentence out of my mouth, he pushed me against the wall, right under her bedroom window may I add, and snogged my face off. I was flattered and for the first time since we got together, I felt like his girlfriend. This was a massive thing for me and for the notches within my adolescence. Okay, so I had been in a relationship before, but with a schoolboy, who wore trackie bottoms, and this was a grown man, who wore trackie bottoms. I'll let you decide the difference for yourself.

Following his physical declaration of togetherness (although it did occur in an alley in the dark) things changed between us, it became like a real relationship We stopped stalking the local pond in the dark and quickly jumping into cars and speeding off, and instead laid snugly watching films together. Don't get me wrong, there were no exciting dates, nights on the tiles or such like. Instead we would lay on his sofa wrapped around each other, gently kissing. He would hold my hand and stroke my arm through the entirety of the film, staring at me rather than the screen. He allowed himself to go as far as to lay the sweetest of kisses down my neck ensuring that his hands never wandered beyond the safe places, as if simply touching my skin was enough. Now I have written that down it does sound extremely boring. Maybe that's why my feelings for Brian began to change.

I'm sure you are asking yourself why that was all we did. No foreplay? No sex? Nope, nothing. Why? Looking back now, I must admit I'm not too sure? At the time I was just grateful that he wasn't forcing his knob into my mouth. I was not ready for that, not with him anyway. With Kayden that would have been another issue I think, but he was a young boy, like I was a young girl. Brian was 23, he would obviously have a grown-up willy! Surely that meant it would be bigger? Hairier? Browner? Hence, ultimately scarier? I was too young to handle a grown-up willy, but I kind of expected that he would want me to. After all, he was surely experienced. Sex was important in relationships, so why would he want to be with somebody that wasn't ready for that? Although I was nervous about him wanting to take things further (which is a perfectly natural response to undertaking sexual activities with a new boyfriend no matter how old or experienced you are), I was willing to consider his advances. But there were no advances? Not even a measly offer?

Ok, I will admit it, finally after all these years, there was a boob fondling sesh. Whilst he was attempting to erotically kiss me, he began to rub his body hard up against me (which to be fair was a bit odd in itself), when without

warning he (embarrassingly for us both since I had feck all to grab) boisterously began to grab at my non-breasts. He plunged his fingers into them and
squeezed causing my eyes to stem a little. It clearly must have been something
he did to arouse himself. He can't possibly have imagined that would turn me
on? As his fingers continued to knead my breasts as if he was in the final on
Master Chef, I prayed for him to stop, it was both uncomfortable and embarrassing and, totally fucking purposeless.

His lack of forwardness could be put down to one of three things. Firstly,
that he was just a gentleman; that he liked/respected me enough to wait and
that his brain and feelings were not ruled by his cock (yes, I know this would
be a very rare man wouldn't it). Or it could have been that he was well aware
of the laws that govern our country and he didn't want to go to jail. That
would contradict the fact that he would dabble on the drugs scene though,
although admittedly I'm sure drug dealers and paedophiles get treated very
differently in prisons. Maybe he was afraid to ask my age, I certainly didn't
look 16 and strangely enough he had never once asked. Whilst questions
such as this might be less rare with the millennials who can easily do a CSI
style check with a few clicks through Facebook it was the norm pre-social
media stalking days. Or lastly, it could just be none of the above and could
be that he didn't want to have sex with me, again this could be for a list of
reasons all of which would make me feel very negatively about myself, so I
would rather not list them if you don't mind. I mean who wants to make a
list of reasons why somebody would not want to sleep with you.

It would be fair to say that I loved all his attentiveness at first and I'm not
sure at what point I became totally sick of it. Maybe it was the time he turned
up at school, whilst I was relaxing in a science lesson? No not the romantic
rose event that you are imagining. Instead he turned up banging on the science room windows demanding my immediate presence outside. The teacher
dragged the chalk down the board in annoyance. Bitch! I hated that noise.
She wanted to be careful or I would crush that chalk up into her latex glove
again. Being allergic to chalk can't have been fun when you were a teacher.

I groaned as I laid my head on the desk.

"Who does he belong to?" the science teacher yelled.

"That will be her," giggled my classmates, as they pointed in my direction.

"Get out there and sort it," replied the inexperienced newly qualified teacher as she struggled to take control of the unruly science class during an imperative science experiment. Thank you to the dumb bitch for sentencing me to a bit of domestic violence from the scary man outside.

Surprisingly, as I walked outside, I wasn't afraid of his reaction at all, but I was embarrassed and fucking angry. After I had filled my friend's heads with images of this gentleman who treated me like a goddess, I was embarrassed that he hadn't exactly presented himself to fit with that same perception.

I threw the door open and came face to face with Brian.

"Hey up babe," he said as he showed off in front of his friends suddenly behaving like Kanye himself, picking me up and waltzing me up and down the path.

I stared at him for a moment and I pitied him. I knew this wasn't the real him, I had seen the real him. I knew better than to argue with him. I was a bright girl (despite the way I acted sometimes) and wanted to go about this without getting anybody (especially myself) hurt.

MILESTONE = GAINED AN UNDERSTANDING OF WHEN TO GET OUT

That was the end of it, for me anyway. To some maybe it would have been flattering, an older man demanding their attention and taking the time out (in actuality, he had no job, so time was plentiful for him) to stalk her, but for me I saw an alternative view to it. I saw it as a demanding man who showed his utter disrespect by treating me like a dog who he had thrown a stick for and the mutt had refused to run after it. What on earth was this feeling? It seemed the desperation of putting up with whatever a man threw my way was beginning to leave me. I was once again evolving. Shit, I loved the empowering feeling of this growing up lark. Shrewdly, I took his hand and urged him to come with me. The only way to talk to Brian (for a real conversation) was alone, he was a completely different person in front of his friends, something that I know that he lived to regret later.

I led him down the street knowing that as I squeezed his hand that this was truly the end. Inside I was torn and if I am totally honest with myself, I wanted to help him because I cared for him. I could see that his life was on a downward spiral, he was an addict and that severely affected his personality at times (and no doubt his sex life). But on a more selfish road, I was a kid and I wasn't ready to commit my life to helping someone else, especially when I wasn't in love. There I had said it. I suppose I hadn't realised it until that point.

As he walked me home, like many times before I nodded when needed and told him everything he wanted to hear. He asked me to come straight home with him that night. This was unusual for him, so I think he had an inkling of how I was feeling that day. I began to convince him that I needed to prepare my luscious self for his wandering hands. He tried to sway me otherwise. After lots of strained kisses and cuddles I persuaded him that I would meet him at our normal stomping ground at 6.30p.m. Reluctantly, he agreed, he had no other choice.

Philosophy – The Line between Flattery and Fear
Admit it we like it at first, somebody demanding your attention, being so hungry for your time that you felt so important. It feels particularly warming after you have had a boyfriend that drops you like a hot potato, proving his complete and utter 'I don't give a fuck about you' stance. It is flattering, you are somebody's everything. Damn that feels good! But when it gets to the point of stopping 'warming' you, when it no longer feels 'good', you have crossed the line of flattery. Now, you have to be careful that you are not crossing the line of fear. It either feels good or it doesn't, it isn't rocket science – but it is a warning!

Aware that I was playing with fire, as soon as I got home I jumped on the phone to arrange with my friends the next step. The plan to bunk the village and bunk it fast. Yep, it meant yet another bus trip with our heads down. Sounds tragic, but at the time it was probably the most exciting thing that had happened to us all that month. I knew what the repercussions of not meeting Brian that night would be, but as with most young people, I lived for the moment and wasn't going to let my fun be ruined by the little matter of a psycho boyfriend who was going to flip his lid for being stood up.

I don't think that even I was ready for exactly how bad Brian was going to take it that I had stood him up, he took it so bloody personal. It really wasn't like that. I was at that age where I just liked to have fun and he had just stopped being fun. I expected that he would catch up with me at some point to give me some kind of humiliation exercise but I didn't anticipate it being that very night. I didn't know he cared that much, I certainly didn't. I'm still not sure whether it was me that he cared about or just his reputation. Either way I was just a few hours away from feeling his full wrath.

Having successfully fled our village, we met up with our friends in Comby and recounted the day's events. Yep, we actually went out into the streets to 'recount the day's events' and we did this through the good old art of conversation and not a scroll through the virtual lives of our mates, a strange concept I know. Imagine the terrifying reality of all being sat together – the cold air, the smell of B.O. We couldn't even do laughing faces at each other, we had to laugh for real. And then there was the extreme anxiety of trusting your friends to meet you when and where you had arranged. You couldn't give them a quick ring to check on their whereabouts and you certainly couldn't track them with scarily, snoopish technology.

Anyway, my friends had just finished congratulating me on escaping Brian and I gratefully received lots of admiring comments from the guys. I was feeling pretty pleased with myself I guess. I didn't feel guilty about hurting him, I didn't imagine for one moment he had feelings.

Philosophy - The Disappointment of Dating Your Fantasy

Finally bagging that person who you have had your eyes on forever, should be like gaining entry to the promised land. Except I had fancied Brian for ages and it didn't even remotely feel like an achievement. I suppose putting somebody on a pedestal can only lead to disappointment (said nobody ever, after laying Anthony Joshua). Or maybe it was just that I never truly did like him in the first place? The person that we present is often so far from the person we are that maybe we should accept that a fantasy is named that for that exact reason – it doesn't exist.

My celebrations were very short lived. In my life I very rarely wore my smile/smirk for very long, it was always wiped off my face one way or another. I'm guessing it was one of my so-called friends from Detton that informed Brian of where we were going to be that night, they were mostly willing to slay you to satisfy their own needs. He never struck me as the mind reading psychic kind (psycho, yes - psychic, no) yet here he came tearing along the school drive in his mate's car, while we were sipping happily on our bottled cider.

He stopped, jumped out and ordered me to, "Get the fuck in now!" I was guessing this kind of meant that he wasn't too happy!

I had never seen Brian like this, not with me anyway. Undeniably, I had seen him be a total wank puffin on many occasions, none more so than when he knocked my brother out, but never, ever had he even crossed a bad word with me. I don't mind admitting that I was frightened and quickly began to realise that I had played with fire and was quite likely about to get burnt. Although I knew this, I still had my reputation to protect. Come on, I was an adolescent girl, there were only two things that were important to me, boys and my reputation, as doleful as it now seems. Nonchalantly, I responded with a very firm 'No', knowing I had plenty of strong men around me for backup. Looking around for support I realised those same strong men/boys, had already done a runner. The very same boys who had boasted about protecting me and who were allegedly ready for a fight with any boy from my village, had begun to scatter in all directions upon the sound of the screeching of the wheels. They pitifully abandoned me at the first sign of trouble, up the drainpipes, behind the bushes, even sliding underneath parked cars. Maybe they could have taken advice from millennium boys on how to look tough as they have it nailed. I mean biting your t-shirt whilst looking sullen into a filter with dog ears is a damn sure way to demonstrate your masculinity.

I will never forget the look on his face as I gave him a firm 'No'. He was furious, and my eyes were quickly drawn to the clenching of his fist.

He marched over to me and put his forehead against mine aggressively, "I will tell you one last time, get in the fucking car, please," he mumbled through desperate gritted teeth.

Quickly, his fury had turned to anguish. I was so shocked. He was upset, very upset. I couldn't work him out and had no idea why he felt this way? I was under no illusion as to what this relationship was, a bit of fun, something for him to brag about to his mates and no doubt I was still one of many. So why was he behaving this way now? Was I wrong?

His eyes were filled with tears and as he took my hand he was shaking.

He changed his tone completely and whispered to me, "Please, babe!"

My heart saddened for him and I weakened. I did not want to be responsible for doing this to him! I remembered how Kayden had left me feeling, questions unanswered and his refusal to satisfy my yearning for the truth deeply haunted me. I couldn't do the same thing to somebody else. I told him I wouldn't get in the car, I didn't have a bloody death wish and I could tell by the look on my friends' faces that they didn't feel like it was a good idea. But I would go for a private walk with him. The level of private had to be interpretational since I didn't want him to beat me to death. He looked at me for a while as if he was trying to work out my sincerity.

I took his hand and he gripped it so hard I instantly knew I had made a mistake. He walked around the corner and dramatically broke down in tears. As he angrily began to wipe his tears away, he was totally unrecognisable to me, I did not see it coming. Although I was so sorry for making him feel that way and it was certainly not my intention, there was just something missing. It didn't feel even remotely like it did with Kayden. Now that I had experienced such intensity, I just wasn't willing to settle for less than that. I knew I couldn't spend the rest of my life comparing every relationship I had to my first, it wasn't realistic I know, but it wasn't that simple, it was more of a craving for that intensity: an addiction.

I tried to explain this to him in the nicest way possible without offending him and risking ending up in the boot of his mate's car. I had listened to Eminem's *Stan* enough times to know exactly how that worked. He stared at me for a while before he pushed me against the wall, took my hands and placed them above my head. He slid his hands down my body as though taking in every contour for the last time and then kissed me passionately. I was never sure what that kiss was? Was it a kiss to remind me of our once shared passion or was it simply a goodbye kiss? Maybe he had laced his lips with Rohypnol, okay maybe my anxiety disorder was getting the better of me here.

Romantic notion interrupted .... I hate to tell you all this, but the kiss meant nothing to me in all honesty and I knew I was making the right decision. He pulled away and asked me if that was it, was it over? I nodded and looked at the floor. I couldn't bear to look into his eyes. He walked away, back to the car. He would have left without any more drama if ....

.... I had not uttered, "Yeah fuck off!!"

If you have just asked yourself WTF happened there, I'm with you! As soon as I said it, I wanted to shove the words right back into my cake hole, but it was too late. Don't even ask what I was thinking. I have no idea. It had all gone so it was over. I suppose if I am honest, I did not expect him to hear but he did. It was an exercise in saving face. I had spent the last hour telling my friends how I would handle him if I saw him and then I had done the absolute opposite, I was embarrassed. Like we discussed earlier, it is very important to save your reputation during your adolescence. Although what was about to happen, did not help my reputation.

He slowly turned around like 'The Godfather' himself. I heard my friends gasp and even my heart seemed afraid to beat. He took one look at me, came charging out of the car and tried to physically pull me back into it, much to my friends' distress (the girl friends, obviously, as the boys were still shimming the drainpipe and peeking out from inside the bushes). He dug his fingers hard into my arm (yep just like your mam used to do when you mouthed off at her in front of her friends) and my eyes met his. I had never seen him this angry, actually I should say hurt, he was hurt! What had I done?

I burst into an elaborate display of tears. I was a girl and I was always going to use the weak female thing to my advantage, ok, maybe I was shitting myself too. Ultimately, I knew I had behaved like a total bitch and my tears were also recognition of this. Once again, 'welcome to adolescence'.

The tears worked. He released his firm grip and took a moment to stare (okay, maybe penetrate my deep dark filthy soul), before he pulled me back out of the car and shoved me back into the direction of my friends. I didn't look back, I didn't dare, I only heard the door slamming and the screech of the wheels as they sped away.

MILESTONE = DUMPED SOMEBODY

As the cars disappeared, our so-called friends slithered out of the wood work. I was so disgusted in them. We promptly left the weak-kneed boys alone to reflect on their lack of heroics. We punished them – we didn't go to visit them for at least 2 days!

Juggling Potentials

There was no time to waste, time was 'a ticking' and in more ways than one. I had just celebrated my 16th birthday, so yep, I was all legal and shit and could no longer state the law as the reason that I was still a virgin. I know, it sounds so cruel but having put Brian behind me (if indeed he was ever in front), I was feeling well and truly up for being back in the hunting game and I had little choice unless I was going to become *Ms Havisham*. It wasn't hard to move on since I already had a few victims lined up. The key word being 'few' and there was the complexity. Why did I let this happen? Because I was a reckless teenager.

If there is any part of your life that you can let this occur, it's in adolescence. It's not considered the 'done' thing to have a few boyfriends as a grown up, oh no, your slut rating would be through the roof! But pah, 16? You are just finding yourself! I don't buy this shit about gender expectations. If it is good enough for the goose, it is good enough for the gander. Other acceptable reasons could be: don't put your eggs in one basket, greed, mis-understanding of societal norms and expectations oh ok and maybe a tad of sluttiness. Why did I do it, my first answer would be, that it happened before I even realised it was happening. One minute there was nobody, the next minute there were three. My <u>honest</u> answer would be, because I could!

Who are these victims? Bear with me, whilst I give you the background. But promise me one thing? Don't hate the player, hate the game.

Firstly, I may just have been brushing lips with one of Kayden's friends. Honestly? He was more than his friend, it was his best friend: Mitchell. You remember Mitchell? The one that continuously encouraged Kayden to dump me? Yes, him. The twat. How? Come on, you didn't see the signs? There are only three reasons why a boy would go to extreme lengths to break up his mate and his girlfriend. 1) He wanted his mate back 2) He wanted the girlfriend 3) Both 1 and 2.

More importantly – why? Again, obvious really. Getting with Mitchell was the thing to do in the hope that Kayden would realise that the old matron with a moustache had nothing over the purity and innocence of a blonde 16-year-old virgin. It never worked. The idea of a virginal girlfriend is everyman's fantasy until the frustration of the padlock on her chastity belt leads to an increase in the muscles of the right hand and balls so large you need a wheel barrow to get from A to B. The irony is, if only men realised that the persistence with the belt was worth it. Do they not know that once the animal in the virgin is released she is unstoppable? Why it is that girls can be so pure until their cherry is popped then they can ride like a fucking Harley Davidson. I can tell you why. It's a novelty like anything I suppose: a new puppy, a golden-brown tan, a new car, a wedding ring, a cock! You spend your adolescence craving these things only to very quickly bore of them once you have them. So, although I cringe when I say it, hope did remain that Kayden would come galloping back into my life and if this helped him realise how much he loved me, then it was a terribly small sacrifice. Some people (mostly, young girls) just can't be helped and I was one of them.

He wasn't my type. He was too tall for me. I'm a midget at the best of times without being paired with a bloody giraffe. Even a small act like walking down the street holding hands was embarrassing. I had to hold my arm so high that I felt like I was a 5-year-old walking hand in hand with my dad. Funnily enough that didn't make me feel very sexy and definitely didn't turn me on. He was a bit on the skinny side too. Don't get me wrong I didn't want 'fat' (aka Rag N Bone Man), but neither did I want 'skinny' (aka Rowan Atkinson). I may have only been a teenage girl embarking on the ladder of lust, but I was becoming particular on what it was I wanted (finally). When I didn't have a bottle of Thunderbird in my hand anyway. Maybe that was why I was close to choosing to have a few boyfriends at once. I could simply collaborate the good attributes of each one and theoretically, I would have my perfect man. If only I could still get away with that now. Anyway, in all fairness, he was a good-looking boy, he just didn't tick the boxes that were required to push my buttons, that's all.

Philosophy – Crime of Not Being in Love

I was realising by this time that falling in love wasn't easy. I had thought once upon a time that all I needed to do was to find a guy and voila. Except the tiniest little things put me off, do you know what I mean? You know like the clothes they wear, the way they eat, the way they walk ... the way they breathe! It isn't a crime not being in love, but people sure fucking made you feel like it was. It honestly feels more acceptable to lie and pretend that you love someone than to tell the bloody truth and set them free – how can that even be? My advice? It goes without saying that you will be judged whatever, and if it isn't for this, it will be for something else (although if it is for wearing Crocs, then you are a cunt and you deserve all the judgements – just saying), so you have one life, do it YOUR way.

Was it all about Kayden then? I am a big girl, so I will admit this and accept the fall out. No, it wasn't. I also used Mitchell when I needed a bit of company and avoided him like the plague when I didn't. Yeah, I said it. And don't go pretending you never have. On that note, I remember him turning up to my house unannounced once. As I caught sight of him walking down my garden path from my bedroom window, I quickly shouted down to my mam to tell him that I wasn't in, today wasn't a Mitchell kind of day. To ensure it worked, I hid, just like my mam used to when the doorstep loan man used to call for the weekly debt.

Unfortunately for me, my baby sister opened the door and boldly announced, "My sister said she isn't in."

"Oh," he replied looking confused.

"She's laid on the landing if you want me to get her for you," she innocently replied to him trying to resolve his confused state.

I didn't worry what he thought of me, I knew he would still be chasing my tail. Yeah, so I had become a little bit confident. Too confident? Maybe. Something I had found since I had entered my relationship with Kayden was that I wasn't short of people willing to give me a piece of their time.

The next guy in the lust triangle/square was Shane. Remember I had lusted after him since my adolescent hunting days in Combe. Quick recap: fucking gorgeous, total slag. Somebody that I should have totally steered away from, so I wanted him a million times more. He was somebody I should have run a fucking million miles from but let's face it, the more of a loose cannon they are or the more they shit neatly upon one's head the more we desperately desire them. Whilst Shane was a mere 16-years-old, his tactics were evolved beyond his years. He would cleverly pledge enough time to me on his fleeting visits to our group to let me know that he was interested, but not enough for me to lay any claim to him. Until that day .... THAT DAY!

As of late, he had begun to spend more time with us, and was no longer as keen to flee to his next destination as he had been previously. His flirting was getting more obvious, but god was he good at it. He was one smooth operator. As he walked me to the bus but a week earlier, it was obvious that night was going to be the night that he moved from the seductive slow pecks on the lips that he occasionally blessed me with, to something a little more. There were no clumsy kisses from his lips and his hands didn't shake as they slid down my back, I wish I could have said the same for myself. A seasoned professional, he placed his hands upon my face while enforcing me to make direct eye contact. I'm talking proper movie star shit. He pulled me closer ensuring his firm chest touched against my bare stomach leaving me struggling for breath. 16-year-old boys with a six pack were rare before the demands of *Instagram* you know. Seductively, yet passionately he encompassed my lips with his, pulling away dramatically slow after a few minutes, leaving me puckering up, eyes closed reaching out for him as he disappeared as nimbly as he came. My heart and loins figuratively exploded simultaneously.

Before I get lost in a horny haze of nostalgia, I still need to introduce my final potential victim: Neil. Neil was the total and utter epitome of a 'bad boy', and boy was he hot, but hot made him dangerous. But arguably, dangerous is damn sexy! I may have just mentioned to you my confidence had grown since the days of being afraid to kiss Kayden, but when it came to this bad boy, I had no confidence whatsoever and so there had been no such contact. But he wanted there to be, badly! He was as smooth as Shane but in a slightly more aggressive way, which while I loved it did scare the fucking shit out of me. He was very unpredictable which also made me weary. But in terms of looks, he so had it. He wasn't your typical dark, tall, handsome kind but he was tall and definitely handsome. It was his personality that captured my heart. He was confident and oozed charm, I loved that. He knew what he wanted, and he went for it. Now that was a trait that had my stomach doing back flips.

Did I ever tell him? No way! He was far too cool for me to let anything like that become public knowledge. I mostly admired him from afar. Not because he didn't gaze my way, but because I still didn't have enough confidence to play around with somebody as cool as him! I knew my league and he was way out of it. Although I felt that he was too good for me, it didn't stop him chasing me. And in all honesty, knowing men the way I do now, it probably turned him on that little bit more that I didn't fall at his feet, like all the tall, blond girls did.

Neil and I had an odd 'relationship'. Whilst we had flirted with each other since I could remember, it was nothing more than banter and we hadn't so much as laid a finger on each other until that very week. After stumbling upon him and his friend whilst walking home, up Detton Hill, he pulled me to the ground to sit with him for a while. He ordered his friend to leave us alone there and almost immediately pounced on me.

It is funny how personality comes over in a kiss isn't it. Neil kissed exactly the way I expected he would: total control, with little room to escape. It was a leader-led activity and I wasn't given little chance to influence the situation. But, I must admit, that the lack of control I had over the situation, really turned me on. Whilst it was very controlling, it wasn't intimidating – maybe I could handle this guy after all?

Whilst, I put it down to a one off after he dropped me at my front gate later that night, he had spent every day since eagerly attempting to enslave me into a relationship.

Philosophy - Bad Boys

What is it about females and bad boys? I don't think this is as complicated as people often make it out to be. All that bull shit about women wanting to try to change somebody and want to claim the title of being the one who tamed the shrew. It is fuck all to do with that. It is usually quite simply because they are more exciting than the other boring bastards that we can choose from. That or we don't realise what cunts they are before we commit ourselves and by the time we realise, it is too late.

The Big V

The big day had finally arrived, Anna's 16th birthday party. Whilst we usually let our birthdays pass in a hazy blur whilst smashed on a street corner, this one was different, we were having a party! Anna had convinced her dad to have a night away, so we could take over the house and we had spread word on the street.

This was going to be the best party ever, Anna and I had been planning for this day long before we even hit double digits, and whilst there was the little matter of my virginity, I had no doubt it would all be sorted by the end of this life shaping night. That oh so special moment was to be given to the choicely picked man of the moment at tonight's party, Shane! Oh, I liked this carefully chosen guy, I didn't make this decision lightly, in fact I was in love with him for all that month before this event, he just might not have known it. Even bigger fact - I was maybe a little bit entangled with a few boys at that unforgettable party (as I mentioned in the last chapter) that made for quite a post pubescent love triangle, or should I refer to it as a square due to the amount of people involved? Life shaping it was, as I was dealt my cards when all three of the afore mentioned guys turned up to the party. As if I didn't even contemplate that this might happen?!

So quick recap: there was the gorgeous man of the moment, Shane; my new date, Mitchell; and just to add the last side to the oddly formed triangle was the bad boy of our notorious mining village, Neil. Now, I know what you are thinking. That I lost my virginity in a mind blowing but sensitive and special, foursome! Not this time guys. Although I am thinking that would make such a better story, no?

Instead, I upset Neil (details later) who then proceeded to kick shit out of several of the partygoers. Although I did not want this to happen at all and I did try to intervene, I knew it was all in vain. The situation really was inevitable the minute that Neil arrived. We didn't exactly think the plan out for the party that well. We were adolescent teenagers and we were having a house party. There were no rules really. You just invited as many people as you could, consciously considering that at least half wouldn't turn up, unfortunately for us, they all did. It was all about creating the atmosphere, it was in the ambience. Ambience to us in our late 20's may be a candle lit room, but as adolescents it was as many people packed into a room as possible, regardless of whether you knew them, think your virtual *Facebook* friends list stood, smashed in your house. This was pre-Facebook, so we relied on good old word of mouth to spread party invites. An easy device in a gossip ridden ex-mining village.

Ambience we may have had but maybe I should have been a bit smarter when realising that if you are seeing several boys, it probably doesn't take Einstein to conclude that you shouldn't probably invite all the boys to the same party! Try to remember though that any excitement was better than no excitement, surely? Let's be fair about this I did try to advise Neil not to attend. I would have instructed him not to come. But he wasn't the type of person you could control. The order would have made him more determined to come. It wasn't that I didn't want him there, but he was just so unpredictable. So, it wasn't hard to guess what would happen.

In he waltzed to the party and demanded an immediate meeting with myself outside in the privacy of the darkened urine-ridden gennel. Why? Simple. He wanted to demand that we start an immediate monogamous relationship, although we were both aware that it wouldn't be on his part. That and probably the immediate release of a hand job. What did I say (to the relationship issue not the hand-job)? Again, simple "No" (to the hand-job also had he asked).

Why? Like I said, I did want him and to be frank, to be his girlfriend would have been an honour to any hood rat such as myself, but I was scared and just not that confident in my capabilities of a girlfriend. Did I have it in me to make this guy happy? I doubted it. He seemed so experienced, yet I hadn't even lost my big 'V'. It surely could have only led to humiliation and I had had enough of that to last me a lifetime already.

Obviously, "No," didn't go down too well, especially as I wasn't really able to give him a reason. What could I say? *"No sorry Neil, I am far too afraid of your cock to become your girlfriend?"* What about, getting naked in front of him? Him seeing my dirty knickers on the floor? Farting during his presence? All the things inevitably we would do in front of each other, once a couple.

I couldn't share these deep dark fears, so instead I cockily replied, "I do like you, but I like a lot of boys."

Philosophy – Boyfriend Fear

Initially it seems an alien concept to consider this issue as an adult. The chance at bagging a guy we fancy is a dream come true not the onset of a nightmare. But I guess it all comes down to the issue of insecurity doesn't it, and there is no species more insecure than adolescent girls? But if we are honest with ourselves, how confident would any of us feel climbing aboard Channing Tatum after many years of bedding the same guy night in, night out? I hold my hands up, I would totally shit myself. Having said that, I would face my fear and get on with it and take one for the team (Team Channing).

Admittedly, that was not too smart a move considering the events that followed, but I was the queen of making the wrong move. Let your mind wander back to the Brian saga. It didn't matter anyway, mostly because I had Shane waiting for me inside and in layman terms, I had waited just too long for the opportunity to lure him to be alone with me. Sounds awful now when I say it out loud, but I just knew I could pick Neil back up at a later point should I learn to overcome my fears. But maybe this party was the only chance that I would get to corner Sexy Shane!

Subsequently Neil's proposal took a nosedive and I refused to stand around and be abused so I sulked back inside, around the safety of my friends, not that I thought he would never hurt me. He swiftly followed me in. He took about 30 seconds to pick a fight with one of the strangers and the violence ensued.

During the bloodbath, I had no choice but to quickly shift upstairs with the man of the moment, Shane. I don't know if it was me or him that began the mission of escapism. I think we probably both had the same idea at the same time. Please do not get me wrong here, it was not a selfish flee, but I needed to save his face of perfection from a quick stamping from Neil's size 12's.

Once we were upstairs the charm filled the room like a squirt of *Ambi Pur*. The events downstairs were quickly forgotten, and we were back to being horny adolescents. He slammed the door behind me, took my hand and led me to the bed. His charm was unlike any other that I had experienced with a boy of his age. At the time I took it as being the fact that he was a genuinely nice guy. Now I can clearly see that this was more an attribute of being so experienced at trying to get girls knickers off, that he had it down to an absolute and perfect T.

Abruptly, his manner changed. He pushed me back down on the bed and his focus turned onto himself as he began to routinely remove his trousers whilst I laid awkwardly on the bed awaiting the next steps. Being that naive (translation; thick as shit) little girl, my knees buckled as I laid back thinking of wedding rings and trendy pushchairs as he fumbled around on top of me ... erm sorry, I mean, the magic filled the room as the fireworks exploded and he made me feel more amazing than I ever felt in my life. Then we lived happily ever after ...whatever!!! The reality is he hardly spoke to me while he rocked back and forth on top of me for all of 40 seconds before that magical event was over.

What you want detail? I'm afraid that really was it! It was nothing like the sexual experiences I had enjoyed with Kayden. I wasn't excited, neither in a sexual way, or a giddy way. I was simply nervous, although nervous is too weak a word, petrified would be more accurate.

I suppose I convinced myself that I was bound to feel this way, not only was he way out of my league, this was my virginity. This was big shit! Let's not pretend that the thought of a large object entering a small (delicate) hole on your body isn't horrendously unnerving. You have no idea how it will feel, if it will hurt and to put it bluntly, it is just ridiculously embarrassing to lay there with your muff out, to what was practically a stranger. And then there is the trickling of the love juice – what the fuck was I to do with that? This is no jest when I suggest that when schools armed us with our 'Record of Achievements' upon our embarkment into the world, that they should have also given us something useful like a 'Manual on the Practicalities of Copulation'. If they had, I wouldn't have pulled my underwear back on so hastily and uncovered both the heartbreak of a ripped condom and the joys of the failure to mop up gizzum!

But in reality, it wasn't the taking of the virginity per se that was a disappointment, it was his treatment of such an important event. Not a single word was uttered from his mouth, grunts maybe but no words. The only skin contact he made with me was his hips slamming into mine, it was the headboard he was gripping tightly, not me. Oh, don't get me wrong he wanted sex alright, but I'm not too sure he was fussed if the vagina was mine. In all honesty, I could have been a hole in the mattress and he would have been equally as pleased/disappointed, although in all fairness, so would the mattress have been.

I would like to tell you about the foreplay, but it's a short story to deliver. He reached into his wallet, the moment we entered the bedroom and pulled out a strip of condoms. I was elated at his health and safety awareness, but I did wonder about the amount of health and safety contraptions that he was armed with. I could have trustingly assumed they were there because he planned on making love to me all night, but I had a gut feeling that this would not be the case. I think it was a case that there were several vaginas to be pounded rather than the ideology that he would stick to pounding one multiple times. He skilfully applied the fruit flavoured condom in a matter of seconds and placed his hot rippled chest upon mine for a split second.

"Take your dress off," he commanded.

Now that bit I could do, it didn't sound too scary or arduous. Until you go to do it. How can you suddenly forget how to get fucking undressed? I knew that I could have playfully pushed him from me, rose to my knees and seductively began to sway the dress from around my body, insisting that he touched only with his eyes. But I didn't, I was bloody terrified. I grabbed the bottom of my dress and routinely pulled it over my head taking no care of the mess it created of my hair. My shaking body may have led him to believe that I had the onset of Parkinson's Disease, but if he noticed the fear pulsating through my body, he skilfully chose to ignore it. He pushed me back down (probably to stop me from entering into a convulsion), took hold of the base of his penis and guided it into the correct position whilst paying more attention to his own cock than what was laid beneath him. He held his manhood like it was the Olympic Torch and he was so fucking proud to have been chosen to carry it. It was an awkward 30 seconds as I laid there whilst he admired it from all angles in his hand before he clearly decided it was time to treat his little chap.

Due to the lack of arousal techniques, not to mention the fact that I felt like I was hanging off the side of Mount Kilimanjaro, I was evidently not gushing in the sexual fluid department. I say evident, I'm not sure Shane noticed, he was too busy staring at his own ass in the mirror at the side of him. I however, could not fail to notice the searing, burning pain ramming up and down inside my loins. Pleasure? Errmmmm no! It seemed there was none. No sweating behind the knees, no tingling toes, no desire to scream the fucking house down? No, absolutely not! Just a desire for this thing to frigging end as soon as possible, and I certainly got my wish, about a minute into it to be precise. End of story.

Not exactly, I missed quite an important event out there. I have spent years trying to block it out as it has become one of those haunting events that always comes up in those cringe worthy moments when reminiscing with friends. Ok, what happened, I hope you are ready. 10 seconds into my memorable rendition with handsome bloke, Mitchell burst in only to see his purer than pure (ok, maybe not) virginal 'kind of girlfriend' being punished by a stranger. Funnily enough that relationship ended there along with my virginal reputation. Ironically, I became a lot more popular with the boys after that event!

Ok I hear you. You want more details of this humiliating episode, you sickos! You want more detailed imagery of Mitchell's eyes glazing over and his bottom lip beginning to protrude? No, you don't. You want to know about naked me with my legs akimbo, being caught getting laid by the entirety of the party, don't you? Immaturely, Shane's friend, decided it would be a great party trick to sneak into the bedroom and pick my crumpled pre-sex stained dress off the floor whilst Shane and I were temporarily distracted (probably him by his own love stick and me in awe of this fascination), and run around the house with it informing the party that he had stripped me. He led everyone to believe that I was sat upstairs naked just waiting to be humiliated (as you do). Ok so maybe the latter part was true if the next two minutes were anything to go by.

Believing I was naked and with images of my pasty waif like self seductively cuffed to the four-poster bed circulating, the entire party stampeded upstairs lead by none other than my very best friend, Anna. Like Judas she opened the pit of betrayal for all the congregation to witness in full glory. As she flung the door open, her excited grin quickly turned to horror as she witnessed my white legs wrapped around the hunk. Quick thinking on her behalf very nearly saved me, as she was only too aware that hot on her heels was Mitchell (luckily Neil had left by this point, keen to avoid being arrested for the GBH he had just carried out). As she desperately tried to close the door to the can of worms, time was not on her side. The party wanted a taste of naked me and they were not going to let a flimsy pre-formed panelled door stop their fun. Mitchell pushed her out of the way and slung the door open only to reveal the afore revealed image. Yep just in case you need a reminder, it was me, legs akin, boy in-between, no covers, no clothes. I'll let your imagination do the rest. Great party, great reputation!

You may be asking yourself what atonement awaited me and where that left me with my love interests? I'm thinking that you could probably write the next paragraph yourself and I don't think it's because you are psychic. Evidently, I never saw Shane again! He had gained what he wanted, so he had no need to return. I probably thought about inflicting myself with a bit of self-harm because I was that heart-broken, but I never did really like pain.

Whilst Shane and I never discussed it, I certainly heard many fictional recounts of the losing of my virginity! As stories such as this do, it certainly took on a life of its own. I could be forgiven for forgetting that it was even me who partook (mildly). He took great delight in telling his friends how dissatisfactory I was in the bedroom department. No shit Sherlock! It's funny how men (or should I say boys) of this age often quickly make this judgement and are very vocal with the declaration. Even funnier that he thought that I had the time to give him the ride of his life in 40 seconds. Watch out for this kind of man girls. You are sure to end up with one of these at some point. Put it behind you as a sleazy mistake and promise yourself you will never do it again.

Philosophy – Shit Sex

It didn't take me long after this event to quickly realise that it isn't about being good or bad in the bedroom department. It is about the 'chemistry' between two people (or maybe 3 or 4 if you are more adventurous) and it is that 'chemistry' that is needed to seal the bedroom fate. If it isn't there, you can't really make it happen, but if it is, it has the potential to be mind- blowingly, explosive. So, I guess the fact that Shane behaved like such a cock womble and ignored the existence of the encasing surrounding my vagina, didn't exactly make me want to swing from the chandeliers. Lesson noted!

I did kind of get some answers when it came to Shane. I heard on the grapevine many years later that the over-confident, cocky twat did come out of the closet. It's always the ones that you least expect isn't it? Why did it make me feel better? It relieved me of the humiliation that he told all our mutual friends about my bedroom failings. Let's face it, I clearly was never going to make him hit the ceiling with my slender physique and my refusal to carry out anal sex. Admittedly, I guess my pancake tits were probably more akin to a 6 pack than I would have liked and therefore probably helped him at least achieve an erection.

So, what happened with Mitchell? Now that was a tricky one. I think in his heart he knew it was never to be, but he must have seen something in me that he just couldn't let go of (just like me with Kayden). Hence, we weren't quite finished just yet. He just couldn't seem to hate me no matter what I did. Finally then, where did the episode leave me with the last corner of the rectangle, Neil? He was a law unto himself. He told me in no uncertain terms, "It just makes me want you more!"

Settling Down

Everybody has one person who ripped their heart out of their chest, threw it on the floor and stamped the very life and feeling out of it. I fell in love with my 'Special Bastard' when I was sweet sixteen. He fell for me a lot sooner than I fell for him, but boy did I show him the true form of a woman scorned when the tables finally turned.

His name was Chris, but that isn't really what you want to know is it? I know you are dying to know what this one looked like. In all honesty he was better looking than most of my earlier conquests, but sadly still not even remotely in Shane's league. My first encounter with Chris was nothing to do with me. Ok, let me clarify, it wasn't supposed to be anyway. It just so happened, that one of my friends fancied the pants of him and being the brazen bitch that I was, I decided I would take the role of arranging their little rendezvous. Confidently, over to him I strolled, whilst him and his friends were chilling on the grass at the bottom of Detton Hill.

"So," I stated bluntly, "my friend fancies you, you going to get with her or what?"

Yes, I was one of those lovely, attitude ridden, teenage girls that we (as adults) all love. And I was so subtle, I was not however, prepared for the response.

"God no," he declared with a glint in his eyes (of which surprisingly I found I really liked), "nice tits, but I'd rather be with you," he swiftly added.

Although at the time I wouldn't have touched this boy with a barge pole (not part of my preferred pickings you see), I obviously enjoyed the fact that he wanted me. Not only was I a teenager, I was also a girl, so would be lying if I said I didn't like the attention, I loved it! Even if that attention should have belonged to my friend. However, it didn't make me want him, I just noted that somebody wanted me, and shelved that feel good feeling for a time when I would most definitely need it.

Philosophy – Less Attractive Friends

A difficult subject to explore, I agree. But it can't be ignored that having less attractive friends is of great benefit during adolescence. Standing out is hard during this difficult period and so, put simply, this is all the easier if you have friends who don't, let's just say, outshine you. Now I am not suggesting that you purposefully search out 'ugly friends' but I am just saying that there are certainly huge benefits should you happen to have some.

After Chris had made his feelings clear, he inevitably appeared around every impending corner that I ventured down. Annoying? Flattering? Neither. Initially, I had liked the attention as I confessed, but on the whole, I didn't care to the extent that I wanted him to stalk me. Like I said before, the adolescent rule goes, my mate had clocked him first, so he was untouchable to me (yes, yes, I know that I had broken this rule previously, but you don't have to label me a serial rule breaker) not to mention that I didn't like him anyway.

The 'relationship' all started with a bit of convenience. You see at the time, I lived at the top of a very steep hill and often we would party at the bottom of that there very steep hill and boy was it a very long walk home. I could cope with the extreme weathers on the long walk home up this obstacle should I have a strong man to literally carry me there, and my very strong man/boy just happened to be Chris. Look I wasn't taking him from my friend at this point – no, not at all. I was just taking advantage of having somebody to get me home safely. This boy had dedication; he was even happy to backie me up the hill on his bike, no honestly. God knows he must have had his protein shake to make that expedition. Either that or wanking was just getting extremely boring and the lure of the real thing was just natural adrenaline. I had also learnt, from previous experience that to get, you had to give, if only a little. And in Chris's case it was only a little conversation, he had never even tried to kiss me. Therefore, I felt it was worth that little sacrifice to gain a little bit of company on the long road home.

Our friendship began slowly but steadily, the odd bit of flirtation here and there. You know, a bit of a shove and a punch where appropriate. Or a well-placed insult that was simply a way to get you to go over and begin to punch them. They could then restrain you and pin you to the floor, using it as a guise to get you in an uncompromising situation so that they can have a little skin to skin contact, or maybe a little accidental fondle. But that was as far as it went.

The first-time Chris made any real advance towards me, was a sunny June afternoon in 1995. I was seated upon the floor outside one of my usual teenage haunts (the shops) chilling with my friends. I remember the day so vividly as we sat grief stricken around a solitary candle (of which I stole from my mother's 'leccy' cut out emergency stash) mourning the premature death of hip-hop legend, Tupac Shakur!

Whilst contemplating that if his life was over then so was ours, I was confused to hear a, "Hi," infiltrating my dark thoughts.

Hardly a knight on a white horse, instead a shy looking boy peeked out from underneath his baseball cap, hardly daring to make eye contact with any of us, it was Chris. Frantically, he began searching his head for some way to make conversation in any menial way with me. After some panic searching he managed to stutter an invite to his house that night. His parents were out at the local working man's club (W.M.C) watching the Saturday turn and he was having a bit of a shindig. Being popular socialites (please detect the sarcasm here), we considered the options for our very valuable Saturday night and decided that Chris and his equally geeky entourage just wasn't important enough to waste our Saturday night on.

"Erm ...no tar," I awkwardly stated, avoiding my friends' gaze so that I didn't burst into laughter, as he gawkily left.

The candle burned low and we had decided to find some company for the evening. After an hour of tramping the streets and not bumping into any desirables, we decided that wiling the night away at Chris's (especially if there was free alcohol) was probably the better option than tramping the streets in the dark, so maybe we should have said yes after all. So off we went. In all honesty we shouldn't have even been contemplating partying when our idol laid cold in a mortuary!

The party at Chris's was in full swing by the time that we arrived. Chris seemed a little surprised when he answered the door. Surprised but pleased, he clearly didn't expect us to come! Again, yet another bit of ego boosting for me.

I sense that this would be an appropriate time to give a few more details about Chris. Visually anyway as I didn't know him well enough at this point to tell you anything else. So visually he was mediocre, nothing special but definitely acceptable and he had some of my desired mesmeric points. For starters: he was the red, shy type (but strong don't forget); he was tallish (that means he was bigger than me but not a giraffe type); widish (meaty but not fat); dressed sporty (which I liked), wide shouldered (mmm my favourite); and big arms (my all-time favourite). It is hard to describe his facial features to you because he didn't have any jaw-dropping striking features like gorgeous eyes or anything, but all his features added up to make quite a little cutie. Maybe I hadn't noticed that before?

He didn't give me flutterings in my belly or make me catch my breath but neither did he make me feel sick, which made things much easier. If I am completely honest, at that time, he was not someone that I wanted to be knowingly connected to. As I most feebly admittedly earlier, I liked popular/naughty boys as many adolescent girlies do and Chris did not seem even remotely able to fit this category. Now we discussed the notion of popular earlier but perhaps it also needs saying that often 'popular boys' were only called so because they were a touch handy and were able to frequently demonstrate their masculinity through violence and whilst it may sound odd, I've watched enough David Attenborough to know that, this type of savage behaviour is normal for mating animals.

In truth, I wanted a trophy boyfriend who would look good on my arm, not somebody I could conduct scientific experiments with in his secret lab. Experiments yes, but not of the scientific kind. In all honesty though, I was still hoping that somewhere, somehow, Kayden would fall back in love with me. Yes, I know, simple, surely? And, yes, I was still on that path! It's first boyfriend syndrome isn't it? It may be about 100 pages to you, to me it was 6 months, and much more than 190 days of snot sobbing is needed to rid the heart of the stench of 'not love'. I wasn't interested in starting new relationships, however, I was amid adolescence and I needed to keep myself occupied whilst I was hatching my master plan. Therefore, as a distraction, Chris would do!

Chris welcomed us into his home and genuinely seemed excited that we had turned up. His house was very different to mine, there were even family pictures on the wall. It is important that you readers remember this is my adolescence, choosing a partner at 16 is very different to choosing a partner as an adult. Different things were important to me then. For example, it mattered to me whether he was a mammy's boy, what his school photographs were like and what style of underpants he wore. These days, I am more interested in whether he can clean the cooker to my standards, in fact, that's all I'm interested in!

He eagerly led us through to the back garden where the majority of people were hanging out: the ones who were not making out on the sofas anyway. I was pleasantly pleased with my findings in the back garden. Standing as a centre piece to the party was only a bloody bouncy castle. Ok readers hold your horses, no I wasn't impressed with the castle itself, but more of the fact that he and his friends were not sat around playing Scrabble or Sonic the Hedgehog on the Mega drive. They didn't exactly ooze cool, so I hadn't expected them to know how to have fun and I certainly didn't expect to be able to have fun with them, but maybe I could! I had to grin at his creativity. Everybody smashed out of their faces jumping on a bouncy castle whilst techno music pumped out of the speakers, I loved it (ok maybe not the music)! As I scanned the room, I realised Chris had been staring at me, watching me taking in the atmosphere. He witnessed my grin and cheekily grinned back. Chris – cheeky? Maybe I had underestimated this boy?

It took me and my girls about 30 seconds to take over the party and, more importantly, the bouncy castle. Chris was still standing back admiring his part: I liked this too. Ok so I was beginning to like quite a few things, but then I was slaughtered. The night was successful; we had fun and got pissed. Those were the main requirements for an adolescent party. I say main because there was one part missing - the canoodling. Chris's party was that good that he was about to complete the trio!

I had barely spoken to him all night. I had just used his hospitality to enjoy myself and give me and my girls a good night out, *Gatsby* style. The final bonus of the night was that we got free booze, yay! And for us broke arse ghetto bitches, that was always a bonus. As the night was coming to a close and we were all partied out, we took the opportunity to lay on the bouncy castle watching the stars. Unexpectedly Chris plonked himself down next to me on the inflatable.

"You had a good time?" he asked.

"Funnily enough I have," I replied laughing.

It was no secret to Chris that I wasn't desperate to be in his company.

Without warning our eyes locked and I was shocked by the reaction in my stomach (always refer back to the butterflies in the stomach; it's a sure-fire love indicator). I remember thinking that he was quite good looking when I was up close, albeit I was more than slightly sozzled, so the beer goggles could have been blamed for this particular viewing.

He slowly, yet eagerly, leaned forward (yes just like in the movies) and kissed me. Now equally, I was not prepared for this. Not the kiss, no, I had kind of guessed from the staring session seconds earlier that he was about to pounce. It was worse than that; I wasn't ready for the lack of standard in regard to the kissing. I know that sounds so obnoxious and makes me sound like an utter bitch, but I did promise the whole truth and nothing but the truth. What could have been a magical moment was destroyed by the fact that he totally ate my face. I may have been pissed and probably even a bit desperate, but I still knew a bad kiss from a good. It wasn't just a case of him eating my face and leaving a total pool of spit around my face. Maybe I could have dealt with that and eventually put it behind me, but it even consisted of the extremely embarrassing situation of teeth smashing. Yes, it seemed this happened to me often. Oh boy, did I want it to end.

Philosophy – Kissing

I think people underestimate the importance of kissing. If we think about kissing as the starting up of the engine on a car for a moment. If we can't get that step right – the car isn't fucking going anywhere, right? Voila – same analogy.

Although, admittedly I wasn't in the slightest interested in any sort of romance with Chris, I was still a bit sad that he didn't excite me in this department, because by the end of this party I suppose I had kind of considered that he could have been a good stand in piece of entertainment, just while I convinced Kayden that I was the one. But on a more positive note, we did end up having a good laugh with his mates too. Shock, Horror! It paved the path to our new 'hang out' group and some lifelong friendships, who would have thought it? I mean after stealing Josh from Susan and failing to appease

Shane in the bedroom department, Comby had just lost its appeal. No boys = no point (just saying).

Following the kiss, I quickly made my excuses to leave and avoid the awkward situation of Chris wanting to take it further but instead he offered to walk me home. Now that was something I rarely turned down. As explained previously I did like the company on the long road home. I just had my fingers crossed that he wouldn't attempt the face eating, teeth smashing experience again. The journey home was an interesting one that night, if nothing else. We (yes, I did use the plural pronoun there, don't read into it) embarked upon the long road and almost immediately, he grabbed my hand. I was shocked, but I hasten to add that I liked it. Confused? I'm sure you are, I was too!

We walked in silence most of the way. Maybe this was my opportunity to pretend for a while, pretend I was in a real relationship, or maybe I just didn't want to hear his voice, as that would simply remind me that I was not walking up the hill hand in hand with Channing Tatum, but it was just young Chris. He occasionally muttered a few conversational questions that I chose to give minimal answers to.

"You have a nice time tonight?" he nervously blurted out, repeating his earlier question.

"Yep," was my minimal 'please do not talk to me' reply.

We finally arrived at my front gate. And yes, you would be right in your thinking that he was about to pounce on me again. As I tried to slip my hand from his and reach for the gate, he pulled me back to face him. We didn't speak but, it was clear that he wanted to collect his fee for the walk home. Darn it, I supposed I should give it to him really, my street was one hell of a climb in all fairness.

His hands kept a tight hold of mine as he reached down, and the face mingling began. As much as you might like me to say that this time it was the passionate heart stopping kiss I had been waiting for, but I just can't, because it just wasn't. Actually, it wasn't 'as' horrendous, granted. His depth perception had improved greatly since the kiss an hour earlier and thus he managed to keep his teeth in his own mouth and therefore on the whole it was a much less painful experience if nothing else. Honestly? The thoughts of him becoming my plaything were even re-surfacing. As I wiped his saliva from around my mouth, we quickly uttered our goodbyes and I swiftly ran into the house.

Philosophy – Awkward Teenage Moments

Whilst they will haunt your forever, they are unavoidable when it comes to sexual adolescence. And if it is any comfort, absolutely nobody escapes unscathed. So, you have to just put your grown-up pants on and deal with it. What we often fail to realise is the person that you are sharing your awkward moment with, is too busy worrying about their own fuck ups to even identify yours most of the time. And when they aren't, they have empathy with you as they too are often moronic in the carrying out of intimate moments. You know, people in glass houses shouldn't throw stones and all that.

As I laid in bed that night, I mulled over the night's events. I had to admit to myself that not only had I enjoyed it, but I had acquired a different opinion of Chris and his friends. Maybe they weren't as geeky as I had first presumed. A friendship gained I thought, but that was all. The decision was made, right there and then whilst laid in my box room snuggled up in my Forever Friends pyjamas laying staring up at the woodchip that adorned my ceiling. I decided that he would be my side-line for when I was bored, to aid me in my survival during the difficult periods throughout my master plan in winning back my first boyfriend.

It wasn't long before our paths were set to cross again. That weekend, my friends excitedly called me whilst I was babysitting to let me know that they had seen geeky Chris walking through the village. And the relevance? They were shocked. It was a particularly hot July day and Chris was wandering around topless, and I must say, my friends were very impressed with what they saw. Apparently underneath those baggy sweats he had a little bit of an Adonis going on. Now before I get into this, let's just remind ourselves that as young girls what we felt was an Adonis was probably not even remotely anything akin to *Magic Mike's* Crew (again I'm just saying). Still, I got the feeling that this was going to get interesting. I may have passed comment at this point that should they bump into Chris again, then they could send him my way with immediate effect.

I thought no more of it until I was raiding the fridge (the best bit about babysitting obvs) and I noticed heads bopping up and down behind the conifers in the front garden. Upon investigation, I witnessed Chris slinking down the driveway. He looked nervous when he saw the confused look on my face.

"Your mates said you wanted me?" he muttered, staring at the floor nervously.

Oh shit, why had I got myself into this situation? What the fuck was I supposed to say here? Maybe I could have tried, *"Yes I wondered if you could strip so I could inspect your body and decide if you were good enough for me to take this relationship to the next level."*

I don't know about you, but I was too young to have the confidence to blurt that out, with my ageing wisdom now, that would be no problem though. If I couldn't say that, what on earth was I going to say?

I settled on, "Yeah, I wanted to know if you wanted to start seeing me?" and this time it was my turn to look at the floor.

MILESTONE = ASKED SOMEBODY OUT

What the fuck? I know. Did I mean it? Yes and no! I could always change my mind later, right? I only committed to 'seeing' him after all.

I might have acted all cocky and confident on a day to day basis but when it came to boys and love, I was most definitely a novice as you know, so the fact that I had uttered those words was nothing short of a miracle, even if it was just Chris.

"Yeah," he replied, much more confident than I sounded, not to mention enthusiastic.

Voila. it began: our relationship and the next chapter in my adolescence.

Philosophy - Relationship Terms

I thought some of you might need some help with the terms here. Whether it is an age or culture thing, these kind of slang terms are never self-explanatory, are they? So, in the nineties we had two phases of relationships not too dissimilar to those that exist today.

1) Seeing (now generally referred to locally as talking)

2) Going out with (in an official couple)

3) Chucked (dumped somebody – sounds violent but hopefully isn't)

Seeing covered a whole heap of variations of a relationship too. You could be seeing five people at once if you wanted and that was quite acceptable, as long as it had been agreed previously with the other person. Or there was the option to agree to 'see' each other exclusively. Whilst this sounds similar to number 2, it was a less serious option. It would be the option where the control freaks and bunny boilers in relationships would refrain from showing their true colours just long enough to make it to the more serious betrothal of an official couple. Number 2 was harder to get out of, you would have probably met parents by this point therefore tying the partner into the inner woven parts of your life. Think of it as trying to get a dog hair out of a wool blanket. Tricky shit!

Unfortunately, my newly betrothed, kind of partner, stalked me much more than he ever had after our little agreement. Ok, I knew this was completely my fault. And, I know you are thinking, poor him! I didn't really have the heart to explain to him that I didn't really mean what I had said. Or maybe I liked the idea of having him there when I wanted him. He tried so hard to arrange dates, time alone etc, but I would either agree and then fail to turn up or I would pull out excuse after excuse to avoid committing myself. I know, if you weren't feeling sorry for him before then you are now, right? What did you want me to do? I was too young to be responsible, wasn't I? Besides I wasn't doing it to hurt him, I just didn't fancy going on a date. Where's the crime?

Alright, I will admit, my behaviour did get a little childish during the times that we legged it when we saw their bikes approaching, just to avoid the awkward situation. But again, I relinquish all responsibility as I was only 'seeing' him! My playful avoidant games did come to a head one day when I walked around the corner and was immediately faced with Chris. There seemed to be little chance of escape and so a conversation it would have to be.

"Did you forget to meet me for the pictures?" he clumsily questioned.

I suddenly felt like a complete bitch! Suddenly? Alright I know, I was a complete bitch. Maybe that is the first time I had looked at him like a human being rather than an annoyance.

"Erm .... yeah I did," I said as I avoided his gaze, "I don't really like the pictures," I blurted out to break the deafening silence.

What else could I fucking say? *"Soz bud, got a better offer this week pal?"*

We began to communicate, albeit very awkwardly, and I suggested, out of duty rather than fascination, that we all meet up later to hang out as a group rather than the awkward two-person date thing, surely that had to be a better option.

Philosophy – Dating

Dates are just awkward, aren't they? It doesn't matter how you look at them, they are an interview really? And worse than an interview because in this situation you are not selling yourself or your skills, somebody is actually buying 'you'. Like some kind of human cattle farm. It is just a horrendous situation, but what is the alternative? God knows. Try before you buy sex?

Over the next few weeks Chris and I hung out a lot and I often let him accompany me on the walk home. I suddenly began to wonder why I had been so reluctant to spend time with him, it wasn't that bad after all. The walks to my gate helped me get to know him better. Consequently, the nights that he didn't walk me home, I began to miss him. Yes, you read that right, maybe my icy soul had begun to thaw. We didn't spend much time together during the evenings that we were socialising together, we didn't need to. We knew we had our private time together at the end of the night during our long dawdling walks home and at that point, that was enough for us. I am not afraid to admit however, that there was no part of me that wanted to have a relationship that people knew about, not yet.

You're wondering about the kissing, aren't you? Ok I will tell. Obviously, the kissing got better. It had to, or I wouldn't have stuck around. I think we showed each other the way and worked on it a bit. Maybe I was being a bit harsh earlier on in the relationship, and now realised that it might not have been his bad kissing skills but more that we were a bad match (kissing wise) and we needed to work on it. I'm back tracking here, but a girl can change her mind, right?

I suppose you could say that we began to fall for each other over the garden gate, it seemed Chris was not just a curio. Whilst Chris and I were alone, there were no pressures from friends, nothing that we felt we had to live up to and no pressures of the sexual kind. I may have lost my 'V' but it wasn't exactly an amazing experience and was one I was in no rush to repeat. It was hard to believe that I had been so desperate to lose my virginity and here I was now with a complete and willing partner and I had no desire to do anything about it. The anti-climax had really stayed with me. That and the fact we were walking up a hill on a residential street. Receiving oral sex in the middle of the road during the *News at Ten* was likely to get us arrested.

Chris was also no stranger to delving into the realms of sexual adolescence which made it all the sweeter that that he placed zero pressure on me to undertake any activity of a sexual nature. He was willing to wait. A strange concept, but nonetheless it was true. That is not to say that I had asked him to wait and I certainly didn't want a zero-touch policy. I wasn't a fucking Jonas Brother!

There were lots of good things about Chris. He was sweet and attentive but the obvious attraction to him was when he dropped his geeky drawers. His manhood was something to be feared. Mind, looking back now, I was sixteen, five foot nothing and was a virtual virgin. Anything bigger than my 10-year-old next-door neighbour (of whom I played you show me yours, I will show you mine under the stairs) was a stomach churner. How did I know? It was well documented by his friends, and, once it has been said, it's down to the owner to prove it! Not that Chris minded this one bit, as I'm sure you can imagine. Don't get too excited, I'm not talking an intimate private viewing. I am literally talking a drop your pants, show your length and quickly withdraw it from sight again. Bragging to my friends about his manhood was the ultimate in conversations but taking charge of the beast was another thing. Thankfully, I did not lose my virginity to him, oh perish the thought, it makes my eyes water.

It became obvious that our relationship was changing when he would pull me to stand in-between his legs when we were chilling with our friends, whilst he wrapped his arms around me and snuggled me hard into his chest.

Obviously, I knew it was a way to remind me of the solid frame that lay just beneath that Helly Hanson coat. Oh, I hadn't forgotten, it was the main reason I was there. I would slide my freezing cold hand up his top and bite my lip whilst sliding my hand across his carved abs. We so had to get this relationship moving.

He did some serious wooing too. It was the small things. If he thought my hands were getting cold, he would stick my hands in his hoody front pocket and then the next day he would bring me a spare pair of gloves. Or he would bring me a bottle of booze to our drinking sessions, tell his mates to shut the fuck up if they spat an insult, squeeze my ass as I passed and more importantly I would feel his gaze fixated on me constantly through the night. What captivated me about this was that his look may have had the hint of a lustful gaze but the core of it was adoration. He looked at me with adoration over lust. What even was that? It was something that I had never experienced, and Jesus, it felt good!

My friends were totally in awe that I was giving this boy so much of my time and attention. They constantly questioned how I could fall for somebody like him, but could it be that I had? Maybe. He was not my usual bad boy type admittedly and had never even broken into his mam's fridge never mind a house. Yet there was something about this lad, something that seemed to have me hook line and bloody sinker. Why? Do you know, I just couldn't put my finger on it. He had a smile that only turned on one side of his cheek. He could easily be mistaken for somebody who was partially paralysed, but no that was just his cheeky side-smile trait. I loved his shy rosy cheeks, he looked so coy and innocent and that really turned me on.

Another tell-tale sign of my new-found love interest was that you may remember that I had previously been a little notorious for stringing a few boys along at the same time. Don't judge, I was simply exploring who I was. That was all over. My days of being a major player were behind me (temporarily mind) and Chris became the only one that I even wanted to spend time around. Whilst I was nowhere near the realms of being in love, I certainly did like him, I liked him a lot.

Philosophy – Decision Making

Damn, this is how you knew if you wanted to be with somebody. You could feel it! It isn't a decision after all, it is a feeling. Whilst we can make every excuse in the world why we do or don't make a decision, in the end all we have to do, is feel the answer.

Ok I hear you, you have had enough of the fluffy stuff – now you just want the filth! Who am I to deprive you? Our first intimate session was at the ultimate teenage sex haunt, babysitting (yep again)! The lady that I babysat for would frequently offer a bed for the night to Chris and for me, the panic would set in! Panic? Yes, that's right. For a couple of reasons, firstly, I was quite scared of doing the actual 'do' with him but more poignantly, I was definitely not ready for him to witness me drooling down the side of my face and snoring as I slept and was certainly not ready to face him make-up-less in the morning. I was falling in love and for now I wanted to keep him, I wasn't sure he would feel the same after witnessing those sights.

When he eventually did stay over we finally got intimate! We built up to it slowly, it made it more exciting, I guess. My nightmare experience of virginity loss made me feel more terrified than I had felt as a virgin. I suppose that's because I really liked this participant and it was important to me how he felt about me. Yep, my hard-faced attitude was changing somewhat and maybe it was down to Chris.

As I mentioned earlier we had overcome the rubbish kissing phase (otherwise I would have made tracks long ago). Besides I had realised by this point that kisses were only a small part of it, the way that boy slid his hands all over my body made me weak at the knees. So, to be fair he could have been pecking me with his teeth and I doubt I would have noticed. Now, Kayden had given me my first taste of foreplay, but I had never had the chance to return the favour. Not for lack of trying may I add. It just so happened that he was very eager to please me and there was no bloody way I was going to discourage that. Not to mention that our time together was so short. So, when it came to my turn to give Chris a bit of attention I was petrified. I had prolonged the kisses for as long as possible, but the time had come.

I wasn't sure whether I had been eager or hesitant at putting the children to bed that night whilst babysitting. The tightening in my chest and the dizzy spells tell me it may have been the latter. I wanted to be alone with Chris, I spent every day dreaming about being alone with him lately, but I was also scared to death. What was I scared of? To put it bluntly, I was afraid of him lumping his large penis in my hand and expecting me to know what to bloody do with it, that's what. It is so much easier for young girls in today's society, when they are short posed for an answer to such a humongous question (no pun intended), they have a silent but knowledgeable partner to confide it. GOOGLE! What choice did we have? A sniggering friend? A furious parent? An unforgiving partner? Porn? In reality we had no-one, so it was learn as you go in the nineties I'm afraid. That could be not only an embarrassing but a painful learning curve.

I returned downstairs, to my very own hunk laid lovingly waiting for me on the sofa. All images I had been conjuring up of him, angrily parading the living room in his leathers, boisterously banging his whip against the sofa whilst waiting for me to don the crotchless PVC catsuit he had purchased for me, were non-existent. He was just laid there, snuggled under the duvet, sleepily watching the back of *EastEnders*. My presence at the door caused him to turn and look at me, the smile he threw at me said it all, I was in safe hands!

Not a single shred of hesitancy was flowing through my veins, I wanted him no matter what the consequences were, under the covers I dived. I melted into his arms the second his lips touched mine and his hands traced the shape of my hips. Although his hands were happy to explore every single crevice of my body, my hands remained firmly glued to his back, although I occasionally let them roam to his face. I wanted them to sliver down to his bum (oh, what a mighty fine ass he had), but he may have then been waiting for them to sneak around the front and begin to perform certain duties. Certain duties that I'm afraid my hands just hadn't been trained for.

Imagine my relief, when he advised me on the best way to please him. I certainly didn't take it as an insult, I took it as a young man being quite grown up and talking to me about our sex life instead of behind my back to his mates. Don't get me wrong, he didn't whip out a flip chart and whiteboard marker and start mapping out complex diagrams of the most pleasurable avenues to explore. No, he took the more simplistic way of monkey see, monkey do.

It seemed he wasn't willing to wait for me to prise my own hands off his back and to take my own initiative. He probably smelt the fear. Instead he took my hand and bluntly shoved it down the front of his trousers. I may not have known much, but I knew I couldn't do a hell of a lot with a cranked wrist and a tightened cord around his tracksuit bottoms. Now this part I could do. I pulled my hand away to make this situation a bit more .... erm .... do-able?

With all restrictive barriers removed, he gently took hold of my hand as I was carefully guiding it up and down his firm skin, he signalled to me with his hand, that gentle guiding was the last thing he wanted.

And just to ensure that I really got the message he heavily breathed in my ear, "Harder". Ahhhh, my first lesson in wanking!

MILESTONE = MALE MASTURBATION COMPLETE

It was only a hand job, I wasn't brave enough to humiliate myself by taking the tool in mouth. Oh no, I would have had even less of an idea about that, especially due to the mis-leading name given to the deed. No, it was just a bit of tugging and pulling and surprisingly wasn't anywhere near as difficult as I imagined it would be. Admittedly it ached my arm and I yearned for it to be over, but it wasn't too difficult a task. Especially as it took him about two minutes to bust his load. I would learn to become grateful for this as the years rolled on.

I can't say that I enjoyed it as much as my 'oral treat', or if I enjoyed it at all but maybe I needed to learn to be less selfish. As mentioned previously, I didn't find them attractive and they certainly didn't make me want to touch them, but I did want to touch him, and I certainly wanted to please him

So, he had given me my first lesson in man pleasing and this would prove very useful to me over the years, cheers Chris. He however, did not need a lesson in lady masturbation. It was my turn to be pleasured. Maybe I should have been concerned to realise that not only did he know exactly what he was doing but he had undoubtedly perfected his technique. Funnily enough we had never discussed his previous experience, it was clear that he had much more experience than me. But concern was the last thing on my mind as he took me back to that place that Kayden's tongue wiggling, had transported me to many months before. I was more than pleased that it was not a one-off visitation to that very mind-blowing land.

He seemed to know that my clitoris was not in need of sanding down and instead he began with gentle touching and taunting building up his pace to ensure my longing would build. The tingling began in my toes and slowly ensured the spasm in my legs helped me fight the urge to stop him as the pleasure became unbearable. I needed him to stop, but I needed him to carry on much more – the strangest of sensations (similar to the urges I have when eating chocolate now). As if he had judged my body to be ready, he began to slowly edge his way down, he was to taste me for the first time. My hands were quivering as I placed my sweaty palms upon his head trying to push him away, only to find myself pushing him right back down hard between my legs. The feeling of his warm breath between my wet legs too over whelming to keep my groans to myself. Unable to stop the screams, I felt his warm, wet fingers against my mouth, reminding me where we were. He skilfully took me to the tip of my orgasm and then pulled back to watch me melt into the sofa with pleasure. From the look on his face, this clearly was his favourite part. And mine! It had never happened to me before. So, that's what all the fuss was about? It was a fuss worth kicking. My first orgasm, complete with still shaking legs.

MILESTONE = FIRST ORGASM

How did his technique bear up in comparison to Kayden? I must admit that with Kayden, I could barely catch my breath and was so brimming with emotion. It was a natural high that I could imagine would be very hard to beat, it had been the first touch. Chris certainly knew what he was doing, but it just couldn't be comparable to that. My stomach may not have flipped quite so much at that point, but it certainly was getting there. Perhaps it would be a fair point to say, that I had more physical feelings than actual emotional ones at that point. The best thing was the nerves had gone, it just felt right. And what about the feeling of completeness? It came the next morning whilst wearing his footie shirt!

There was still the main event to go though. Why didn't we have sex when we had the chance? Because we didn't need to, although I'm sure we both probably wanted to. We had covered as much ground as we needed to that night, and in a way, I felt that had we gone all the way, it would have tarnished the memory and feelings that we had created. It would have made it about having sex, rather than getting to know each other. But I was now ready. And not ready like I was before where I needed to get rid of 'it', no this time 'we' were ready.

First Love

I had already lost my virginity (the oh so magic, unforgettable, for all the wrong reasons, night), so surely handling the beast would be like sweeping the stairs. If only! You know what it's like at 16, fresh into the sexually active crew, you want to be at it like rabbits, if only you could find that special place and perfect time for that first taste of your new bloke. Our 'special' place was in his mate's recently deceased grandma's council house, only a matter of weeks after our first taste of foreplay. Following her recent demise from this world and in celebration of her memory, we decided to have a weekend of house parties, in her home before his family handed back the keys to the council. So, decks at the ready mics in place, we bought the house down. Actually, I did not see much of the party as I was upstairs getting to know Chris even better. It was time for the big event!

Drawing your attention back to the size of his manhood this was no local operation so armed with a bottle of Thunderbird (as pain relief), the process began. All mocking aside and unbelievably so, this was the magical event that I never had the first time around. Chris was attentive, sensitive, loving and looking at him from my horizontal position, he had blossomed into a little beauty too. I had never really found him super attractive, maybe I didn't now, but maybe I had found the beauty within? Maybe this was deeper than the surface of his skin. The kisses, cuddling and talking (yes, this one spoke) was perfect. He made me feel like a goddess. He kissed every crevice of my body expertly knowing that getting me horny enough for foreplay just might get him that bit further. He told me he loved the way my skin felt, the way it smelt, even his words left me melting into the floral sheet. With his stroking and touching of every part of my body, there was no way I was not going to feel him inside me tonight.

He laid on top of me face to face, noses touching, the tips of my toes brushing his legs. And as he took off his trousers, I felt his penis against me for the first time. The excitement of being here with him reached my chest so quickly that I dared not speak for fear of sounding like an excited child. There was no fear, just an absolute desire to be as close to this man as I could possibly be. I had to have him, right then!

As our bodies expertly began to explore each other, the process was so natural that I couldn't believe that I was ever nervous. This is what it felt like to be ready, and this is what it felt like to be with the right one. The actual insertion however, was slightly more complicated. Fuck it, it wasn't complicated, it was impossible.

Without speaking, it was clear that we had both decided that it is was time. In all honesty, I couldn't wait. We ceased 'preparing each other' and we began to position ourselves ready. In a total mix of lust and tenderness he moved the focus back to kissing. I felt his erection slip in between my legs and naturally wrapped my legs around his sweating body. But kissing was clearly a distraction theory from the fact that he was trying to ram a screw into a pin hole. Nope Chris, I could still feel it despite your tongue exploring the caverns of my mouth and I still knew that there was no way that is was going to fucking fit. How embarrassing, I just needed the bed to open and swallow me. Or my vagina to do the same to the cock would be helpful! Did things like this really happen in real life? I mean come on, these organs have to fit together in order to ensure the continuation of life. So what the fuck was wrong with us?

As I pulled the pillow over my head in embarrassment, Chris laughed along with me.

"Shannon, these things happen," he assured me.

"Oh, do they, Mr Fuck a Lot?" I said smirking, "glad to hear that roughly my vagina experiences the same issues that the other vaginas that you have attempted to slip into do."

As we laughed, I saw it again. That look of adoration. I sat up, took hold of his face and kissed him differently than I had before. I kissed him like I meant it.

Eager to continue, I sent for more alcohol to ease the pain and as we shifted around the bed to find a possible solution something sharp latched onto my behind. As we scrambled for the lights, the night was ruined. That's how I felt at the time anyway because now it is probably the most entertaining sex I have ever had in my life. In a humorous way of course, granted that is not the aim of sex I know. You see the lights revealed that dead Grandma's false teeth had been left in the bed. It was then that the reality sank in that our 'amazing' first time, 'our magical place', 'our perfect experience' was in fact the dead woman's bed. Eeeeeeeeuuuuuuhhhhhh! Kind of spoils the imagery doesn't it?

In all honesty it wasn't ruined (I'm just being a drama queen), it fact it aided the situation. We began to laugh (a lot) and as we eased up and relaxed, bingo, things began to happen. He was so sensitive and caring that this couldn't have felt more right. He pulled me back down onto the bed, dusted the teeth nonchalantly onto the floor and kicked them under the bed. This time it happened so naturally. He pressed himself down hard on top of me, controlling yet caring. No strategic placing or dramatic pushing of the penis was needed. Instead a natural, desperate exploration ensued. Whilst immersed in the rhythmic union of our tongues, there was no focus needed on the uniting of our loins.

I felt him pushing into me this time, although admittedly it was slightly painful, but the pleasure, desire and excitement overrode any of the un-comfortableness and being this turned on certainly helped. As he entered me, I heard myself gasp for breath as I struggled to keep a hold of myself. My breathing quickened and my body gently convulsed. And married women complained about doing this? I grasped at him pulling him against me, so I could wrap myself around his magnificent frame, feel his skin against mine and thrust him deep inside me. As we moved together in unity, I pulled him close towards me and sank my finger nails into his behind. I let out a deep groan as I struggled to catch my breath.

The physical sensation of him being physically connected to me, quickly turned into an emotional one as I could never imagine being without him again. We had been united! Like some pervy kind of blood brothers – I liked this version better! His flawless abs rubbed against my breasts hardening my nipples and ensuring the buzzing sensation under my skin slowly took over the entirety of my body. I felt the sweat run down my arms from his back and knew that he felt it as strong as I did. We reached orgasm, the pleasure was so immense for me that the emotions became too much, and I felt the tears well up in my eyes. Crying? Yes, I know, I thought it was so strange, but I also loved it. His body shook on top of me just before he collapsed in a heap beside me, leaving me totally fulfilled and completely wanting more all at the same time, a complete juxtaposition. I had never experienced so many emotions in such a short space of time in my life. I was completely walking on air. He pulled my face around with his manly hands so that our eyes could meet. He stared silently for a while before he pulled my face forward and kissed me so gently on my lips.

Philosophy – The Most Natural Process in the World.

It is so normal to worry about having sex, yet how odd that it is normal, considering that sex 'should' be the most natural process in the whole world. Let's compare to the likes of 'Animal Planet', you don't see the lady bears pacing up and down quivering over the prospect of letting their partner down whilst being aggressively taken from behind in front of their friends, do you? But us humans, we obsess over the perfection of one of nature's most natural processes. That is an oxymoron if ever I saw one. You can't tame a natural event and there is no point in worrying about something that you can't control. You also can't put a wise head on a young one's shoulders!

Intercourse is very different in comparison to masturbation of oral sex. The emotions and feelings stemmed from the latter are about self-pleasure, pure sexual enjoyment and the heightening of an amazing sensation. But Intercourse is something in its own world. Ironically, intercourse to me, seemed nothing to do with sex but more about getting to know each other, being as united as two human beings could possibly be, showing how much, you loved each other, and I guess that's where the term 'making love' came from. A term I could now fully identify with. There was categorically an absolute difference between having sex and making love. I had now undertaken the act of intercourse twice; once I had partook in the act of sex and the second I had made love!

MILESTONE = MADE LOVE

I would be lying if I said that I hadn't become unashamedly besotted with him by this stage because I was. It was hard not to be. He was such a charmer. He said and did exactly the right things. I do remember the first time we admitted we loved each other. But don't worry, he was the one who said it first. I must say the sex had to be one of the key aspects of my falling in love with him. No, not in a slutty way. Come on, people in glass houses shouldn't throw stones! Surely, we are all living in a fantasy world if we are still denying that sex is a major factor in any relationship. I mean how do we know if we are really in love until we have discovered if we are compatible. And I can tell you now, Chris and I were definitely compatible. It was either that or the fact that my chastity belt had been released and I was taking full advantage of my sexual liberation.

Back to the sloppy stuff then, let me set the scene for you. This time we were babysitting with Anna. I imagine by this point in the book you have all cancelled the idea of ever having a babysitter ever again and who could blame you? We were laid on the hessian striped sofa snuggling together, so as to avoid the uncomfortable rubbing of the unfortunate sofa upon our skin. Due to our levels of maturity we also added a blue bobbly blanket that smelt ever so slightly of dog. We didn't care about that though, it may have been a dog stained blanket, but it was our block from the world, it created our own private cell. It was irrelevant that the twenty people packed into the heavily smoke laden living room, could hear every single word we were saying.

"Shan, I am so in love with you," he said holding my face still to ensure I didn't break our gaze. He didn't need to. I had no intention of taking my eyes off him. I wanted to savour this moment for as long as was physically possible.

"Right back atcha," I threw back nonchalantly, grinned and pulled him closer for a kiss.

My heart was exploding, life was beautiful!

Philosophy - 'I Love You' Phrase

Growing up, I had always believed that 'Love' was a word that you needed to hear. I eagerly awaited Kayden to tell me that he loved me and felt that it signified something. But what Chris taught me in the beautiful early stages of our fatuous relationship, was that when love was real, you didn't need to say it, you could feel it. I was glad that Chris had said it and I am not going to pretend that it didn't set my soul (and sexual organs) on fire, but mostly I was glad because it meant that I could say it too. And again, not because I 'wanted' to say it but because I 'needed' to say it. Because it felt like the most natural thing to do and say every second that I was near him.

There you go. He had told me he loved me, and I had told him. We had said it, declaration complete. I was on a complete natural high. The spell was broken, my longing for Kayden had finally been shelved! And it seemed it was those words that sealed the step to number 2 (an official relationship), without needed to say anything more.

It seemed then, that little shit with his arse out, who flies around shooting people with dangerous (and illegal) darts, fucking caught up with me. How he gets away with it is beyond me. I mean if I ran around with no clothes on and began shooting people with arrows and proclaiming it was in the name of love I would be locked in an asylum. I hope you have all realised here, that I am in fact referring to Cupid and not some dirty psycho nymphomaniac flasher.

MILESONE = COMPLETELY AND UTTERLY MOVED ON

Sex, Sex and a Little Bit More Sex

I must admit, I loved having sex at this point in my teenage years. I guess that goes without explanation. I was young, kid free, responsibility free, too poor for hobbies and kept my friends to a minimum, so all I had to do was 'fuck'! Oh, and I was raging with hormones. You tend to think it's down to that person. It's more likely to be attributed to the fact that it's new, there is so much to explore, it's a high without the cost, or the come down, and let's face it, it had to be more exciting than sitting in a field with your mates freezing your arse off!

Chris obviously loved this period too. Or maybe I'm being too specific here and it wasn't the period (or even me) he loved. It was just the fucking? Maybe that was me too? However, I do remember him hurriedly hushing his young cousin once, when he was in danger of telling me just exactly how much he was loving that stage of his life. It was too late though, too much information had already been spilled by the young innocent mouth. See readers, like me, you may be under the illusion that it's only the female species that hold relationships, virginity and number of times you have made love to that special person in high regard. Maybe even keeping a record? Like me, you would be wrong! Little cousin very innocently informed me of Chris's special calendar. The one that he used his secret code upon to detail how many times and when we had sex! Did it put me off? It should have done, but it didn't. I liked that idea much better than a little black book. Maybe we need a novel that takes on a guy's perspective of adolescence? Now there is a gap in the market, get on it boys!

Now I am not sure any girl could recall her first Mouth et Cock with great splendor. Detailing how she licked and gobbled her way to liberation. And if she does, she is talking utter shit!

By now, I was well versed with the art of hand-jobs but surely taking it in mouth was a whole other ball game. While with hand jobs the male counterpart can offer a little guidance, you know, putting your hand in place, helping you pull a little harder etc, but in this game, you are riding solo. It's not like he can just show you how he wants his bell end sucking.

"Oh, excuse me darling, watch me whilst I do a demonstration. Just a little lick here and a suck there. Then right to the back of one's throat."

I realise that in the 2000s there is quite a realistic answer. It comes in the godly guise of 'YouTube', however in 1996, you just learnt shit the hard way. Once again you want the juicy details, right? This could be the least glamourous part of the novel.

Philosophy – Sexual Slang Terms

Let's take a moment here to reflect upon the pet name given to fellatio. Now often words do not have obvious links to their uses. Let's take cunnilingus as an example. You wouldn't look at that word choice and know how to perform oral sex, fair enough! But neither does it lead you astray. Therefore, I honestly think a group of cruel bastard boys at high school got together to show the virgin up (think Carrie, without the pig's blood). There was just absolutely no need to put the word 'blow' in there! Why not 'suck' or 'lick'? But, I can understand the plausibility behind the 'job', it is something that you must get completed to get the money in the bank. Seriously, I'm not being nasty: Oxford dictionary definition; a task or a piece of work, especially one that is paid. That is the definition of job, not blow job by the way. I saw you all rubbing your hands together thinking of back pay then!

You won't be surprised to learn that it was Chris's suggestion that I relieve him with my mouth rather than my hand. I say suggestion, but do we as a female species have a choice really? In all fairness, a man who wouldn't go down on me would be totally useless to me, so I can't say that I disagree with this notion. I suppose Chris just presumed I would know what to do, maybe he hadn't even considered that it was my first time? For no other reason than duty I dropped to my knees whilst we stood behind the abandoned garages at the bottom of Detton Hill and prayed to god that instinct was about to kick in.

I treated it much like I did anything that I didn't want to eat, I tried not to look at it and I certainly tried not to 'taste' it. Once my lips closed around his very erect penis, he threw his head back and groaned loudly, so I figured that I must be doing something right. As I began a dramatic performance of covering his entire penis with salvia and kisses his groaning increased. Okay, I was still on the right tracks. Wow, this wasn't too bad after all, as long as the penis showed perfect signs of cleanliness, I wouldn't be opposed to undertaking this activity more often. As I began to masturbate him at the base of his penis he took the opportunity to thrust to the back of my throat. If he was testing my gag reflex, then it worked.

I wondered why on earth he would do that until I saw the absolute look of ecstasy on his face as his whole body convulsed. Ah, that's why. Perhaps him (and millions of other men) haven't yet grasped hitting the gag reflex at the back the throat with a large (hopefully), hard object can cause one to erm, GAG! No shit sherlock. Luckily for him, I didn't release my Chinese takeaway on his very erect penis and instead pulled my head back just in time.

Despite the horrendous situation of having a limited opportunity to draw breath whilst trying to avoid spewing on my boyfriend's cock, I didn't hate it. And seemingly neither did he, since it became his favourite pastime. Yay, lucky me!

MILESTONE = ORAL SEX GIVEN

I chuckle when I think back to some of our sex-scapades. Why is it that most of my memories of this time are of sex? Ahhh yes, because I didn't have piles of washing, curious children, still had a mildly attractive body and I still had some fucking energy. I particularly remember the first time I met Chris's parents. Unfortunately, not because I was bubbling with excitement because I had gloriously made it to that 'important phase of our relationship'. Nope, it was far from a normal affair. There was no invitation, no time choosing out the right outfit, no formal introductions, no awkward dinner. It was all Chris's fault really. One of our main aims around our first months (who the fuck am I kidding, it was our only aim) was to find a place to exercise our skills in aerobic sex sessions. It was because of this mission that we were slowly becoming banned from all our friend's houses. We snuck off to parent's bedrooms, bathrooms, living rooms, gardens, sheds (anywhere really), and when needs were at an all-time high, in the corner of a very packed bedroom!

Oh, come on, we have all had sly sex in a highly occupied space, haven't we? Problem is, I am thinking we were probably not that sly. #lostinthemoment

Therefore, when we discovered Thursday nights, they were a godsend. Hallelujah! Thursdays were *Asda* shopping night for his parents, and I, for one, have never been more appreciative to *George* for presenting such a wide array of value and choice amongst his aisles. Honestly it was like some major outing, to his parents. They were gone hours and hours. But it was long before Gastro pubs. I'm not even sure Asda had a café! Hey, thinking about it, they were probably playing our game and were probably having some 'grown up' time in the back of their *Ford Sierra*!

That Thursday night, we must have got particularly carried away and the squealing out of hand. When you don't have to have quiet sex, why would you? It was compulsory to add the dramatics when you were usually suffocated by somebody's hand due to your secret location. Cringingly, we never heard the shuffling of the green and white bags or the dragging of the freezer drawers, just the frantic opening of the bedroom door by his furious, disgusted mother.

We could not have just been in a forgiving missionary position with maybe a tiny covering of clothing, no it had to be, butt ass naked, doggy style with my tiny lilies hanging. Chris had nothing to fear. I mean Okay, I'm sure his mam had seen him naked many, many times before, even with an erect penis maybe? But it mattered not, since I was sat aboard his manhood, covering every bit of his modesty. Me however, I was sat upright, mid thrust, legs akin, sliding up and down. squealing like a banshee! We had been so excited to be alone that we had torn every shred of fabric from our bodies, leaving me vulnerable to her penetrating glare!

I would like to say that the rest is a blur but unfortunately it is crystal clear, and I am sure it always will be. After Chris managed to convince his mam that it was for the best, if she waited until we were dressed to have a nervous breakdown and to explain to us how disgusting and disrespectful we were, she slammed the door shut. Thinking the worst was over, I eagerly pulled my clothes on, put the hood up on my hoodie (in the hope of shrouding my embarrassment) and embarked on the walk of shame downstairs. Un problema. You see to get out of the house, I had to walk through the living room consequently facing 'Mother'. Obviously, the worst was still to come.

The room was like an episode of *The Royle Family*, all the family were there including Grandma and little sister. What had she bloody done? Phoned all the family to come and witness my public flogging or what? I began the dash for the kitchen door avoiding the tar and feathers on my walk of atonement, and nearly made it too, she bloody gave me a false sense of security.

My hand was on the handle as she sweetly began, "Excuse me."

"Yes?" I nervously answered.

"Can you keep your bloody clothes on in my house in the future," she snarled with a look that could kill, glaring at me like I'd just bloody raped her son.

Bring on the ring of the bells and the chants of shame, it was all very *Game of Thrones*. Needless to say, I steered clear of 'Mother' for a while.

She wasn't the only one who was unfortunate enough to catch our reckless abandonment of morals. When the cold weather kicked in, we had to spend more time with our friends (of whom we had tended to spend less and less time with, as of late), as laying in the corner of a field 'fucking' wasn't as exciting a prospect whilst covered in frost (I'm sure that there is a fantasy group out there so completely into this). We needed somewhere that we could be alone together that was warm and dry and as a group of friends we would all take it in turns in dossing in each other's bedrooms when the weather was bad. Our friends clearly sussed that we were only tagging along in the hope that we could sneak off to some private time somewhere in their homes for some loving. Often it worked, on good days there weren't even any parents home. Bonus! But our friends were fast becoming tired of this.

Cringingly, we were always, always, getting 'discovered'. From his parents, to my parents, aunties, sisters, brothers, but the worst kind of 'get caught sex' just has to be by your friend's parents. I have lost count of how many times this happened to me and Chris and the shame never got any easier to bear. The ones where we had more clothes on were always slightly easier to explain to angry parents but the likes of getting caught in Anna's bath by her mam, or doggy style by Chris's friends dad in his living room, were just total armadillo time!

What you need to know specifics? Haven't I made you cringe enough yet and we are only half way through? Ok, I'll begin with Anna's mam. She was never ever around, she mostly stayed with her boyfriend, so that initially gave us a false sense of security, which is never good when the ingredients are teenagers and sex. Chris and I liked to be adventurous and so were making our way through the hypothetical list of 'places you have to have sex'. We realised one day that we had never got down to the deed in a bath. Sounds super trivial but we were only 16 and didn't live together, so taking a bath together was no easy fete. Besides there were no 'Groupon experiences' in our day, we had no money for nights away and so we were super limited in terms of entertainment. Yes, even I felt sympathy for myself here.

One boring Saturday night we took the opportunity to satisfy this gap in our love making history, but no sooner had we disappeared under the bubbles for some slidey fun, did we hear Anna's exasperated yelps from downstairs. We knew instantaneously that we had an intruder, although to be fair, she did pay the rent. Knowing somebody was there and doing anything about it however, was a little tricky when you were soaking wet from head to toe and your clothes were far from being neatly folded up on the radiator. Whilst dwelling on this memory, I must admit, I am wondering how we broached this subject with Anna?

"Erm excuse me Anna, can we fuck in your bath, whilst you lot watch *Coronation Street* please?"

"Yes, sure mate, knock yourself out," must have been the reply!

Come on have some empathy here. You know what it's like in the swimming baths, when you are in a rush to get changed, not because you had some important place to be or somebody special to meet, or even because you were always really conscious that some gawper would be copping a load of your cellulite and hairy nipples, but just because you were still damp (no you weirdos, not that kind of damp), the clothes you were hastily trying to drag over your love handles would cruelly cling to your bulges, totally refusing to help you cover up your private regions. So, imagine our utter dread when not only did we have the cruel clothing to contend with, we were not only damp but wringing bloody wet (explain that one then) and to top it off finding the right clothes was like an exercise out of the *Crystal Maze*! I'm sure you will be pleased to know we failed the task, although getting locked in would have been a welcome punishment rather than sat on the sofa receiving our grilling from Anna's mam whilst Chris sat uncomfortably inserted into my tiny Nike jumper.

Philosophy – Parenting in the Nineties

Parents in the nineties were so different to millennial parents. They had so few responsibilities that it gave us a much greater sense of freedom than any adolescent would have now. There was no way for them to trawl through your private conversations about wine and willies. They weren't obsessed with carving out the perfect childhood for us, hence ensuring that every second of our lives were routinely filled with 'things to do'. They also didn't have to live up to a pretence on social media, ensuring that the whole world knew that they were involved in every second of their children's lives. Therefore, in complete contrast, they kicked us out first thing in the morning and we knew to be home by 10pm (or for the younger ones, when the street lights came on). They continued their own lives and hobbies, which were usually attending the local club in fancy dress with their Tupperware full of pork pies and pickled onions or sitting on dining room chairs in their friends' gardens on an evening drinking tea whilst screaming for the kids to shut the fuck up and get off the windowsills.

Similarly, one evening, we were lucky enough to acquire our friend's living room. Since his dad had gone to see *Meat Dog* (clearly a tribute to the legend that be *Meat Loaf*) in the local club, we presumed he wouldn't be back for some time. That meant there was no need to be sly, we could have sex with no clothes and everything, wooo hooo!! This is the stuff dreams are made of when you are a love sick/horny teenager.

If I remember rightly I think we were somewhere around doggy style when his dad opened the front room door and caught us right at it. Once again, my poor tiny titties were hanging in full view of the world. I really felt for the poor man, he was either very used to this kind of thing or he was too much in shock to react. In fact, he apologised to us and told us he wouldn't be a moment he just needed his lighter!

Not all the sex was so ill thought out. My 17th Birthday had finally arrived. Chris and I had spent a year together already and it had passed in a blur of …. sex really! But not all the sex was so ill thought out.

"Happy Birthday beautiful, I've got a surprise for you later babe." Chris told me over the phone that morning, "come down when you are ready."

Upon walking into Chris's an hour later, tears brimmed as I laid my eyes on his living room. The curtains were drawn, and the room glowed majestically from an array of candles scattered around the room. The flooring was covered with a quilt and a single red rose was laid romantically upon it. There was only one thing to do ....

And, we really entered the world of grownups when we decided to head to the East Coast with my sister, Clair and her boyfriend, for a bit of fun during that summer. I didn't spend nearly enough time with my sister since I had entered adolescence, so I was looking forward to some family time. Whilst I was encompassed by my 'sexual adolescence' it was hard to make time for anybody but boys, but I am sure that is pretty much obvious from this narrative and I'm even surer that it is standard for most adolescents.

Going on holiday with my boyfriend, even if it was just for one night in some scruffy B&B was all so exciting, you would have thought that we were heading to the Caribbean. I didn't mind the unkempt B&B we ended up in, if I'm honest, but to be fair I was offended by the owners, pink velour bobbly tracksuit. She was about 70 for god's sake. Not that I'm suggesting for a moment that somebody of less digits could have carried it off, because that just wasn't possible.

MILESTONE = HOLIDAY WITH A BOYFRIEND

Chris was a dream boyfriend in those couple of days by the sea. I even woke up in the morning to a bunch of roses! Who cared about the green urine stained hefty armchairs, the World War II evacuee blankets and the not so faint smell of OAP's. I was in love and I was with the man I adored. We could have been in a refugee camp and you would have been hard pushed to wipe the grin from my face.

We conducted all the usual cliché in love activities whilst on our little trip: going out for meals (how very grown up), strolls down the sea front, seeking the thrills at the fairground so that I could conveniently cling to him in my petrified state! Aside from Kayden taking me to see Disney's *Toy Story at the local Odeon*, my experience with dates was very minimal and so I was in total heaven. Although I remember it all only vaguely, what I mostly remember is the 'sex' (I did tell you that my memories largely consisted of this, didn't I) and the seaside was no different. We tried our best never to leave the comfort of our weekend sex chamber. No furious parents or interrupting friends, no begging for the use of their facilities, no watching the door with half an eye but most importantly .... no clothes .... we were free of the need for a quick cover up.

Falling out of Love

If there was one key thing that would sum up mine and Chris's relationship after that first year, it would be, ups and downs. Were we falling out of love, is this what happened? It became such a power struggle and the focus of our relationship became more about who was in control than how we could make each other happy. It took around 18mths before our total devotion to each other began to wane. Sometimes I loved him (in a fashion), sometimes he loved me (again in a fashion), but it rarely happened at the same time. The problem is, when you are not happy at home, you look elsewhere. And whilst there was absolutely no doubt that I was utterly in love with Chris, we couldn't seem to give each other what we needed to make each other happy anymore.

It was clear that Chris's attentions had begun to wander as had mine. The small things he used to do, had begun to be the things that I would have loved him to have done at that point. We spent less time together and get this, we no longer had sex every day. This was a huge shift. Maybe there had been far too much emphasis on sex within our relationship and now we had begun to settle down, I didn't like the shift. On the other hand, I had plenty of admirers, as did he, so it was hard to resist when your boyfriend no longer looked at you with that adoring look that had made me fall in love with him in the first place.

To be totally honest (don't be cross at me) I had begun to string Mitchell along again at this point. It sounds cruel to them both, but I needed Mitchell to comfort me in the times when Chris was sure to either smash my heart to smithereens or lower my self-esteem to the bottom of the Grand Canyon. So, you see, I just couldn't completely throw Mitchell in, besides I had no intention of doing anything with him, I wasn't about to cheat, I just needed him close by, that's all. I was an adolescent, I found it hard to be alone that's all and thus I needed a backup. Sometimes adolescence requires you to be selfish, period.

The time eventually came when Chris got annoyed about this tiny matter of my attachment to Mitchell. I didn't hide things from Chris, I had male friends just as he had female friends.

"We need to speak Shan," Chris blurted out the second I had walked into his bedroom.

"Cool," I replied.

"I don't want you anywhere near Mitchell, it is clear he is just trying to split us up," he banged his door shut so his parents couldn't hear his irrational whinging.

"Where the fuck has this come from? I am not going to stop being friends with somebody because you don't trust me all of a sudden," I retorted.

"He is in fucking love with you, you fucking idiot."

"In that case, maybe you should spend more time with me to convince me you are the one that I should be with, and not him. And that might be a hell of a lot easier if you weren't trying to scour the village for somebody else to lay your length to every fucking night."

I stormed out as he was screaming some demands at the back of my head.

Perhaps we should have realised that Chris would turn up to Anna's that evening. Once upon a time, I had to have Chris there every night whatever I was doing, maybe for physical reasons. But since I was seemingly on rationing, and I was no longer guaranteed a fumble when he visited me, I didn't always see the need for us to spend every night together. Chris rocked up demanding entry. I didn't have a good enough excuse not to let him in, so we all stuck on a film and began to chill.

To soothe the situation, I went over and sat on Chris's knee. And yeah so, I could slyly rub his penis a little, of which we all know is the easiest way to fix any situation when it comes to men. I had no idea what to say to him about any of this, but I knew this boy inside out and I knew exactly how to make him putty in my hands and I wasn't afraid to use it. As my hand made gentle (accidental) contact with his dick, he turned to look up to me, still wearing a frown. I grinned cheekily as I let my hand drift back over for a second time. This time, he grinned!

Philosophy – The Power of Sex

Sex has many uses. But don't be fooled into thinking pro-creation and pleasure are the only ones. There is also power! I'm sure that you have all learnt this by now but if you haven't – go out there right now and test out your superpower. It is damn right fucking amazing! There are people all over the world who only have their job, house, relationship, money all because they rocked somebody's world in the sack. It truly is a much more powerful currency than money. The deeds that can be forgotten with a quick deep throat of a willy is phenomenal. Somebody is sad? Give them a quick shake. Can't have that dress? Can't have that pussy! You get the idea!

The problem occurred when the phone rang, of which happened to be next to Chris.

Cocky and confident, he answered the phone, "Yo."

His cockiness didn't last long when he found it was Mitchell on the other end! I knew what had happened by the quick sudden furious stare he threw straight at me, but especially so when he picked up the poor plant at the side of him and lobbed it at the wall. Charming! He didn't have any bloody proof of infidelity, it could have been innocent? He wasn't stupid though and he knew exactly what was happening. Anna told him to leave and he did exactly that, but not before he turned to face me so that I could see the flood of tears falling down his face! I was shocked to say the least. This was the first time I had seen Chris cry in front of his friends. He was raw and hurt. I didn't really know how to feel, and I definitely didn't know how to react.

Did I feel guilty? Not really if you want me to be truthful. The problem was that I knew that I loved Chris and I knew that Mitchell meant nothing to me, so I didn't really have anything to worry about! Mitchell was my back-up, my security blanket, my spare loo roll, my emergency tampax, my clean pair of knickers, do I need to go on? I had planned to tell Chris in due course and explain just that and he would be fine, right? I had to apologise a lot sooner than I thought I was going to have to, since 10 minutes later, Chris was pounding at the door.

In all honesty, I did feel terrible by the time we were stood face to face at the gate. As innocent as the phone call was, and it was innocent as I had never

ever had any sexual contact with Mitchell, I could see that it had clearly hurt him and for once, that really wasn't my intention and I did care! It didn't help that Chris had clearly totally got hold of the wrong end of the stick, convincing himself that not only was I having an affair, but I was also about to leave him for Mitchell. As a result, he had come armed with a speech to convince me to stay with him and even, let me add, a proposal. No chill out, it wasn't a marriage proposal. No. It was ten times bloody worse, he decided that we should try for a baby!

Philosophy – Men Fixing Problems

Whilst we have just discussed a really cool way of fixing issues in relationships through the use of sexuality activity, I thought that this was a perfect way to demonstrate how men think that the way to do the same with women is to offer them a ring or a foetus. And again (similar to before) there are so many men with wedding rings and babies that they traded for forgiveness for playing around with the best friend. I like the earlier way better – it is less of a life restricting fix isn't it. Now maybe if Chris had offered me a spot of oral sex that might have worked better than the idea of a screaming baby, stretch marks and an empty purse. It is also strange how men think that babies are less of a commitment than a marriage isn't it?

Yep, no shit, this boy was crazy, but I kind of loved him for it. I obviously had absolutely no intention of taking him up on his offer like (unless he wanted to change it to my philosophy suggestion of oral sex?), however, I liked the fact he could see me as a mother, but not only as a mother, but as the mother of his children. Yep, he was surely hooking me. Confused? You should be!

Sometimes, I wasn't sure if I was still in love though. Or had I been in love at all? The indecisiveness had really kicked in. Why did adolescence and love have to be so confusing And often I had panic attacks at the thought of him not being in my life, and then at other times, I didn't want to see him for days. Maybe I was beginning to get cold feet. The intensity of that first year had passed and we were, just 'normal'. I didn't like 'normal'. It was fucking boring. I thought that perhaps when I stopped finishing with Chris just to see him cry, then it would prove that I still loved him. Yes, I know, it sounds terrible doesn't it? It was, and I must say I am quite embarrassed about it. Maybe I'm telling you now in the hope that you will tell me also that you did the same, then I will know that I can add it to my list of 'embarrassing activities in a normal adolescence' and stop cringing about it whenever I saw his picture on Facebook.

Don't get me wrong, it wasn't a planned act of torture or anything like that, it just more or less happened a time or two, or maybe three or four. Who's counting? Maybe he was annoying me a tad or maybe I just wanted a bit of attention or something, I really don't know why I did it. But I would sit him down and tell him that I didn't want to be with him anymore, that we needed a break or some other cliché. He would then cry, no sorry, beg me not to leave and hey presto I would have a change of heart and momentarily our relationship would be that bit better following our 'rocky' patch!

How I can say that when I spent the rest of the relationship snottily sobbing into my crusty pillow, I'll never know.

It was shortly after this that my lovely Chris forgot to use the litter tray and preceded to shit all over me. Maybe he wanted to punish me or maybe he had quickly bored of dedicating his penis to the love of one girl. Before the year was out he decided it was time he gave his attached friend a little treat, even at the expense of my pummelled heart. This one particular evening he informed me that he wouldn't be accompanying me babysitting that night, as his friends were fondly missing him – aaaaahhhhh! Such an unselfish boy always thinking of others. I have to give it to him, he was not lying, he was going to be with his friends and one particular big nosed freaky bitch by the sea. So as the caravan was a rocking, I came a knocking. I wish! No, unfortunately, the deed was done before the pigeon brought the news.

MILESTONE = BEEN CHEATED ON

I was heartbroken, horrified, torn apart, devastated, betrayed and any other heart wrenching verb that you could conjure up. I had never felt pain like this, emotional or physical. This shit was painful and torturous. How could he? Why would he? Ok I wasn't the best girlfriend in the world, especially in the beginning, but the truth was I loved him, and I didn't deserve this. This was the key moment in my life where I learnt the lesson required for the transformation into womanhood. The lesson that all men are bastards, regardless of the puppy dog eyes, flattering one-liners, bulging biceps or large cocks. In fact, what generally tends to happen is the more the man/boy may seem to have to offer the more they feel they need to share themselves with half the population of the country.

In all fairness, in my case, it was the population of the village, luckily for me he wasn't well travelled enough for it to be the whole country. Lately there was always one rumour or another detailing Chris in some kind of fix with another woman, not that I ever had any proof. It began to feel like one of those communal marriages where the one so-called stallion has several wives and they all become one big happy family, apart from ironically, I wasn't that happy and certainly wasn't going to pretend to be just to be honoured with his presence. How had this all happened? Where had our infatuation gone? Maybe if it happened now, we would get our own show on MTV or something?

The truth was, he had absconded to the seaside with crow nose (real name: Brooke) and left me licking my wounds as I mulled on his promiscuity, but as the tears began to stop, my anguish turned into anger quite quickly. Learning the art of revenge (ironically this came quite naturally to me), I decided to pay his dear parents a visit, who by this time had seemingly grown fond of the naked imp that had previously raped their son (and I of them).

As I burst through their kitchen door with a handful of *Bounty* kitchen roll (much required for the amount of snot making its way down nose mountain), I bravely announced to his entire family, through my sobs and sniffles, that their beloved and dearly treasured little boy was in fact a very dirty little bastard who'd been caught letting his snake play with a stray dangerous pussy, who I'm sure had had none of her inoculations; dirty little bitch! His dad was undeniably horrified and phoned knob jockey who confirmed the accusations through his sobs and sniffles. As I ate the salty chicken sandwich his mam made, I sobbed my poor broken heart out.

Philosophy – Realising People Lie
Part of the pain through this kind of grief is accepting that 'people lie'. We know people in general, lie. I mean, parents are the biggest lying bastards going. Don't want to accept the blame for shitty Christmas presents? Blame Santa.

Can't control your kids? Tell them that the Bogey Man is coming. Need a drink of water when you are pissed up? Tell the kids you are unwell. Realising your parents lie is one thing but learning that the person that you are in love with lies, is a different kettle of fish. Learning that they lie to 'you' is unbearable.

On a more serious note, I did believe that he would never ever hurt me. Fool, I hear you shout! I know, I know, but I was only a little, wittle 17-year-old, I'd tried so hard not to fall in love with him, not to get hurt and the minute I did it was like he was dancing around shouting *'Ha, got you sucker'* and pissing all over me at the same time. Therefore, this is probably the biggest most important, major adolescent lesson I could ever teach you guys. The sooner you learn this, the better and hence you will savour more of your heart and ultimately/hopefully your pride! Everybody (absolutely everybody) is capable of breaking hearts.

I cringe when I hear folk saying, "He wouldn't do that to me."

Bloody idiots. Half of the heartache is the fact that you believed them when they said they would never hurt you, so prepare yourself from the beginning and it will make it so much easier! I'm not trying to insinuate that they don't mean it when they say they won't hurt you. I'd say, 8 out of 10 times they do, but feelings change, and things happen, sometimes intentionally, but mostly unintentionally!

I couldn't stand the fact that Chris and Brooke may have had secrets that I didn't know, it was killing me. I hated that they had shared the intimacy that we swore to only share together. It was haunting. I couldn't close my eyes without imagining them together. What did he say to her? What promises did he make? Had he treated her the way he had treated me? Was he about to leave? The pain was unbearable. There was no other way, I just had to speak to her, so that I could match up stories and attempt to find out their secrets. At least that way, I too could be part of it (weird and perverse I know). I soooo wish I hadn't bothered. If I thought I was heart-broken before then this was the car crash that I could have avoided been ensnared in.

"He has told me everything," I screamed in her face as I pinned her against the brick wall by her neck, when I had finally tracked her down.

I scrutinised her face whilst squeezing her neck so tightly that she grabbed at my hand and was struggling to speak. She had attempted to make herself look older, there was no disguising that nose though. Her back-combed hair and huge hoops in her ears, told me that she too today felt like a woman. Fuck! He had done that to her. What the fuck was this. Was he going about with his magic wand, turning girls into women like he was some kind of sexual wizard?

"Today girls, is the special day where I transform you into a woman, how cool is that? It won't take me but a flick of my tongue and the stab of my penis wand and it is all done. So, let's be having your knickers off, womanhood awaits."

Let's be honest with each other, this kind of severe hurt and betrayal has the ability to turn you into a cold-blooded killer. The idea of watching her lifeless body drop to the floor relieved some of the anger that was totally consuming my body. Maybe bumping her off was the way to go. Maybe death is the only way to solve this after all and if not hers, then it would have to be his. Petrified tears streamed down her face.

"What do you want from me then?" she sobbed, desperately pleading with me through her eyes, to let go of her neck.

"Because I want to hear it from you, I think you owe me that?"

Silence. Even the tears stopped as she dropped her head. Consumed by grief, I couldn't even bear to look at her. I was close to tears and there was no way I was going to let her see me cry. I let go of her.

"He said you were a shit lay anyway," I spitefully spat the words at her as I turned to leave.

"We didn't sleep together," she shouted back.

My heart raced. I even almost, prematurely, grinned, "He just fingered me and went down on me, that's all," she added, quickly causing my heart to plummet to my toes as I forcibly swallowed my vomit that had arisen into my mouth.

Fingering? Yep there was that minging term again, as discussed earlier what a repulsive term. All the fuss created over the 'C' word, yet this one seems to have escaped the obligatory universal hate. Brooke the slag's statement made me feel so much better. Note, curiosity killed the cat!

Philosophy – Blaming the Woman

It is impossible not to be angry at the one that engages in sexual enjoyment with your partner and to some extent, so you should be. But it is important to also lay the blame exactly where it should be, at the door of your partner. They are the ones that have betrayed you, they are the ones that have broken the promises made. Isn't it funny how often we forgive our partners for breaking our hearts, but you still want to kick the woman in the fanny when you bump into her in the supermarket a decade later.

Whilst I had semi dealt with Brooke, I still had to face my very own Judas. He eventually appeared back at his house later that day and after a long conversation with his Mam, she convinced me to come and speak to him. I finally felt that I had an ally. His parents stayed present while he tried to worm his way out of the situation, using every bullshit excuse in the book. I particularly liked the part when he uttered something that his Mam wasn't happy with and therefore he received a nice slap to the cheek. I listened for some time and bored of hearing his dismal reasoning of how his tongue accidentally slipped into this hoe's pussy.

I slammed the door behind me and left them to their domestic, I had heard enough. I left! He chased! I ran! He ran! Did I want him to? I was wholly confused at what I wanted at that point. The hurt had totally washed over me, and I was temporarily unable to think or feel. Probably for the best. I stopped at the bottom of Detton Hill.

"Why the fuck are you following me?" I shrieked, "you clearly didn't give this kind of a fuck, whilst you were laying your length to her, did you?"

He seemed speechless, or maybe he just knew that it was pointless. What exactly could he say? "You are right Shannon, to be fair you were the last thing on my mind as my penis hardened from the joy I received from tasting the wares of her vagina."

I had finished listening. What could he do? He took the only other available option. He dropped to the floor and grasped at my feet as I attempted to head up the steep hill.

"Please don't leave me. I don't know what else to say to make you stay. I love you!"

I looked down at this tragic man-boy who had resorted to physically laying on the floor, begging, sobbing to save a relationship that days earlier he
had seemingly convinced himself that he didn't even want.

Philosophy – Begging

*Fact: men will do anything to get you to do what they want you to do. You
need to be aware that there will be little truth or meaning in their words, it
doesn't work like that. You can't seriously sit and weigh the options up dependent
on the words they utter. It is all bullshit. Think of the things you would say to
parents whilst trying to gain their permission to camp out. You didn't seriously
mean that you would wash the pots or take your sister to the fair. They are all just
words, words that when jumbled into the right order and spoken with the right
amount of emotive imagery will enable you to manipulate the person in front of
you.*

I'm sure it won't shock you when I say I took the scumbag back. In fact,
keep this to yourself, but I was already preparing a game plan to win him back
before he even set foot back on Yorkshire soil. Aren't women crazy bitches? The plan was along the lines of dressing in something extremely smutty
and riding him until the cows came home. Not very imaginative I know, but
I think you'll find it usually works. This was all in the hope that he would
conclude that nobody could satisfy him in the entirely selfless way that I
could, especially not 'Crow Nose'. As it happened the suspenders seemed to
be unnecessary as Chris had clearly come home with his tail between his legs
(again no pun intended), begging like the naughty little dog who had forgotten where he lived and sneaked elsewhere to be fed. In fact, she did me a
favour as puppy once again became his attentive old self, forsaking all others
etc. The puppy soon forgets having his nose rubbed in the urine and always
seems to do it again.

Philosophy – Why do People Cheat

*I do not have the answer to this million-dollar question for every individual.
But I do think I can sum it up through a couple of stabs in the dark.*

1) They don't like their partner

2) Because they are greedy mother fuckers/because they can

Let me make this clear, I do not believe for one minute that every partner who cheats, does so because they are not in love. I don't go to work to make money just because I am poor. I could be rich, and I would still go because I would want more. We as humans are a little bit like that. Life can be fucking great and we would still want more, the analogy doesn't change when we are talking about relationships. Things can be great, but why would we not want more?

I am sure some of you are saying, "What is wrong with getting that 'something more' with your partner?"

To that I would say, chocolate pudding every night is tiresome eventually.

By this time, we had discovered the joys of the good old working men's club. Whilst W.M.Cs are almost a thing of the past, back then they were the shit. Now that I am 'of age', I will hold my hands up and admit that we were not old enough to follow in their footsteps at all, and mostly the committee knew this, but still as long as we behaved and put money behind the bar – we were welcomed. We had eagerly awaited the days where we could follow in our parent's footsteps and become a member of 'the club'. Maybe even one day becoming a member of the Committee? Imagine the power of being able to bar every bitch you hated. Sweet!

Philosophy – W.M.Cs (Working Men's Club)

W.M.Cs were akin to a very large living room and they were to be treated as such too. Firstly, you were not welcome in the club if you were not from the village. If you dared to walk into a club in another village, expect to be treated as if you have just walked straight into somebody's home without even knocking. Secondly, there were designated seats, not physically labelled, but if you dared to sit in somebody's place, shit was going down. And that somebody might be 98-year-old Doris, but you were going to get it. 'You rude little shit'. Also, there were activities that were run in the club and they were to be taken very seriously. The most important one being 'Bingo'. And repeat after me, 'We do not speak whilst bingo is being played.' There were beer tokens riding on this so was held in very high regard. It was a similar situation with 'the turns'. It was fine to bit and bob with conversation with your table mates, but if you got a little loud and you weren't paying enough attention to the turns, you risked being pulled up in front of (drum roll please) 'The Committee', which as gangster as it sounds, was a panel of 90 odd year-old blokes exercising their power over the village the only way they could.

Our club was called *'The Pipe'*. Oh, just the name of this scruffy old hole (I mean quaint little village watering hole) brings back thousands of memories. You know how that works, like when you open a bottle of aftershave or perfume and that certain smell can trigger a thousand memories that you'd long since forgotten about (not sure whether that is a good thing or not). When it comes to a smell, it is not just a memory in your head, it is a memory that is there, around you, an instant smile bringer (or a vomit inducer). This particular one brings back a mix of good and bad memories. I suppose you have probably already gathered from his previous adulterous episodes that Chris had by this time began to shed his geeky status and started getting noticed by the over teeming female population of our village. I loved this at first because it felt good that people wanted 'my' bloke. However, once the blonde skinny beauties started gawping, my insecurities stepped in as his attention once again began to wander.

The Pipe was fantastic at first, it made us feel grown up but with adulthood comes drama and our outings to this place could be likened to *The Jeremy Kyle Show* most of the time. Chris had this special little trick that he had learnt, clever little boy. He would spy a bitch that he took a fancy to and suddenly he would slip the leash and manage to avoid/ignore me, all night. Every night would start out perfect with us, this golden couple perfectly turned out, I would liken us to maybe, Marilyn Monroe and Marlon Brando. I'm not sure others would have done though, maybe it was more Sharon and Ozzy without the money and fame. Walking down that long road to the club, we would be all smiles and kisses, promises of long life love and floaty happiness. But walking through those rickety doors of the club was like entering the twilight zone. My precious, loving, baby, hastily turned into the boyfriend from hell. Even to this day it is the most amazing transformation of the male species that I have ever witnessed.

It wasn't just the pub, he too had a strange effect on me. The seemingly confident and outgoing person that had been formed by adolescence had seemingly disappeared and left in her place, this anxiety ridden, jealous, naive little girl. The more he ignored me the more of a whinging, whining bitch I became. No man had ever managed to reduce me to this.

Just as the beginning of the night always started the same, the end of the night always mirrored the one before. He would take his pick of the bunch of drooling, flirty bitches and proceed to pick a big fight with me. He was very clever though because he would always make himself out to be the victim and me 'that psycho bitch'. After I would let loose on Chris, he would always need comforting and there was always some sly one, willing to lend him a shoulder to cry on. As I was being held back by several sticky beaks, pretending to prevent me from landing the pair with a chimney, when really just wanting to be in the front line of action. The sneaky cow would then lead him to the safety of her abode, or more likely, behind the village factory.

One particular girl (not that there was only one), let's call her big lips (for reasons better known to her and her lovers), had made quite an impact on mine and Chris's by now already very volatile relationship. Michelle (her real name) had originally been one of my best friends before we all fell into the realms of adolescence. It quickly became obvious to us all that Michelle was not the type of female friendship we should be taking into our teenage years. She had one aim and one aim only – boys, boys and more boys, regardless of who they belonged to. So yes, she was a total fucking whorebag! And said, whorebag, had been flirting with my Chris for some time now.

That alone I could deal with but the fact that she did it in front of me, I could not. Not because I felt threatened by her, she was facially disfigured with thunder thighs that complimented her swollen ankles, but because of her attempt to render me invisible and insignificant. However, persistence pays off with knobs like him and all too soon she temporarily became 'the chosen' shoulder to cry on. Being unable to follow them through the twilight door, due to the interfering bastards preventing my wrath, I had no choice but to send one of my spies. Wes was a perfect choice as he was one of Chris's close friends, but we had become good friends. Choosing between Chris and I was no competition, I was clearly his favourite and who could blame him?

Even way back in the very early flirting stages of mine and Chris's relationship, Wes and I formed a very close relationship. Okay let's be honest here. He obviously just wanted to fuck my brains out, but I wasn't averse to using my pussy power as a form of manipulation as you know! The morons in our village (every village has them), liked to fantasize in their sordid little gossiping conversations that I was clearly taking a daily spit roasting from Wes and Chris. But unfortunately, Wes was like my brother, so any sexual relationship or longings would have been nothing short of incest. It's that small-town mentality of 'a man and a woman cannot be friends, unless they are gay'. Wes was one of the loveliest men that I would ever meet in my lifetime thus far, he was my protector.

Without hesitation, Wes followed them, only to return to me with heartbreaking news. He'd caught the dirty little fuckers at it, no shock there then. He detailed the witnessing of their giggling, hand holding partnership of the pair as they entered her house. Wanting to gain as much evidence as he could, he peeked through the break in the curtains to watch them sprawled out together in front of the coal fire. I hoped that the fire would spit hot ashes onto their naked asses. More heartbreak. He had only gone and done it again! What the fuck? I barely had time to get over one episode of his dick sharing before I was faced with another.

I knew Michelle was not the type to place being faithful at the top of her 'to be' list, but it didn't make it hurt any less that she knew exactly how I felt about Chris, yet she still pounced upon an opportunity to ride his dick. When I thought about the times that I poured my tears into her ears, only for her to have used it to fuel her own agenda, I felt like a fucking idiot. Admittedly these things happen from time to time, even between friends, but this wasn't an accident, she wanted it to happen, she made it happen. She broke my heart with total and utter disregard for what would become of me after. How could she? And more importantly – how could he?

MILESTONE = BECAME A TOTAL AND UTTER DOORMAT

My fury turned into pity for Chris. I suddenly realised that his high sex drive was having a negative impact on his own life and not just mine. It was leading him to have sex with the ugliest of bikes, therefore tarnishing his sunshine boy reputation and his rep was very important to him, it did help him pull the ladies after all. Without sounding like a bitter bitch, Michelle was not the kind of girl that boys rushed to sleep with. She was single for a reason.

Philosophy – Men Cheating with Ugly Women

Being cheated on is painful experience regardless of who is involved. But it is a double-edged sword when the girl is a munter. On the one hand you feel relieved that you don't have to feel intimidated by her good looks and fantastically carved body. The thought of him imagining grafting her whilst grafting you is not going to boost anybody's confidence is it. But on the other hand, it is really hard to understand why your boyfriend would want to graft something that was of a lesser value than what he had at home.

Obviously, my pity stopped with Chris, as I only had deep rooted anger for big lips as she too was about to learn the true wrath of a girl so pissed off with desperate slags playing hide the sausage with her bloke. I decided to bide my time regarding my carefully plotted revenge.

MILESTONE = GREW SOME BOLLOCKS (KIND OF)

So, we were over. What choice did I have? You don't stop loving somebody because they break your heart, but you can choose to limit the amount of damage they can do to you. I didn't deliver the message to his face. Why? Fear of looking at him and wanting him probably. It wasn't easy to tell your heart the things your head already knew. I told Wes to tell him never to frequent my personal space again, and Wes was more than happy to oblige.

Letting Go

Although we weren't officially together anymore, it didn't stop Chris laying claim to me whenever it suited him. Whilst he attempted to convince me that 'I' was making the biggest mistake of my life, he seemed quite happy to dive into his own new-found freedom, he just wasn't necessarily so keen to let me do the same. Funny how that works isn't it? I realised that Chris wasn't the only man on the planet that would be interested in me. He liked me to believe he was though, often telling me that 'nobody would want me for anything but sex'. Did any man want any woman for anything more than sex at that age? If they did surely sex was the most important thing? So there, I had the most important factor, I could live with that! To me it just confirmed my qualifications in the bedroom department. Fuck You Shane!

It was Xmas Eve and it was time to let my hair down and party. Whilst I no longer excitedly awaited Christmas Eve awaiting Santa and his present bringing, Christmas had taken on a whole new meaning for me in adolescence. It was now just a complete and utter excuse to get fucked up, even throughout a work day. What a great time of year!

Excitedly, I dug out the very inappropriate short, lacy, see through, little black number. That, I decided, would be the perfect attire for a 'no Chris' night out. It was a fitting choice for this occasion. It was quite demure, which was exactly the reason that not only did I take the scissors to it to make it a more acceptable length, but I also refused to wear the underdress with it and instead wore my black Wonder bra complete with black hot-pants. Think Lilo-Lill from *Bread* and you have fantastically accurate imagery. I had created the finest me I could conjure up. With tinsel draped around my shoulder, baubles hanging from my ears and a complete and utter desperation to belt out *All I want for Christmas*, I was ready for the perfect Christmas night out.

And it was ... until he appeared at the back of the room! I can't say I was disappointed because, I was too smashed to care either way. Besides he was there all of 10 mins before he stormed out of those double doors with a face like thunder. I didn't enquire why, nor did I need to, because as I continued to throw myself around the dance-floor with his friend, one of the old nosy gits that religiously lined the sticky chairs of the club came over to give me a piece of her mind.

Apparently, I had upset Chris by dancing with his friend. So, what? He did realise that we weren't 'exactly together', didn't he? He was taking advantage of the 'space' and ensuring his dick got appropriate massaging, so what was good for the goose! Oh, he was upset? Me – 1, Him – Nil! I'll tell you why he was upset. Because he had dragged his sorry ass into the city and hadn't managed to find anybody to massage his ego/cock. And just to add insult to injury, his yo-yo bit of familiar sex didn't fall at his feet the minute he walked through the door.

Apart from that little hiccup, I had a good night and I did manage to acquire that walking home partner. Let me set things straight here though, never ever did I have any intention of anything happening between me and my chaperone (who just happened to be one of Chris's bessies, Paul). We were friends, ish! I suppose then, I was a little unprepared for him clumsily shoving me up against the wall and trying to snog my face off whilst heavy handily attempting to shove his hand up my faff. Oh Romeo, Romeo, wherefore art thou Romeo? Was this the one I had been searching for my whole adolescence?

I shoved him so hard he fell against the car at the side of the road before he attempted to hurriedly explain to me why he had just tried to molest me. I gave him a few choice words before leaving him shouting about how he was, "in love with me" and, "how we should be together." Oh, the joy of the drunken revelation.

Philosophy- Beginning to Adjust

Whilst no part of me wanted to be apart from Chris and I won't pretend I didn't feel like my life was over, I had begun to accept that life was going to go on. And more excitedly, that life could still be great. Once, the nausea of breaking up with somebody begins to pass, you begin to see the gains that single life can bring. Sure, the thought of my baby laying in somebody else's arms crucified me, but the thought of laying in somebody else's arms, it excited me! Having sex with the same person for a long time, can be amazing. You really tune into each other and often it is a guaranteed orgasm. But let's be honest – it can be shit too.

If I wasn't prepared for Paul's advances, I was even less prepared for the 5 o'clock telephone call from a very distraught Chris. I had steadily become used to the fact that Chris didn't give a fuck about me, so I mean it when I say, it took me by complete surprise. I was at the point where I was sure that Chris could have not only 'rented' me out to his friends but could have stayed to supervise and still wouldn't have shown a flicker of fuck giving. It seemed that Paul's ego was more than a little bruised from my rejection and probably out of fear that I would tell his best friend exactly what had happened, the pathetic little boy had resorted to awakening Chris from his slumber by throwing stones at his window in an attempt to save him from wretched old me. He saw it as no more than his duty to tell Chris that I had just tried it on with him. Yep you better believe it! Scum.

Philosophy- Rejected Men
Rejected men are the worst. They can't just accept that somebody doesn't want them, apologise and move on. I mean none of us can be everybody's cup of tea, can we? They are so easily offended, and it seems they feel if we don't find their receding hairline and puffing stomach attractive – then we shall be punished. Woe betide!

Paul did me a massive favour though. It just happened to be the shake Chris had needed to realise he wasn't willing to stand by and watch me with somebody else.

"Shan, this is killing me, let's give it one more go?" he pleaded, "I'm a different person, people are just trying to break us."

I didn't buy it, but I was missing him so much, that just hearing his voice on the phone melted me. He immediately became his old self once again (I know this is getting repetitive isn't it) and did everything he could to make me happy. Ok maybe not everything; I would have perhaps liked him to legally sign his soul over to me for eternity and have my name tattooed on his head, oh and maybe it would finish it off nicely if he was to wear a male chastity belt, and only I had a key? But anyway, we could sort those things out later but for now we were officially back together.

Philosophy – Game Playing

It isn't rocket science as to why Chris wanted me back. You may think that he suddenly realised what he had. I believe the truth is that he knew what he had all along, but he was confident enough to be willing to gamble it if it meant he could get his rocks off. To men, it is all a game. Dodging the bullet. Getting as much as you can, with as little flak in return. Chris re-entered a relationship with me, not because he finally realised how much he loved me, but because he thought the game was nearly over.

It was Utopia once again, we went on dates, he phoned me regularly, he slept over lots and he was beginning to look at me like he loved me again. So why did it feel like something was missing? There was no denying that I was still totally in love with him, but during the time that he had been depriving me of attention, my eyes had begun to wander elsewhere. It is a natural process surely? Adolescence or not? I was a woman, I needed attention and if my boyfriend wouldn't give it to me, I would just take it from somebody else. You may also feel that is also a dose of good old-fashioned karma.

It was always the same, as it is with any man, the minute I threw in the towel he began chasing me as if like Hermione, I had put a love spell in his pint of bitter. No, I mean it, even the magic of the twilight door in the pub didn't have the power to overcome the spell. Wait for it, he even sat next to me in the pub. A previously unwritten law that stated that he could not even be seated anywhere within my vicinity, never mind on a seat directly next to me whilst in a public house. He couldn't seat himself next to me previous to this, as it would lead potential punters to believe that he was a young man involved in a monogamous relationship and we couldn't be having that now. The idea of depriving the village of such a stud filled me with guilt and I had no desire to be responsible for that.

Now let's face it, adolescence is full of drama and Chris and I were nowhere near out of the woods yet. Not to mention that the saga with Michelle was not over, the girl that we had split up over in the first place. Seemingly, she had had a taste of my thoroughbred and decided that she wanted to dine on him more frequently and since she had seemingly escaped not only my physical punishment but my vicious tongue too, there did not seem much to stop her. The next evening whilst in *The Pipe*, Chris and I, were cosily loved up surrounded by ringlets of nicotine and listening to the DJ pumping '*Children of the Night*' into the dingy four walls as we bounced up and down on the spot, ahh it was bliss. But bliss, more often than not, is broken and this was no exception. Michelle bounded over with a tightly sealed Christmas card addressed solely to him, MY BLOKE! That was it, the cheeky little bitch. Although at first, I was speechless, I wasted no time snatching the card from him and tearing it into tiny pieces (followed by regret that I hadn't read it first). Another lesson, think first, act later. That was it, I was about to lose my shit.

As she smugly strolled back over to her friends, I was about to explode. If she knew anything about love, she would know to never fuck with a broken woman. I quickly followed her back to her group of geeky followers and calmly seated myself in the middle of them. My friends sensing danger (or more the fear of getting barred from our local) immediately appeared behind me. My head was empty and what I was going to say at that point I had no idea, so what did come out of my mouth shocked me as much as it did everyone else.

"Did I taste nice?" I blurted out, shaking with adrenaline.

Her face looked shocked, nervous, but admittedly, confused. She obviously needed further clarification, to be fair, so did my friends. So, like any decent human being, I helped her out.

"Did I ever tell you how much my boyfriend likes oral sex?" I said whilst watching her brain tick away, "he particularly likes giving me oral sex just before we come to the club, in fact that is our routine every week, a touch or oral and then a few pints," I casually added.

"So, like I said, did my pussy taste nice?"

That smug grin was wiped right off that bulldog face of hers. Anna spat her drink across the table. Yep, this was savage, even for me. Job done! Even her friends could not stop themselves from being amused as they failed to attempt to try to even comfort her and instead buried their faces in their hands. Who would have thought I could have handled this without smashing her face in. The power of words.

I finished off the night by walking straight out of the pub, head held high and Chris running behind at my heels.

The One That Got Away

As you can see, being his girlfriend wasn't easy but being in love with Chris was even harder. But not everything in my adolescence love life was so negative. I don't want to lead all pre-adolescents (who really should not be reading this by the way) into a meltdown over the path that they must tread.

By now, I had started college and left the drama of high school behind, as I began to prepare for my future. If I could just focus more of the content of the business course that I had enrolled on, rather than my love life, then the next step would surely be University.

Whilst Chatfield College was still local, it wasn't in Detton, so it was still my escape from the village. And whilst meeting new people as an adolescent can be terrifying, it is also bloody exciting when you have exhausted all the totty you know. Just as Chris needed the filthy bikes in *The Pipe,* I often needed a shoulder to cry on too (or 2...or 3...).

Let me introduce one of these strapping shoulders: Leroy. I see you all puzzling over this one, who the hell is he? He was the one who got away and we all have one of those don't we? Let me set the scene for you. It's a shame I can't pop some soothing music on for you and love hearts could float up the page. Yes, that might just help with the imagery.

I met him at *Chatfield*, this was actually a great part of my adolescence, but maybe/unfortunately not <u>sexual</u> adolescence. Yes, believe it or not, not all of adolescence is about gobbling cock. Going to college showed me what a big world we live in. Albeit I was not jetting off to Tenerife and was still in the same town. But I'd had the realisation of just how many fishes there were out there for me to capture. Phwoar! Had I been mooning after Chris this whole time? Really?

On the very first day, Leroy and I immediately hit it off and quickly became the best of friends. He was very good looking, but not in a turn your head way, in a stylish, wore very trendy togs, spoke nice, made you laugh kind of way. This didn't just make him attractive, this made him fucking delicious. Ironically, he was the exact opposite to Chris and unlike any man I'd ever met in Detton. We clicked because we had all the same interests, unlike myself and Chris. I just wasn't really into downing handfuls of pills, dancing in derelict warehouses, loving every smack rat in the room, whilst dancing like a prick and blowing on a fucking whistle. So, it was quite hard for us to find common ground. But with Leroy it was easy; we didn't even have to try. We would sit for hours chatting in the common area, while some Jesus look-alike would strum hymns on his guitar (every college has this clique). I was oblivious to any goings on around us and I'm not ashamed to admit, I became very obsessed with him. No need to worry, obsession is a normal adolescent past time they tell me. We would talk about music (both hip hop heads), films (anything linked with hip hop), sport mostly basketball (okay, I knew none of the rules, but I knew that I liked to watch the men in shorts bounce around the court) and 'Love'! Yes, a bloke who was cool, sexy, intelligent but spoke about Love. See you all love him already don't you? Fuck *E.L James* and her depiction of *Christian Grey*. Some rich tosser who kicks fuck out of his bird and rewards her with an *Audi Spyder*. To be fair she lost me at 'he ran his bony finger down her back'. Who did? Fucking *Skeletor*. Oy *James,* that is not attractive! All hail Leroy instead, despite his lack of bank balance.

I had spent the last few years convincing myself that nobody could possibly have a connection like Chris and I. Except I was fast coming to the realisation that our connection wasn't the only kind of connection possible and maybe it wasn't that unique after all. I was facing up to the fact that it was a sexual connection. I used to think that was the most important kind of connection that you could have. Yet without laying a solitary finger on me and with total and utter ease, Leroy had me. He totally had me!

Maybe it goes without saying though, there was a hitch. And this one in adolescence, we call the 'one you have to fight for'. No, he wasn't a transsexual, the opposite actually, he was a very horny hot-blooded male. The catch was that he had a girlfriend. Oh, and it gets worse: she was an absolutely stunning blonde, tall, sexy girlfriend. It couldn't possibly be my luck that he would be shacked up with some crossed eyed, bun wearing fatty. Nope, she was so stunning that she was already a model at the tender age of 16. Even worse still, he loved her, boy did he love her! How did I know? Because he never fucking shut up about her. I wanted him to love me like that. But for now, I had his friendship and I adored him for that.

We spent so much time together that tongues wagged on our college campus. I didn't care because he kept me going most days. Whilst Chris and I were still bumbling along, I had long since come to the conclusion that maybe we were not soul mates after all. Leroy was nothing more than a name to Chris, he wasn't interested in meeting my friends at college, and funnily enough, I never encouraged it.

On the days where I was full of self-pity because my boyfriend was a twat, Leroy was my saviour, especially on the days where I thought that suicide was the only way to rescue me from all the drama and heartbreak of adolescence. He had a knack of making me feel good about myself. How? Not because he sucked my ass, tried it on with me, or gazed lovingly into my eyes (I bloody wish). No, just simply because he told me things that nobody ever told me with a truthful heart. He would casually tell me I was beautiful with no expected return (yes, long before the days of like for returns on Facebook) and he just spent time with me, even though there was no sexual release in it for him to be gained. However just for the record, I would have so done that shit! And, swoon, he was soooo protective. If I needed cuddles, he gave them. If I needed a lift, he came for me. But most importantly he was always searching for somebody to rescue me from Chris! I regularly deliberated with myself, that if he thought that much about me, why didn't he want me for himself? That is the million-dollar question isn't it. Ok you twats, no I hadn't forgotten about the smoking hot girlfriend!

I remember one day when we were sat together eyeing up passers-by through the common room area. I had spotted a particularly, completely out of my league, very gorgeous bit of hot shit on the other side of the room.

"Oh my god, he is fucking hot," I muttered to Leroy.

"Oh, he is my friend, Tyrone," he replied as he shouted him over. My jaw hit the floor.

Shit, Shit, Shit! I didn't want him to do that, I was more than happy to admire from afar. But it was too late. He was on his way over complete with a dazzling Hollywood smile. I sat red faced and embarrassed as Leroy introduced me to Tyrone.

This guy had it all, tall, dark and handsome. He was a basketball player and so had a ridiculously stacked frame and it was extremely tricky to breathe whilst he was within my eyesight. I was already mapping out in my head how I was going to hang Leroy by his man parcels, when Tyrone decided to free me from this awkward meeting.

Leroy introduced me and we all made small talk, I was dying with embarrassment, couldn't he bloody tell? Leroy introduced us, and I became a self-conscious mess. Was my voice too squeaky? What clothes had I thrown on that day? Had I rubbed my make up in properly? A very real problem for teenage girls, and all you readers who are giggling at this thought it is probably because you remember the orange face white neck problem only too well. I was careful not to breathe too near him, I had just finished a bag of pickled onion *Space Raiders,* and was especially careful not to spit on him when I spoke. These are the very real traumas that girlies on the pull, face on a daily basis. It was a hard knock life. I had also never really tried to encourage anybody to like me, except maybe Shane and look how that turned out.

After what seemed like an hour of Leroy and Tyrone catching up on small talk about music and families, Tyrone got up to leave and I felt relief swamp over me, I couldn't have taken much more of that kind of intensity.

As Tyrone lent down to kiss me goodbye on the cheek, I felt like I was having a post-menopausal hot flush, especially when his amazingly sexy husky voice said, "Hey, you fancy catching up sometime?"

I was obviously going to make a total utter fool of myself, wasn't I? I barely knew what to say, so instead I just stared at him struggling to find the words, until Leroy butted in.

"Yeah, she would be cool with that, right?" he said nudging me.

"Yep," was about all I managed to utter, as I completely cringed at my behaviour.

When Tyrone left, Leroy was so shocked at how I had behaved.

"Really? What was all that about?" he asked in bewilderment.

Seriously, did he not know that Tyrone was completely sailing way up out of the lowly realms of my existence. Yeah sure I wanted to look at him, I wanted to imagine his body pinning mine to the bed, I wanted to ... ok sorry I was about to go all erotica on you guys then, I'll toy with that on my own later.

Realistically, I knew that I didn't have a shot so was completely ok about a bit of window shopping. I just didn't feel comfortable in such hot company. This should have been because I was in a relationship, but this fact didn't even enter my head. I didn't know why, I just didn't. Maybe I was embarrassed about myself? I explained this to him whilst playfully punching him for putting me in such a teeth-pulling situation. He just couldn't believe what I was saying, he looked genuinely shocked as his eyes fell pitifully on me. What happened next was just about to make me fall head over heels in love with him.

He looked deep into my eyes, like he was searching my soul for an answer to something, stroked my face as he whispered, "You really don't know what an amazing person you are both inside and out, do you beautiful?"

Time paused, and I understood something new about love. I thought intensity was a physical display that could only really be bought about by the intimacy of sex. I was wrong. There was an intensity here, right now, whilst we were fully clothed and surrounded by people, and there was no chance that it was going to be any different. The intensity wasn't sexual contact, it was friendship, it was a love that travelled above the realms of physical pleasure, it was absolute adoration. This time I really didn't know what to say and I couldn't take my eyes off him. What does one say to somebody in the moment when they have just realised that they are in love with them?

As per usual something would always break moments like this and this time it was the warning bell for the end of lunch. Damn, fucking damn. If only I could have remained in that poise for just, maybe, like ... FOREVER! He kissed my forehead and picked up his bag as he shouted back to me, "Come on we are going to be late."

Ok so I was in love with Chris, but it didn't stop these feelings for Leroy and he was just about the only person that could have stolen both my attention and heart at any point that he chose to. I knew it wouldn't happen though, I could tell even then that he saw me more as his sister than anything else. Nope this was not just me misreading the situation. So many times, we were smashed out of our faces and I ended up sleeping at his, in his bed, butt naked and he just held me while we slept. That kind of spelt his feelings out for me. Oh, and the fact he kept setting me up with his mates too. I think he just so wanted to get me away from Chris. He hated seeing me so down on myself and he just seemed to want to save me, but I had to want to save myself first.

Philosophy – Can you Only Love One Person at a Time?

Although I think we complicate it purposefully, I think this debated question is once again, so much simpler than we allow it to be. Nobody wants to think that their partner is capable of loving anybody but them. It is also an easy way to deal with the situation 'you can't love me, if you love her', the truth is, you can! Who made these rules? Humans apply their crazy laws of thinking to every natural process imaginable. Shit, they even tell us what love should feel like. The truth is when it comes to love, there are no rules. It is not a tangible entity, it is just a god damn feeling, it isn't a 'thing'! With millions of individuals inhabiting this planet, I think it is fair to say, that as sure as we all differ in facial features and characteristics, that we all experience the journey of love in completely different ways. And let's face it, doesn't it sound a little bit stupid to suggest that once we turn on the tap of love to an individual, the valve shuts off somewhere else?

Oh, you want to know about the spooning? I suppose this is a diary of sexual adolescence. You picked this book up for the dirt, right? Ok, who am I to refuse? This particular day, we had fled college lectures and swapped them for comfy beds, a smoke-filled room and a bottle of chilli flavour vodka that somebody's wise parents had refused to drink. Being the ultimate show-off at times, I had no problem with necking this stuff back, shame I couldn't do the same with the sick.

Sensing my inability to function in an acceptable manner, Leroy was quick to remove me from the situation, forever my gentleman and hero. He organised us a lift with his friend and got him to drop us off at his house. He ushered me upstairs, clearly not wanting his parents to witness me in such a state and who could blame him. Carefully, he laid me in his bed and covered me up. I was never one for sleeping in my jeans, so in my semi-unconscious state, I began to strip.

I may have been beyond hammered, but I still caught his grin as I did so. Don't get me wrong, it wasn't a 'I'm so going to fuck you in a minute' grin. Had it have been such, I would have been on it. Okay, maybe I wasn't capable right at that very moment. It was more of a 'you crazy bitch' grin! I can't explain though why he too decided to strip and climb in snuggling up behind me, bare naked skin to skin contact.

As his body touched mine, I felt a comfort I'd long since forgotten existed. A comfort I had felt with Chris once upon a time. But that seemed so long ago, and I yearned for that feeling more than I yearned for Tom Hardy sex nowadays, which to be fair is pretty hard stuff. As he wrapped his arms around me and pulled me closer to him, I easily forgot that we both belonged to somebody else. His fingers stroked my arms bringing goose bumps to rise up my back. I left a trail of gentle kisses up his arm as it he wrapped it more tightly around my neck and pulled himself closer onto my naked skin.

I hated myself for being so absolutely rat arsed that I was unable to do anything about it. I had no choice but to shut my eyes to prevent the room from spinning and therefore cease any vomit from ending up in his bed. But in shutting my peepers, I was unable to avoid myself drifting off to slumberland. Oh, what a waste of a golden opportunity. Give a girl a fucking golden goose, aarrgghhh. Never had I wanted to rewind time so much in my life.

By the time I awoke, Leroy had sadly replaced his nakedness with clothes. Bollocks! I couldn't stay mad at him, since his t-shirt clung so beautifully to his abs and his jeans shaped the perfection that was his ass. But still, it went without saying that I preferred him in the buff.

He was perched on the edge of the bed when I awoke, cup of tea in hand, watching me as I slept. I was glad for the tea, even if just as a mask for my beer breath but wasn't so keen on him staring at my make-up-less face and bed hair. He didn't seem to look at me like that anyway. He was smiling, no doubt re-collecting the previous day's events. I grabbed the tea from his hand and smiled back- not a single scrap of awkwardness.

I often wondered if Leroy ever worked out how I felt. I was never sure really, but there was an uncomfortable moment once whilst we camping in celebration of the end of our college education.

There is always that one girl who feels the need to enable a rite of passage through her vagina to all the men in your class at college. For us, her name was Sarah. To be fair, Sarah and I were friends. Girls like that always have plenty of boys around them and therefore she was always fun to hang around with. But she crossed the line when, knowing exactly how I felt, she chose to attempt to share a sleeping bag with MY Leroy. There was instantly a weird unspoken unease as his eyes met mine. I looked away uncomfortably swallowing the lump of both anguish and anger in my throat. I looked back up to see that he was still staring at me, willing to save him maybe?

As he vocally tried to encourage her to vacate his sleeping bag, she fought harder to retain her place within it, physically pinning him down to kiss him. He tried to laugh it off and playfully kissed her back. Ouch! Without any rights, my heart gave way. I won't pretend it didn't feel like I was watching somebody seduce my boyfriend. I had felt many emotions during my time of adolescence, but jealousy wasn't often one of them. But this is how it felt. A mix of pain, frustration and an absolute desire to slash her throat and kick her in the mary.

MILESTONE = BECOME AN ENRAGED JEALOUS BITCH

As she reached down into the sleeping bag to begin the process of molestation, I decided to release myself from the torturous pain of being present and sleep in the car.

"Shannon, where are you going?" he yelled as he attempted to prise Sarah off his face.

I ignored him and didn't look back, "Shannon," he repeated.

We never discussed what happened that night and I never did tell Leroy how I felt, although I fantasized of 'our' life together all the time. I imagined him to be an amazing lover, strong but sensitive, perfect. And what kind of husband would he make? One could dream. Yet, I must admit, I had never even considered anybody else as husband material, so probably, I had never felt like this about anyone before. So, I never told him. I never even pounced on any of the many given opportunities I had to dive upon him: even as we laid spooning in his bed semi-naked. Fuck, I bet fate is a bloke!

Whilst Leroy and I remained friends for the reminder of my adolescence, I learned to keep my distance from him, I could do without the complications to my already complicated life. Had it been possible though, I would have chosen a very different path for us both and therefore he would forever be known as, 'the one that got away'.

The Awakening

It was around bonfire night that we, no sorry, Chris, decided that we should have, yet another, break. Yeah 'a break'! Nothing specific had happened. Things were okay, but that simply meant that we weren't arguing every second and I wasn't catching some other bird on her knees sucking his wiener.

Philosophy – Having a Break

What the fuck does 'a break' mean anyway? I suppose its definition would depend on who you asked. If it was the person demanding the break, I would say it meant 'you're boring me, so I'm going to take some time out however, if I don't find somebody to entertain me, I'll be back. But if I do happen to find whoever/ whatever it is I'm looking for, you're binned!' Basically, it is a pussy's way out of saying 'it's over'. If, however, you are being put on a break through no choice of your own, you often choose to create a different meaning for it. You choose to interpret it as meaning 'I love you and I want to spend the rest of my life with you and only you and a break is the only way that this can really happen'. Huge sigh.

Sat in his bedroom upon his stripy bed covers having 'the talk', I guess is where I stopped believing in fate and destiny and all that crap. How could my fate be without him? Unless it was to be with Leroy, which it clearly wasn't. I loved 'mostly' everything about Chris. I must have chosen to ignore all the foul bits about him. You will all sympathise with me here. There are always certain elements of a person that we do not like, or it simply turns us off. You know like brown 'Y' fronts with a cream trim, a bent willy, slippy shoes, bad dress sense, shoes with a tracksuit, you know where I am going with this, right? The point is, we can all find faults with our loved ones. But in all honesty with Chris, I liked everything about him, his dress sense, his personality, his manhood, his naughty ways, his sensitive ways (once upon a time), the way he smelt when he came home from work. Yep, see I was in love with him,

I even liked his sweat. I was addicted, he was my drug, I craved him, needed him even! The further we drifted, the more my heart yearned for him.

Yet it seemed, the end had begun. We began our trial separation and the hurtful part was, I had never seen Chris appear so happy and ironically, I had never been so miserable. I watched from the side-lines while he had the time of his life, shagging his way through the village, getting pissed paralytic every night with his friends, new clothes, new haircut, new tattoos and then even new friends. This was his transformation to single man.

Philosophy – Break Up Transformations

It seems part of the process of breaking up, involves a physical transformation of the person into a new hotter version. Sad really that often relationships can break up because people let themselves go. Strange then that following being dumped, they have a wash, get on the weights and throw the t-shirt away that they have had for the last 5 years. Obviously, people want to increase their chances of pulling, understandably. But spare a thought for the broken hearted. Already heavily laden with the dealings of a shattered future, they now must accept that the frog that they had been kissing for a ridiculously long time, was now a prince. But not your prince, some fucker else's.

Chris had completely changed. There was no longer a single trace of the boy beneath the blanket that I had fallen so deep in love with years before. Whilst we were still to some extent an item, we would begin to separate our existence and try to find out whether we needed each other at all. One rule we did ascertain, was that we would absolutely not get involved with anyone else whilst we ensured we were doing the 'right thing'. That conversation was obviously one way, as while I stupidly stayed completely 100% faithful, Chris broke every single promise he had ever made to me.

His nonchalant attitude, regarding our relationship, didn't last long when he found out about my planned trip to the strippers at *The Pipe* one weekend though. He suddenly made every excuse under the sun to see me, anything really as long as I didn't make it to that club. He even asked me to stay over at his! Yes, you heard me right, he had honoured me with an invitation to spend the night in his very chambers. This had been a rare occurrence as of late even when were still officially together. Fortunately, I had grown to know him too well and knew his game plan in detail. He really didn't have anything to fear though, did he? Well actually he did!

My friends and I arrived at the club all lusted up. It was my first such event and I really couldn't wait. Seriously ladies, now you have the delights of *Magic Mike* (I am on that damn train too), but in the nineties, it was the Chippendales that the women lusted over, although of course, they didn't visit *The Pipe*. So, the fact something similar was going to be in our club was exciting shit.

I'm sure you are all aware of the concept of the *Dream Boys* but for those of you that are not let me enlighten you. It is a show for horny ladies who, for a multitude of reasons, feel the need to ogle naked men, not that you need an excuse for that. Men had always had an array of such material and experiences to choose from long before the internet was even a twinkle in Khan's eye, but women had limited resources in that department and so, to women, this shit was the bomb. And to adolescent women who didn't have the pleasure of a top shelf porn mag, it was the only bomb!

It sure did live up to my expectations and my pent up sexual frustrations could so have been sorted out there. What were my expectations? This is where you guys are stamping with frustration at the conventions of adult novels. Where are the fucking pictures? So, there were seriously hot, totally naked, extraordinarily well-endowed, over excited men, with their splendid cocks out. I know, I had previously mentioned my repulsion of willies, but it was hard not to be in awe of these rare beauties.

The crowd whooped and gawped as the boys seductively peeled their clothing from their perfectly prepared skin. They sure were brave around these seemingly sex starved women. The old timers were the worst, "Get your mother fucking cock in my mouth," yelled an elderly lady waving her walking stick in the air.

The next hour was filled with seedy dance routines, women being sexually fondled in chairs, penises being stroked, yanked and admired, drinks being stirred with dong-a-longs and unsuspecting (ok, petrified) volunteers from the crowd being engulfed with whipped cream.

The end of the night came quickly as I got last orders in at the bar. Just as I was ordering three pints of lager for eight of us to share, I felt a protruding hand attempt to slide across my front bottom. The hand belonged to the very gorgeous, well hung, clearly very confident, stripper. I looked across at my friends expecting to see them pissing themselves laughing as they witnessed their little set up. But nope, they were oblivious to my event and were still reeling from said stripper's special cocktail making skills.

"What you doing later?" he asked, without giving me time to reply, "fancy coming with me for a drink?"

Fucking hell. What was this? Surely this bloke had just been carrying out this deed to win a bet he regularly placed with his friends, crack on to an ugly bird?

Obviously, I nodded as I was unable to string a sentence together.

"Great," he replied, flashing me that smile that told me, it wasn't a bet after all.

I grabbed the drinks and hazily headed back to my table. I had barely made it back to my friends before I began spilling the tale. It wasn't everyday a bloody stripper/model cracked onto me and I wasn't against a bit of bragging. They didn't believe a fucking word I said. They are funny, girls from villages, you know. They didn't believe my story because they hadn't witnessed it with their own eyes, so it clearly can't have been true. However, they believed any shitty bit of gossip that flew about the village, whether they had been present or not. Irony? No, just double standards. I knew better than to fight my corner, either that, or I didn't really give a shit what they thought.

I contemplated going with him for a drink, but that dick head Chris just kept creeping into my thoughts. After all, I did have the prestigious invitation to consider and I suppose if I'm honest, I wanted to go back to him 10 million times more than I wanted to go for a drink (which was probably code for sex) with Mr Stripper. So, I indecisively put my coat on and left with my friends. I had barely walked ten steps up the street when I heard somebody shouting behind us. We all turned around to witness the vision of hunkiness that was 'Mr Stripper' running towards us.

"I thought we were going for a drink?" he asked confused.

"I'm sorry, I've got a erm .... sort of .... boyfriend, I can't," I replied smiling, knowing I owed this stranger nothing, but happy that I had proved my tale to my friends.

"Sort of? If it's sort of, he doesn't deserve you," he replied before kissing me on the cheek and walking away.

No shit Sherlock, I thought as I traipsed back to Chris.

MILESTONE = PULLED A STRIPPER (ok admittedly this may be not a milestone of adolescence in general, but it sure is cool as fuck)

Whilst attempting to enjoy myself out with the girls in *The Pipe* on the eve of the New Year, it was evident that whilst Chris and I were trying so hard to save our relationship, it was momentarily different. It felt false, forced, hard work. I was so scared to set one foot wrong that it felt like we had just met. I sensed his heart just wasn't really in it and felt like an intruder when I spent time with him. As a result, I had gone to *The Pipe* alone with Anna, whilst Chris went to a family party to bring in the New Year. We had loosely arranged that I would join him at some point that night, but something just didn't feel right. I contemplated not turning up, not intruding even. But the very sad truth is that there was nobody else in the world that I wanted to spend that night with.

Philosophy – Forgetting Who You are to Please Someone Else

We all change as we grow, that is normal. But in desperate times, we can allow our growth to be distorted or hampered by our fears of losing someone that we love. Again, maybe this is normal? Maybe we are supposed to learn to grow and adjust together, just like a forest of trees, learning to lean towards each other to create a perfect covering. But does that work when only one of the participants is doing the changing. When they are bending over backwards only to seemingly lose that person even more. Before you know it, you are in danger of looking in a mirror at a person that you don't recognise, looking at a person that you don't even like. I no longer had a scrap of confidence. Not about the way I looked, the way I acted, my future. I was a mess. A miserable, needy, mess. And if the person that I loved and adored more than life itself had done that to me, then who needed enemies.

Anna and I had done nothing but bicker since Chris and I had declared we were an official item after the Michelle saga. While I was happy, she was happy, but as it became evident we weren't exactly living a fairy-tale, she couldn't bear to see me so hurt. Being the one in love, I failed to see the things that she could see. I believed his lies and manipulation whilst she saw right through it. I wasn't sure if I loved her or hated her for this. I was grateful she had my back don't get me wrong, but I preferred the head in the sand approach and didn't appreciate her wake up and smell the coffee effort.

NYE was to be the night that all this frustration would all come to a head and she would do the un-thinkable and give me an ultimatum. Yes, a fucking ultimatum! Him or her? Was this some kind of joke? Choose between the two people that I loved the most? Whilst I appreciated and loved her passion and desire to protect me from the painful path that Chris was inflicting upon me, she clearly had no idea how much I wanted him, needed him, loved him! How would I breathe without him? If I had to suffer his pain to endure his pleasure, then that was a small price to feel his love. And if that meant sacrificing our friendship ....

This is something I could have never willingly have chosen. No doubt I don't need to preach to you guys how important friends are during adolescence. In fact, during life. I hope you all realise just how important Anna was to me? Of course, as an adolescent, boys completely take over your life. You stop calling for your friends and begin to sacrifice everything you ever had just to be alone with the boyfriend. I mean a threesome is surely only cool if the third person joins in, right? So, I didn't feel that an angry arms folded friend glaring furiously at our intimate fondling would have been useful or productive for any of us. The sex is to blame, it is addictive and that is something your bessie, just can't provide (although no judgement here if your Bessie does).

Anna was my soul mate of the non-sexual kind, it was true that I had never once contemplated a bit of muff diving. She had been my constant source of friendship during a time fraught with heartache, frustration and abandonment. Being a girl growing up is not easy. This will be no shock statement here, but girls are bitches. I had more of my 'friends' steal my boyfriends than I had strangers do the same. Okay, okay, I was a player of this game too, tomato, tomatoe. The girls who made me question my beauty, my fashion sense, my body shape, my self-worth, were not the bullying strangers in the girl's toilets, they were my closest friends. But Anna was not one of those manipulative scheming little girls, she loved me, and I loved her right back. She removed the knives before they had even hit my back and had dusted me down more times that I could even remember.

As, I emerged from the toilet cubicle, of which may I mention was door-less (typical feature in the club) to wash my hands, Anna was stood there with a rare stern face with her hands furiously placed upon her hips.

"He did sleep with her," she blurted out.

I pushed past her and searched for the soap on the sides of the sink, which clearly was also not in existence since we were in *The Pipe*.

"Who?" I asked nonchalantly, knowing full well this was a conversation that I had no desire in which to partake.

"Brooke," she spat!

"It doesn't matter now, fresh start," I turned around and smiled at her, blinking away my tears.

"Oh, for fuck's sake, you are thick as shit and I can't .... I won't watch this car crash anymore!" I refused to make eye contact with her as she continued her rant, "choose now .... I mean it .... me or him," she bellowed. I didn't really have time to take in her words and I certainly didn't make my decision fast enough for her. "Fuck it, I'll choose for you. We're done," she angrily declared before she stormed out of the toilets.

I slumped my head onto the grimy sink counter and stared into the heavily graffitied mirror. Was life ever going to be simple, or was I destined to carry around with me, this constant source of heartache thrown at me from every direction? I thought about her ultimatum long and hard after she left, but she really misunderstood. Either way I would have lost one of the most important people in the whole wide world to me. It was like asking a mother to choose between her children. Maybe that is a bad analogy for obvious reasons. But nonetheless, there was no possible way I could/would do it. I needed them both.

I didn't feel comfortable returning to the table I had been sharing with Anna, so I grabbed my belongings and left with no farewells. If she had chosen, then my path was set. There was only one person who I 'could' share this evening with.

Philosophy – Best Friends

Best friends (a bit like teachers) have the ability to make your life wonderful, or miserable. And on a general scale, they probably do a bit of both. But best friends in adolescence are like a partner. You spend all your time together, you share detailed dark secrets and you have an emotional attachment that adults find it hard to secure. For adolescents, their first experiences of a non-blood relationship are with their best friends. Friendships are intense, and it is not an exaggeration to say that your best friend is your entire world. Therefore, it can become totally confusing when you meet an 'actual' partner. I mean who the fuck is this thunder cunt stealing my bitch. It can put a complete kibosh on your plans to buy a caravan together, adorn the walls with posters of Patrick Swayze, whilst breeding guinea pigs and living off the fat of the land. The lines become blurred and it isn't unusual for bessies to feel an extreme sense of jealousy. Not jealousy in terms of wanting what you have, but more of a fear that this 'partner' is about to change the life that you have carved out together. More importantly, you can't share that kind of emotional attachment without feeling the other person's pain, think E.T and Elliott. Anna was so feeling my pain.

Hogmanay was in full swing at Chris's aunts'. Whisky was flowing, and neighbours were in and out of each other's home delivering shortbread and black bun. They may have left their country, but their traditions had been well kept. When I arrived at the house I was told Chris was upstairs. I dashed up, biting my smile to hide my excitement to see him. I threw open the bedroom door to witness Chris and his sister's friend startled and jumping to their feet. Why? I wasn't sure, but it was very suspicious. I couldn't imagine he would have wanted her? Not because she wasn't gorgeous because she was, and besides Chris hadn't ever made looks his priority before, but surely it would be a tad incestual? She was like his sister.

While these thoughts were circling my mind, Chris quickly bound over to me, grabbed my bum, kissed me on the cheek and pulled me downstairs by my hand, diffusing any conversation that he seemed worried may have been going to occur.

"What was going off in there then?" I asked whilst passing the family portrait that donned the stairwell wall.

"What? We were all just chatting," he said kissing me for a second time menacingly on the cheek.

That was the last of my questions. I wasn't about to cause a scene at his family Hogmanay and fighting with him was the last thing I wanted. Ostrich, head, sand!

He tugged me into the living room just as everybody was joining hands ready to drunkenly belt out *Auld Lang Syne*. Chris took my right hand and as I turned around to see who had seized my left hand, my heart sank to see Paul grinning at me. This really wasn't a good sign. I still couldn't figure how Chris could even talk to him after the lies he told about me? Behind that grin of his I had a feeling there was a master plan brewing.

"Babe I'll kiss you as the clock strikes 12," Chris shouted at me over the revellers excited exchanges.

But before I could answer, Paul angrily butted in, "I thought we were going to chink bottles at 12 mate?"

"Oh yeah," Chris smiled, "I'll do that first, then I'll kiss you Shan," and sealed this promise with yet another kiss, but this time it was on the lips (about time). He swiftly broke from the kiss to begin the annual sing song.

I didn't reply or challenge, but I did contemplate. I had clearly fallen even further in Chris's order of importance. It was then that it all fell into place, it was that importance that had changed. We may have been back together, but we weren't even nearly on the same page and it was becoming apparent that we were never going to be the same again.

I got my kiss as soon as Chris had fulfilled his promise to his friend and although it rung with lust it didn't leave even a slight taste of love. I thought this usually happened the other around, lust to love. Trust me to get a backwards version. As Chris moved around his family and friends wishing them all the best for the coming year, I made a slinking exit out of the back door. I needed to be alone.

As I walked home alone amongst the party goers returning home and the whoops of excitement for the new year, the pain became overwhelming. I began to sob uncontrollably as I began to accept that my forthcoming year was unlikely to feature Chris and me. As my heart

seemingly ceased to beat, it seemed as if life as I knew it was over.

By this time in my adolescence, I was working in the local supermarket to subsidise my studies and so were many of Chris's friends. Although working in a supermarket isn't exactly a suits and heels ambition, it wasn't a bad occupation for my age and status. Not that I'm implying that there was an array of varied occupational positions in our parish. No, there were five main jobs and these five jobs had a very specific hierarchal structure.

1) Hairdresser
2) Shop Assistant
3) Bar Person
4) Factory Worker
5) Cleaner

So, as you can see, I was not doing too bad to be 2nd in class at only 17. Although working at the likes of *Topshop* might have helped my street cred a lot more than the cheapest supermarket in Europe but hey ho, I had time to progress yet. In all honesty to have any job in our village was a bonus.

There certainly was nothing like laying on the conveyor belt with the hangover from hell, looking up only to be greeted by a snot-sniffler. I would like to be nostalgic about listening to the old silvers drumming on about their external haemorrhoids, but they barely got a word in, in-between my moaning about how much I hated my job, how much Chris had broken my heat and my gipping to save them being covered in last night's Chinese chips and gravy and half a bottle of Thunderbird.

Whilst working in the shop, through Chris's friends, I had access to the gruesome heart wrenching details of the life that he had forged whilst I had been desperately trying to salvage our relationship. The brutal truths I learnt in that stock room, whilst loading the cardboard cruncher made me sick with hurt and anger. Although by now, I was no stranger to this, I still can't see a carton full of Crunchy Nut Cornflakes without mentally harking back to those torturous days.

Paul, who had previously tried to molest me and destroy mine and Chris's relationship, explained to me, that Chris had every intention of getting back not only into my knickers but my heart too, just as soon as he had sampled a wide array of the choice of splendid looking ladies that had begun to pop up in our village. If only they had all been splendid looking that would have been a tad more bearable.

I really could not believe that this unfeeling evil bastard was the same boy who had been so sensitive in our many failed love-making attempts. That he was the guy that kept a diary about our sex life, that he had laid on the floor crying when I had tried to leave, the guy who had begged me to get pregnant so that we could be a family.

Philosophy - Wanting the Best of Both Worlds

Was Chris a villain or did he just fuck societal norms off and not pretend that he gave a shit about other people above his own wants and desires. Let's face it, we mostly only hold back from perusing our own interests because we know that 'we shouldn't'. We know that society will frown upon us and we will be viewed as bad people and nobody really wants that. We are encouraged, probably rightly so, to put other people's feelings above our own even at times to our detriment. And it seemed that Chris didn't give a shit about societal norms and more importantly didn't give a shit about me. Maybe he knew that perhaps, I could be the one he should spend his life with? And perhaps that was still a valid, favourable option for him? But he also wanted to shag lots of random women, experiencing lots of dick dipping so that he could feel both fulfilled and widely experienced. Maybe he felt like he shouldn't have to choose and maybe, I made him feel like, he didn't have to choose. Maybe, just maybe, I was a complete and utter fucking moron.

The Long Goodbye

I probably had some plans to discuss this with Chris, but I really had no need. Unsurprisingly, not too far into the new year our new start was over.... for good! The weekend after New Year's Eve, we had a minor disagreement about my not wanting to spend the night in *The Pipe* and he jumped at the opportunity to throw the towel in. The fact that I had envisaged this situation saved me from falling into the shadowy depths that I had been thrown to, by him before.

Experiencing this kind of pain is comparable to grieving a death and I often thought that it would be easier if he was dead, maybe that situation would have been easier than facing the reality of rejection. I knew it was over but that didn't mean it didn't hurt, it didn't stop me loving him, it just meant that I had reached acceptance.

Philosophy – Grief of a Lost Love

It isn't overdramatic to feel that the loss of a relationship is comparable to the death of a loved one. There is little difference really and, in some ways, maybe it is worse. When somebody dies, the biggest thing you have to get your head around is that you will never see that person again. I am not sure you ever do accept that fully, the finality of it can seem too much to bear. But then is it any better, to know that you may see the one you love again, except his arm will be twisted around some other hoe, and after watching them interact with each other for a few minutes, your mind is plagued with the imagery of him playfully playing with her pussy whilst looking upon her with total adoration, with a stonking hard erection. Yeah, I would go with the death thing every time.

If I had thought that Kayden had broken my heart, I knew absolutely nothing. How do you describe first time heartbreak to somebody who has yet to experience it? Multi-car pileup maybe? Purgatory? Hanging in between life and death? 1st degree burns? I would argue with anybody that heartbreak isn't a physical feeling. Oh, it very much is. I wouldn't be surprised if there was a similar imp to Cupid that takes care of this. He can be the 'Heartbreak Cherub'. Ok, let's just say it 'Heartbreak Cunt'! Instead of a bow and arrow he carries a baseball bat and a lump hammer and is sent by the gods to give a lengthy violent beating to those that have been dumped. That sure would explain the soreness and aching that comes with being chucked.

Everyday aspects of life become suddenly unbearable and pretty much pointless. I remember listening to my friend's everyday conversations and thinking, what is the point in this conversation ... in talking ... in breathing ... in living ... yes, I might as well die. Yep, that's how my macabre trail of thought went in those gloomy days. Tragic I know, I feel pretty much the same now when faced with an over brimming washing basket, a sink full of pots and no idea what to do for tea.

Similarly, there is the requirement of food. There really is no point in nourishment when you are heartbroken. Food magically becomes flavourless and so swollen that it is impossible to chew. I bet the Heartbreak Cunt has something to do with this too! I bet he injects all the contents of your fridge with some kind of solution that dissolves the flavour and renders it unchewable, a bit like school dinner beef. This isn't all bad though is it? The broken heart diet can perform miracles in helping you re-invent yourself in the just beyond heartache days when you begin to re-present yourself on the single's market.

I doubted very much, that by this point Chris had any feelings whatsoever left for me. No let me be more honest, I knew for sure that I meant jack shit to him. Still, I had so much I wanted to say to the twat. I felt that putting my feelings down on paper so that I didn't have to look at his smarmy face whilst I poured the contents of my heart upon his knee, would help me to close the door. Now, there aren't many perks to not having the ease of social communication, but this was one. Back then, the letter would be delivered, we would then presume that he will have read it and that would be the end of that. But the sending of a message over social media now is only the beginning of the issue. There is then the issue of checking obsessively to see when they have finally read it. And woe betide if they appear online but then still don't read your message. Potentially, you also risk the heartache of the ultimate rejection, being blocked. Ouch!

Dear Chris,

I don't even expect you to read this, but I feel before I close the door on us, I have things to say. I want you to know just how deeply you have broken my heart. I know that it is not cool to admit this kind of shit, but I think I have embarrassed myself enough over you to forget any attempt at ever claiming cool again. You could never understand because you have clearly never loved anyone like I loved you. You can't have, or there is no way you would have treated me this way. It's not a crime to no longer be in love with someone, to choose to back-track upon your promises or even to move on much quicker than they can bear. The crime however comes in the form of abusing that person's trust, in refusing to acknowledge that they are human and that they have feelings. The crime is using that other person to ease your own confusion and pain, because you can't make it alone. Yet choosing to let go of that other person's hand whether they are ready or not. Especially after you have emptied them for your own desires.

I doubt you would know how hard my life is at the moment, you are too busy whimpering and feeling sorry for yourself to even contemplate how long it takes me to get the courage and motivation to get out of bed in the morning. I haven't eaten in a week, my stomach refuses to accept food because my heart is sending signals to it to stop accepting food to end this pain quicker.

I have lost most of my friends due to your promiscuous ways (sleeping with my friends has to be your finest hour), so funnily enough I don't feel I can talk to them about how much my heart is breaking as I think secretly whilst I am weeping upon their shoulder, they will be having flash backs to them on their knees with you knocking your tent peg in. Not the kind of support that is going to help me through this heart break Chris, I don't think.

Who could have helped me through? You! Do I need you to be with me? I don't, and neither would I expect you to be if you don't love me, but I do expect you to still care about me. How can you go from loving someone to having no feelings whatsoever? Could you not call me to ask how I am, rather than to let me know how you are? Or maybe you could actually turn up when it's you who has asked to meet me. I don't think I need to say anymore, I think I have given you about as much emotion as I can bear to give.

I'm not sure you will ever find anybody who loved you the way I did, who believed in you the way I did and I'm just hoping that I never find someone who loved me in the perverse way that you did. I just have one last request? If you ever loved me at all, or even if you have any shred of feelings for me, please, please, please, leave me alone.

All my love always and forever,

Shannon xx

I emptied both my head and heart into that letter, it was drenched with emotion. Did it make me feel better, which surely was the aim? No, not really. Why? Because I wanted him to feel, care, love or even in its most basic form, show some humanity. Maybe the truth is, nothing could. Ok, maybe a bit of sexual experience with Cillian Murphy would?

The weeks ahead were predictable, it consisted of me laid in bed, slowly dying of torturous anguish and bitterness. Funny isn't it, the pain you feel over your first love you never really feel again, thank fuck. Although I am not a psychologist and am instead simply a mere mortal, I predict that this has nothing to do with the fact that they are your soul mate but it's more likely because once you have witnessed the unfeeling, coldness of the male species, you prepare yourself to understand that despite how perfect they may seem, they are all capable of this! I cried my poor broken heart out, contemplated suicide, tried a touch of self-harm etc. You know all the erratic, irrational things you do in the hope that cutting your arm will mend your broken heart, erm nope, there is absolutely no connection there is there? Nonetheless, I had to do something.

In complete contrast Chris more than got on with his life, along with his new haircut and new clothes, he even bagged himself a new girlfriend. Yes, that really helped my healing process, such a sensitive soul. Take that knife boy, that's it, dig it a bit deeper. Fuck it, go on finish it off, why don't you give it a little twist? Yes, so while I was lying on the floor, nursing my wounds and my burning eyes, knob jockey preceded to jump on me from a great height.

The girl (and girl is the correct word) in question was a mere 15 years of age, whilst we were knocking on the door of 18. Sure, what is a 3-year age gap in the grand scheme of things? It is nothing when you are both adults, but 15 is young, immature and let's face it, illegal! I know you are all thinking about Brian. But it was only sinful to go out with someone younger, not older, therefore I committed no legal or moral crime.

What the fucking hell could a school girl have to offer over me? Obviously, something? Maybe he enjoyed picking her up from school, or taking her to the park? No, it seems obvious to me now many years on, that it was probably the school uniform. You see that is where he made a big mistake, he could have had somebody with physical attributes e.g. breasts (albeit not exactly bazookas), bum, love handles, etc in a school uniform instead of a pre-pubescent shrimp. If only he had had asked. In a bizarre twist of adolescent fate, I had been victim to opposite ends of the binary, where my first boyfriend left me for an old woman and my second, left me for an underage bit of fluff.

I started hanging about with one of my childhood friends again at this point, Lucy. We had grown up together and had a ridiculous amount of background together. These are the kind of friends that you don't ever really forget, and it is easy to see how they are responsible for shaping the person you are to become. From collecting frog spawn in jars, to playing 'May I' and 'Kirby' in the street, we began to enter the stage in our lives where we were interested in men. No that wasn't a typo, I mean 'men'. Even as 10-year-olds, girls don't really start fancying their peers. No, they are drooling over Shakin' Stevens and Patrick Swayze just like every other woman in the country. Bit weird isn't it really when you think about it? But Swayze was responsible for many a late night out on the street, practising the 'time of my life' lift with each other, until the street lights came on.

Lucy was desperate to pull me out of my deep dark depression (not an easy job, I tell you) and she knew there was only one way to do it. Help me to get laid! She would drag me out of the bed that I used to lay in and cry convulsively for my lost love, get me extremely wasted and make me hit the bright lights of the town's hottest clubs extremely regularly. I was very grateful to Lucy for the dedication she showed in assisting my recuperation, especially when if we are all honest, broken hearted friends are annoying as fuck. Sure, we may have a little empathy in the beginning, but it just drags on too long every time, doesn't it? Whilst whispering words of comfort, you can't pretend that you don't want to say *'pull yourself together, you pathetic mongoose.'*

Like a snake shedding its old life, I knew I had to get back on my game, changing my friendship group wasn't going to solve this on its own. Years had passed since I had to worry about attracting a new man, and it was very doubtful that my baggy Eclipse jeans and Caterpillar boots were going to do the trick. It was time for me to make the most of the slender physique that had once repulsed me during the beginning of my adolescence. Lucy would be my perfect mentor. Eagerly, she encouraged me to replace my wardrobe with short skirts and plunge tops and for the final part of my transformation to ditch the trainers for heels. Who was this sexy bitch? Why hadn't I attempted to look attractive before? This was going to make going on the pull so much easier. I looked hot if you don't mind me saying so myself. Oh Chris, you silly boy!

MILESTONE = DRESS LIKE A GROWN UP

My job was the next thing to go. I could no longer subject myself to heart-breaking conversations while putting out cartons of baked beans. Besides what better way to check out the single scene then getting a job in a nightclub. Ok, I'll admit it, they sacked me from the shop! Apparently, the customers didn't appreciate my constant hangovers, moods and state of depression and the boss didn't appreciate my tardiness. Not to worry, everybody has to lose a job in their teenage years. Mission accomplished!

MILESTONE = GET SACKED FROM YOUR MUCH-NEEDED OCCUPATION

I wasn't yet 18 and had never been to a nightclub in my life, yet here I was about to have a masterclass in pint pulling. They never asked for I.D and I doubt they cared that much. With the structure and order of present day it is hard to understand this relaxed attitude, but in the nineties the world of work was very different. For one they trusted you, probably far too much, and took your word that you were old enough, good enough and were legally allowed to work. You were even trusted with your own money if you believe it? There was no waiting for the end of the month to get paid, nope, you received it every week in a little brown envelope accompanied by a handwritten payslip of which you were well aware wasn't really paying fuck all to your national insurance.

I loved this little job, it opened my eyes up to just how many men there were out there and, whilst this is by no means the sole reasoning behind a job, this was undeniably the way to mend my broken heart. Now that I was happy to share my figure and assets with the world, I loved the attention it brought. The drunken punters would lavish you with drinks (and the women would lavish you with dirty looks), the other bartenders would offer to do your menial tasks like mop the floor for you and the doormen became your personal bouncer whilst trying to woo you. So, this is how women were to rule the land? Why hadn't my mother introduced me to this art? Since she had never ditched the art of wearing her pinny around her lengthy skirts and wrapping herself up in home made cardigans, maybe it is safe to say that she didn't know herself?

The story of one particular doorman always makes me smile, or should that be cringe? He tried a touch harder than the others and I decided to take him up on his offer of a lift home in his convertible one night. Now having a car is impressive to an adolescent but having a soft top is some orgasm producing shit. It wouldn't have mattered to me if it was a Golf GTI Cabriolet, since we had never even had a family car, but it was a touch classier, maybe more KFC than McDonalds, he drove an Escort Cabriolet. It was an absolute shining perfect example of a man who cares more about his car whilst probably having fuck all in his house, all speakers and no todge, so to speak. You know those types where their car takes on a more visual representation of what they wished was in their fucking pants.

He was a very sweet guy on the outside, but I was in no doubt that it would have been an act and I was glad because I didn't like my men too nice.

He was much older than me, but after dealing with men my age for the last few years, I was totally ready for a touch of maturity. His years had not affected his looks, this guy was hot, and he knew it. Whilst Chris had a luscious frame, in comparison this guy had an epic frame. Being the protector of a club, I suppose the muscles were necessary. Necessary or not, they certainly did it for me.

He drove me home and we made small talk, I lied to him about my age, understandably I think. I wasn't trying to lead him astray and turn him into a criminal, I just didn't want to lose my job. I only told him the nice things about me, that's how it works isn't it? I'm sure you may judge me on this choice, but really, I just extenuated my good points. It's not as bad as today's generation of girls, who not only play on their strengths but undertake a complete makeover making them not only unrecognisable to their own parents but put *Ru-Pauls Drag Race* to shame.

I'm serious, in my day if you were ugly you just dealt with it. Now you just go to *Boots*! In all fairness, these men could bring a libel case for fraud or at the very least false representation. These poor unsuspecting fools think that they have pulled Beyoncé but wake up next to Caitlyn Jenner! After removing their 'hold you in' pants (revealing the extra 3 stone of rolls they were holding in), scrubbed off the fake bake (from Whitney to Celine). Not to mention the ladles full of make-up, false eyelashes, the blusher that allowed them to have cheek bones, lip plumper to allude to Rihanna's lips, chicken fillets out of their bras (enough said on that one), off with the sexy slinky long nails (revealing the half chewed half painted numbers underneath), unclip the hair extensions revealing a less than flattering barnet and finally the heels have been shred, revealing that they aren't 6ft 2 after all but more the size of Warwick Davis and about as attractive too.

Everything was going well with Mr Doorman. I am not even going to pretend that I remember his name #notevenslightlyembarrassed. We had arrived home and were laid on the sofa with a lot of heavy petting going on. His kisses were working, they were soft and sensual, there was no doubt that my body wanted him. His hands began to creep underneath the little clothing that I had on and I began to aid him by slowly undressing myself.

Maybe it would have moved on to the next stage too, if he hadn't spoken (let that be a lesson to all of you boys)! He was so good looking, clearly had enough money to make me happy, beautiful car, large house, wasn't an overly terrible job, but he spoilt it all with his choice of vocabulary. I know, it sounds so petty, but I just had those kinds of niggles about things. The smallest of things put me off people. Although, language choices are quite important I think. Wait until you hear what he said though, you may even agree with me. So, whilst I slowly undid the buttons on my dress, he enthusiastically placed his hand upon my stomach.

That was fine, I had no problem with the groping, I was waiting for his hands to take a detour down slowly to start shit getting real, but then he said, "Nice Tummy!"

Tummy??? Oh no he didn't. Oh yes, he fucking did! Like I said, this guy was a little bit older than me. Not enormously but let's say I was 17, he may have been about 30, or so. Let's face it 30 seems sooooo old when you are 17, but for him then to mention such a childish word and apply it to me, to my body, made me feel awfully sick. I'm sure I don't need to tell you that I ended that right there and then. I didn't like it and that was that.

How did I end it? Easy, pants up, front door open!

Philosophy – Searching for Perfection

As an adolescent, what are we looking for? In fact, as a woman, what are we looking for? I had absolutely no idea. What type of guy did I want? Did I want a guy at all? Did I want it to be casual? Did I want it to be serious? Why did stupid little things repulse me? I had no idea what I was looking for at the beginning of my adolescence and there in the midst of it, I still didn't have a fucking clue. I don't profess to have the answers here, but I do have a suggestion. Go out and explore and make those mistakes. Only from these experiences can you ascertain what it is you are looking for. And let me just tell you something, exploring is fine and making mistakes is even finer.

There are Plenty of Fish in the Sea

As my confidence boomed, I bagged myself a brand-new man. Ashley was his name and a handsome fella he was too. He had a fantastic body, a <u>really</u> fantastic body, ambition, drive and he treated me with respect (yes, some men did this you know), but, yes ladies and gentlemen there is always a but, he was just too damn nice.

I know I am a sadist, it's not the pain I love, it's just that damn rollercoaster. That feeling that you never know what is going to happen tomorrow, the butterflies it brings, pure unadulterated lust. To juxtapose this, it also brings heartbreak, overeating and in extreme cases, venereal diseases. Nonetheless, I was back in the world of coupledom, although I do admit that it was largely to show bastard features, that I was also in demand. The problem with that little bright idea was that Chris did not give the slightest shite. So, I was lumbered with the ideal bloke, who unfortunately annoyed the shit out of me, whilst my ex congratulated me on moving on.

Ashley wasn't actually an entire new meet for me. I had met him a long time ago, during one of my illegal drinking sessions in the local town whilst I was still with Chris. Maybe I should explain this to you all. As I have explained above, he was defo a looker and 'Wow' what a body. Yes, I know I keep repeating this, I am currently reminiscing with a large glass of wine thinking about this very nice body. He caught my attention straight away and it didn't take us long to lock lips. He had the largest of lips so was a delight to kiss and let's be fair, alcohol mostly always improves kissing scenarios, doesn't it? I had no intentions of seeing him again though, especially since I had really started to like Chris at that point but still wasn't averse to necking on with a bit of hot totty while inebriated. Therefore, I was totally panic stricken when he called me at my parent's house whilst Chris and I were house sitting for them during their holiday.

"Hi, do you remember me?" he asked with the kind of voice that buckled knees.

I didn't remember him, I was smashed. But, once he began to reveal the time and place, I cringed. Shit! I sly shifted into the other room with the phone so that Chris couldn't overhear the conversation.

"How the fucking hell did you get my number?" I questioned him, "and more to the point, wasn't it an indication that I didn't want you to call me, when I failed to give you my number?"

Imagine the frustration of not being able to look somebody up on Facebook when you wanted to find somebody. When trying to track down the fumble from the night before, there was often no choice except to go full out Erin Brockovich.

He went on to explain that I had partook in a very brief (two day) relationship with his cousin who I had met in Combe back in the day. Oh yes, I remember that little hottie. He dropped me like a steaming piece of dog shit for Hot Heather back in 95! Apparently, they had been discussing our little rendezvous and they worked out that 'I' was the same person. This boy had done some serious investigating. He thought he would call to make sure I got home safely. Great, I had fucking Sherlock Holmes on my hands.

"Yes, I got safely home to my BOYFRIEND," I attempted to whisper and shout all at the same time (which is so difficult you know).

I put the phone down quickly before I went to seat myself on Chris's knee to make up for my extreme guilt. Nothing like a bit of guilt to make you want to suck cock. I imagine any guys reading this might not be comforted reading that line. Clearly, if they are not getting any head, it probably indicates that their partners are faithful and if they are getting head, let's look at this positively, maybe she is just keen!

He was a labourer on a building site, and he was the same age as me, there was more but let's face it, I wasn't listening. I was contemplating sex with this guy, how much did I need to know about him. In these circumstances it might be appropriate to list your sexual history rather than names, ages and job titles. Okay, let's leave the age in there for obvious reasons. Something a little like, *"I don't have AIDs, syphilis or genital warts. I also don't have a girlfriend, which is beneficial knowledge to you and I don't usually receive complaints in the bedroom department, so sex with me is unlikely to be something you would regret. Now, would you like a drink?"*

See, how much more useful would those kinds of introductions be? We go about everything arse about face really, don't we?

Anyway, the point was, that there was nothing exciting about him really. I had nothing to lose so I didn't see the problem with having a bit of fun with him. Who am I kidding, I was desperate for this. Unfortunately, I hate to admit that I was struggling to rid myself of the heartbreak of Chris, so 'fun' was just about all I could offer anyone at that moment. I played my cards close to my chest. I wasn't going to lay my poor damaged little heart open to a beating ever again. She was firmly cushioned in a secured box.

I happened to mention meeting Ashley one day to Leroy whilst we were pretending to study in the library.

"I know him," he stated nonchalantly.

"Really?" I replied.

I hated the fact that Leroy knew him. I didn't want the two of them talking about me and I didn't want Ashley to know anything about me either. If there was one thing that my stint through adolescence had taught me so far was, the less you got to know each other, the less you got hurt.

"He hasn't been totally honest with you though," Leroy grinned.

What was fucking new? I thought to myself. He was a bloke since when were they ever honest?

"He is a little puppy, my friend," he laughed uncontrollably, "he is only 16!"

What a dick head! I know you are all probably thinking that this was no big deal. So, he bumped his age up a bit. Yes, when you are adults that wouldn't make a difference, but I was nearly 18. Yes, so if you can work it out readers, I praised the lord that the first time I met him that I didn't touch his tail, because that would have made me an unsuspecting paedophile! Mmmmm, maybe I was more like Chris than I would have liked to have thought.

Ironically, that situation totally made me feel for men who end up in that position. I met the guy in a bloody pub in the town, why should I even have had to think about asking him his age? If I had asked, I am in no doubt that he would have lied to me anyway. It's terrible to think that before you make an advance towards anyone you must ask them to provide I.D to prevent you from having to be sent to jail. Hold on, idea number 2, sexual health and I.D cards all combined into one, now there is a gap in the market. The whole situation made me feel nauseas. Thank god I was too drunk that night to molest him. A word of warning to you readers here I think. No I.D? No licky, licky, no touchy, touchy and defo no ..... okay you get the picture.

Leroy's revelation made me so angry. But there was more. Now I have to tell you that the second revelation calmed me a little and was probably (ok it was) the reason that I didn't call his ass to dump him straight away. It seemed that Ashley had also lied about his occupation too. He was in fact a footballer. And not just for some lowly team such as Doncaster Rovers, oh no! He only bloody well played for Newcastle United reserve team and England Under 21s! Admittedly, we weren't talking super stardom and he wasn't going to cover me in bling for the time being, but I sure called it a step up from being a labourer in a visy vest. Superficial, yes, I suppose. But it wasn't as black and white as it sounded. I liked ambition and drive, which ultimately led to success. Power is just as sexy as money, don't you think?

MILESTONE = BAGGED MYSELF A FOOTBALLER

Although that was enough to raise my interest in him ever so slightly and maybe even enough for me to forgive him for his lies and for potentially trying to lead me into sexually molesting a minor, he was going to have to work hard if he was to stay my official boyfriend. I may of at times displayed a little bit more than a tad of sluttish behaviour, but one thing that I wasn't, was a fake. I couldn't pretend to love somebody because of what I could get out of it. I was too deep for that and (although I hated to admit it) I had realised that I needed love. For now, being interested would have to be enough.

Ashley and I didn't seem well suited from the start. He was so much more serious than me and tended to disapprove about absolutely everything that I bloody did. If this was his way of wooing me, it was a warped way. But I liked him. He was more clever than Chris and we had conversations about real life things, not just discussions about sexual positions. I can't deny that he also treated me like a total princess.

I prepared myself in the usual manner for another night (and morning) on the tiles. Looking more like a stripper than a partygoer, Lucy and I made our way to the nightclub. It was the routine to meet Ashley by the pool table during regular intervals, just so he could make sure I was still there I think.

This was fine for me, at least I did not have to sit with him all night. Oh, god forbid, he would have bored me to death. After all it is true what they say, all brawl and no brains.

Do not get me wrong, I was finding that Ashley was a lovely bloke, but doesn't that just say it all? The irony here is that he was good looking, but I had just had the boyfriend from hell for the last couple of years, the contrast in niceness was just too much for the system. I needed breaking into the world of decent blokes in a very fragile manner. Unfortunately, Ashley was like the bleeding Mallard. He was steaming ahead faster than I could say 'Fuck Off!'

As I queued for my bottle of Hooch, my personal space had become invaded. I span around ready to launch the perpetrator to the other side of the club …. I stopped. The infamous Chris! My heart ceased to beat, ok raced, whatever. I couldn't even think straight. Fear? Excitement? Shaking legs? Yes! All rolled into one. That smirk that might as well have been shouting *"You know you wanna fuck me baby!"* The thing is I did, oh I really tried not to think that, but I was powerless against his witchery. I know I had moved onto fresh meat, but my heart just couldn't get used to the change in my diet. Believe me, I was trying harder than you could believe, but the wanker had charm oozing out of him like a bottle of Hi-Karate (off putting but nicely familiar).

The charmer and I locked eyes and that is not all we locked. This episode really was like something out of an extremely sad chick flick.

We were surrounded by friends and as I walked in, he smarmily stated, "You're not going to knife me, are you?"

I just giggled.

I know, it's shameful isn't it. Yes, he was ever the allurer and I was oh so mature. We then proceeded to stare at each other for what seemed like hours while our friends talked over us. They were simply amazed that World War III had not broken out. I mean this was a big step, Chris and I were in the same vicinity and there were no glasses flying, hold it, the night was still young! I knew I had to break away from him quickly, maybe not for the whole night, but at least to avoid Ashley coming to find me and catching sight of my jaw scraping off the floor and drooling over my ex.

"So, are the rumours true? Are you shacked up with a footie player?"

It was hard to interpret his emotions to be honest, he was a strange one. I had expected him to be upset, or at the very least, jealous that I had replaced him with somebody that he couldn't rival. But he didn't seem to see it that way. Dare I say it, but he looked a little bit proud? It was clear that he was confident of where my heart still lay despite seemingly having the world on my doorstep. Arrogant bastard!

"Who is he then? You going to introduce us?" he said his eyes darting around the nightclub looking for a clue.

"Well, friend, I am glad that you seem as excited about this relationship as I am," I spat angrily as I began to walk away totally unsure of how to continue the conversation and totally bewildered at his eagerness to meet the one that I now belonged to.

Reluctantly, I sloped off to meet Ashley by the pool table. Okay, that was what I set off to do, until Chris pulled me to one side and stepped extremely close to me. To be more honest (and crude) Mr Peni Pickle Eye was protruding my nether regions. Look, we have explored fingering, B.Js and wanking, what is a simple discussion about a protruding penis now? God the boy was a fucking sex maniac (as well as being nicely endowed, I am sure that I mentioned that). Did he ever not have an erection? I pushed him away, I *tried* to push him away, no really, seriously, I *thought* about 'trying' to push him away. They do say it is the thought that counts. As he gently stroked my skin with his fingers, I was well and truly putty in his hands as my whole body began to remember.

The truth is what was said or done next was lost in a hazy blur of horny lust as we found our way to the fire exit. I know, what a romantic reunion! As soon as we had smashed our way through the heavy doors (don't even go there, you filthy lot), there was no doubt what we were there for and it was nothing to do with a tearful reminiscent reunion. He shoved me hard up against the wall and it took seconds for us to free enough of our flesh for us to be able to begin to touch each other. I was going to say arouse each other, but who the fuck am I kidding, I was nearly at orgasm when I laid my eyes upon him never mind as his hands began to enter me.

Sliding me up high enough to place me around his hips, I pulled my skirt around my waist and dragged my knickers to one side. Grabbing furiously at my hips, he lowered me hard and fast onto him as I let out a deep groan.

Hastily, he wrapped my hair around his hand and pulled it just hard enough to elongate my cries. I dug my nails into his back with pleasure and slowly dragged them down his burning skin. With every thrust he eagerly caressed my neck with his lips unable to stop his own groans as he dug his fingers furiously into my behind. Oblivious to the cameras and lacking in fear of being caught, we grabbed at each other like a pair of hungry predators reunited after a long period of starvation. As he kissed my neck, the desire to crawl inside him returned, I needed to be as close to him as possible. Oh, I had missed this type of intensity.

Pushing him away, I dropped to my knees and took his penis in my mouth, enjoying the sound of his groaning, driving me to thrust it deeper to the back of my throat. I was shocked as he pulled me away from him but was mistaken in my thoughts behind this. It was far from a plea to stop, but I sensed the sensation of needing to be inside me had returned for him too as he lifted me up against the wall for the second time and thrust himself inside me hard and fast, letting out the ultimate sigh and pausing at the innermost point of depth, allowing us both to enjoy the moment. I let myself fall against his shoulder, gasping at my breath and holding on to him as tightly as I possibly could. I wrapped my body around him and felt his heart racing against my chest. He began to thrust again, the railings digging into my back each time. Upon the last thrust he stopped as he leant heavily against me and pulled me close to him.

Gently, he used his right hand to pull my face up out of his shoulder. He examined my face before placing a lingering kiss upon my forehead and pulled away from me. I didn't want it to end. Ever! I had allowed my mind to consider what might happen when our bodies parted. Would we talk? Did he want me back? Did he still love me? Who was I kidding, we had just fucked each other in a fire exit with cameras pointing at us, and I knew in the back of my mind that this wasn't some firework exploding reunion. No, we simply returned our underwear to its rightful place, although it was now slightly damper admittedly (sorry), kissed each other goodbye and exchanged a few meaningless words.

"Let's not finish this here," he said avoiding my gaze and buttoning himself up.

Wonders never ceased with this runt. What the fuck? Clearly, I wasn't even worth a few minutes of finishing up in a fire exit. Ouch! I'm sure the truth behind it all was that he had somewhere more important to be. What was new? When would I bloody learn?

"Meet me tomorrow?" he posed. I ignored and began to make myself presentable for the return to the real world, my real world, not this fantasy here with him.

He firmly grabbed my face and forced me to make eye contact with him. "Please," he said.

I tried to break free of his grip, but he placed his other arm around my waist pulling me back to his still firm erection. Sharply, I pulled his hand from my face and wriggled out of his grasp. I snatched my bag up off the floor and pushed him from the door as I hastily left, refusing to look at him. Why? Anger! Repulsion! Fear! Pain! Take your pick.

As if having sex with your ex in a fire exit whilst your new boyfriend is at the other side of the door isn't bad enough, the even more cringe worthy part of this is that I gave him oral sex. Eeeeeeeeeeessssssshhhhhhhhh I know, I know that was so wrong, below the belt, unforgivable! Why did I even tell you guys this? Nevertheless, I was a girl trying to win back her first love. Oral sex is therefore a prime tactic. I never meant to hurt Ashley, I did it in the name of love! It is probably one of the only times that I haven't been jealous of millennials. Imagine the days where you could free style fuck in a fire exit without the fear of it being leaked on 'spotted in Detton'. We were still yet to feel the fear of an unexpected tag notification appearing on your phone after a heavy night out.

"Where have you been babe?" Ashley smiled as he grabbed my arm to stop me from hurrying past.

One look at him and my eyes filled with tears, I threw my arms around him, probably selfishly only to appease my own guilt.

"Shannon, I haven't seen you in ages," a voice interrupted. I knew before I even turned around who that voice belonged to. This man had no scruples whatsoever. I couldn't find the words to even attempt to deal with the situation, "Is this your new fella?" Chris asked.

Ashley reached out to shake the outstretched hand smiling naively back at a grinning Chris, who was clearly enjoying this situation. Maybe we got our kicks very differently to each other these days.

MILESTONE = BECAME A CHEATING BITCH

What a total bitch I was. But still, I agreed to meet Chris the next day. Yes, I know, I stormed out of the door, I refused to look at him – blah, blah, blah. But I weakened later in the night. Come on, congratulate me for not ending back up in the fire exit for a second time. Clearly, I had consumed far too much Lemon Hooch. I didn't fall straight at his feet, I will have you know. Firstly, I enquired where Lily (the girlfriend) could be while our secret rendezvous was taking place. The answer was obvious, doing her homework. While the good girl was studying, someone had to keep her boyfriend entertained, didn't they? Why not me? It was so painful to refer to him as her boyfriend. So, while Ashley had a lazy Sunday morning lie in at his mam's, I snuck out to get myself a full English breakfast.

Nervously, I awaited Chris's arrival at the village pond, both my heart and my sanity in my mouth. I was so bloody confused. I really wanted him to turn up, but it would just make my life a lot less complicated if he didn't. Not to mention saving me from being tarnished with the same brush as him himself and stop me from taking two steps forward, ten steps back. I found it possible to think like this before I got there but when he failed to show, I was devastated. Absolutely fuming might be a more accurate statement but more at myself really. I hated myself for letting him shit on me all over again. Aaaaaarrrrrrrrggghhhhhhh.

I tried to stop myself from launching tears down my perfectly made up face. Hesitantly, I began to sulk away down the rocky back alley.

"Where you going like?" announced the bastard from behind me.

He had turned up after all. Relief washed over me. Although this was short lived as it became clear that the pure and simple reason for this engagement was that he had his lipstick out again (you will probably only understand this metaphor should you be lucky enough to be of northern origin).

Our business was obvious, we were there to have sex and that's what we did. It was completely mechanical and routine. I wasn't used to this kind of sex, not from anyone, but most definitely not from him. I figured this must have been the kind of sex that married women complained about. We kissed, removed our own trousers and underwear, I laid back on the rocky grass, he laid on top of me and we carried out the expected routine of 'shagging'.

I was turned on so there was no difficulty that way! Why was I turned on? Stupidly because I loved him, I think? I still wanted him deep inside me, just as I had done on that very first night that we slept with each other. But did my heart race? No! Instead it was breaking. Did I cry due to orgasm? No, just because my heart had started to separate.

He pushed himself inside me, I didn't hold him close and force myself closer to him to feel him as deep as possible as I usually would. Instead, I threw my arms around his neck and buried my face into his shoulder. I took a deep breath smelling him, feeling him, knowing this was probably the last time I would. I revelled in the feeling of his skin against mine and the deep sliding of his penis within me, but the hot sweats were gone! The shaking, along with the uncontrollable desire to scream as his body pulsated against mine as he took himself to his peak had all vanished too.

He was alone at that peak as he ejaculated within me, for the first time, ever! No longer was I comfortable to lay there with him as he kissed me and attempted to stroke my face whilst moving my hair out of my eyes. I hurried to my feet, eager to retain my dignity. Dignity, what fucking dignity, I was a complete cock womble? I was uncomfortable around him, we had become strangers.

MILESTONE = UNDERSTAND THE DIFFERENCE BETWEEN SEX AND LOVE

This was the first time I had slept with him, where I could feel that there was absolutely no feeling in it, on his part anyway and to some extent, mine too. It was purely sex and he made that more than clear. Not with words though, in fact I can't even remember him speaking all that much. A few grunts and groans but that was about the brunt of it. Lucky me! Needless to say, we didn't arrange another meeting, he didn't even stop to kiss me good-bye. The film *Pretty Woman* springs to mind and feeling, erm, like a prostitute. Perhaps it may be true to say, that I had acted like one too, however the cheeky twat didn't even have to pay me! In brutal truth, I stood there numb, big fat tears rolling down my cheeks as he strolled back down the alley like the cheap tom cat he was, swinging his arms like he was fucking king of the swingers. What was I even? The 2nd, 3rd, 4th best thing. I was a pussy, the hole in the mattress. Chris was using me for a release, just in the same way Shane had used me all those years earlier. It seemed adolescence was not so much a fucking rollercoaster as it was a merry go round. I needed to get off this shit!

I was right back where I had started. I felt like I'd just been raped. Except I had even laid there and let him do it, wanted him to do it even. What was wrong with me? The truth probably is that he didn't even contemplate what he was doing to me. He had an erection and I had a vagina. There was probably not much thought in-between that. Nothing personal, I suppose just business.

Despondently, I wandered back from the pond, I felt like somebody had half beat me to death, I must have looked like it too.

"What the hell has happened to you, are you crying?" Ashley gasped wrapping himself around me and lovingly kissing my forehead as I approached my back door.

Shit! I had forgotten that he was coming over. I considered making some story up to get a bit of sympathy, have somebody to hold me and say that they loved me, but truth be known, I just couldn't be arsed. It would all be fake, I didn't want it from him, I wanted that knob head who had long since forgotten that I even existed to bring such comfort. What was I doing with either of them? One who was using me for his own physical desires and the other whose physical desires I sought to avoid. I was a train wreck. I made my excuses and went for a bath. A locked door was just what I needed.

Philosophy – Dead End Relationships

It is easy to fall into a relationship because we think it is the right thing. They tick all the right boxes and you can't work out for the life of you, why the chemistry is not happening. So, you convince yourself that it needs time, convince yourself that it will come naturally. Why don't we just leave? I believe it all comes down to fear, fear of being alone, fear of hurting others, fear of not feel-

ing anything. And as usual, a bit of honesty, because I wanted to show the world that I was over Chris.

Getting My Kicks

S hortly after this significant event, things were about to start looking up for me. In every which way you can imagine. I like to think of this period as my 'slutty' adolescence and I quickly realised, I should so have started this phase earlier. I started renting a house from Sarah's parents. It wasn't that I had forgiven her little stunt with Leroy, but it was hard to lay claim to somebody who clearly wasn't mine.

MILESTONE = LIVING ALONE

I would have been renting it if I could have ever afforded the rent. I tried really hard you know, despite what people may have thought. I did lots of things to pay that rent ... except that! Bloody hell, I know I liked sex, but I was picky, unless I drank Vodka, that was. I even started selling good old *Avon* to bump up my wages, which weren't too high since I was still studying full time at college. Whilst this may make you snigger, I think it is entrepreneurial. It was true though that nobody ever wanted to buy anything except from the clearance pages, of which you didn't receive commission anyway, and if I did manage to make any money it went straight back to them. The allure of their cheap make up was just too much. They are marketing gods. The free nail varnish when you have bought 99 items across pages 5 - 12 is just too much to resist.

MILESTONE = STARTED A BUSINESS (it is a business goddammit, I even had to excitedly complete order forms)

Besides, my new side business was to come in handy more than I knew. Chris clearly had no shame or even a shred of guilt, so I really wasn't shocked when after dropping one of my *Avon* catalogues at his Mam's house, he had the nerve to order his sun tan lotions ready for his boy's Ibiza holiday. Not one to miss an opportunity to seek revenge, I jumped on this unique prospect. I didn't have a problem with him ordering his lotions and potions from me, in fact, I was so grateful that I would offer a bit more of a personalised service and tailor the goods to his needs, how I'm not a millionaire with this kind of customer service, I will never know. Kindly then, I poured out half of the bottle, and proceeded to top it back up with *Daz Washing Powder Liquid.* It did say on the bottle *'keeps items whiter than white'* and I wanted to give him the best sun block ever! I was worried about his health around all those nasty UV rays and thought I would give him the best chance of survival possible. Payback! Immature, but necessary. High 5 readers.

MILESTONE = STOOPED TO PSYCHOTIC REVENGE

Although this act filled me with glee and pleased me no end, and still does to be fair, it didn't stop my heart skipping far too many beats when I found out Chris had suffered quite a nasty bout of sunstroke whilst basking on Las Salinas Beach. Esssh! It could have been much worse though. Still, I hoped he had shared his sun cream with all the lovely ladies that may have had the pleasure of his company for the fortnight.

Philosophy – Petty Revenge

I know revenge isn't a low that everybody chooses to stoop to, but I fucking loved it. We can kid ourselves that it is to teach somebody a lesson, but that is not true. If you take my example, how was Chris potentially bleaching his skin going to teach him not to slip his widge to every girl who passes him by? It wasn't, was it? It couldn't even teach him what he should have already known, and that is – DO NOT TAKE THE PISS AND BUY YOUR SUN CREAM FROM YOUR EX GIRLFRIEND, therefore rubbing her nose in the fact that you are off for sun, sea and shagging frolics, because he would never know what I had done. So, the truth is, revenge is for the perpetrator, for sure. The only power it has is to make you feel better. You have one over on them, and it feels mighty fine. Come on guys, sometimes it is just necessary to snatch back a tiny bit of that power, and if it makes you smile again, is it really that bad?

Petty revenge wasn't the only thing making me feel better at that time. Let me tell you about the time I was accosted by a workman. It sounds a bit cliché, but he just happened to be my plumber (at least it sounds better than my gynaecologist), and I just happened to have a blockage, it's true I tell you. I was more than pleased then when I opened the door to the man who was going to fix said blockage and he was the hottest thing that I had ever laid my eyes on in Detton, so he clearly couldn't have been from the village.

He must have been about 26 and was built like a house, just the way I liked them, and just in-case people might not notice his spectacular physique, he wore a teeny weeny tight little short sleeve top that was seemingly cutting off his circulation. His mush wasn't too bad either. Put it this way, I doubt there would have been many that said 'no' to him. He had all the required: chiselled cheekbones, perfectly placed locks, just enough stubble to look sexy not homeless and to top it off he looked cheeky. I liked a bit of cheeky as you know. I also liked his trainers so that helped. What? I was a bloody teenager, kicks were important.

I coyly flirted right from the off, because I was a teenage girl and that's what we did. However, to my surprise he flirted back: outrageously flirted back should I say. I couldn't believe it, I thought this kind of situation only arose in porn movies.

"So, you live here all alone?" he enquired, clearly trying to find out if I was either home alone or shacked up with the boyfriend.

"Yep," I replied, and grinned.

"How the fuck are you single?" he asked whilst biting his lip and running the back of his fingers down my arm.

Naturally he couldn't drag out the small problem of the sink blockage too long, so our flirting came to an end and I grudgingly saw him out of the door.

I was then, utterly flabbergasted when I opened my front door to him the next morning.

I was unsure of why he was there at first and he must have observed the perplexity on my face when he announced, "So, we having sex or what love?"

Yep, I think that's what he called foreplay. What did I do? I undeniably shit myself and made some excuse about my mam coming over soon. What was I thinking? Obviously, I think like that now that my adolescence is over, but at the time whilst I may be no stranger to activities in the sack, the truth was I had slept with two people in my entire life, I wasn't exactly Megan Fox and despite my confident exterior, inside I was anything but. So, in answer to, what was I thinking? Who was thinking? I was petrified!

Once he knew obtaining a lay was out of the question, he made his excuses and left, never to be seen again. I watched him walk away down the drive, asking myself, why on earth couldn't he have just asked me out on a date? Huge sigh for the male race.

Factually, I was officially in a relationship with Ashley, but I suppose I never threw myself into it and we hadn't even slept together yet. Beyond a bit of fumbling, we had barely touched each other. Why? Too hurt? Too knowledgeable? Too scorned? Too disillusioned? Too filled with guilt? All of those actually. And, if I am totally honest with you, when I cheated, it didn't even feel like cheating. Besides he was away all week playing at being a footballer, so it didn't feel like a real relationship, not like I had with Kayden and Chris. My friends were well aware of his existence, but it was easy to forget that I had a boyfriend at all. I'm serious. I didn't even have a home phone never mind a mobile, so communication between us was limited and the time he was willing to spend away from the pitch was even smaller.

You stopped reading at the 'haven't had sex with my boyfriend yet' bit didn't you. It wasn't that I didn't fancy him. This was the one thing that Ashley and I had from the off. I completely fancied him physically, but there was something holding me back, a total lack of sexual chemistry perhaps? We did have one or two close calls whilst we were drunk. Alcohol does that to us, doesn't it? I'll never understand why people would buy an expensive bottle of vaginal lubricant when a cheap bottle of *Lambrini* would no doubt solve the issue. But none the less, despite the lowering of inhibitions that drinking brings, it just never happened. It seemed, subconsciously, that I had never emotionally opened myself up to him and this was seriously affecting the physical.

Some confusion may arise here as it is clear that I wasn't totally against the idea of getting laid. In fact, I was not against getting laid at all. Sex I could handle, wanted to handle even. No feelings involved, just sex. So why didn't I just sleep with him, if for nothing else than physical pleasure? Firstly, he didn't really try it on to that extent, he seemed happy with third base. Don't get me wrong though, that wouldn't have stopped me, if I had wanted him, as you well know. Secondly, it could be argued that sex with a partner requires an element of emotional togetherness, that I just wasn't ready for. And so, for now, Ashley would have to be a slow burner and we would see where it went, if anywhere. I was drastically hoping that the desire to sleep with him would arise soon and in the meantime, I would live my life and get my kicks. I couldn't fail to learn from my past experiences, and so would not dedicate myself to one man whilst he spread himself out over the town and neither would I force myself to sleep with him, simply to appease expectations.

MILESTONE = BECOME AN EMOTIONLESS BITCH

I suppose then, that the plumber wasn't too much of a conquest, but let me tell you about my next bedpost notch. Still, I suppose as I think of them now, they too could probably not be counted as any great mountain climb in terms of bed notches. Now there was Chris's mate and surely the fact he was my ex's mate, made that a victory?

Zak wasn't your typical stunner because, because he wasn't exactly good looking. But he was really nice, no not in an ugly way either. He wasn't ugly, he wasn't fit, but he was nice, and we had a good time. There was a slight problem with him though, he had a girlfriend, but I didn't see her as my problem, she was his problem! Now my head had been torn apart by strangers, friends and the love of my life, leaving me with little empathy for anybody. If I saw something I wanted, I took it. Maybe this is where the prologue should have started – Welcome to my fucking Adolescence!

I often flirted with him but in all honesty, he used to act like a rabbit caught in the headlights when we were simply within the same vicinity. This was not attractive to me admittedly, but everybody loves a challenge, right? I was never sure if that his insecurities were about himself or if he just didn't bloody fancy me and he felt slightly embarrassed for me when I did give him the come on.

Taking everything that you want can be damn hard, sometimes it meant not only lowering my standards but burying them under a concrete path. After one night of particularly large amounts of lager and cider, I decided that was the night that I was going to have him. Yes, that's right I was going to make him have sex with me whether he wanted it or not. Don't be concerned for the boy, there was to be no rohypnol involved. I may have been interested in a relationship with him, I also may have not. I really didn't know at that point, but I needed to find out if we were compatible in the bedroom first. This wasn't about me being an out and out slut, but I needed to know if he was another Shane or another Chris? And not in terms of being one of them per se, but more how compatible we were with each other in the bedroom department. You know the sex v's love thing!

It wasn't hard snaring Zak. He was Wes's friend and since I had started living alone, Wes and the boys were a constant fixture in my home much to Chris's annoyance. It seemed I had been awarded their friendship in the break up custody battle. Anybody with their own home suddenly became very popular ironically, so I wasn't flattered by their presence.

It was a normal Saturday evening at my shack. The room was adorned with empty cider bottles, the tunes were pumping, the boys had their checked shirts off whilst bouncing around the living room in their Adidas poppers, and the vibe was definitely there. I sat trying to catch his eye for roughly an hour before I tired of the game playing. I had no time for this shit anymore. I jumped up, grabbed his hand and dragged him up the stairs. It was clear from the reaction of our friends that this wasn't going to stay a secret for long.

Fair dos, he came willingly but he still looked scared out of his wits. I suppose I should have let my catch free at that point, but I was sure deep down inside that his fear wasn't because he didn't want to be alone upstairs with me but more about the fallout that this little rendezvous was about to cause.

I didn't have to wonder long about his frozen state as one of his friends bellowed up the stairs, "Be careful with our little virgin!"

Oh no! It could only bloody happen to me couldn't it. So, there I was, so bloody horny, and well overdue a good seeing to, and who did I choose for that mission, a fucking virgin! Just bloody, twatting great. I dropped my expectations right there and then and if I'm honest, I wanted a 'get out of jail free' card and thought about fleeing right there and then. This was to be the first time that I had sex with somebody other than Chris (omitting Shane of course) so it was going to be hard enough, I didn't need this pressure too.

I know I should have been caring and sensitive and that I was disgusted in Shane's treatment of my special event, but this wasn't the best time for me. I was trying to have revenge sex, sex that would make me feel good about myself etc. This kind of sex was going to be hard work and challenging and if that's what I wanted, I would have bought a Sudoku book.

Zak was just an unfortunate part of my healing process, not that I am making excuses for my poor behaviour. And of course, I could see how similarities could be drawn between Shane and I.

Despite wanting to act on my instincts and flee this sticky situation, I wasn't about to lose my manners. I just couldn't be a Shane. So, I set about getting the deed done just about as fast as I could (which I was hoping being his first time, might be seconds rather than minutes). And this might have been the case had he let me take control like I tried to. I suppose in his head he had lived this moment out and knew how he wanted it to go, and thus he refused to let me sit astride him as I tried, and he instead twisted me back around to lay on my back as he laid awkwardly upon me.

He wasn't a great kisser, but neither was he terribly bad. As we struggled to find a kissing sync, I began to remove my jeans since it was obvious from his erection, that we could skip much of the foreplay part. Small mercies.

The problem with Zak was that he didn't seem able to combine two physical functions simultaneously. So, kissing and trying to get his cock out and into the right place just wasn't happening for him. He was struggling so much that I was afraid to help him. I felt that it might draw attention to the fact that I knew that he had no fudging idea what he was doing. So, I let him struggle! Yes, I know that wasn't a good idea either. I know I could have handled this so much better, but I just fucking didn't. At this rate it was going to take him so long to undress himself that we would both be sober, and it would be game over anyway.

I think he was relying on magnetism to get his weapon in the right place, but he spent more time humping my leg then he did humping me. His face showed no signs or understanding that he had not even remotely entered my vagina, and if I am honest, my vagina and me, really didn't mind anymore. I did think at one point that I might just carry on and pretend that the crevice at the top of my leg that he was currently pulling back and forth on was in fact my lady garden, but it didn't seem like it was going to be a short affair, so I thought that I better guide him into the right place at least to bring the end a bit closer. Even when I placed the end of his penis against my vaginal lips, he still could not seem to give it that last push and actually get it inside.

I tired of the situation and pulled myself from under him, pushed him down onto my freshly prepared bed, straddled him and lowered myself onto his semi-erect penis. Yes, semi! There lay the difficultly, the penis was wilting. I don't bloody know why? Maybe he just actually didn't want to have sex with me after all, although in my defence, his frantic snatching at my body told me otherwise. But still the semi-erect penis truly led me to feel like I a total and utter rapist. Whilst the willy (probably because it had bloody folded in half, hence making in stronger) did manage to enter my vaginal cavity marginally, it was short lived....

I heard a commotion outside of the bedroom door, clearly the immature sexually deprived boys from downstairs had climbed the stairs to check on their friend's progress. It was at this point that my eyes caught sight of Zak's pants adorning my bedroom floor. No, surely not? I couldn't quite believe what I was seeing. That was it, game over, I was truly done. I let go of his fast-shrinking willy and scrambled off him as fast as I could clamber. Why had the item caused such offence? Zak's underpants only bloody had cars on them. Cars! And I'm not talking novelty Lamborghini boxer shorts. No these were proper underpants, and they were peppered with tiny logos of multi coloured cars. I would have coped better at the sight of a pair of Y fronts, at least they would have had a cool retro feel, instead of making me feel like a bloody paedophile? As if it wasn't enough that I already felt like I was raping the boy with his floppy purple headed warrior and robbing him of his virginity. I think that spelt red curtain.

MILESTONE = TAKEN SOMEBODY'S VIRGINITY

I quickly stole away to the bathroom, telling him I needed to get a bath. Don't ask why I used this excuse, it just came out. If I had said the toilet he would have sat and waited for me surely? And that's the last thing I frigging wanted. I thought the bath bought me a bit more time. He rapped the door a few times in confusion of why I hadn't returned, I took the silent approach and pretended I had fell asleep. If all else fails, fake concussion or extreme drunkenness.

Philosophy – The Importance of Test Driving

Let's discuss the issue of pre-relationship sex. I think in contemporary society we have more or less accepted that anybody who gets married without having sex is a total fucktard. Why would you tie yourself into not only a relationship with a partner you had no idea if you had any chemistry with, but a financially and legally binding situation, with a partner you had no idea if you had any chemistry with? I think our ideals and morals need to evolve even further than our 'acceptance' of sex before marriage and we should actually be 'encouraged' to have sex before relationships altogether and not just marriage. Test driving a potential partner should become part of the normal pre-dating process. Okay for some people I suppose it is. Imagine all the time and heartache that would be spared if we all took this approach. Take me for example, I had liked Zak for months, I had even cheated on my 'kind of' boyfriend for him. When in the end, he was totally not the one for me. Test driving seems to be the way forward.

Zak was my friend, so we still saw each other all the time, but I think we both must have chosen to banish the unfortunate memory to the far corners of our minds, for we never discussed it again. Our friends tried to, but I was in the fortunate position of being the one who paid the rent on our hangout. It was winter, and it was cold outside on that open field, therefore one mention of the outside and it was a sure-fire conversation stopper. Sure, it was awkward around Zak for a while, but I was fast getting to the point where I didn't care about anyone or anything (especially every week out of 4) so we soon got over it.

Unrequited Love

B efore I knew it, I barely thought about whatshisname? Chris was becoming less and less of my focus, probably due to the amount of fresh
meat that was entering my head space/bed space, whatever! And even Ashely
and I were beginning to get on considerably well, despite my lack of acceptance that I was actually in a relationship. The taking it slow approach
seemed to be working. I had asked him not to expect anything of me and I
wouldn't do of him in return. It was this much more relaxed approach that
saw us begin to get to know each other. He was good company at times and
we were develop the onset of a possibly beautiful friendship.

I suppose that is where the problem was. Pure and simple, there was just
no spark. Whilst the friendship was going swimmingly, the relationship side
was not. When we were in a group of friends, he made me laugh and I was
in awe of the way other people acted around him. People liked him, he was
kind, sensitive and made everybody feel at ease. But when we were alone, he
made me feel like a god damn lesbian. Not because of my lack of desire to
fuck him, but because he behaved more like a woman than I did. He constantly nagged me about my lifestyle, it was so unsexy. I was no angel but nor
did I want to be. I guess I just wasn't the 'lady' he craved, and for me, he just
too pure. I needed a bad boy, or at least a hint of some badness, or at the very
least just let *me*, be fucking bad. I could cope with that.

Our relationship had developed however, and the time had come for us
to take things to the next level. It wasn't as mechanical as it sounded, and as I
suggested in the test driving philosophy, I wish we had done it sooner.

After a night on the tiles in the 'Toon', he invited me to stay back at his
mam's. I knew what this meant, and to be fair I was up for it, as we often are
whilst heavily inebriated. We snuck in quietly eager to not awaken his parents. This in itself was super exciting, considering that it had been a long time
since I had been required to sneak around. As I began to take my coat off, he
slipped behind me and began gently kissing my neck. I had refrained from as

much physical contact with Ashley as I could, so his confident approach to carefully moving my hair from my neck whilst he seductively began to arouse me, shocked me somewhat. I let my coat drop to the floor and turned around to face him. I grabbed his face with both hands and frantically began to kiss him. I was awakened.

The frantic anticipation of what else was to come, saw us both throw caution to the wind and begin to uncontrollably tear away the reminder of our clothes and abandon them on the floor. His confidence took my breath away as he stood there naked, I had never noticed how beautifully alluring his body actually was. Had I really been running back to Chris like a little bitch, whilst I had this little gem the whole time? It was clear he was an athlete, his exceptionally well-trained physique had me weakening and, for the first time, desperately needing him inside me, right now.

I suddenly realised why I had been reluctant and let's face it, avoidant of this moment. I had slept with the same man for years, sleeping with somebody else, just felt weird. The last thing I wanted to do was compare, the last thing I wanted to do was to be thinking about Chris whilst I was with somebody else.

He joined me on the sofa and set about preparing me for what was to come. I always admired a man, who chose to go immediately down on a woman. It was so much expected of women, that I only felt it right to expect the same back, he didn't disappoint. Clearly eager to please, he took the time to ensure that my shaking body could no longer endure his soft tongue a second longer before he pulled away and expertly pushed himself deep inside of me. Shit!

Eager to ensure that this episode was as elongated as possible, I pushed him away and rose to my knees. I caught his eye as I turned around and it was clear that I had him. That look of adoration was staring down right back at me. My heart stopped, is this what I wanted? Did I want him to look at me that way? The sinking feeling in the pit of my stomach suggested that I didn't. My thoughts were soon shelved as he began to thrust taking me back to the ecstasy that had engulfed me only seconds earlier.

As he groaned through to climax, he collapsed, exhausted onto my back. His heavenly body touching my naked skin as his sweat trickled onto me.

If I had been worried about comparing, I really shouldn't have been. All thoughts of Chris had been erased from my mind the second that our bodies entwined.

"I wasn't expecting that," I smiled coyly as he lay next to me in his naked perfection.

"That is because you were a hard one to break," he replied kissing the hand that he had taken hold of, "but Shan you are so worth the wait. I love you!"

He had said it. Why? The moment had been perfect. I hadn't had sex like that in forever, and he bloody said it! It was the last thing that I wanted to hear. My mind was racing, why didn't I feel the way I absolutely know that I should feel? No part of me wanted to travel this weary road of love, not now, and maybe not ever.

I didn't return the words he had so lovingly given. I had already proved that I was unworthy of his love by refusing to be faithful, but I wasn't going to go to the lengths of convincing him that I was in this for the long haul. Using him for his company was one thing, destroying his heart was another. I wasn't quite that cold, just yet.

Aside of one little argument, we barely crossed a bad word. This was obviously very alien territory to me. But sooner or later, he was bound to question my lack of verbal when it came to discussing feelings. Now that we had connected on a sexual level, there was absolutely no problem there, and I certainly no longer avoided his touch, in fact, I was quite encouraging of it. But I had no desire to lay and discuss our future plans.

"I love you," he whispered again as we lay together watching Sunday afternoon movies the next day. I passionately kissed him to re-direct his thoughts. As I pulled away, it was clear he was about to re-instigate the conversation. "Shannon," I kissed him again and this time I reached down into his jeans to ensure none of those silly thoughts were to return any time soon. He pushed me away angrily, "Do you love me?" he demanded to know, whilst seemingly searching my face for answers.

"No," I let go of his face and dropped my gaze.

I hesitantly awaited his reaction, I am not sure he knew how to react, whilst it seemed obvious to me, it clearly took him by surprise. He preceded to push me violently off the sofa we were cozied up on. Unfortunately, I hadn't yet had time to lay a carpet in that room, so I was left with a lovely imprint of the floorboard on my head. That was our first big row and it was probably the most I had ever fancied him. Yes, I have to admit I liked this snippet of the more violent him. Bad I know, but it was no contest against his nagging whinging streak. It didn't stop me kicking him out though. Yes sure, I wanted him to be bad, but it was still in my nature to rebel against his badness. There was also that simple fact that I also wasn't in love with him, so I was obviously only going to take so much of his shit. Not to mention that I wasn't even 18 yet and I had had enough of men, boys really, to last me a lifetime and half.

We weren't over though, oh no I still needed him, albeit probably only purely for a selfish time filler. I had no idea how we had made it this long, we had been together over six months already, but it is important you know, that I felt great sympathy for him, and if truth be known, I wanted to love him, I really wanted to love him. He was smoking hot, great career prospects, he clearly cared for me and the sex was more than acceptable. But it seemed I couldn't make my heart understand any of these things. So, for tonight, I wanted to be on my own in solitary confinement.

I never thought that I would say that, I often craved company, but I wanted to get drunk on White Lightening (cheap cider £1.99 from the beer off) and feel so sorry for myself that I sobbed myself dry. Don't we all love doing that? Women are so good at mulling over their unhappiness and we even get a weird perverse pleasure out of it, don't you think? Nothing more satisfying than slamming a few broken-hearted tunes on whilst torturing yourself with past memories, add a bit of liquor on top, bingo, perfect suicide scenario!

I trotted to get stocked up on the percentage for my night alone. I was feeling better already, until I bumped into Ken and Barbie themselves. It was 10 o'clock in the evening and Chris was walking Lily home. Bless, early bedtime, school in the morning.

He had the cheek of the devil, "Hi babe" he waved at me from over the street, whilst walking hand in hand with his new beau.

I swallowed the huge lump that immediately formed in my throat. Fuck, that hurt! That cunt knew no barriers. I know the use of such a profanity is rather severe, but it is the most appropriate word for the scenario, you must admit.

He must have carried her home at great speed, because by the time I'd had a quick pint in the pub next door to the off licence and left clutching my plastic bottles, he was there waiting for me like a bad penny. Perversely, I thought it would rather turn me on to watch an articulated lorry ram his fucking body right down the middle of the street.

"We going back to yours for a drink, babes?" he blatantly asked grinning like a fucking Cheshire cat as he began to paw at my waist.

"No thank you," was the swift intended reply but, "Die bastard," was probably more accurate a description of the wordage. I was more persistent than I had ever been, but Chris was oblivious to this and the patronising bastard just kept telling me to stop trying to prevent the inevitable.

"Shannon, you are doing a great job of pretending that you don't want me," he said mockingly, "and to anybody else in the world, it would be a pretty convincing job, but I know you better."

We neared my back door and I warned him one last time to leave but instead he backed me up against the wall in the dark back alley and kissed me whilst mimicking the dramatics of a movie star.

"Please let me in," he whispered in a seductive attempt.

Oh, for god's sake I was a sucker for a bloke with manners, besides I couldn't even move for 30 seconds after the kiss. God he still turned me on (I still think the hit and run would have worked better), my legs were shaking. Inevitably, I let him in.

I am so mortified to admit that this kind of episode repeated itself many times over the coming weeks and he became quite a regular at my back door. Following mine and Ashley's rather sexy fall out, I had really begun to distance myself from him. But the more I distanced myself from Ashley, the more I began to fall back into Chris.

Ironically, I had inadvertently become the other woman. How the fuck had this happened? Maybe the question actually was, why had I let this happen? Being T.O.W had its good and bad points. He couldn't lie to me, I knew I wasn't the only one. In fact, I had begun to see him more than I did when we were together. He chased me now, I never went to him. The bad points were, he didn't say he 'loved' me anymore and I would have sacrificed the time and the sex just to hear him say those words. Oh, I'm an old romantic, aren't I?

No, not really, just a 17-year-old girl desperate to be loved by the man that she loved more than life itself.

I knew that things were getting worse (in terms of my mental state) when I found myself waiting for Chris's little visits. The sad bitch that I was/or had become! It was inevitable then, that things were about to go pear shaped. I was sick of playing second fiddle to some little girl, he was 'my' man, not hers! I hadn't served all this time in purgatory with him, to play this lowly part.

The May bank holiday had arrived, and it was a ritual for all of us to go on an all-day drinking session to one of the neighbouring villages. All day drinking was one of my favourite parts of adulthood. Sitting out in the sun, getting slightly sozzled whilst it was still daylight just seemed so naughty. So, I was more than a little bit heated when my friends decided not to show this particular bank holiday. I was not merely angry but livid. I didn't know what the crack was? There I was dressed in my finery: bell bottoms and a tube top. I had worked hard on this midriff (starving myself to death, whilst sustaining hydration through pressed apples, okay, cider) and I was going to flaunt it. My hair was twisted in a painful manner with a million hair grips strategically placed to ensure my bun did not let me down. I had carefully chosen the front strands to fall down my face and curled them to perfection, so they fell beautifully down my forehead. Not to mention the hours wasted on creating the perfect facial features with my war paint, only to be left home alone, gutted!

Wes turned up around tea time. What a nerve. By this time, I had shred my gorgeous attire and swapped it for my t-shirt and thong (please note: there is no point in getting dressed when heartbroken). My face was strewn with angry tears.

"Come on," he said, "get dressed and come to the club." My reply cannot be printed due to the graphic content. "Chris bought Lily to the club with him, we didn't want you to come and be around that."

MILESTONE = STOOD UP BY YOUR FRIENDS

Chris, the swine! At that moment I never wanted to see his smarmy face again. I sent Wes packing, I needed to be alone, so the voodoo ritual could begin. I was going to rid myself of this guy whatever it took. I ran around the house collecting photos, letters, presents and anything that reminded me of him. I piled it in a big mountain on top of my glass coffee table (a must have feature of any 90s home, although what is attractive about seeing all the shit you shove under your coffee table is beyond me). My actions might sound more acceptable if I explain that I was extremely liquored up by this point. I began to desecrate the pile, ripping, burning and destroying. It was the first step to eliminating Chris from my life.

Philosophy – The Right to Cry and Mull

Now listen to me, I don't care what Jeremy Kyle or Dr Phil say about this kind of self-indulgence, I am telling you straight – you have absolutely every right to cry and mull. In abundance. You have been brave enough to tread the creaky boards of love and you failed that shit. And it absolutely does hurt! It is painful, frustrating and fucking unbearable and you need to cry that shit out. And if a little desecrated mountain of ash memories eases that pain a little, then you go girl.

Sounds good and strong, doesn't it? It was, I really meant it, until I was groggily woken by a sharp knocking on the back door. Forgetting that I was semi-naked, and the embers were still glowing within my visible sacrificial burnt mountain, I answered the door. Surprise, surprise, my little visitor was back. I wasn't surprised, I couldn't even be bothered to react or argue, and I just sloped back to my sofa with him trailing behind. I curled back up on the sofa when he (thinking he had a main part in The Godfather) strategically placed himself in the middle of my sofa and proceeded to untie his shoelaces to make himself more comfortable. Was this kid for real? I just stared in disbelief.

Here was my ex-boyfriend, walking in and settling down like he was my husband fresh off night shift. "Been having fun, have you?" he remarked whilst taking in the carnage on the table. He turned towards me and grinned.

He, fucking, grinned!

"The heart-breaking thing Chris, is that to you, this is fucking funny," I replied, "that fire is symbolic of the fuck up that be my mind, and you Mr Fuckwit are the sole cause."

I headed for the stairs. He grabbed at my hand as I passed and sighed deeply at my dramatics.

I paused to stare at him. I could never describe to you neither the thoughts going through my head or the feelings pumping through my body at that very second in time. A very important note to be taken here readers, and it's that there is an extremely fine line between love and hate! And by fine, think invisible. I learnt this little corker of a piece of information that there, very day, whilst laid very hung over on my sofa dressed only in my knickers. Could I love him anymore than I did? No! Could I hate him anymore than I did? Absolutely not!

I wanted him, ached for him even, with every bone and breath within my body. But equally as powerful as this was the desire to plunge the sharpest implement to hand, deep into his body and to watch him become lifeless in front of me. Confused? Yeah, I was too. So, I did the only thing I could think of. I fucked him senseless!

I'm not sure if I even wanted to have sex with him, I had no idea what I wanted, but I was completely twisted in my web of desire for him. On one hand I was totally repulsed by him, on the other hand I was willing to hurt just about anybody if that meant that I could have him in my arms even if only for a second. This wasn't too much of a problem because most often it was only me that was getting hurt and at that time, I was willing to take the pain if it meant I got my fix. Lust was my addiction and Chris was my dealer! The reality though? Other people would clearly be hurt, if only they knew!

MILESTONE = LEARNT THE HARD WAY THE FINE LINE BE-TWEEN LOVE AND HATE

As he climbed into bed with me, my heart was still pounding but my head was telling me to run as fast as my legs could carry me. Unfortunately, I was too young to follow my head, just as a man is too weak to follow his.

As I proceeded to scrape my nails down his back, partly out of sexual ecstasy and partly due to the fact that I had a deep-rooted desire to cause him extreme pain, he shockingly blurted out, "Don't, Lily will kill me!"

Suddenly, after all this time, it was as if somebody had smashed me in the head with a lump hammer and said, *'Wake up stupid, not only is this randy dog having his cake and eating it, but your bloody baking it for him too'.* The fine line had snapped. I wasn't angry, hurt or upset, he just repulsed me.

In a flash the line had been crossed and my feelings couldn't have been clearer. I looked at him and realised I didn't even fancy him, his once handsome face appeared haggard and pathetic and I realised that I had never noticed how terrible his back acne was. His smarmy grin now made me shudder and finally, he appeared before me as the disgusting excuse of a man that he had become, warts and all (I wouldn't have even put that past him). He was just like a stranger, I didn't even like him. I pushed him off me, like a sweaty rapist. Bring Zak and his car pants back instead. Now that I could see him clearly for all that he was, there was no reason for him to stay.

"You need to go," I stated emotionlessly whilst pulling the covers around my naked body, suddenly feeling very vulnerable in the presence of this stranger.

His smarmy smile returned, "You're joking right?" he sniggered.

Who the fuck did he think he was? Cue, nasty bitch.

"Look Chris," I began, "The truth is you repulse me, you make me sick, so get yourself out of my bed, out of my house and out of my fucking life once and for all ... please."

Not an exciting choice of words I admit, but I hadn't planned this speech you know.

Not even daring to even look at me, he just stared at the floor for a while in the deafening silence before he picked up his stuff and left.

MILESTONE = LEARNT HOW TO LET GO (shall we celebrate?)

Ironically, that was the best night's sleep I'd had in a long time. It was a weight lifted from my shoulders. All I felt for him now was pity, I was so sorry for the person he had turned into when once upon a time he had so much to offer, and extremely, bitterly sorry for the person he had temporarily turned me into. Although I wasn't in love with Ashley, I had no right to treat him the way Chris had chosen to treat me.

Philosophy – Sleeping with the Ex

Yes, we are long overdue discussing this philosophy and I have no doubt that the saga with Chris has left you all wondering what the fuck I was thinking? I was thinking what many other grief-stricken women stupidly believe, that whilst he was in my bed, I was still in his heart.

Drum Roll ... that was it, we were finally over! Although that was mine and Chris's last sexual episode, our volatile relationship was not dead and buried yet. In fact, the next day as I alighted the bus after work, I bumped into the village 'bike'. If you are unfamiliar with this term, let me help. Bike being something you 'ride' a lot. Ironically, she was a lovely girl and as I discussed earlier, we should be free to explore our sexuality. But the problem here was that she didn't have any other hobbies other than getting laid. It must be said however, that you can get too much of a good thing, especially when you rarely visit the same bed twice. The fact that she was a little unsanitary, to say the least, didn't help either.

She began in her monotone voice, "I'm really sorry about you and Chris, you were a really lovely couple."

I could have thought of many ways to describe us but lovely was not one.

She continued, "It's shit how many people he has cheated on you with thought isn't it? I mean when he came on to me, I was so shocked, I told him to fuck off."

I just stopped and stared at her, as the molten lava began to smoulder inside me. As lovely as the girl was, I know damn well that she didn't get the pet name 'bike' from saying *'No, thank you'*. Besides I knew through his persistence and charm most of the time he got exactly what he wanted. Let me make it clear though, I wasn't angry at her. Those days of blaming the woman were over. It was all him, they owed me nothing, as I hadn't Zak's girlfriend. In my humble opinion, girl code was only relevant to friends. I politely said my goodbyes and seated myself on the bottom of Detton Hill to think.

By this time Lucy had settled herself down next to me and was adding her fuel to the rapidly expanding fire too. He was not a popular man amongst my friends. They had watched me suffer under him and change into this control freak, of which he had created. Like a gift from the gods, there appeared an average sized iron bar next to me, I felt like Perseus. Now I had never believed in God before, but come on, are you seriously telling me that this was a coincidence? I think not! Some higher being clearly wanted me to have my revenge.

I picked it up and hastily slotted it up my sleeve. It must be stated here that I do not recommend violence in any shape or form and definitely not with an iron bar, but Chris was an unusual character with a skull so thick it was crushing his brain, clearly causing it to malfunction, hence making him act like a complete tit. At least this way I could give him the chance of a decent life by removing some of his skull, therefore relieving the pressure from his brain, and he would then be more able to act like a normal human being. So that was the plan.

Right on cue my Lucy's boyfriend pulled up in his car, "Do me a favour mate," I begged, "take me to find Chris?"

He reluctantly agreed, I guess because he knew exactly what was going to happen. We were not even 10 yards down the road before I spotted him, or at least I thought I did. Even to my own surprise, I found myself doing my Charlie's Angels bit and jumped out of the moving car, no really, I did. I probably looked really stupid at the time but hey it helped with the adrenaline and anyway broken-hearted teenagers rarely care about how much they embarrass themselves. Hell they barely care if they live following being chucked.

I ran over to the crowd and dramatically pulled the iron bar out of my clinging sleeve ready to give Chris a hand with that skull. There was no need for words, which was unusual for me. I wasn't there to talk, we'd spent months doing that. Okay, mostly we had sex and there was absolutely no talking, but you get what I mean. I just wanted to share some of that pain he had lovingly given me and if I couldn't do it via the heart then via the head it would have to be.

Just as I was about to bring that bar down on his head, Wes spun his head around.

"Jesus, what the fuck are you doing?" he screamed.

Shit it wasn't even him! What a close call. I'd never realised how much alike Chris and Wes were, especially from the back.

The crowd remained silent and as I looked over to the bench my eyes fell upon Lily, silently watching.

"Where the fuck is your boyfriend?" I said between gritted teeth.

"I don't know," she stuttered trying to avoid my gaze.

"Don't fuck with me kid, I'm not in the mood," I said lunging at her.

The words had barely left my mouth when some anonymous voice from the crowd shouted, "He's up there," while pointing at the passing bus.

As I looked up the moment was comical. He was lovingly waving to his group of friends when he spied my angry face. Realising that he had finally driven me to meltdown, the smile quickly disappeared off his face and he dropped his hand. I pushed the bar back up my sleeve out of sight as I began the mad dash for the bus stop, swiftly followed by both of our rival groups of friends.

As he stepped off the bus his ugly mug said it all, *'What the fuck does she want?'* How dare he? This knob head, whom turned up on my doorstep every night wanting to relieve himself of his daily build up was looking at me, like I was pestering him!

If I hadn't lost it by then, then that was the blowing point. As I walked up to him shaking with pure hatred, I managed to utter, "Sorry for bothering you, bollock breath, but did you happen to shag the Bike behind my back?"

The crowd waited with baited breath, aware of the protruding weapon up my sleeve, unlike him. The smarmy bastard looked at his adoring public and with the smirk to end all smirks he gloatingly said, "Might have!"

As I raised my arm up to his head, the poor asshole didn't even flinch. He must have thought that it was going to be a girlie slap. Oh, how wrong he was, I thought as I watched him hit the floor like a squatted fly. He quickly pulled himself up off the floor and made a run for it. I gave chase fuelled by the desire to beat him to death. He was so dazed he couldn't even run in a straight line. Maybe I shouldn't describe to you here the feeling of complete fulfilment and pleasure tingle through my body. Wes however, must have felt bad for his friend as he jumped in his car and opened the door screaming for Chris to get in. It was probably the first time I had seen him choose Chris over me. He dramatically threw himself in, as the car quickly disappeared up the street.

I left my friends and went home alone. I thought beating him would make me feel better and it did, for all of 2 minutes, much better, but that feeling had left my body by the time I arrived home and I probably even felt a little bad too. I was after all only human. What had I allowed him to turn me into?

Philosophy – Violence in Adolescence

From this yet another violent episode, you could get the wrong idea of me and I really don't want you to. As mentioned Detton was rather ghetto. Violence was the way most people solved problems. My mam and dad didn't exactly cradle each other with affection. Once my dad disappeared it was my step-dad and brother's fights you woke up to, then swiftly followed by my own and my step-dad's. So, as you can see, it just became the norm. I didn't seem to be able to handle emotion without frantically lashing out and Chris really hit me on that emotional level that I just couldn't deal with. So unfortunately, violence was often the outcome. It really didn't make me a bad person, it made me a frustrated adolescent who immaturely had no idea how to deal with emotional turmoil. Although it did often leave me battered and bruised and prevented me from growing my nails!

You would think that would have been the end of it, but I had one last thing to do. I wouldn't allow him to treat anybody else the way he had treated me. So later that night, Wes and I went to the Offie to stock up on our lethal potions and I decided that it was the right time.

I knew Chris and Lily would be snogging (I know 'snogging') behind the pub. Hence, I decided to pay them a visit, it was time she knew everything. Oh, and they were so pleased to see me. Chris was seated on his super dupa mountain bike, GT Terra Outpost, while cradling his baby in his arms. Such a moving scene, if it all weren't so damn fake!

I immediately noticed the gold chain that I had lovingly purchased him for his 17th birthday hanging beautifully from his neck. We are not talking any Elizabeth Duke shit here. We are talking, gold dealers on lay away and painstakingly paid for over a horrendous number of weeks. I strolled over and demanded the big fat piece of gold bling that was draping round his neck. I had scrimped and scraped and sold my soul to buy that chain for him and there was no bleeding way he was going to keep it.

Philosophy – Taking Back Gifts

Whilst taking back gifts that are given in a relationship is frowned upon, my thoughts are, so is fucking other people, so I feel we had no need to adhere to the rules.

He obviously refused to hand over his beloved neck piece (it was sad that he wanted to hold onto that more than me) and the bitching session commenced. But in all honesty, words weren't releasing my anger in the way that I had hoped. I pulled his bike from his grip, threw it on the floor and started stamping on it. If you had clocked his face you would have thought it was a Porsche 911 that I had just taken a baseball bat to. Never underestimate the importance of a bike to a teenage boy in the pre-technological age. In the way that the millennials pledge themselves to the latest phone, teenage boys drooled over each other's latest set of wheels in just the same way.

It had been a long time since I had seen this much emotion on his face, and boy was it worth it. The boy was nearly in tears, oh what pleasure I derived from this. As he began with the insults, he was digging his own grave. If my intentions had not been to reveal our affair to Lily, they certainly were now. I wanted to reveal him as the sniffling, sobbing wreck that he really was underneath that fake identity that he had somehow managed to carve for himself.

He was no exceptional catch. The sensitive, caring and protective guy that he presented himself as was utter bullshit. The more he insulted me, the less I was able to control myself. Some would say he bought it on himself. I lashed out physically by wrapping my cider bottle repeatedly around his head. Please note, this did not make me feel anywhere near as good as the iron bar thrashing. Wes was trying desperately to stop me, but not out of concern for Chris's welfare, just the fact that he was gutted about the amount of alcohol I was wasting.

Philosophy – Keeping Cheating Secrets

Why do women stay silent about men's cheating actions? They have such power within their grasp, yet even when their lover is destroying them quite openly, they choose to remain tight lipped. I will tell you why, because nobody wants to win by default. Nobody wants to gain their man because somebody else has rejected them. More importantly is the fact that often they are in love, often that means that they are keener to feel the pain themselves than inflict it on the man that they so ardently love.

Don't however think for one minute that Chris was the innocent, injured party. His mind set was exactly the same as mine. Today however he was just playing victim because Lily was there. She was the one who hammered the last nail in his coffin.

"Why can't you just leave us alone?" she blurted out.

Chris turned a greyish colour as his eyes darted around, clearly looking for an escape route.

He knew that she had just signed his death warrant. I hadn't planned to drag her so deep into this, breaking her heart in the cruel way I had had mine broken was not what I was there for. But she left me with no choice. Besides, I suppose she had a right to get out now before she too wasted her adolescence on this loser. Maybe somebody could have saved me? Oh yes, I guess they tried telling me, a few zillion times. Let's face it, it had been the sole reason that I had lost Anna. My best friend throughout my whole life, thrown away for him. Him, who currently stood cradling another right in front of my eyes.

Telling Lily was quite a heroic deed. Firstly, I assisted Chris with the swelling on his brain and now I was about to save Lilly, from wasting her adolescence on this fuck knuckle. Arise Lady Shannon Black, you mother fucking legend you!

I began to smugly laugh, his panic excited me more.

"Come on Lily, we are going," he stammered as he urged her onto the back of his bike. This was hilarious. Think a scene out of Benny Hill and you won't be far wrong. I had kicked his bike so much his wheel was bent. It seemed that I couldn't break his heart, but I damn well could break his fucking bike. Now a cute little backie on the bike is usually lovely imagery but shuffling the bike up the road with a bent frame with your bird on the back, is nothing short of hilarious. A total classic picture of which, even now many years later, never fails to raise a smile. Since she was now the one to be seated upon his bike and not me, she could deal with all the shite that came with it.

I stood in front of his bike and I knew I was going to love every minute of my outburst.

"Why don't you ask him where he was last night then honey, in fact ask him where he was the night before and the night before that?" It was my turn to be smug.

"Move out of my way, you fucking liar," he screamed.

"Lying about what?" I calmly smiled, "I only asked her to ask you where you were, is that a guilty conscious darling?" I sweetly stepped aside, winked at them both and strolled home.

I didn't need to say another word, she knew!

MILESTONE = ENGAGED IN WHISTLING BLOWING

Now that did make me feel better. Not because I hurt her, like I said before, that wasn't my intention, I didn't care about that, she was an insignificant part of our whole love affair, but because somebody, no sorry 'I' had stood up to him and stopped his cheating ways, albeit probably only temporarily. He wrongly presumed he could go through life shagging left right and centre and presuming that nobody would have the guts to inform his dearly beloved (whoever that may be at the time). He'd done it to me and now he was doing it to them. I wasn't one of his pawns, not anymore anyway. No, I was the king, so I believe my last move made us check mate!

I wasn't surprised when I heard through the grapevine that Lily didn't believe me, although didn't want to believe me would have been a more accurate interpretation, but neither did I care. We all know she knew the truth. I also wasn't surprised when I found out he'd dumped her a few days later. His reason being that she was boring. Which knowing Chris was clearly code for, *"she tends to not want to fuck me at the drop of hat and as for cock sucking, she was dismal"*.

Coming of Age

It had finally arrived, my 18th! Jesus, it had been a long slog. Despite being bombarded with a huge variety of experiences during adolescence, I will admit I still felt like I had learnt jack shit. Whilst I felt super old, I absolutely did not feel super wise.

Ashley and I were still 'kind of' together, how (or why might be more appropriate) I'll never know but we were. In all fairness, we rarely saw each other due to his football schedule and he hadn't been the same since my refusal to commit to the 'L' word and I had seen him all but once a month since the incident. Like I had been with Chris, there just seemed to be a refusal to let me go. It was clear he was distancing himself, and not only could I not blame him, but he was absolutely doing the right thing. The damage had been done and I doubted there would be any going back.

That evening, I had a party that I'll never forget, no matter how hard I try. I had organised the party myself to attempt to bring to a close my adolescence in style. I never contemplated until writing that down now, how sad it is to throw your own party.

By the time the evening was nearing, I was absolutely trollied, as you would expect. I started the day with a champagne breakfast, actually, it was just champagne, I skipped the breakfast. Followed by champagne for dinner, that is a total lie, it was more like beer and cider since I had consumed the one bottle of imitation champagne that I had been given as a present. You can imagine then, that I wasn't exactly in a good way by 6pm. When my friends turned up to accompany me to my party I hadn't even started getting ready. Besides I was too drunk to put my war paint on in any decent manner. I did try to straighten my hair but after several burns to my neck and ears, I gave up. Sporting yellow welts upon my skin was never going to transform me into a birthday beauty was it? Tip: never handle heated hair styling equipment whilst piffled – adolescence or not.

But none of that mattered because my outfit was the bomb. It was the outfit to have that year. Cute white little hot pant shorts teamed with a, erm, now how can I describe it. A dress top? Yes, that would do it. Effectively, it was a floor length dress with a split up the front rather than the back. Except the split went up to the breasts. I suppose when it was designed for super-models who can carry anything off, the idea worked (a bit like the only male that could carry off a fur coat without looking like a twat is 50 cent). But looking back now, I guess people could wrongly assume that the dress had been put on backwards, had then split its seams and I was simply saved from embarrassment because ironically, I had matching shorts on underneath my dress. So I guess what I have been trying to say throughout this lengthy ramble is that I arrived at my party looking like a total twat!

Shall I say what you want me to say? It was great to have all my friends in one room? Or the truth? I couldn't fucking stand half of the people that were in the room, as is the norm with parties. As I began to circle the room to speak to my guests, my eyes laid upon Anna. She had come! I had dropped an invitation through her door, hoping that an outstretched arm would be enough to end this ridiculous situation. If she had missed me, half as much as I had missed her, then I knew she couldn't bear to stay away. And if she hadn't, then I would have to get used to a life without her.

"Thank you for coming," I blubbed as I threw my arms around her.

"As if I had a choice," she smirked. She put a smile on my face that would have been hard to remove. God I'd missed that girl and I was so relieved to be leaving my adolescence with her back by my side.

Originally, that morning, Ashley had called me to say he wasn't coming to my party that night. Oh, Happy Birthday Shannon! Although, who could blame him, the last party I had where Comby lads attended, it ended in a blood bath. I had already made the decision to end it with him, I just hadn't gathered the courage to deal with it. This was not helped by the fact that I was beginning to forget what he looked like, except for his abs, I could never forget those! The fact that he blew me out on my 18th, wasn't of the slightest bit of a disappointment. If anything, it just confirmed that I was doing the right thing.

But for now, there was someone else who had caught my eye at this party and it just so happened to be one of my old love interests actually, Neil. Whilst we didn't exactly hit it off at Anna's 16th, things hadn't exactly stopped right there. Throughout my relationship with Chris, we had constantly flirted with each other and I was more than a little tempted on numerous occasions, but that was a fire that was nowhere near worth playing with.

He had always made it more than obvious that he wanted me, he had even resorted to telling me whilst I was sat on Chris's knee at times. He was very brutal, and Chris was not the type to pick a fight, and definitely not with Neil. It wasn't that I didn't fancy him because I really did. So now that Chris was removed from the scene and Ashley was about to be given his marching orders, there really was not much, bar my own confidence, stopping me.

I had just starting to talk to him when my birthday 'stripper' arrived. Now maybe my previous dealings with the stripper made me a tad over confident, or was that the alcohol? The shame of this situation is that I seemingly momentarily forgot that I was in a room surrounded by people. And many of those people, were sober people. So, I do thank the lord above that I was blessed to grow up in a world free from camera phones and such like, I would have so made it as a viral meme.

Music, percentage and a delicious bit of naked totty were clearly a recipe for one hell of a debacle. With a sense of charm, he began to dance around me, sucking his fingers and wiping my hand down his sweating abs. I was marginally impressed. Although Ashley's body rivalled his, so I wasn't hitting the ceiling at this point. But I playfully began to join in as I ditched my Tia Maria and coke and let him begin the seduction routine.

Clearly, the nymphomaniac in me, must have been triggered by the last swig of my drink, because as he whipped his masterpiece out of his trousers, I decided to take complete control. I snatched the whip from his grasp and brought it cracking down on his mighty fine ass. The look on his face, told me that the leather arseless pants he was sporting, were completely for show and did not reflect his sexual desires at all.

I vaguely remember the stripper fleeing looking totally humiliated. The irony of this, when he swings his cock around in the faces of desperate woman for a living. But after that, I remember nothing, and I absolutely promise you that even to this day, I cannot recall the events that led to me being laid on the floor upstairs in the gent's toilets carelessly.... let's just say, I was more than stroking Neil's ego!

"What the fuck are we doing?" I asked when the realisation of what we were doing hit me.

"Thought that would be obvious," he replied intrigued if not a little bemused. He attempted to re-engage me with a kiss.

What the fuck was I doing? Jesus Christ, there was a party going on downstairs, my party! How had this even happened. On a brighter note, I guess the deed was done. Let's face it, half of the reason I hadn't done this before is because I was worried about getting my body out in front of him, but it was done now. So really there was nothing stopping me doing it again. All the same, this probably wasn't the time or the place.

"Neil, just stop!" I demanded angrily.

"You only had to say, princess," he mocked me, "you are one hell of a strange find Ms. Black, but I fucking love it," he shared, whilst buttoning his checked shirt back up.

I had stopped listening, my mind was ticking wildly, I began to make myself look presentable. After unsuccessfully fumbling with my dress, I scrambled to find a mirror to assess the damage. This was when I came to the stark realisation that there are no mirrors in men's toilets. I mean, what the fuck? I am sure this must have evolved by now. I can't imagine today's prissy, face mask wearing men would survive without them. Anyway, I suppose that I had bigger things to worry about – right?

I couldn't believe that I had done this to myself. Now that I had reached the end of adolescence, I had hoped things would be slightly better for me and that somehow, age had gifted me the ability not to make such stupid fucking decisions. I quickly made my way downstairs, whilst trying to look as inconspicuous as possible, which was tricky since the ladies' toilets were on the ground floor. As only my luck could bloody have it, I bumped straight into Anna and my sister who just happened to be stood with Ashley. Ashley, my boyfriend. Mother Fucking Holy Shit!

Without thinking, Clair boldly announced, "As if you two haven't been shagging!"

I was horrified and suddenly found myself unable to breathe! I tried to speak, but not only could I not think quick enough, my tongue and lips couldn't form words. In fact, I just stood there staring at him.

"Well?" Ashley yelled, in clear distress and wanting answers.

My brain finally engaged, sort of, "What are you doing here, honey?" I replied awkwardly as I stumbled down the last few stairs and tried to put my arms around him.

He shook his head in complete disbelief and stormed out of the bar. To be fair, I was with him, I even joined him in his head shaking. What a fucking muppet I was.

MILESTONE = CAUGHT IN THE ACT (maybe it has to happen to everybody, once?)

I was just about to defend myself to my sister, when a brawl similar to a football match feud luckily broke out back in the party. I say luckily as it gave me much needed time to think. My village always came up trumps when it came to a bit of a battle. Believe it or not, my uncle had started it over the strength of the alcohol. Everyone was screaming, glasses flying, fists throwing, hair pulling, heads butting. God knows what had happened, but who cared. It prevented me from dealing with a sobbing, angry boyfriend, for then anyway. Embarrassingly enough it took six police cars and three riot vans to suppress the madness, a proper village family do!

Philosophy – Village Dos

Villagers haven't evolved that much from cave men really. They still feel the need to stomp their feet, wave their club and defend their territory. They clearly can't do that with words, motivation or encouragement. Just a knuckle duster and a well-trained right hook. My uncle wasn't from Detton, so him taking a stand against the club, meant he would pay the price, for disrespecting one of their own. Like football hooliganism, there is always another side to it. Footballers claim it's passion, and maybe villagers would claim it is honour. Either way, they're all a bunch of dumb fucks.

Afraid to walk back into the bar for fear of bumping into Neil or Ashley, I snuck out from the party and seated myself outside on the cold concrete steps, wallowing in self-pity and wondering if life could possibly get any more complicated? It could! Especially when Brian (yes cast your mind right back – the older bloke) plonked himself down on the steps next to me. This was all I bloody needed. I couldn't have possibly written a diary of adolescence unless it had been a complicated one, could I? Truthfully, it was nice to see Brian, it had been a long time and he had always been lovely to me really.

"Can we talk?" he asked softly.

Ok, so let me sum up my mental and emotional disposition at this point, it may help you to understand my answer to Brian. So, the little geek that I had unfortunately fallen in love with had turned into a heart battering slag and completely stolen my cool. I had therefore thrown myself into a completely pointless relationship with a man who I couldn't possibly have anything less in common with, although I liked his abs, oh and his ass, nice legs too – okay admittedly, he was very aesthetically pleasing. I had then finally given into the temptation of wanting to sleep with the bad boy of our village, who was possibly the only bigger slag than Chris at that point in time. He had been begging me for two years to sleep with him and finally the temptation seemed to prove too much. My pointless boyfriend had therefore just caught me post shag, which I suppose didn't matter too much since I had been sleeping with my ex, more or less since day one of our relationship anyway. As if my world wasn't caving in enough, my birthday party had turned into smash a glass/face fest all because my uncle knob head had decided the vodka had been watered down. The man that I did love, didn't even turn up to say, 'Happy Birthday,' because he couldn't give less of a flying fuck about me, and just to add to the very complicated/highly emotional night, here was one of my ex boyfriends seating himself down for 'a talk'. Mmmmm, so there could only really be one reply!

"No sorry Brian, we can't," I said coldly as I stood up to walk home.

"I'll be quick," he replied as he grabbed hold of my hand and pulled me back to the step. I had no energy left to fight him. I found myself slouching back onto the step, "I need to tell you that I still love you, I think we can make a go of this Shan. I want us to be a proper couple, I should have never let you go. It's been years and I still can't forget you."

His words turned into a total blur as I put my head into my hands and wondered if my life would ever just be simple. I remembered the days when I longed for something so simple as a kiss, where the idea of a boyfriend was my happily ever after and absolutely nothing else mattered. Yet adolescence had given me all these things in abundance, and all it had brought me was misery. I supposed I could try batting for the other team, maybe dating a woman would be less complex? I hear the irony here, don't panic.

I turned around to face him and took his face softly in my hands, I was suddenly very sober. I knew he was hurting and I knew exactly how he felt. Chris had turned me into a person that I didn't want to be. What on earth was I doing going around breaking hearts the way he had mine. I didn't deserve it but neither did they. I kissed him and felt his tears on my face.

I hated myself and wondered if Chris ever felt this way about himself too. I felt so unloved, so lonely and so reckless that I could have taken Brian and made love to him right there. I had always wondered what our sexual chemistry would have been like, that is normal isn't it? I was sure fucking him would have made me feel better, but I owed it to him to end his hurt the way Chris should have done with me. Chris would never do that, it was far too selfless. He had shelved me so that he could use me when needed for regular ego boosts, and I could have done the same to them all. But enough was enough! This wasn't me and it certainly didn't make me happy.

As I pulled away from our kiss, I looked him straight in the eyes, "But I just don't love you back! As much as you think that I'm being a bitch, I'm trying to stop you from getting hurt because believe me that's about all I could do for you right now," I paused to compose myself, as the wreckage of my life was becoming too much for me to bear. "I'm really not worth it and you definitely don't deserve it," I picked up my handbag and shoes, slid my hand from his and walked away.

I had done the right thing, finally. But I had a lot more to do if I was going to put everything else right. As I began to stagger home thinking of the disaster of my party, ok maybe the disaster of my adolescence, I heard a familiar voice shouting my name.

"Shannon, hold up," Ashley shouted as he ran to keep up with me. Outrunning him obviously wasn't an option since he was an athlete and the only running I did was the bath, "I think we need to talk" he said sternly, more reflective of a father than a lover.

He was determined to get his answers instantaneously, but I was drunk, emotionally drained and as bad as it sounded, I just wanted to ram a doner kebab covered in garlic mayo in my mouth and sleep for the next 12 hours. I know that sounds unsympathetic, and you would be right, it was. But alcohol did that to me, it made me hungry and unable to give a flying fuck.

"Yes, we do Ashley. But not tonight. You may have noticed that my birthday is not going to plan, let's fuck tomorrow up instead of tonight, what do you think?" I said sarcastically.

"I think you are a straight up fucking bitch," he retorted angrily.

"I totally agree," I said and walked the rest of the way home in silence whist Ashley got everything off his chest that he had ever wanted to say.

I couldn't take it any longer. I wish I had some sympathy for him, empathy would have been enough. Don't get me wrong, I was sorry for what I had put him through and thoroughly ashamed of myself for the things I'd done, but this day had been bad enough without it ending with a lecture on how it is appropriate for a lady to behave. I was 18, I'd made a fool of myself, so fucking what!

Ashely and I had barely waked through the door, when my friends clumsily threw themselves into the house singing, *'happy birthday'*. I had no intention of carrying on this party, this day was definitely over for me, the torturous pitfalls of adolescence had clearly taken their toll. I was far from a party pooper though and didn't mind them carrying on in the slightest. Thus, I crawled, literally up to my bed and yes, Ashley closely followed behind me. Lucky me! I was determined to get some shut eye, but this bloke was glutton for punishment.

"Did you sleep with him?" he asked.

"Yes!" I begrudgingly replied, having no desire to cause him any pain.

My hangover began to kick in prematurely. I covered my head with the pillow, both to dull the pain and his voice.

"Why?" he repeatedly asked, his soul destroyed! I couldn't give him the answers, I didn't even know myself really.

His anger soon started to simmer. A lot sooner than I expected actually and then he bizarrely just wanted to make up and forget everything that had happened. Not everything because he didn't know everything did he? Aren't there just so many *'what the fuck'* moments in adolescence?

"Let's just start again Shan, a fresh start. Just tell me you love me, and I will forgive you. That is all you have to do. Just say it and I'm yours."

I saw this as my opportunity to end it and took the bull by the horns, "It's over Ash. I don't deserve you. I mean it when I say that I am emotionally disturbed and am sure that I will never have the capability to love ever again."

"Don't be so ridiculous," he said kneeling at the side of the bed whilst grasping at my hand.

"If it is so ridiculous Ash, why the fuck don't I love you? You are everything, absolutely everything, that I ever wanted on paper, but nothing is happening in here," I had sat up by this point and was pounding heavily upon my chest. I wiped streams of tears from my face.

What did I have to do to make him hate me?

Oh lord, this sounds very familiar doesn't it? How very embarrassing! Is this how Chris felt about me? Was I as foolish with Chris as Ashley was with me? Yes, I'm afraid I must admit that I probably was. But more to the point was Ashley feeling about me the way I felt about Chris. I really hoped not! Not only would I never wish that pain on anybody, neither did 'I' want to be responsible for inflicting such wounds. Right, I had to be strong, harsh but strong. I had to make him hate me the way I had begun to hate Chris. I had no desire to hurt this guy any longer. Clearly, I never had (I can see how this would be unclear to you, but he was an unfortunate victim of my circumstance). At least that way he could move on quicker and therefore so could I. This was clearly an additional perk. He would know that there could never be any type of reconciliation and shouldn't waste his time trying like I had done with 'Chris the Heart Crusher'.

"I've been sleeping with Chris for months behind your back!" I blurted out whilst burying my head in the pillow.

Ok, so I had braved hurting this man with the truth, but I wasn't even nearly brave enough to look at him whilst I destroyed him.

"No, you haven't, you liar!" he stuttered as he slowly pushed himself up off his knees.

"Oh. for crying out loud I have, I fucked him, I loved it, I love him, and I don't regret it, so get out," I screamed. I was crying inconsolably by this time as the humiliation and shame began to shroud me with guilt. This human being who loved me, for what reasons I wasn't sure, but he did. He unconditionally loved me. I wanted to tell him that I loved him too, I yearned to stop him from hurting but I couldn't tell him something that wasn't true. I couldn't even convince myself and I couldn't make myself love him, I had tried!

The memory of his face in that moment will haunt me forever. He was unsuccessful in blinking back his tears. He wiped them away awkwardly with the back of his hand as he began to grab at his possessions from around the room. The hurtful part is that I knew that I had punished Ashley for the things that Chris had done to me, not intentionally, but nonetheless that is what I had done. He grabbed at a framed picture of us from my bedside table.

"What an absolute joke," he threw it against the wall.

As he got to the door, something came over me. I needed to fix him, make him feel better, his pain was evading me. I jumped out of bed and grabbed his arm. I whispered my regrets to him, with honest and truthful regret. He simply shrugged me off with disgust as he walked out, slamming the door as he left. I slumped down onto the bed and began to sob.

The door flew back open, "And you fucking owe me 50p, for that coke earlier, the coke I didn't even get to give you because you were too busy fucking somebody else," he commanded.

Oh yes, he did! Never mind the fact that I had lied through my back teeth for many months and had broken his heart, yes it was the 50p that got him in the end. All emotions I may have been feeling within that nano-second, flew right out of the window and into the gutter. Clear vision, I had obviously done the right thing and at least he left me with a smile! It was just a shame it wasn't for the right reasons!

I never thought about Ashley after that night. In the end, it seemed it was easy come, easy go as much as I hate to admit it. Perhaps he was right, maybe I was an ice maiden after all. I had finally come to the conclusion and acceptance that I was single now and boy was I going to enjoy it. At least no one could get hurt, right?

Philosophy – Regret
You are simply damned if you do and damned if you don't. You don't experience the world before you settle down and then people say, 'it will never last, she has never been with anybody else you know'. Yet, you sow your wild oats and you are a fucking whore. You don't give that man a chance, you are being too picky.

You give him a chance and the spark doesn't catch, then you are an ice-cold bitch and you used him. You cheat on somebody and .... ok you got me there. Maybe not everything is as clear cut as it sounds, and not everything can be explained away in a bit of philosophy at the end of a troubled section of memories. But the truth is, this adolescence lark doesn't come with a manual, and sometimes the only regret that is the one worth pondering on, is the one where you allowed other people's opinions and superficial (often sexist) judgement stop you from exploring who the fuck you actually are!

Accidental Sex

The problem with being single in a village of which you have grown up in, is that you are usually both (a) sick of looking at the men available in that village and (b) the men that are there, feel more like brothers and unless you liked to dabble in a bit of incest (which I can promise you, I did not) you were foookkkedd! I had done nothing but re-evaluate my situation since my birthday. Maybe it was time that I accepted that I had outgrown this village? Besides I had bedded everybody here that I wanted to bed.

There seemed a realistic and quite simple solution for this sudden growth spurt. I could just fucking leave? Wooooahhhh! Did people really leave their home village and survive? This wasn't a tale that I was familiar with. So, what were my options. I could move to Comby? Admittedly, not very adventurous but it would be a start. Or I could really push the boat out and move into the city? The boat I would need to push out would have to be a yacht, there was no way I could afford that. But there was still one unexplored option that was just nagging away in the back of my head. London! Like Dick Whittington, I could pack up my possessions in a napkin tie them to my bindle and skip all the way down to the <u>real</u> city – the big smoke. The potential was enormous.

Okay, I couldn't afford to live there by myself but whilst adolescence hadn't given me an easy ride, it did give me a dad who resided in that their city with its streets paved with gold. The idea of moving in with my dad, wasn't a new prospect, my Dad was more than keen for me to come and live with him after moving there when I was young. It might be too late for me to build a relationship with him, but at least it was a roof over my head. I had posed these threats to leave before, firstly to my mam and then later to Chris, but there was nobody to make threats to anymore, just a promise to hold myself to. My mam and I hadn't been close when I lived with her, and I barely stayed in contact with her nowadays. If I stayed in the village, there were only two things that could happen, Chris's death, or mine and sadly I believed, that I would more likely be responsible for both.

I suppose in all fairness, there was never any choice to make. This wasn't just about escaping, this was about growing. I was leaving behind the village that I had barely ventured out of, my family, the friends that were just as close, my job, my home, my entire world. But you know what, I was ready for a new entire world, I was more than ready, I was excited. I would embark upon my adult years in a totally different life, a much-needed chance to start again.

The following weeks were full of house parties, drunken pub crawls and lots of goodbyes! I suppose that it was obvious that the first goodbye would be to Chris. Don't get me wrong, I didn't seek him out to sing our farewells, no nothing so dramatically nostalgic. He simply turned up to mine one night to join in my regular weekly house party. My love life may have been in tatters, but I still knew how to party. I was in a particularly good mood, so feeling particularly carefree, I let him in. The truth was I was always comforted by his presence. Lately, I had become accustomed to not having him around and no part of me wanted us to work things out, but that didn't mean that every single bone in my body didn't ache for him at times. I remember wondering at that moment, if I would ever not feel this way about him? Would I ever be able to look at him without my stomach doing flips whilst my heart broke into smithereens all over again?

MILESTONE RETRACTED = MOVE ON BITCH

"Can we talk?" he announced in front of everybody.

Shocked was not the word. The whole room seemed to stop (you know like that dramatic record scratch on films) and focus on Chris in the doorway. Even in the midst of our affair, it had been top secret and now he wanted to talk to me publicly. To what did I owe such a bestowed pleasure? Curiosity got the better of me and since he'd asked me so nicely, I didn't decline.

I followed him into the emptiness of my back room, silent at first. As he sat himself down on my dining room carpet, he pulled me down towards him. At first, I thought that in true Chris style, he wanted a free style fuck amid our friends, but as I nervously sat cross legged on the carpet in front of him, I caught a very different look in his eyes. What on earth was this about? My head was a mess already, as if I needed this!

"What's wrong," I asked, genuinely intrigued, maybe excited even. Don't ask, even you want to beat me now, right?

"Nothing," he replied, "just wanted to talk to you."

I recognised this person to some extent, he reminded me of a boy who once spilled the contents of his heart to his young girlfriend under a dog stained blue bobbly blanket. My heart warmed to the boy's return and I leaned onto him to snuggle into his chest as he intensely wrapped his arms around me and squeezed so tight.

Awkwardly, no one spoke, he simply began to queerly look me over, studying every line and contour on my face before he let his eyes drop back to the floor. He didn't smile, and he didn't frown, he just seemed to be scanning me. I had never seen him look quite like this before, something was happening. Whilst he reminded me of his old self, this was an older more worn look. He was sporting the bloodshot look, which was attributed solely to drink, drugs and rock and roll. Although this was Detton not L.A, so it was a lot less glamorous then you may be imagining.

I would have gone as far to say that he looked emotional. Could he still have some humanity in him after all? Is this what our relationship did to us both? There was no denying that our relationship was destructive. We seemed drawn to each other unable to breathe for too long until re-united. Then once back together we would fasten upon each other like vampires, quickly leaching the life and blood out of each other, breaking again only to prevent the final wisps of life evaporating from each other.

I quickly began to figure out exactly what was happening. I grasped that this was not an old friend calling by to share some MD 20/20. Neither was it a confession of past events in an attempt to rekindle what so obviously, could never be. I must admit this thought had crossed my mind though when he asked for some privacy. I knew instead it was simply his way of tying up our beautiful disaster and ultimately saying goodbye. He must have caught wind of my impending departure?

We spoke for hours in the end. We snuggled down in the corner of the room, temporarily like teenagers in the early throws of a lustful relationship. We asked a lot of questions and received some answers and we got things off our chests that had previously been eating away at our very sanity. I wanted the truth in all its filthy form. Despite the pain I wanted to know, I needed to know! He gave it to me and I took it because knowing from him was better than learning from somebody else. We cuddled, kissed and held each other's hands, forgiving each other of our sins. We talked about everything, where we went wrong, why he had lied, why he had hurt me, why I had hurt him, why we had to fight, why we weren't friends, why we could probably never be friends!

I didn't know what had made him turn up that night? Or what urged him to say the things he did? But I was convinced that he meant every single word. He wasn't exactly trying to rip my clothes off, so I'm not sure what he was trying to gain if not? I found myself not only in acceptance of his words and feelings but in agreeance too.

"Did you ever love me?" I challenged the silence. His slow response twisted my stomach inside and knotted my throat. I looked into his eyes and I once again glimpsed (and fondly remembered) a young Chris and I couldn't help but remember why I loved him. He looked into my eyes, like I mattered, for the first time in so long, took my face so gently in his hands and sensitively kissed my lips.

"You were my first love, I loved you, I still love you, but I'm young and I need to experience life. If we were older it would have been different," he continued as I laid weak in his arms, "I will only carry on hurting you and I don't want to do that. Forget me, I will never change." He had finally done it, he had let me go!

The realisation was stark. Stark and damn right painful. I knew then that this teaching was not something that I would forget for a long time, if ever. It had taken me months, maybe it had taken him the same, but it was finally as clear as day to me. He didn't love me, like I loved him. Age or life didn't matter to me, not beyond him anyway. So, he was right, he had to go out and find that one girl that made him not care about life too.

How did I feel? That's a hard question to answer. I felt strangely calm, happy even! I suppose that I knew we could never be together and so the closure that we got that night was the next best thing. He had said everything that I wanted to hear. Ok, I didn't want to hear him talking about taking Cindy Lou Who from behind but at least there were no lies, no surprises for me to uncover in the months to come, no regifting of the pain or anger. It was the perfect end, but it was also probably all total bullshit. I believed him because I wanted to and for my sanity at that point in my life. But now leaving my teens, I wonder if that was yet another attempt of him clawing back his sunshine boy reputation and making sure he kept me sweet should he ever need me for any purpose in the future, such as erm.... I don't know.... let's take a wild stab in the dark, sex? Still the closure was nice, the perfect end to the relationship from hell.

He stayed the night and I knew for sure it would be the last time we would lay together like this. I was sure to take in his every contour with my hands as I ran my fingers up and down his chest and I breathed him in as he slept, in a desperate attempt to preserve his memory in my mind. Nothing sexual happened and when I awoke, he had gone.

On the village vine, I'd heard a rumour that Chris had decided to take a job working away. It didn't shock me, he'd talked about it before, but I was shocked that he was actually doing it. He was usually all talk, like most of the people in Detton. Ok, so I was moving away to London, but moving abroad felt different, more final. It seemed this time, we were in for a real goodbye. The kind of goodbyes where in 10 years, you could barely recall their face. The finality was more painful than I thought it would be and when he would come to say goodbye, I needed to make sure he knew how important it was that we stayed in touch.

But, he never came to say goodbye.

No matter how hard I tried to understand his blasé approach to leaving, I couldn't. Did his sick perverted mind, come and offer me reassurance of his love simply to watch me begin the process of repair. so that he could destroy me now? Despite being 18, was this all still a game to him? I didn't understand how we could have once been so close, so in love and despite insisting his love for me was still there, only a couple of days earlier, he was going to move half way across the world without saying goodbye.

I recalled our final conversation. I knew that we weren't lovers anymore, but I thought that we were friends. Boy, was I a dumb ass, but you guys already knew that, right? If this didn't prove how little the wanker cared for me then what would? As I put two and two together, the pieces feel together, his visit had not just been a goodbye to our relationship but a goodbye altogether!

I didn't think he could have ever hurt me more than he did during the midst of our relationship, when he fucked his way to liberation. But his decision to walk out of my life not only as my partner but as my friend, forever without even so much of a handwave, was a new kind of pain. It was beyond heartbreak, this was akin to grieving a real death. I just couldn't get my head around the fact, that we would never see each other again, I found myself struggling to cope with the tightening of my chest and an inability to breathe every time I dared to get my head around this concept. How could he leave without saying goodbye? I'll tell you how, because no matter how much I, or he, tried to convince myself otherwise, he didn't give a flying fuck about anybody but himself. I don't think his tiny mind had wandered over never seeing me again, probably because he assumed that I would still be sat waiting for him when he returned. Although if I am completely honest, I had relied on the fact Chris would be here on my visits home from the capital too.

Philosophy – The Real Goodbyes of a World without Social Media

We covered goodbye earlier, but this was not goodbye, this was certain death. A death that millennials will never understand. It was the finality. That knowledge, that you weren't going to bump into them in the supermarket and as the years passed by, you would just become a tiny figment of their memory, if you were lucky. In contemporary society when somebody moves away, we have the option to ease our grieving soul with a bit of cyber stalking. You often don't need to speak to the person, often knowing that you wouldn't like to hear what they said, but you are appeased by watching their life continue from the back seat whilst pathetically tracing your finger over their silhouette on photos. Although, there are always 'the blockers', this can be a similar pain admittedly.

.

Like a bad penny, Paul had popped around to see me the night before Chris left. Yes, I jumped up to the door, hoping it was Chris who had finally come to his senses and couldn't bear to leave without saying goodbye.

"Ta da," he stumbled on the step whilst waving a bottle in his hand.

Why was he there? The obvious reason would be to tell me how much Chris loved me and couldn't carry on without me! I'm afraid it wasn't for that reason. Why then? There was no one as confused about this as me. As he stepped through the door, he quickly took my hand and pulled me down to sit next to him.

"There is no point in beating around the bush," he quickly said as he squeezed his clammy hand against mine as the stench of alcohol hit me heavily.

I quickly pulled away, sensing by the way his eyes were trying to molest my cleavage that this conversation was nothing to do with Chris and I.

"How about we get down to some naughty shit?" he stuttered as he patted my hand of which he had taken a firm grip of.

Oh yes, this village was full of charmers and it seemed the older they got, the worse they got at it. I wish I could leave this little memoir right here, but nope, there was more.

"I've heard a little rumour about you," he said whilst tracing patterns on my hand with his finger.

I pulled my hand away from him, my anger rising, what was he doing? Playing round and round the garden on the palm of my fucking hand? I didn't care about any rumours, I had dealt with people's opinions on me my whole life. I wasn't going to get upset about some receding hairline, pissed up loon judging me either.

"What are you bloody talking about," my voice raised, and I was fast losing my patience.

I stood up, hands on hips. I was about to lose my shit.

"Calm down, calm down. It is nothing bad. In fact, it is terribly good, I can tell you that," he smirked perversely, "Chris tells me that you … erm … how do I put this, that you 'taste' very nice, if you get what I mean" he winked and reached back for my hand.

Oh, I know what he meant ok, it was a line Chris had used on me a thousand times. Was I supposed to be flattered? My jaw dropped both at the fact that this man had come around to discuss the succulent flavour of my vagina, but that Chris had, for whatever fucking bizarre reason, decided to share this extremely private information with him. How do conversations like this even occur?

"I think it is time you left please," I demanded opening the door ready for him.

"So, is that a no?"

"Is what a no? What do you want?" All patience had left me by this point, besides my focus was on what the fuck Chris had been thinking whilst having this conversation with this guy.

"Isn't it obvious?" he said genuinely perplexed, "I want to give you oral sex, I want to taste you!"

I had to stop myself from visualising their sordid conversations. Had Chris been aware that he had come here? Had he even suggested it? Had he agreed to hand me over like a toy he had long since bored of. I couldn't bear to think about it. Maybe that is all I had ever been, a toy?

"Get the fuck out you perverted twat and tell your friend that I hope his plane crashes," I said shoving the manky piece of shit into the garden.

Philosophy – Desperate Men

You may be asking yourself, what the fuck that was all about? Even my ageing self wonders the same thing. Admittedly, I haven't met many men like that, but I have met enough desperate men to know one thing, they are desperate because they have no fucking idea how to pull. Clouded by their complete desperation to get laid, they dive straight in, making it obvious to the victim that they are hungry for one thing and one thing only. They may claim it is honesty, it is not honesty, it is total and utter desperation. Women can confuse this general desperation as an innate hunger specifically directed at them. And they would be wrong, in fact it tends to suggest that nobody of sane mind in the world wants to sleep with this specimen and hence their longings are spilling over and causes them to act in this embarrassingly distressing way.

It was finally my last weekend before I moved to the Big City. I was sad to be leaving my friends behind particularly Wes and Anna. We had all become so close. My circle of friends had gotten smaller (as inevitably it does during adolescence) and they were my family and I wasn't sure how I would cope without them.

Philosophy – Friendship Circles

Growing up in a village you tend to know everyone. Not that you are friends with them all, but it is comforting to walk down the street and know more of less every face in one way or another. Your friends are usually the people who you

have played with in the gennels since you can remember. From dirty faces mak-
ing mud pies and collecting ladybirds in jars, to whacking out the stereo, lining
the path with cardboard and breakdancing until we were called home by the
yells of our parents from our front doors. But adolescence shakes the foundations
of all friendships and by the end of it, you are only left with the sturdiest, most
robust of them all. Losing friends is inevitable, sometimes because you are now so
different, sometimes because you settle down, or sometimes because they fucked
your boyfriend (which seems to be the more repetitive one for me). But none the
less, it is normal, and adolescence should be looked upon as a filtration system. It
weeds out the liars, the cheats and the ones who seek to do you harm and it leaves
with the pure rocks of friendship.

We had our own farewell party, just the three of us. We listened to cheesy music, nothing wrong with a bit of *Don McClean's American Pie* busting out of the tape deck. We reminisced about our childhood, our teenage years, we slagged people off and generally rubbished anybody who didn't idolise us (as you do). Anna got wrecked sooner than usual and sulked off home earlier than typical, probably before she ended up puking on my pots in the sink, which to be fair, wouldn't be the first time.

Wes and I were left to carry on the session for as long as we could, but the curtains were lightening with the breaking of dawn and if I had to listen to Don McClean one more time I would have to break the tape. I accompanied Wes to the back door to bid him goodnight.

As I pecked him a kiss on the doorstep, as I had done many times before, something strange happened. There was a connection, a pull that clearly wasn't there before. Although I failed to consider that it might not be there after either. I had never noticed his dark hair falling over his eyes, their dark aurora peeking out from underneath. I had failed to notice how strong his hands were as they grasped my neck as he reached in to kiss me back. And I have definitely never noticed how deliciously huge his arms were as he wrapped his arm around my waist. Before I could consider anything proper-ly, our bodies were wrapped around each other and we were recklessly shov-ing our tongues down each other's throats!

I didn't know Wes had this kind of passion or was so domineering, had I known earlier ..... Anyway it was a matter of minutes before the kissing wasn't enough to satisfy either one of us and he was pushing me against the kitchen cabinets literally ripping off my clothes. He left me breathless as he hoisted me up onto the worktop and slid his hand up my nightie. My skin forgetting this was the hand of my friend, the goose bumps rising up my back told me only that this was a lover. This was no time for foreplay, I needed him right away. Sex without emotion, this is exactly what I needed!

Let's forget the fairytale sex though, this is adolescence after all. As I pulled him towards me due to a deep-rooted desire to feel him inside me, we came across a bit of a hurdle. It seemed the variation in our height was going to make it pretty fucking impossible for him to take me on the sideboard. Doh! The realisation that sex like they do it in the movies is often impossible, is a hard pill to swallow. Never one to give up, especially when horny, I made a quick decision to lay on the floor to enable easier access for the, clearly far too tall one.

Although greatly inebriated, sod that, let's be honest, greatly inebriated is usually better. It lowers inhabitations and, erm, generally makes you do stupid shit you may not have done previously. I laid upon the floor steering him away from wasting any time on foreplay and pulled him deep inside me. He let out a deep nosie making sure I knew how much he had wanted this to happen. He broke my control and thrust hard and deep within me taking full control of the situation. I didn't mind. I lay back twisting beneath him as his rhythm took me to the edge. He grabbed at my hips dragging me closer to him, moaning with every thrust.

His fingers gripped deep into my thighs, ensuring I knew his wanton, his urge, his need! I liked his eagerness and the more I felt demanded upon, the more I was pulsating, the faster my heart was racing and the quicker this was about to be over. He had barely finished making 'that face' when I grabbed his hand and pulled him upstairs to my bedroom in anticipation of round two.

He may have been in control downstairs, but it was my turn to show him. I pushed him down onto the bed, pulled up my t-shirt and carefully lowered myself onto his erection. It seemed he was already ready. He slid inside me with ease and I rode up and down while he covered his face with a pillow to appease his screams. We didn't need a dose of s & m to make this sex work, it was unforbidden and that was enough for us.

In true teenage style, I wasn't rodeo for long before the show was over. Just saying! As I threw myself back onto my pillow, I was rudely awakened by the realisation of the offence that I had just committed. Ok, so to the normal person I, a single person, had just had sex with another single person. No great crime? The crime was that this guy was my friend, one of my best friends. He was more like a brother than my actual brothers. Whilst Wes was admittedly quite attractive, I had never looked at him that way and quite frankly it didn't feel right doing so. What had been quite fantastic sex suddenly made me feel sick, it felt so wrong. What the fuck was wrong with me? Why as soon as I had a drink inside me did I do such stupid shit!

MILESTONE = SLEPT WITH A MATE (tell me everybody has done this?)

"Set the alarm for me babe," Wes broke my thoughts as he reached out for me to snuggle up to him.

Alert, he thought he was staying over? I had to think fast to avoid laying next to my incestual conquest for the entire night and even worse, having to wake up next to him too! Fuck this, I didn't have time to think, I just had to get rid of him. There was no time for niceties here.

"You can't stay, just go!" I anxiously stuttered, grasping the bedclothes tightly around my naked chest and burying my head in my other hand. I suddenly felt like I was stood muff out whilst doing a class presentation. It took Wes all of sixty seconds to realise that not only was I not joking but I was also full of regret. It pained me to see him so confused and clearly hurt as he quickly dressed himself amidst the uncomfortable silence. Unsure of how to bid me farewell, he awkwardly leaned down and placed a kiss upon my forehead and headed for the bedroom door. Now head kisses may have been my favourite kind of sensual kiss, but not this one. I failed to stop myself from pulling back in repulsion as he did so. He noticed. He stood frozen and eventually shook his head in disbelief at my actions.

"Maybe Ashley is right about you Shan, you are one unfeeling bitch."

Philosophy – Sex with a Mate
I'm sure for some people this is the norm and they are totally fine with it. I suppose in different circumstances, I too wouldn't be averse to a fuck buddy or

two. But I think it has to work a different way around. You must become friends through having sex. Being friends and then starting to have sex, is just a total fucking no-no. Unless that friend is Tom Hardy, Channing Tatum or some other hot piece of ass, that to be frank, you would fuck even if they were your grandfather.

So, I had fucked up that friendship and I knew that we could never bury this totally weird fucked up situation, there was no way I could ever look him in the eyes again. How would I deal with this? I usually find that total avoidance does the trick.

He rapped the door loudly the very next morning at the crack of dawn, not that I had slept a wink, I had taken myself off to some personal form of purgatory in punishment for indulging in brother fucking the night before. I quickly hit the living room floor and crawled into the dining room. I hid behind the wall not daring to breathe until I heard his footsteps down the path and recognised the click of the garden gate. I'm sure you'll agree, a mature way of handling the situation. Who cared about mature? I was done with the drama.

If I had thought that by removing Chris from the village, it de-complicated my love life and daily movement, I was very much mistaken!

As I walked through the doors of *The Pipe* that last evening before my demise, I saw Neil's body propping up the bar. I ordered a pint from Seedy Shelley and rebelliously seated myself next to Anna, in a chair that was usually reserved for somebody else. Come on every club has a barmaid that fucks more punters than she pulls pints. Now a book on her adolescence, I wouldn't mind reading. I could even think of a great name: 50 shades of cock!

I quickly got down to enjoying myself but had a constant feeling of unease as Neil's gaze did not leave me. We hadn't seen each other since the incident at my birthday party. I had avoided all his calls and had refused his demands to let him in when he called at my house. I was after a really wild happy night tonight and maybe even one last village fling? But that clearly wasn't going to happen as everybody was too aware that Neil had a major bee in his bonnet for me. Therefore, anybody of the male species was highly unlikely to even glance my way, never mind take me for a quickie! How I could want sex after last night's episode was beyond me. But I was 18, saying no to someone fit tended not to happen. I almost hear sighs erupting from society not to mention the age 30+ readers that are mooning after the days when sex was a sought-after activity and not a chore or a trading tool for getting him indoors to fix the fence.

Philosophy – Women and Sex

Now sex had always been important to me, I'm not going to lie, and neither should you. Society tells us that women shouldn't feel that way, that if they do, they are dirty whores. I say that there must be a god damn lot of dirty whores wandering this earth, so hold your hands up and tell society to spin! Be you male or female, you are equal, and so are your desires. Sex is an important part of anybody's adolescence and life thereafter. So, I for one say, let the days of shame for enjoying the most natural act of humanity, be left in the dark ages!

As Shelley shouted last orders at the bar, it was obviously home time. I nostalgically took my coat off the wall pegs and took one last look around the old place. I had made a million memories here, good and bad, and I wanted to remember them all. The paper may have been peeling from the walls and the ceilings yellow from the abundance of nicotine pumped into the room every night, but it was beautifully familiar to me and I would miss it.

The toilets were revolting, and soap and toilet roll were a rarity but the deep philosophy that had been shared in those toilets, had enabled me the right of passage through adolescence safely! And the people? The place may not have been filled with Oxford and Cambridge graduates, or people that were lucky enough to be blessed with a silver spoon in their mouth. I had no doubt that plans for space travel were not going to be conjured up amongst the revelling of the turn, but that didn't mean they weren't clever, and it certainly didn't mean that they weren't good.

Ok, maybe I didn't always feel that way about them, but at the root of it, it was true. They were a community that I have never experienced in my life since. Even within that tiny club there was a social hierarchy where generally people were nurtured. The elders took care of the younger ones, offering them worldly advice and a shoulder, should they need it. Ok, maybe at times this was done through a committee panel meeting, a bit like a kangaroo court. Where you would be threatened with suspension from the club should your behaviour have been unacceptable. But you know what, it worked, and people behaved, because they wanted to be part of it, this exclusive community, where we belonged because when it all boiled down to it, we were all one and the same.

Despite all the drama and heartache that this place had brought, I was so going to miss it so much. Although I can't pretend that I wasn't going to enjoy going for a drink, and being able to have a shit and wipe my arse on toilet roll, and not the cardboard middle. I reached for the door and took one glance back. If I tried hard enough, I could picture us all there. When times were good, and we were all still together, the dance floor packed, us pounding up and down with our arms in the air, screaming out to *Children of the Night*. None of us missing, none of us sad and none of the hatred that had inevitably occurred between us all. Just a carefree, happy bunch of kids that were enjoying being slap bang in the middle of a totally fucked up, but frankly quite fantastic, adolescence. A lump formed in my throat and I couldn't stop the tears from streaming down my face.

"Come on dick head," Anna was holding the door open for me, for us, to leave together, for the last time.

"Shannon, wait up," Neil was running to catch up with us.

"Oh, I am so going to leave you with this one," Anna giggled throwing her arms around me and kissing my cheek, "I'll see you in the morning." She sauntered away leaving us alone. We would say goodbye amongst the smog of the bus station in the morning, it would be brief and there would no tears, as she was just about the only thing, that I would never be leaving behind.

"I am going to ask you this one last time, and I swear you are totally done with! Can we start a little something? You won't regret it, I'm not the person you think I am."

He didn't know? I thought he had come to say goodbye, but he didn't know. I was leaving tomorrow, whatever could have happened, couldn't happen now. I could do without the complication of amazing sex and feelings and flutterings and anything else that could potentially arise from this discussion.

"You know what, I can be honest now, because I have nothing to lose. The answer would have been yes, it would finally have been yes...," he interrupted my declaration as a big fat smile spread across his face as he swept me straight off my feet and spun me around. His aftershave encompassed me, and I allowed myself to be swept away for a few minutes.

I waited until he had given me lots of extremely amazingly luscious sexy kisses before I slowly broke the news that the answer was insignificant! It was all just too late, that I was leaving the very next day!

The light from the street lamp revealed his confusion and disappointment, but it seemed to be something that he thought he could fix.

"Now you don't have to go, you can stay here with me?" The begging had begun. In all honesty it just didn't matter what he said. In a way, I wanted to stay. I believed in what he was saying, that we could at least attempt to make it work. But the truth was I didn't have anywhere to live, I had left my job, and I had used my bond money from my house on tickets to leave, I had nothing!

I know the Beatles had stated that *All you Need is Love*, but they were obviously talking shit. I can't imagine Neil would have even contemplated taking my knickers off when I'd had them on for two weeks thanks to my homelessness! No, the path was set, and we were both powerless to change it. But, we could say goodbye in a titanic fashion, without the untimely death.

I had never realised just how normal Neil was. I had placed him so far up on a pedestal that I was nervous to be around him. I needn't have been. If only I had opened my heart up to him earlier, I would have known this. Hindsight is a wonderful thing and I would learn this lesson many times over throughout my adolescence. We had sex all night. I'm not bragging, just saying!

We lay on top of the sheets talking until the sun came up.

"So, you finally, got me to have sex with you, well at least sex that I can remember," I playfully laughed, mocking his lengthy journey into my bed.

"We didn't have sex tonight Shan, and you know this."

"What are you talking about?" I replied in bewilderment.

"I love you Shan, always have, always will. I have no idea why. Maybe it is because you are a fuckboy, like me. You were the conquest that I could never quite conquer. And whilst chasing you, I fell for you."

I leaned back onto the bed in complete silence.

"And if you are honest, you feel the same, but you are petrified! Petrified of being hurt, and who can blame you, because nobody knows how they will feel tomorrow. And you are just not willing to take that risk. Not yet anyway."

He couldn't have spoken a truer set of words, and maybe I had failed to realise the truth for myself. But who would have thought that Neil in all his Neanderthal glory, would have so eloquently conveyed such a philosophical message. Being here was akin to a final night on death row. As we walked the metaphorical green mile of memories together, there was no situation we were scared to explore. We had nothing left to lose now and we were both only too aware, that this would probably be the last time that we saw each other.

Neither one of us said it, but we both had accepted that it could never be, even though we made vows to speak to each other every day on the phone and promised that we would visit, and one day, who knew, maybe we would even be together? I think that we both knew deep down, despite our promises, this would never happen.

And unfortunately, the morning came! Without so much as a wink of sleep, I walked him to the door to say our final goodbyes. I looked at him one last time on that doorstep. His perfectly gelled hair, his checked shirt, unbuttoned just low enough to reveal a glimpse of his smooth perfectly balanced chest. His narrowed eyes that just held so many memories that I couldn't help but smile. I could easily forgive his ballsy grin, and I slid my hands down his cheek in desperation of remembering his touch!

"Don't you dare forget me, bitch," he smiled and hugged me hard, crushing me in between his enormous arms.

"As if," and I meant it.

Whilst my heart and head were completely torn, there was no doubt about it, that it was time to move on. I know, no shit *Sherlock*. In every way possible, physically and emotionally! I was only 18 yet I felt about 50. Surely, I had experienced every emotion that existed and in such a short time, and if I'm honest I felt like I had made every mistake possible already. I packed my bags with tears rolling down my cheeks like Niagara Falls. I was totally torn. While one part of me, not only knew that the fresh start would be good for me, I thought it probably necessary to stop me from turning into a drug-fuelled, beer-filled, violent, stalking manic depressive maniac. I was destroying myself bit by bit like some bloody lemming on a self-destruct mission. As a little girl, this is not how I imagined my adult life would be. That bitch, Cinderella, gave us all the wrong impression, didn't she?! *Walt Disney* has a lot to answer for.

Conclusion of Adolescence: Farewell Friends

My friends you might ask yourself what the hell I have learnt from this rollercoaster of adolescence? That would be yet another book, wouldn't it? I could coin quite a few sequels here I'm thinking. Though I am very far removed from being a philosopher, I have learnt that life, love, luck, however you want to refer to it, hasn't got a set template. We cannot plan for it or assume how things will turn out. It just isn't possible to predict the future, not for us average folk anyway. This is very cynical of me I know, but nothing is forever. However, I feel the fact that this is true means it enriches our life and allows us to sample a wide array of fellas (sorry I mean choices), allowing us to make wiser choices in the future. In effect it allows us to have a past, present and a future. The important thing to learn, is that this needs to stay in this order. I have learnt that bad times are just as important as the good and ultimately, they shape both the person you are and your future.

People and relationships also do not have set templates and to judge such on stereotypical views is foolish. Take each relationship on its own merits and always carry with you through life the lessons that you have learnt. But more importantly remember the tears and sadness and take the time to reminisce. We are raised in a society where looking back at past relationships is a bad thing. I, for one, have decided this is not true, if the past is not allowed to become or affect the future. What is the point in building memories if we are only forced to forget them when we have moved on? You don't need to be ashamed of these transitions/memories (whatever phrase you prefer), they are important. They are something that should be cherished until the end of time. I for one, hope that they still raise a smile when I am 90!

It is important to always bear in mind that it isn't that the older generations (yes even your parents) don't understand the pain that heartbreak brings, it's simply that they have forgotten. My advice to pre-adolescent readers who have taken this journey through my sexual adolescence is to live life, enjoy the sadness as much as the happiness, but move on with grace, relishing in the knowledge that you have your whole god damn life in front of you. Enjoy!

GOOD LUCK XX

(ah fuck it, xxxxxxxxxxxxxxxxxxxxxxxxxxxxxxxxxxxxxxxxxxxxxxxxxxxx)

This autumn, you will be able to continue to follow Shannon on her treacherous life journey. Unfortunately for her, she is about to find out all about the difference between dating boys and dating men!

Diary of an Ageing Twenty Something is the second book in the 'Harsh and Brutal Truth of...' series. Find out how Shannon copes in a world where there is no escaping adulting?

Pre-order your copy of 'Diary of an Ageing Twenty Something – The harsh and brutal truth of adulting' today.

A word from the author

Thank you for supporting my debut novel, I only hope you enjoy reading it as much as I have writing it. Without you, my dream could not be realised.

Happy reminiscing everyone.

Angelina xx

Angelina Kennedy is a British writer who begins her professional writing career with this comedic coming of age novel of which is part of a four-book series 'The harsh and brutal truth of....'

Following completing a degree in English Language and Literature in 2005, Angelina took the path to become a secondary school English teacher. But in a desperate attempt to pursue her lifelong dream of becoming a writer, she began her writing endeavours after penning a parenting blog to provide amusement for other parents.

Her blog 'Diary of a Mental Mother', gave her the platform to bring this series to the masses.

She is a keen writer of many genres and formats including screenplays, poetry, drama, children's fiction and articles.

Check out her website for more details on her offerings:
angelinakennedy.com

Printed in Great Britain
by Amazon